好萊塢 A 咖教你說愛

電影英文

Love Quotes

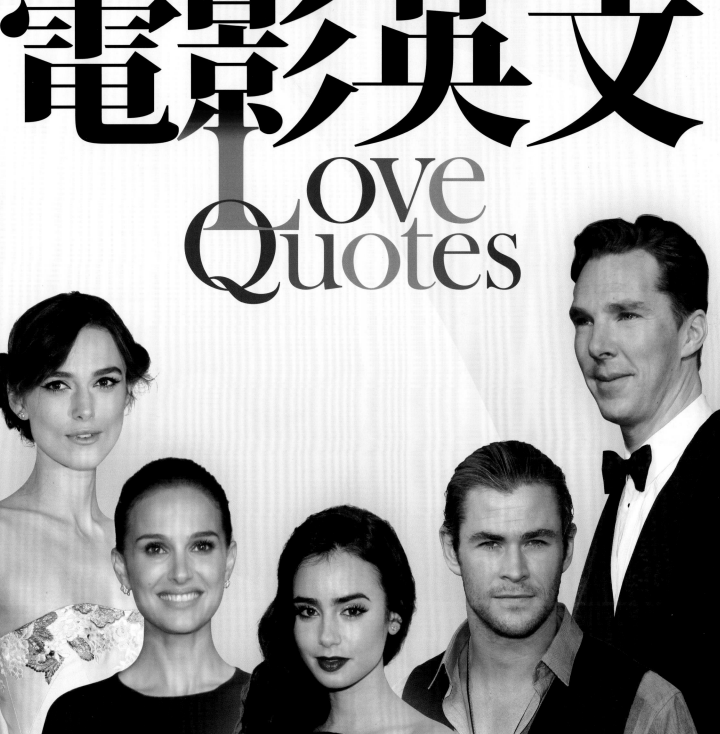

威秀影城

×

LINE@

一起當威秀寶寶的好朋友吧！！
+好友、LINE好康
就愛LINE在威秀影城

加入好友

如果在影城現場，搖晃手機
也可以馬上搜尋到喔！

🔍好友搜尋：威秀影城

頭份尚順威秀影城

COMING SOON

萬眾期待・即將登場

CONTENTS

Love Quotes　最浪漫電影對白

Mr.&Ms. Dreamy

Special Reports 專題報導

浪漫‧電影
All about Romance

Q

請問 romance 和 romantic 這兩個字要怎麼用？到底有什麼不同？「羅曼史小說」到底應該是 romantic novel？還是 romance novel？「浪漫電影」是 romantic movie？還是 romance movie？

Q&A

全面認識浪漫語言、浪漫電影

A

romance 這個字最經常當名詞使用，可以指「愛侶之間的戀愛關係」：

- **The couple broke up after a two year romance.**
  這對情侶交往兩年之後分手了。
- **The movie star says she's too busy for romance.**
  這位電影明星說她忙到沒時間戀愛。

當我們聽到 romance（羅曼史），總是想到男生女生愛來愛去的故事，但其實這個字原本是指「中世紀騎士冒險傳奇」，只不過故事當中的英雄除了遠征異國殺敵，還要屠龍救美，最後總會贏得美人歸。

- **I took a course in college about Medieval romances.**
  我上大學時修過一門中古世紀傳奇文學的課。

隨著時代演進，騎士棄馬就車，美女改穿長褲，國王城堡變成辦公大樓，儘管場景改變，romance 依然繼續上演，形式也從口述故事、浪漫小說（romance novel），進而演變為浪漫電影（romance movie/film），在此 romance 代表這種類型的故事，也可以用形容詞 romantic，變成 romantic novel、romantic movie/film，意思都一樣。

那形容詞 romantic 要在什麼時候用呢？romantic 用來形容「帶給人浪漫感覺的」人事物。

- **Cynthia wishes her husband were more romantic.**
  辛希雅希望她的丈夫能更浪漫一點。

也用來形容「過度美化現實、不切實際的」天真想法。

- **Many people have romantic ideas about life in the country.**
  許多人對於鄉間生活懷有過度浪漫的想像。

我想約女生去看電影，想問「妳最喜歡哪種類型的電影？」，但這句話的英文到底怎麼說呢？

A

說到「分類、類型」，大家應該都背過 genre 這個字，於是「妳最喜歡哪種類型的電影？」直接中翻英會是：**What's your favorite movie/film genre?**

但是請注意，真的講英文的人會這樣說：

● **What kind of movies do you like?**
妳喜歡哪種電影？

就這麼簡單明瞭，國小程度單字就可以講完。其次，要聊電影最起碼要提到男、女主角（actor/actress），也可說 lead、star 或 main character，與男、女配角（supporting actor / actress）的表現。

● **The acting was excellent / terrible.**
演員的演技真好／真糟。

● **The female lead gave a good / bad performance.**
女主角表現出色／不好。

● **The leading man seemed too young for the part.**
這部片的男主角對這個角色來說似乎太年輕了。

● **The actor who played the main character was very convincing.**
演主角的男星很有說服力。

● **The two stars had great / no chemistry.**
兩位主角很有火花／毫無火花。

● **The supporting actors were all well / poorly cast.**
配角的卡司很好／很差。

● **That supporting actress really stole the show!**
女配角的表現真是搶眼！

主要電影分類

電影類型並沒有絕對的區分標準，加上近年來的電影常是複合體，融合多種類型於一片，以 IMDb.com（電影線上資料庫）的分類為例，《超人：鋼鐵英雄》*Man of Steel* 是 action/adventure/fantasy，《少年 Pi 的奇幻漂流》*Life of Pi* 被歸為 action/adventure/fantasy/sci-fi，暮光之城系列（*The Twilight series*）則屬於 adventure/drama/fantasy/romance（還有許多電影的分類比這更長！）。由此可知，要將一部電影簡單歸為某一類是很困難的。

以下是常見的電影分類：

● **action** 動作片
● **adventure** 冒險片
● **animation** 動畫片
● **biography / bio-pic** 傳記片
● **disaster** 災難片
● **family** 家庭溫馨片
● **thriller / suspense** 驚悚懸疑片
● **horror** 恐怖片
● **mystery** 推理片
● **romance** 浪漫愛情片
● **musical** 音樂／歌舞片
● **historical** 史詩／歷史片
● **war** 戰爭片
● **road** 公路
● **documentary** 紀錄片
● **fantasy** 奇幻片
● **sci-fi** 科幻片（sci-fi 為 science fiction 的簡稱。）

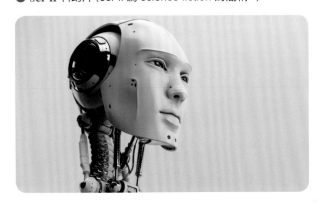

● **comedy** 喜劇片

喜劇片主要是以幽默風趣的情節，搭配誇張的說話方式及動作，讓觀眾笑開懷的電影。一般喜劇片都是美好的結局收尾，像是愛情喜劇片（rom-com，為 romantic comedy 的縮寫），但其中也有例外，像是黑色喜劇（black comedy/dark comedy）除了有傳統喜劇逗人開心的情節，還參雜了荒謬的橋段及元素，以呈現嚴肅議題，讓人感到沉重恐怖，卻又不禁莞爾。

● **comedy** 喜劇片

喜劇片主要是以幽默風趣的情節，搭配誇張的說話方式及動作，讓觀眾笑開懷的電影。一般喜劇片都是美好的結局收尾，像是愛情喜劇片（rom-com，為 romantic comedy 的縮寫），但其中也有例外，像是黑色喜劇（black comedy/dark comedy）除了有傳統喜劇逗人開心的情節，還參雜了荒謬的橋段及元素，以呈現嚴肅議題，讓人感到沉重恐怖，卻又不禁莞爾。

● **drama** 劇情片

劇情片是以劇情發展和角色性格變化串動整個故事的電影。

● **feature film** 劇情長片

千萬不要以為劇情長片是劇情片的一種，劇情長片是依據電影的長度來作區別，而不是內容。一般劇情長片的長度都在一個小時以上。根據美國電影藝術與科學學院（Academy of Motion Picture Arts and Science，也就是奧斯卡獎）的定義，長度短於四十分鐘的電影即稱做短片（short film），因此目前在院線上映的電影皆屬於劇情長片。

● **Western** 西部片

西部片將場景設定在十九世紀的美國西部，以西部牛仔為主題，後來還發展出義式西部片（Spaghetti Western）。義式西部片起源於西部片盛行的一九六○年代，導演和演員清一色都是義大利人，電影內容和傳統西部片一樣，都是以西部牛仔為主。不同的是，義式西部片裡的人物不像是原本西部片中善惡分明，而是顛覆傳統的反英雄角色，內容更為暴力，充斥大量槍戰場面。經典的義式西部片代表作有克林伊斯威特（Clint Eastwood）擔綱演出的《獨行俠三部曲》Dollars Trilogy 以及《荒野大鏢客》The Good, the Bad and the Ugly……等。由於義式西部片廣受歡迎，隨後還意外發展出西班牙的「辣肉腸西部片」Chorizo Western 以及墨西哥的「捲餅西部片」Burrito Western。

● **adult** 成人電影

是指內容描述性愛和色情（pornography [porˋn3gr4fi] / porn）的情節，以激起觀眾性慾的電影。

● **art film** 藝術片

又可稱為 art house film，不像好萊塢電影有著超強卡司和聲光特效，而是著重在意象傳達與故事敘述，於某些特定戲院或電影節（film festival）播放。礙於片型、行銷經費、少廳播放等因素，藝術片一直被認為是小眾市場，但近幾年因拍攝手法獨特和簡單情節，藝術片的觀眾群正逐漸累積中。

● **film noir** 黑色電影

noir 是法語「黑色」的意思。一般是指好萊塢的犯罪偵探片（crime drama），尤其是以性為犯罪動機、道德界限模糊的題材為主，盛行於四○年代及五○年代。現在在描寫黑幫、警界，以凸顯社會問題的電影類型，都深受這個時期的影響。

● **made-for-TV movie** 電視電影

也可稱做 TV movie。電視電影是指由電視公司製作並播放，拍得像電影一樣的影片。這樣的「電影」並不會在戲院播放，只能電視上看到。made-for-TV movie 長度和一般電影差不多，製作成本通常比電影還低，但是比電視劇高。附帶一提，還有一種電影在拍攝完後，沒在電影院上映，卻直接出DVD 的電影則稱做 made-for-DVD movie（也可叫 direct-to-DVD movie 或 straight-to-DVD movie）。

Q

浪漫愛情電影裡經常聽到 blind date
和 double date，請問還有哪些約
會、男女交往形式的相關英文？

A

浪漫愛情片最常見的，要算是 rom-com（浪漫喜劇，romantic comedy 的簡稱）、romantic action comedy（浪漫動作喜劇）、romantic thriller（浪漫驚悚片）及 romantic drama（浪漫劇情片）。

談到浪漫愛情片，chick flick 這個字經常被提起。chick 是對年輕女性的蔑稱，flick 是電影的俚語說法。chick flick 望文生義就知道是專門拍給女生看、滿足女生浪漫幻想的電影，一般男生可能傾向表現出一副不屑看的樣子，但浪漫電影不等於 chick flick，因為像是描述女性情誼（female friendships）的電影也屬於 chick flick，浪漫動作喜劇片及浪漫驚悚片頗多看起來蠻 man 的電影，請看以下例子：

The Adjustment Bureau《命運規劃局》
麥特戴蒙主演的浪漫科幻驚悚片（romantic sci-fi thriller）

The Tourist《色遇》
強尼戴普及安潔麗娜裘莉主演的浪漫喜劇驚悚片（romantic comedy thriller）

Wicker Park《第三者》
喬許哈奈特主演的心理驚悚浪漫懸疑片（psychological drama / romantic mystery film）

Knight and Day《騎士出任務》
湯姆克魯斯及卡麥蓉狄亞主演的動作浪漫喜劇（action comedy romantic film）

此外，浪漫愛情片也常讓人聯想到 date movie（約會電影）。正因為大部分男生宣稱不愛看浪漫愛情片，他們唯一看這種電影的時候，就是跟女生約會了，而背後的目的就是跟女友的關係能更進一步囉！

A

現代人生活步調繁忙，連談戀愛也講求效率，再加上世風日下、人心不古，遇人不淑、視人不明的風險太高，原本在我們刻板印象中，崇尚自由戀愛的歐美青年，也越來越傾向請親友當媒人（matchmaker），和素未謀面的人來個「瞎約會」blind date，也就是大家耳熟能詳的「相親」，來尋找終身伴侶。

● **One of my friends set me up on a blind date.**
我有一個朋友幫我安排一場相親。

但就如同電影 *Blended*《當我們混在一起》，相親結果常以災難作結，因此也有人利用 online dating（網路交友）來尋找另一半，這樣不僅可以不見到本尊就先看到對方的長相，還能利用網路聊聊天，觀察彼此是否心有靈犀。這樣的約會，有一較新的詞彙，稱為 nearsighted date（近視相親）。但由於修圖軟體盛行，結果常常令人失望。

● **I'd rather go on a nearsighted date than a blind date.**
我寧可透過網路交友，也不要相親。

● **The problem with online dating is that people always exaggerate in their profiles.**
網路交友的問題在於大家的背景資料都會澎風。

● **She must have photoshopped her picture—she looked much worse in person.**
她的照片一定有修圖——她本人醜多了。

避免相親災難的另一種方式，就是雙方各找朋友一同出席，兩對男女一起約會，進行 double date，或是乾脆參加商業舉辦的聯誼活動（matchmaking event，或稱 mixer）。多人一起約會的好處是能免除獨處的尷尬，但長相抱歉，或是個性害羞的人，在這種場合就比較吃虧了。另外，商業化的聯誼活動為了提高配對效率，會安排各種快速活動讓參與者有機會跟更多人聊天，因此衍生出快速約會（speed dating）的說法。

● **Your girlfriend's sister is cute—can you set us up on a double date?**
你女友的姊姊真可愛——可以幫我們四個安排一場約會嗎？

● **Did you know that Allen met his girlfriend at a matchmaking event?**
你知道艾倫跟他女友是參加聯誼認識的嗎？

● **At the speed dating event, I met 10 different girls in less than an hour.**
在快速約會活動上，我一個鐘頭不到就認識十個不同的女生

英倫情人
Benedict Cumberbatch
班奈迪克康柏拜區 🎧 1

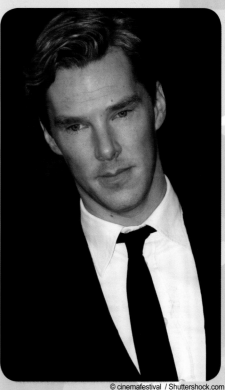

Although Benedict Cumberbatch was born in London to two actors, his parents hoped that he would become a lawyer. But he still followed in their footsteps, studying drama at boarding school and eventually completing an MA in Classical Acting at the top British drama school. After making a name for himself in West End productions, Cumberbatch developed a reputation for playing geniuses on television, including Steven Hawking, Vincent Van Gogh and a modern-day Sherlock Holmes, a role that has brought him worldwide fame. The actor has also found success on the silver screen, appearing in Oscar-winning *12 Years a Slave*, and playing yet another genius—Alan Turing—in *The Imitation Game*, which has received eight Oscar nominations.

© cinemafestival / Shuttershock.com

班奈狄克康柏拜區出生於倫敦,雖然雙親皆為演員,但他們卻希望兒子能成為律師。不過他依然克紹箕裘,先是在寄宿學校研讀戲劇,最後更畢業於頂尖的英國戲劇學校,取得古典戲劇表演的碩士學位。在西區這個倫敦劇院界闖出名號後,康柏拜區以在電視劇中扮演天才建立起名聲,其角色包括史蒂芬霍金、梵谷、以及現代版的福爾摩斯,而後者也令他享譽國際。這位男星在大銀幕上也有亮眼的表現,出演奪得奧斯卡獎的《自由之心》,並在獲得八項奧斯卡獎提名的《模仿遊戲》中再度飾演天才——艾倫圖靈。

影星小檔案

全　名:**Benedict Timothy Carlton Cumberbatch**
（為免麻煩,粉絲都簡稱 BC）

生　日:**July 19, 1976**

出生地:英國倫敦　感情狀態:已訂婚

成名作:《新世紀福爾摩斯》*Sherlock*

© Helga Esteb / Shuttershock.com

Quotes From Benedict

"I've seen and swam and climbed and lived and driven and filmed. Should it all end tomorrow, I can definitely say there would be no regrets. I am very lucky, and I know it. I really have lived 5,000 times over."

我看過、暢泳過、攀爬過、活過、開過車也拍過電影。就算明天一切都毀滅了,我可以篤定地說我死而無憾。我知道自己非常幸運。我真的活過五千次以上了。

BC 和劇場導演蘇菲杭特（Sophie Hunt）閃電訂婚一事,令不少網友措手不及,直呼「心都碎了」。班奈迪克平時對戀情頗為低調,使得鐵粉們不禁對他未婚妻的背景感到好奇。蘇菲曾在牛津大學研讀法語和義大利語,目前除身兼演員與導演身份,還「演而優則唱」,發行了一張法文專輯,並且連騎馬、跑步等運動也是她的拿手項目,可說是全方位才女。好啦,才子配佳人,相信粉絲們應該心服口服了吧!也恭喜 BC 找到這麼優秀的另一半囉!

Q 電影裡的男女主角經常是在咖啡店、酒吧裡搭訕認識的，我要怎麼跟他們一樣，很自然地向有興趣的對象搭訕呢？

A

終於在茫茫人海中遇到心動的對象，從陌生到認識，破冰（break the ice）的第一句話要怎麼開頭？

首先，如果在酒吧中遇見他／她，不要猶豫，大方請他喝一杯，或是借題發揮，問對方喝得是什麼，藉機聊天。

● Can I buy / get you a drink?
　我可以請你喝一杯嗎？

● What is that you're drinking?
　請問你喝的是什麼？

● I'll take one of what she's having.
　（指對方的杯子，對酒保說）我跟她喝一樣的。

如果場合是咖啡店，而你看上的人正在看書，那就好辦啦！

● May I ask what you're reading?
　可以請問你在看哪本書嗎？

● I've read that—I really liked it.
　那本書我也看過，我很喜歡。

● I love that author—I've read all of his books.
　我很喜歡那個作者，他的書我都看過。

● Is that the new Steven King book? Can I take a look?
　那本是史蒂芬金的新書嗎？可以借我看一下嗎？

● I like reading science fiction.
　我也很喜歡科幻小說。

接下來可以利用套話方式，確認他不是跟另一半來的。

● Are you on your own?
　你一個人來的嗎？

若他／她落單一人，就趕快邀請他加入你們，如果孤單無伴的人是你，也可以設法加入他們，藉機拉近距離。

● Would you like to join us?
　要不要來跟我們一起坐？

● Do you mind if I join you?
　我能跟你們一起坐嗎？

此外，聊聊所在的派對或酒吧也是英文超級好用的開場白。

● Do you come here often?
　你常來這裡嗎？

● Is this your first time here?
　你第一次來這裡嗎？

最後，當酒吧裡燈光美、氣氛佳

● Would you like to dance?
　你想跳舞嗎？

或是可以想辦法要對方的聯絡方式，或是約下次再見：

● Would you like to go out for coffee some time?
　你想要找時間一起出去喝咖啡嗎？

● Here, put your number in my phone and I'll give you a call.
　來，把你的電話號碼輸入我的手機，我會打給你。

Q 請教我從「有點動心」到「為你瘋狂」各種程度表達愛意的英文說法。

A

表達愛意，除了 I love you.（我愛你。）之外，還有千百種其他常用說法，都可以用來讓另一半感到你的真心情意，這裡提供幾種可能性：

● I love you from the bottom of my heart.
　我打從心裡愛你。

● You complete me.
　你完整了我。

● We're meant for each other.
　我們是天造地設的一對。

● I'm infatuated with you.
　你讓我心醉。

● I'm addicted to you.
　我上了你的癮。

● I've got a thing for you.
　我對你很有感覺。

● I've got a crush on you.
　我迷戀你。

● I think you're the one.
　我想你是我的唯一。

● I can't bear to be apart from you.
　我不能忍受與你分離。

● You make me want to be a better man.
　你讓我想成為更好的男人。

● I yearn for you.
　我渴望你。

● I'm under your spell.
　我中你的魔咒。

● I'm ready to take it to the next level.
　我已經準備好更進一步了。

● We have a good chemistry.
　我們很來電。

● I have a soft spot for you.
　我對你情有獨鍾。

這樣看來，迂迴地說愛，有時反而更加浪漫呢。快把這些句子學起來，說給你的另一半聽吧

Q

要怎樣提出分手才不傷人呢？
請教我英文的說法

A

對於不合適的對象，怎麼樣用英文不傷大雅地說再見呢？要分的好，可以考慮以這句話做開場白：

● We've shared some good times together.
我們曾擁有過美好的時光。

最婉轉的說法就是：

● I need time to think.
我需要時間思考。（言下之意：跟你在一起的未來令人擔憂）

● I need to move on.
我需要繼續前進。（言下之意：我要去跟別人交往）

若是你需要一些空間獨處，就可以說：

● I need a break.（言下之意：跟你在一起我很累）
我需要喊卡。

● I need some space.（言下之意：跟你在一起我很煩）
我需要一些空間。

如果你心已令有所屬，要據實以告時，可以說：

● I'm seeing someone else.
我正在與某人交往。

● I've met someone else.
我邂逅了其他人。

所以直接告訴他／她，一刀斬情絲吧。

● Let's just be friends.
我們還是做朋友吧！

Q

跟交往已久的男友分手，要如何公告周知？又要如何建議別人分手，以及安慰為分手難過的人？

A

和另一半分手，常見的片語是 break up (with sb.)。

● We broke up.
我們分手了。

● I can't believe she wants to break up with Jason!
我不敢相信她和傑森分手了。

更口語的說法是 dump，該字的原意是「丟棄」，引申為把人甩了。

● He dumped Rebecca.
他把瑞貝卡甩了。

此外，戀情畫上休止符還可以簡潔地說：

● It's over!
結束了。

最後，感情最忌諱偷吃，碰到花心大蘿蔔(player)，還是揮揮衣袖，分手吧。

● My last boyfriend was a player, so I kicked him to the curb.
我上一任男友是個花心大蘿蔔，所以我甩了他。

● If my girlfriend was two-timing me, I'd dump her in a second.
如果我的女友劈腿，我會馬上跟她分手。

感情畢竟很難說斷就斷，如果碰到有人失戀的場合，最經常聽到的一句話就是：

● There are plenty of other fish in the sea.
天涯何處無芳草。（直譯：海裡的魚多得是。）

● I'm sure someone better will come along.
我敢說會有更好的人出現。

● You'll meet someone new in no time.
你很快就會遇到新的對象。

如何用道地英文描述一個人的感情狀態呢？

如果她／他已經名花／草有主，我們會說：

● **He / She is taken.**
　他／她死會了。

● **He / She has a girlfriend / boyfriend.**
　他／她有女／男朋友。

那要如何表示和某人交往中呢？要注意，形容兩人正在交往的片語可以說 dating someone 或 seeing someone/going out with someone。

● **Do you know if Jennifer is seeing anyone?**
　你知道珍妮佛有沒有交往對象嗎？

● **I hear she's dating someone from her office.**
　我聽說她約會的對象是公司裡的人。

當兩人感情穩定，甚至認定對方時，可以說 go steady（定下來了，一般是青少年的用法），或者 (be) exclusive（認定彼此）：

● **Me and Alice are going steady.**
　我和愛麗絲定下來了。

● **We're in an exclusive relationship.**
　我們已經彼此認定對方了。

● **We're in a long-term committed relationship.**
　我們是以長期承諾為前提的交往。

在歐美文化中，還有一種所謂的「開放關係」，意即雖然我有男／女朋友，但我和我的另一半都不介意有其他的性伴侶，這英文的說法是：

● **We're in an open relationship.**
　我們目前是開放關係。

● **I'm dating someone, but we're not exclusive.**
　我有約會對象，但彼此還沒認真交往。

若是已經結婚，但與另一半合不來，感情觸礁，可以用 to be on the rocks 表示。

● **It's no wonder they got divorced. The relationship was on the rocks for years.**
　難怪他們要離婚，他們的關係已經不睦好一陣子了。

另外，若兩人正在「冷靜期」的階段，則可以說：

● **We're on a break.**
　我們目前暫時分開冷靜一下。

Q 有部馬修麥康納主演的電影《絕配冤家》How to Lose a Guy in 10 Days，內容提到一些約會禁忌及戀愛交戰守則，我想多了解這方面相關的英文。

A

有人說談戀愛傷身又傷神，到底要如何才能避免在愛情中受傷呢？在此分享歐美文化中的戀愛禁忌。

1. 避免過度依賴

　　男／女朋友的過度依賴(needy)很可能會嚇跑另一半。要小心，太過黏人(clingy)可是會讓你魅力全失喔！

● **I found Susan attractive at first, but she turned out to be too clingy and needy.**
　　剛認識時，我覺得蘇珊非常有魅力，但她後來變得太依賴、太黏人。

2. 避免識人不明

　　當你陷入盲目熱戀時，很可能會粉飾對方的缺點，一心認定對方，完全忽略可能的警訊(red flag)。

● **I always watch out for red flags when I start dating a girl.**
　　剛開始跟女生交往時，我都會小心觀察。

● **If a guy is always late, that's a big red flag for me.**
　　如果一個男的老是遲到，我就會開始特別留意了。

3. 避免一頭栽進

　　別忘了慢慢來(take things slow)，在正式交往之前，別太快就為一個人神魂顛倒(fall head over heels)。

● **It's easy to fall head over heels for someone, but it's best to take things slow.**
　　戀愛很容易讓人神魂顛倒，但最好還是要放慢腳步。

以下是電影《絕配冤家》當中，女主角 Andie 用來嚇跑新男友 Ben 的一些方法：
● 從公寓管理員處取得他家的鑰匙
　（已經開始以女主人自居）直闖他跟男性朋友的專屬聚會
● 奪命連環 call，留十七通留言
● 把女性用品放在他的浴室和臥室
● 在他賣力煮大餐之後，騙他說她吃素
● 用娃娃音跟他說話
● 在籃球賽最緊要關頭，硬要他去幫忙買飲料

Q 想請問跟結婚有關的英文。還有電影裡經常出現有人給新娘藍色的東西，好像有一個固定說法，到底是什麼？

A

終於找到理想的另一半，成為別人眼中的天作之合(match made in heaven)，也該走向人生的下一階段─婚姻了。首先會有人求婚，一般的說法就是 propose，沒錯，珊卓布拉克主演的《愛情限時簽》的原文片名就是 *The Proposal*。

A: You and Rebecca are a match made in heaven.
　　你和蕾貝卡是天生一對。

B: I know. I'm planning on proposing to next week.
　　是啊。我打算下星期求婚。

求婚較口語的用法還有 pop the question。pop 這裡的意思是「突然提出」，而此處的「問題」想當然就是：
● **Will you marry me?**
　　妳願意嫁給我嗎？

求婚後，兩人決定 tie the knot，也就是結婚了。這個說法的出處是以前結婚時，新人需要在典禮上打結，表示兩人將結合，因而沿用。另一個象徵結婚的片語則是 walk/go down the aisle，指新人將走上紅毯。
● **When are you and Brad going to tie the knot?**
　　妳跟布萊德何時要結婚？
● **The young star is in no hurry to walk down the aisle.**
　　那個年輕演員不急著步入禮堂。

此外，你說的那個「藍色的東西」，是英語系國家婚禮上一個有趣的禮俗，與一首十九世紀的打油詩有關：
● **Something old, something new, something borrowed, something blue.**
　　某樣舊東西、某樣新東西、某樣借來的東西、某樣藍色的東西。

尤其前面四項物品已成為婚禮中帶來好運的象徵，且交由伴娘張羅，電影《結婚友沒友》的英文片名就是 *Something Borrowed*。

愛是什麼？

問世間，情為何物？直教生死相許。
天南地北雙飛客，老翅幾回寒暑。
歡樂趣，離別苦，就中更有癡兒女。
君應有語，渺萬里層雲，千山暮雪，隻影為誰去。

橫汾路，寂寞當年簫鼓，荒煙依舊平楚。
招魂楚些何嗟及，山鬼自啼風雨。
天也妒，未信與、鶯兒燕子俱黃土。
千秋萬古。為留待騷人，狂歌痛飲，來訪雁丘處。

不論古今中外，「愛到底是什麼？」是大家不斷追尋的問題。一起來看看眾多電影角色的詮釋。

《真愛每一天》

提姆（Tim，Domhnall Gleeson 飾）的家族男性滿二十一歲之後，都有穿越時光的特殊能力，他不斷利用這個能力改變未來，追求他所喜愛的女孩瑪麗（Mary，Rachel McAdams 飾），卻也漸漸發現穿越時光能改變的事實依然有限：

Tim: Lesson number one: all the time traveling in the world can't make someone love you.
第一課：世界上再多的時光旅行都無法讓人愛上你。

About Time

《愛，穹蒼》

尼爾（Neil，Ben Affleck 飾）與法國單親媽媽瑪麗娜相戀，原本希望能帶瑪麗娜（Marina，Olga Kurylenko 飾）與她的女兒一起回美國定居，但瑪麗娜的女兒適應不良，母女倆只好搬回巴黎。不久後，尼爾與舊愛珍（Jane，Rachel McAdams 飾）重逢，尼爾在兩個女人當中無法抉擇。另一方面，區內的神父（Father Quintana，Javier Bardem 飾）因當地核電廠有毒物質外洩，每天必須傾聽處理居民的抱怨及恐慌，讓他感到無能為力。一個男人苦於世俗之愛，另一個男人則開始懷疑上帝之愛……。

Father Quintana: Love is not only a feeling, love is a duty. To commit yourself is to run the risk of failure, the risk of *betrayal.
愛，不只是一種感覺，也是一種責任。你對愛的許諾，包括承擔失敗的風險，被人背叛的風險。

But the man who makes a mistake can *repent. You fear your love has died, it perhaps is waiting to be transformed into something higher.
但犯錯的人可以懺悔。你害怕你的愛已經不再，或許它是在等待，等待昇華為更高層次的愛。

***betrayal** [bɪ`treəl] (n.) 背叛

***repent** [rɪ`pɛnt] (v.) 懺悔，悔改

To the Wonder

《安娜卡列尼娜》

安娜卡列尼娜（Anna Karenina，Keira Knightley 飾）是政府高官的妻子，婚姻幸福美滿。有一天她接到哥哥來信，要她趕往莫斯科。安娜在途中認識了英俊的騎兵軍官伏倫斯基（Count Vronsky，Aaron Taylor-Johnson 飾），兩人立刻相互吸引。

Vronsky: I love you!
我愛妳！
Anna: Why?
為什麼？
Vronsky: You can't ask why about love!
愛沒辦法問為什麼！

Anna Karenina

《西雅圖夜未眠》

新聞記者安妮（Annie Reed，Meg Ryan 飾）即將步入結婚禮堂，但總覺得和未婚夫之間缺少傳說中的魔力（magic），正好此時在收音機上聽到喪偶的單親爸爸山姆（Sam Baldwin，Tom Hanks 飾）訴說他對亡妻的思念，讓她莫名陷入必須跟山姆見一面的狂熱……。

Sam: It was a million tiny little things that, when you added them all up, they meant we were supposed to be together, and I knew it.

無數細微的小事加在一起，讓我知道我們註定要在一起。

I knew it the very first time I touched her. It was like coming home, only to no home I'd ever known. I was just taking her hand to help her out of a car and I knew. It was like…magic.

我第一次碰觸她的時候，我就知道了。那就像是回家，只不過那是我還不知道的家。我不過是扶著她的手幫她下車，就知道了。那就像是……魔法。

《金玉盟》

泰瑞（Terry McKay，Deborah Kerr 飾）和尼可（Nickie Ferrante，Cary Grant 飾）在愛之船上墜入情網，為了證明這不只是一時激情，他們相約六個月後在紐約帝國大廈頂樓重逢，如果彼此的感情未變，就與各自的未婚夫妻說明白，再重新開始。六個月後，尼可到達約定地點等待泰瑞卻落空，只能傷心離開。多年後，命運使他們重逢，尼可看到了癱坐輪椅上的泰瑞，原來泰瑞當天失約，是因為一場車禍……。

Terry: Oh, it's nobody's fault but my own!

喔，這不是誰的錯，都要怪我自己！

Terry: I was looking up…it was the nearest thing to heaven! You were there….

我當時只顧著往上看（編註：帝國大廈頂樓）……那個地方最接近天堂！因為你在上面……。

Sleepless in Seattle

An Affair to Remember

Cary Grant 永遠的銀幕情聖

看過 Sleepless in Seattle《西雅圖夜未眠》的人，應該都記得片中有一部讓女人落淚、讓男人翻白眼的黑白浪漫片，那部片就是由卡萊葛倫（Cary Grant，1904~1986）及黛博拉蔻兒（Deborah Kerr）領銜主演的 An Affair to Remember《金玉盟》。

《西》、《金》兩部片的男主角 Tom Hanks 和 Cary Grant 有一個共同處：他們外表都很穩重老實，能演嚴肅正直的角色，也能演陰沈憂鬱的角色，卻又很能搞笑，因此不論男女觀眾都喜歡他們。不過來自英國的 Cary Grant 比起 Tom Hanks 外形俊俏許多，即使昔人日已遠，他的名字仍位居各大「最浪漫男星」排行榜前十名。

Cary Grant 不止受到各世代女影迷歡迎，他在好萊塢的人緣也極佳。與他合作過的超級大咖女星不計其數，像是《北非諜影》女主角英格麗褒曼（Ingrid Bergman），及後來成為摩納哥王妃的葛麗絲凱莉（Grace Kelly）都與他保持終生的情誼。

英格麗褒曼

《給茱麗葉的信》

蘇菲（Sophie，Amanda Seyfried 飾）與未婚夫來到《羅密歐與茱麗葉》故事的發生地：義大利維洛納度假。蘇菲造訪茱麗葉故居，那裡有一群「茱麗葉秘書」，以茱麗葉的名義為來信訴苦的女子回信。蘇菲加入這群志工的行列，因此發現一封五十年前的信，發信人克萊兒（Claire，Vanessa Redgrave 飾）少女時因父母阻撓，無法與她所愛的義大利青年廝守，她為此抱憾一生。蘇菲決定回信給她。

[reading letter]

Claire: Dear Claire, "what" and "if" are two words as non-threatening as words can be. But put them together side by side and they have the power to haunt you for the rest of your life.

（讀信）

親愛的克萊兒，「要」和「是」這兩個字分開完全無害。但兩字並排放在一起卻有糾纏人一輩子的力量。

What if? What if? What if? I don't know how your story ended, but if what you felt then was true love, then it's never too late. If it was true then, why wouldn't it be true now? You need only the courage to follow your heart.

要是？要是？要是？我不知道妳的故事如何收尾，但如果妳當時的感覺是真愛，那就永不嫌遲。如果那時候是真愛，為什麼現在不會是？妳需要的只是聽從心聲的勇氣。

I don't know what a love like Juliet's feels like, love to leave loved ones for, love to cross oceans for, but I'd like to believe if I ever were to feel it, that I will have the courage to seize it. And, Claire, if you didn't, I hope one day that you will. All my love, Juliet.

我不知道如同茱麗葉那樣的愛是什麼感覺，不知道愛到能放手離開親人是什麼感覺，不知道為愛遠渡重洋是什麼感覺，但我寧願相信，如果我真有機會能感覺到，我會有把握它的勇氣。而妳，克萊兒，如果妳之前沒有把握，我希望有一天妳能夠做到。獻上我全部的愛，茱麗葉。

Letters to Juliet

《好友戀習簿》

本片在台灣發行的英文片名為 *What If*，敘述華勒斯（Wallace，Daniel Radcliffe 飾）因發現女友劈腿荒廢學業，遭醫學院退學之後生活潦倒，只好寄住姊姊家幫忙照顧小孩。他原本打算暫停與人交往，卻在派對上邂逅倩翠（Chantry，Zoe Kazan 飾），發現彼此很聊得來……。

Wallace: In fairy tales love inspires you to be noble and courageous, but in real life love is just an all purpose excuse for selfish behavior.

在童話故事中，愛情讓人變得無私，變得勇敢，但在現實生活中，愛只不過是自私行為的萬用藉口。

Chantry: I don't know if you're actually *cynical or a super crazy romantic cheeseball.

真不知道你到底是個犬儒，還是一個無藥可救的浪漫派。

*cynical [ˈsɪnɪkəl] (a.) 憤世忌俗的，悲觀的

羅曼死英文教室

《給茱麗葉的信》對白中的 loved one 字面上的解釋是「所愛的人」，但可不是當下最愛但明年可能會換人的男女朋友，而是真正永遠不變的愛，如家人、最要好的朋友，或是一生摯愛的伴侶。

• *How do you keep in touch with your loved ones when you're abroad?*
  你出國期間怎麼跟親朋好友聯繫？

《好友練習簿》當中的 cheeseball 是俚語用法，當你聽到一個人說些陳腔濫調，做些很土、很俗氣的事，就可以說他是個 cheeseball。

• *Look at that guy's outfit—what a cheeseball!*
  你看那個人的打扮——真是土包子一個！

The F Word

《第六感生死緣》

媒體大亨威廉派里許（William Parrish，Anthony Hopkins 飾）最鍾愛的小女兒蘇珊愛上了死神附身的神秘男子喬布萊克（Joe Black，Brad Pitt 飾），但蘇珊已經和威廉的愛將德魯（Drew，Jake Weber 飾）有婚約。威廉不忍見蘇珊為此所苦，決定要在死神帶他走之前，幫助女兒找到幸福。

William: Love is passion, obsession, someone you can't live without. I say, fall head over heels. Find someone you can love like crazy and who will love you the same way back.

愛是激情、著迷，沒有那個人就活不下去。我希望妳愛到神魂顛倒。找到那個讓妳瘋狂，而他也一樣愛妳的人。

How do you find him? Well, you forget your head, and you listen to your heart. And I'm not hearing any heart. 'Cause the truth is, honey, there's no sense living your life without this.

要怎麼找到那個人？不要用腦袋想，要順從妳的心，但我不覺得妳有做到。因為事實是，親愛的，如果做不到生活就沒有意義。

To make the journey and not fall deeply in love, well, you haven't lived a life at all. But you have to try, 'cause if you haven't tried, you haven't lived.

都來人世一趟了卻沒有深深愛過，等於沒有活過。妳必須試試看，因為如果沒試過，妳就沒活過。

羅曼死英文教室

《第六感生死緣》對白中的 head over heels (in love) 是指「為愛神魂顛倒」，描述墜入愛河，深深迷戀對方且為之傾倒的感覺。

A: Why are you two getting married?
你們兩個為什麼要結婚？

B: Because we're head over heels in love!
因為我們深深迷戀著對方！

至於接下來出現的 I'm not hearing any heart. 字面上的意思是「聽不出妳有順從自己的心」，這並不是慣用句，而是指蘇珊口口聲聲說她愛德魯，但其實她愛的是喬布萊克。

Meet Joe Black

《班傑明的奇幻旅程》

馬克吐溫曾說：「如果我們能夠出生的時候八十歲，逐漸接近十八歲，人生一定更美好。」班傑明（Benjamin Button，Brad Pitt 飾）一出生即被遺棄，因為他是一個蒼老的嬰兒，被好心人收養的他，在十一歲時遇到六歲的黛西（Daisy Fuller，Cate Blanchett 飾），後來兩人在各自盛年時相遇相戀，但接下來黛西會越來越老，班傑明卻會越來越年輕……。

Daisy: Will you still love me when my skin grows old and saggy?
等到我人老珠黃，你還會愛我嗎？

Benjamin: Will you still love me when I have acne? When I wet the bed? When I'm afraid of what's under the stairs?
等我開始長青春痘，妳還會愛我嗎？如果我開始尿床？如果我開始害怕樓梯底下有鬼？

Daisy: What...what are you thinking?
你……你在想什麼？

Benjamin: I was thinking how nothing lasts and what a shame that is.
我在想世事無常，真令人遺憾。

Daisy: Some things last.
但有些事是不會改變的。

The Curious Case of Benjamin Button

《愛在黎明破曉時》

傑西（Jesse，Ethan Hawke 飾）到歐洲旅遊時，與法國女孩席琳（Céline，Julie Delpy 飾）在火車上相遇，傑西說服席琳下車和他同遊維也納，但隔天破曉時兩人便要各分東西。在即將分手時，兩人約定半年後再相聚……。

Céline: Loving someone, and being loved, means so much to me.
愛與被愛對我意義重大。
We always make fun of it and stuff. But isn't everything we do in life a way to be loved a little more?
我們老是拿這類事情開玩笑。但我們一生的所作所為，難道不都是為了更加被愛？

Before Sunrise

《愛在日落巴黎時》

傑西與席琳在維也納分手之後，彼此失去聯繫。九年後，傑西將那一夜的故事出版成書，到巴黎進行宣傳，席琳就在記者會上現身。傑西在日落之後就要搭機離去，兩人在巴黎穿街走巷，互訴這九年來的際遇。

Celine: You can never replace anyone because everyone is made up of such beautiful specific details.
任何人都無法被取代，因為每個人都是許多美麗的細節所累積而成。

Before Sunset

Richard Linklater
美國影壇最成功獨立導演

李察林克雷特曾獲柏林影展銀熊獎最佳導演獎肯定，他和男女主角伊森霍克（Ethan Hawke）與茱莉蝶兒（Julie Delpy）這對曾獲奧斯卡金像獎最佳劇本提名的編劇群可謂「金三角」組合，共同打造了《愛在黎明破曉時》（1995）、《愛在日落巴黎時》（2004）、《愛在午夜希臘時》（2013）三部曲。

李察林克雷特的電影多發生在二十四小時以內，這三部曲也延續相同模式，但三段故事卻又橫跨了十八年，像是在時間長河中掬飲的浮光掠影。他的最新電影 Boyhood《年少時代》則是另一項時間的實驗，全片費時十二年拍攝，從小男孩七歲拍到成年，記錄他的成長過程。李察林克雷特在《年少時代》也是與伊森霍克合作（飾演男主角的爸爸），由於這部片的拍攝時間有夠長，拍到最後李察甚至想過：『伊森，如果我先走了，你一定要替我完成啊』！」

《愛在午夜希臘時》

相隔九年，傑西與席琳在希臘的美景中審視彼此的過去、現在與未來，他們相愛但為彼此的家人帶來傷害，他們相愛卻也必須隱忍對彼此的不滿。原來王子與公主在一起之後，並不是過著幸福美滿的生活。

Jesse: If you want love, then this is it. This is real life. It's not perfect but it's real.
如果妳想要愛，這就是愛。現實就是如此。不完美，但千真萬確。

Before Midnight

Mr. Dreamy 夢幻情人

憂鬱型男
Ryan Gosling
雷恩葛斯林

Raised in a strict Mormon family in small-town Ontario, Ryan Gosling was inspired to be an actor watching *Dick Tracy*. With practice singing at weddings with his sister, he was accepted to the Mickey Mouse Club at the age of twelve, where he performed alongside Justin Timberlake and Britney Spears. But after years in TV, Gosling decided he wanted to be a serious actor,and received praise for his performances in independent films like *The Believer* (2001) and Sandra Bullock vehicle *Murder by Numbers* (2002). But it was his appearance opposite Rachel McAdams in the romantic drama *The Notebook* that brought him to mainstream audiences. Since dating his costars Bullock and McAdams, Gosling has just had a daughter with his latest costar, Eva Mendes.

© Jaguar PS / Shuttershock.com

雷恩葛斯林成長於純樸的加拿大安大略省，一個管教嚴格的摩門教家庭中，因觀看《狄克崔西》而立志成為演員。靠著與姐姐一起在婚禮獻唱作為練習，他在十二歲那年獲選進入米老鼠俱樂部，與賈斯汀及小甜甜布蘭妮同台演出。在電視圈打滾多年後，葛斯林決定他想當個「正經演員」，於是在《狂熱份子》（2001）以及為珊卓布拉克量身打造的《拿命線索》（2002）等獨立電影中參與表演，並因此獲得好評。不過真正讓主流觀眾注意到他的，則是他在愛情電影《手札情緣》裡與瑞秋麥亞當斯的對手演出。葛斯林不但曾跟搭檔女星布拉克和麥亞當斯傳出戀曲，日前更與最近同演的伊娃曼德絲生下了女寶寶。

影星小檔案

全　名	：Ryan Thomas Gosling
生　日	：November 12, 1980
出生地	：加拿大多倫多
感情狀態	：已婚
成名作	：《手札情緣》 *The Notebook*

© Jaguar PS / Shuttershock.com

小生組團開口唱，融化粉絲心

靠著性感又結實的外型，以及一張俊俏到不真實的臉蛋，憂鬱小生雷恩葛斯林不但演戲吃得開，戲外還和朋友 Zach Shields 自組了一個名叫 Dead Man's Bones 的獨立樂團，曲風走輕歌德搖滾，其中幾首還加入兒童合唱團的演唱，營造獨特而詭異的氛圍。在首張專輯現場演唱時，葛斯林還秀了幾段他自學的鋼琴與大提琴，又帥又有才，是不是整個大加分？

© Featureflash / Shuttershock.com

詹姆斯法蘭柯：如果是葛斯林的話，可以喲～

曾被網友票選「最佳性幻想對象」的雷恩葛斯林，不但深受女性同胞愛戴，連好萊塢帥哥詹姆斯法蘭柯（James Franco）都難抵他的魅力，據說他在看完葛斯林主演的《末日車神》*The Place beyond the Pines* 後，寫下了一篇標題為 Burning for Gosling（葛斯林讓我慾火焚身）的近千字影評，裡頭大讚他的傳神演出和健美好身材，直呼：「我實在太愛葛斯林了，看完這部戲，連我都想當他的床伴了！」有沒有這麼誇張啊！

《真情難捨》

小鎮按摩師維吉亞當森（Virgil Adamson，Val Kilmer 飾）自小失明，與來度假的建築師艾咪班尼克（Amy Benic，Mira Sorvino 飾）墜入情網。後來，維吉接受實驗性手術逐漸恢復視力，他必須重新學習一切，不止是已經習慣的世界，還有愛與被愛的方式……。

Virgil: You will see a lot of things, but they will mean nothing to you, if you lose sight of the thing you love.
你會看到很多東西，但如果忽略你愛的東西，看到再多東西都沒有意義。

At First Sight

《綠野仙蹤》

這部一九三九年的音樂片由茱蒂嘉蓮（Judy Garland）主演，是眾多綠野仙蹤小說改編版本當中最成功的。故事敘述小女孩桃樂絲被龍捲風帶到奇異的奧茲國，桃樂絲想找回家的路，在途中遇到需要腦的稻草人、需要心的錫人（Tin Man），與需要勇氣的獅子，只有奧茲國巫師（Wizard of Oz）才能幫助他們。

Wizard of Oz: A heart is not judged by how much you love, but by how much you are loved by others.
一顆心的價值，不在於你能付出多少愛，而是在於你能得到多少愛。

奧茲國巫師另一段關於心／愛的對白，也很發人深省：
Wizard of Oz: As for you, my *galvanized friend, you want a heart. You don't know how lucky you are not to have one. Hearts will never be practical until they can be made unbreakable.
至於你嘛，這位鐵打的朋友，你想要一顆心。你不知道缺了一顆心是多幸運的事。除非一顆心不會碎，否則一點用都沒有。

Tin Man: But I still want one.
但我還是想要一顆心。

*galvanized [ˋgælvəˌnaɪz] (a.)（用電）鍍上鋅的

The Wizard of Oz

羅曼死英文教室

《真情難捨》這部電影的主角失明，而他在上面對白說的 lose sight of 字面上的意思是「失去視力」，但可不是「瞎掉」，而是「無法看見」，可能是「超出視線之外」，也可能是沒認真看，所以「視而不見」。

• *The police lost sight of the suspect when he entered the tunnel.*
那位警察進入隧道之後，就沒看到嫌犯的蹤影。

• *It's important to never lose sight of your goals.*
無時不刻緊盯目標是很重要的。

《戀夏 500 日》

湯姆（Tom，Joseph Gordon-Levitt 飾）是個覺得什麼都好的男孩，他一見到桑墨（Summer，Zooey Deschanel 飾）就無可自拔的愛上她。湯姆與古靈精怪桑墨無樂不作，讓他充滿希望，以為能與桑墨長相廝守，不幸的是，桑墨並不這麼認為……。

Tom: What happens if you fall in love?
妳萬一戀愛會是什麼樣子？

Summer: Well, you don't believe in that, do you?
呃，你不相信戀愛那一套，對吧？

Tom: It's love. It's not Santa Claus.
我們在講的是愛耶。又不是耶誕老公公。

(500) Days of Summer

《101 次新年快樂》

本片由 Valentine's Day《情人節快樂》原班人馬演出，場景由洛杉磯轉到紐約，敘述跨年倒數前男女之間的悲歡聚散、背叛與原諒。這部電影眾星雲集，人物的愛情故事各自發展，卻又彼此交錯，最後由飾演山姆（Sam）的大師哥男星 Josh Duhamel 說出這段片尾旁白作為總結。

Sam: [voiceover] Sometimes it feels like there are so many things we can't control, earthquakes, floods, reality shows. But it's important to remember the things we can, like forgiveness, second chances, fresh starts.

（旁白）有些時候，我們會覺得許多事情都無法掌握，像是地震、水災、真人實境秀。但千萬要記得我們能掌握的事，像是原諒、給人第二次機會、新的開始。

Because the one thing that turns the world from a lonely place to a beautiful place is love. Love in any of its forms. Love gives us hope, hope for the New Year. That's New Year's Eve to me. Hope, and a great party.

因為讓世界從一個孤絕之地變成美麗境界，靠的就是愛。愛藏在各種形式當中。愛能夠給我們希望，新年的新希望。除夕對我而言就是如此。希望，和一個大派對。

New Year's Eve

《藍色情人節》

面對酗酒的臨時工丈夫迪恩（Dean，Ryan Gosling 飾），辛勤工作的妻子辛蒂（Cindy，Michele Williams 飾）越來越無法忍受，兩人不禁懷疑：當初讓他們決定共度一生的真情至愛，到底是如何走到這個地步？

Dean: I feel like men are more romantic than women. When we get married we marry, like, one girl, 'cause we're resistant the whole way until we meet one girl and we think "I'd be an idiot if I didn't marry this girl she's so great."

我覺得男人比女人浪漫多了。當我們跟一個女孩結婚，是因為我們一直拒絕走入婚姻，直到遇到一個超棒的女孩，讓我們覺得不娶她就太白癡了。

But it seems like girls get to a place where they just kind of pick the best option; "Oh he's got a good job." I mean they spend their whole life looking for Prince Charming and then they marry the guy who's got a good job and is gonna stick around.

但女人結婚，似乎就只是到時候挑出最佳選擇，「喔，他的工作不錯。」我是說，女人花一輩子尋找白馬王子，卻嫁給一個工作不錯、不會走人的傢伙。

Blue Valentine

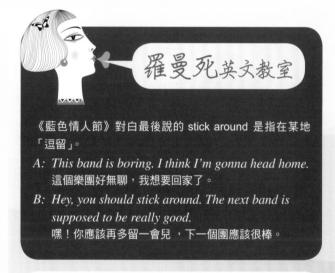

羅曼死英文教室

《藍色情人節》對白最後說的 stick around 是指在某地「逗留」。

A: This band is boring. I think I'm gonna head home.
這個樂團好無聊，我想要回家了。

B: Hey, you should stick around. The next band is supposed to be really good.
嘿！你應該再多留一會兒，下一個團應該很棒。

《愛的故事》

奧利佛（Oliver Barrett，Ryan O'Neal 飾）是含著銀湯匙出生的富家子弟，他與小家碧玉珍妮佛（Jennifer，Ali MacGraw 飾）的戀情不被父親認可，儘管父親威脅利誘，奧利佛仍堅定與所愛的人相守，刻苦生活、自力更生完成學業，眼看兩人就要苦盡甘來，珍妮佛卻罹患絕症……。

Jennifer: Love means never having to say you're sorry.

愛就是絕對不必說抱歉。

Love Story

《理性與感性》

本片由李安導演，改編自珍奧斯汀的小說。故事敘述姐妹花艾琳娜及瑪麗安（Marianne，Kate Winslet 飾）因喪父生活陷入困頓，被迫遷離大莊園，搬到鄉間居住。聰明熱情的瑪麗安在那裡與青年威樂比（Willoughby，Greg Wise 飾）相戀，威樂比最後卻選擇與富家女結婚，令瑪麗安心碎。

Marianne: Love is not love which alters when it alteration finds, or bends with the remover to remove.

愛算不得真愛，如果隨著世事變化就變心，或是人一走遠便離開。

Oh, no. It is an ever fixed mark that looks on tempests and is never shaken. Willoughby! Willoughby! Willoughby!

哦，那不是愛！愛是永不熄滅的塔燈，傲視暴風狂雨絕不動搖。威樂比！威樂比！威樂比！

Sense and Sensibility

《狄更斯的秘密情史》

事業如日中天的大文豪狄更斯（Charles Dickens，Ralph Fiennes 飾）與小他二十七歲的十八歲女演員娜莉（Nelly，Felicity Jones 飾）相戀，兩人的才識相當，相互傾心，卻礙於狄更斯已婚而無法公開。

Charles Dickens: Every human creature is a profound secret and mystery to every other.

對所有人來說，每個人類都是一個難解的秘密和謎題。

Nelly: Until that secret is given to another, and then perhaps two human creatures may know each other.

直到向另一個人揭露那個秘密，或許那兩個人類就能相知相惜了。

The Invisible Woman

羅曼死英文教室

《理性與感性》片中，瑪麗安在狂風暴雨中說道：

Love is not love which alters when it alteration finds. Or bends with the remover to remove.

這段台詞是莎士比亞十四行詩中的句子。which 是關係代名詞指 love，alters 是形容詞子句的動詞，表示「變樣」，when 子句表時間，when it alteration finds 這個倒裝句原為 when it finds alteration，整句的意思是：當愛情找到變心的理由就變質，這就不是真愛。

《枕邊陷阱》

這部古裝異色驚悚片敘述十九世紀末，殷實的古巴咖啡商人路易斯（Luis Vargas，Antonio Banderas 飾）從美國郵購一名新娘，當新娘茱莉亞（Julia Russell，Angelina Jolie 飾）下船時，路易斯馬上拜倒在她的驚人美貌之下。路易斯對茱莉亞的迷戀，會為他帶來什麼樣的命運呢？

I am someone else when I'm with you, someone more like myself.

跟妳在一起時我成了另一個人，一個更像我自己的人。

Original Sin

《戰地情人》

二戰期間，希臘小島被義大利佔領，熱愛音樂的義大利軍官柯瑞里上尉（Captain Corelli，Nicholas Cage 飾）隨軍進駐，與村醫伊安尼斯（Dr. Iannis，John Hurt 飾）的女兒佩拉吉雅（Pelagia，Penélope Cruz 飾）相戀。但橫亙在兩人之間的，除了侵略者與被侵略者的敵對關係，還有佩拉吉雅的婚約。隨著戰事變化，這對戀人能否開花結果？

Nicolas Cage
散發憂鬱氣質的另類影帝

在 Captain Corelli's Mandolin《戰地情人》中飾演義大利軍官的尼可拉斯凱吉本身即是義大利裔，義大利黑幫經典電影《教父》系列大導演科波拉（Francis Ford Coppola）雖然是他叔叔，但他似乎沒沾到多少主流電影的光，反而是以一些半瘋半傻的另類角色闖出名號。

說到浪漫愛情片，大家可能不太會想到 Nicolas Cage 這號人物，但其實讓他獲得奧斯卡最佳男主角獎的 Leaving Las Vegas《遠離賭城》，就是一部浪漫劇情片，他在片中飾演自我放棄的酒鬼。他與美國甜心梅格萊恩（Meg Ryan）也合作過 City of Angels《X 情人》，飾演墮入人間的天使。而他與雪兒（Cher）合演的 Moonstruck《發暈》在影史最佳浪漫喜劇一直榜上有名，雪兒更以此片奪得奧斯卡最佳女主角。

Dr. Iannis: Love is a temporary madness. It erupts like an earthquake and then subsides.

愛是一種暫時的瘋狂。就像地震猛然爆發隨之平息。

And when it subsides you have to make a decision. You have to work out whether your roots have become so *entwined together that it is *inconceivable that you should ever part. Because this is what love is.

當狂愛平息，你必須作出決定。你必須辨明彼此的關係是否已盤根錯節，難以分割。因為這就是愛。

Love is not breathlessness, it is not excitement, it is not the *promulgation of promises of eternal passion. That is just being "in love" which any of us can convince ourselves we are.

愛不在於令人摒息，不在於令人興奮，不在於承諾永不止息的熱情。那只不過是「談戀愛」，誰都能說服自己在戀愛中。

Love itself is what is left over when being in love has burned away, and this is both an art and a fortunate accident. Your mother and I had it, we had roots that grew towards each other underground, and when all the pretty blossoms had fallen from our branches, we found that we were one tree and not two.

愛是談戀愛的激情燃燒的餘燼，是一種藝術，也是美麗的意外。你媽和我曾經相愛，我們的根在地下伸向彼此，待到美麗的花朵從我們的枝幹掉落，才發現我們已經合為一株，不分你我。

*entwine [ɪnˋtwaɪn] (v.) 纏繞，緊密結合
*inconceivable [ˌɪnkənˋsivəbḷ] (a.) 不能想像的
*promulgation [ˌprɑmʌlˋgeʃən] (n.) 公布，宣之於口

Captain Corelli's Mandolin

《心靈捕手》

一位麻省理工學院的數學教授發現年輕的清潔工威爾（Will Hunting，Matt Damon 飾）是數學天才，教授找老朋友西恩（Sean Maguire，Robin Williams 飾）擔任威爾的諮詢師，童年遭遇悲慘的威爾起初極為抗拒，最後終於在西恩及好友的支持下，找到人生目標。

It doesn't matter if the guy is perfect or the girl is perfect, as long as they are perfect for each other.

一個男生或是一個女生完不完美都不要緊，只要他們完全適合彼此就好。

Good Will Hunting

Hugh Grant 休葛蘭

© Featureflash / Shutterstock.com

Hugh Grant was born on September 9, 1960 in London to a carpet company owner and a schoolteacher. Always a good student, Grant was accepted on a [1]**scholarship** to Oxford, where he studied English [2]**literature** and got involved in student drama. In his senior year, Grant starred in *Privileged*, an Oxford-[3]**funded** film about hard-partying students. After graduating with honors, he worked a number of jobs—including writing book reviews and producing radio ads—before considering acting as a career.

Joining the Nottingham Playhouse, Grant [4]**honed** his acting skills on the stage and began winning roles in films like the Merchant Ivory period dramas *Maurice* and *The Remains of the Day*. But by the age of 32, he felt like his career was going nowhere. Just as he was about to give up acting, Grant won the role of a lifetime in the 1994 hit romantic comedy *Four Weddings and a Funeral*. His [5]**portrayal** of the good-natured but [6]**awkward** Charles won him a **Golden Globe** for best actor and made him a big star on both sides of the Atlantic.

Despite a sex [7]**scandal** with a Hollywood [8]**prostitute** in 1995, Grant found continued success playing charming [9]**leads** in hits like Ang Lee's *Sense and Sensibility* and romantic comedy *Notting Hill*. He also [10]**expanded** his range by playing a [11]**womanizer** in *Bridget Jones's Diary* and *About a Boy*. Grant is also famous for his romantic [12]**exploits** off the silver screen. Since his 13-year relationship with model and actress Elizabeth Hurley ended in 2000, he's dated [13]**socialite** Jemima Khan, and recently had three children—two with a Chinese restaurant worker and one with a Swedish TV producer.

Showbiz Words

period drama 時代劇

時代劇 period drama 又稱為古裝劇，指背景設定在特定年代的電影或電視劇，這類戲劇往往透過服裝、場景等表現該年代的氛圍。時代劇通常改編自文學作品或史實，英國廣播公司 BBC 的珍奧斯汀系列，以及獨立電視台（Independent Television）所拍攝的《唐頓莊園》（Downton Abbey）皆為十分受歡迎的時代劇。

Golden Globe Awards 金球獎

金球獎（Golden Globe Awards）是一個美國的電影與電視獎項，主辦單位是好萊塢外國記者協會（Hollywood Foreign Press Association）。此獎從一九四四年起每年舉辦一次，直到二○○三年之前，金球獎的頒獎晚宴都在奧斯卡獎投票日的幾天前舉辦。二○○三年以後，金球獎固定於每年的一月中旬舉行以便與奧斯卡獎區別。此獎的最終結果，是由九十六位居住在洛杉磯、專門報導美國影劇新聞的外國記者投票產生。

休葛蘭於 1960 年九月九日在倫敦出生，父親是地毯公司老闆，母親則為學校老師。向來都是好學生的葛蘭獲得牛津大學提供獎學金入學，當時他主修英國文學並參與學生戲劇的演出。大四那一年，葛蘭主演了由牛津校方資助的電影《牛津之愛》，內容描述一群喜愛狂歡的學生。以優秀成績畢業後，他先是換了許多工作，包括撰寫書評及製作廣播廣告，然後才考慮以演戲為業。

葛蘭於是加入了諾丁罕劇場、在舞台上磨練他的演技，並且也開始為自己贏得電影角色，像是墨詮艾佛利製片公司所拍攝的《墨利斯的情人》及《長日將盡》等時代劇。不過到了三十二歲時，他不禁覺得自己的演藝生涯前途茫茫。就在他即將放棄星途時，葛蘭卻在 1994 年的賣座愛情喜劇《妳是我今生的新娘》裡，得到了一生難逢的角色。他在片中飾演本性善良但言行笨拙的查爾斯一角，為他奪下金球獎的最佳男主角獎，更令他成為大西洋兩岸的巨星。

雖然葛蘭於 1995 年和一位好萊塢妓女捲入性醜聞風波，不過他仍持續在賣座電影中成功主演迷人的男主角，像是李安執導的《理性與感性》以及浪漫喜劇《新娘百分百》。此外，他更拓展了自己的戲路，在《BJ 單身日記》和《非關男孩》中飾演獵豔豔高手。葛蘭於銀幕外的情史也同樣出名。自從他於 2000 年和名模兼演員的伊莉莎白赫莉結束一段長達十三年的關係後，他曾與社交名媛珍美瑪罕交往過，近年來還生下了三個小孩，其中兩位孩子的媽媽是一名中國餐廳員工，另一個小孩則是與一名瑞典的電視製作人所共育。

Tongue-tied No More

get involved in sth. 參與……

involve 是「包含，涉入」的意思，而 get involved in sth. 就是指親身參與某事物。

A: What are you planning on doing now that you're retired?
現在你退休了，有什麼打算？
B: I'm thinking of getting involved in charity work.
我想要參與慈善活動。

Vocabulary Bank

1) **scholarship** [ˈskɑlɚˌʃɪp] (n.) 獎學金
Scholarships are available to students with superior grades.
獎學金是提供給成績優異的學生。

2) **literature** [ˈlɪtərətʃɚ] (n.) 文學，文學作品
Donna studied French literature in graduate school.
唐娜研究所讀的是法國文學。

3) **fund** [fʌnd] (v./n.) 提供資金；資金，基金
Because he is so rich, Bill Gates is often asked to fund new ideas.
比爾蓋茲十分富有，因此時常被邀請資助新創事業。

4) **hone** [hon] (v.) 磨練
Patrick is going to a cram school to hone his math skills.
派翠克上補習班加強他的數學。

5) **portrayal** [porˈtreəl] (n.) 飾演，描繪
The actor's portrayal of Lincoln was widely praised.
那位演員所飾演的林肯廣受讚譽。

6) **awkward** [ˈɔkwəd] (a.) 笨拙的，尷尬的
There was an awkward silence at the dinner table.
晚餐桌上有種尷尬的沈默。

7) **scandal** [ˈskændəl] (n.) 醜聞
The scandal ruined the politician's reputation.
該起醜聞毀了這名政治人物的聲譽。

8) **prostitute** [ˈprɑstɪˌtut] (n.) 娼妓
The woman caught her husband sleeping with a prostitute.
那名女人將嫖妓的丈夫捉姦在床。

9) **lead** [lid] (n.) 主角，主要演員
Both leads won Oscars for their performances in the film.
兩位主角都因在這部電影中的表現贏得奧斯卡獎。

10) **expand** [ɪkˈspænd] (v.) 擴大，擴展
The company has plans to expand into Asia.
這公司有擴展至亞洲的計畫。

11) **womanizer** [ˈwumənˌaɪzɚ] (n.) 沉溺於女色者，花花公子
Dan's father was a drunk and a womanizer.
丹的父親是個沉迷女色的酒鬼。

12) **exploit** [ˈɛkˌsplɔɪt] (n.) 功績，英勇事蹟
We learned about the exploits of Napoleon in history class.
我們在歷史課上學到拿破崙的英勇事蹟。

13) **socialite** [ˈsoʃəˌlaɪt] (n.) 社交名流
Most New York socialites live in Manhattan.
曼哈頓是紐約社交名流的聚集地。

愛的宣言

世上最浪漫的表白，莫過於不用直白地說出「我愛你」這三個字，卻能將心中真摯的情意表達得淋漓盡致。用隱晦的言語傳達，含蓄而深沉，更能打動人心。尤其在電影中，觀眾隨著劇情一起經歷了一對戀人從相識到相戀的過程，中間穿插一、兩句只有雙方才能心領神會的密語，不但能表現出兩人之間的脈脈深情，也能讓觀眾深刻感受到戀人間的默契，成為值得再三回味的經典對白。

《征服情海》

運動明星經紀人傑瑞（Jerry Maguire，Tom Cruise 飾）與老闆意見不合而被炒魷魚後，只有會計桃樂絲（Dorothy Boyd，Renée Zellweger 飾）和另一位二線球員願意與他同進退。隨後三人一起創業，傑瑞和桃樂絲也結了婚，但因事業不順等因素，兩人分居。傑瑞事業成功後，發現沒有妻子一起分享，人生就不算完整，於是來找桃樂絲，為了挽回她而發表了長篇大論，桃樂絲回應了傑瑞這句臺詞。

Dorothy: You had me at hello.
你一開口打招呼，我就已經被征服了。

Jerry Maguire

直接了當！打動人心的英文說話術

You had me at hello，這句話的字面來說會讓人聯想到中文的「一見鍾情」，不過在這部電影裡，這句話出現的時候，男女主角已不是第一次相遇。男主角傑瑞在歷經了事業的起伏後，領悟到與另一半分享人生的重要性，於是去找分居中的妻子桃樂絲，在剛進門時說了一聲「Hello」。接下來說了一段長篇大論，試圖挽回桃樂絲。桃樂絲最後回應他：You had me at hello.

另一句這部電影的經典臺詞 You complete me. 的意思是「你讓我變得完整」，也就是「我的生命有你才完整」。而這句臺詞，在電影前半段也出現過一次。那時仍不熟識的傑瑞和桃樂絲在電梯裡看到一對情侶，男生對女生用手語比了一句話，女生顯得很高興的樣子。傑瑞很好奇那個男生說了什麼，桃樂絲剛好會手語，告訴傑瑞那句話是 You complete me. 在電影尾聲中，由傑瑞口中再次說出來，不但達到前後呼應的效果，還讓觀眾知道，傑瑞一直將桃樂絲說的話放在心上。You had me at hello.、You complete me. 兩句話可說是直白誠懇的浪漫說話術名句，趕快學起來！

《大象的眼淚》

美國經濟大蕭條時期，獸醫學院學生雅各（Jacob Jankowski，Robert Pattinson 飾）因父母雙亡，生命失去方向，決定離開學校。他意外搭上馬戲團列車，擔任起馬戲團獸醫，並愛上馬戲團老闆娘瑪蓮娜（Marlena，Reese Witherspoon 飾），兩人從此展開曲折的命運。

Jacob: You're a beautiful woman. You deserve a beautiful life.
妳是個美麗的女人，妳值得擁有美麗的人生。

Water for Elephants

《幸運符》

美國海軍陸戰隊中士羅根（Logan Thibault，Zac Efron 飾）在戰場上撿到一張陌生女孩的照片，之後每次出任務時，都能逃過一劫，於是將照片視為幸運符。退役歸國後，他找到照片中的女子貝絲（Beth Green，Taylor Schilling 飾），並窮盡一切力量為她帶來幸福。

Logan: You should be kissed, every day, every hour, every minute.
妳每一天、每一小時、每一分鐘都應該被吻。

The Lucky One

《一日一生》

殺人越獄的逃犯法蘭克（Frank Chambers，Josh Brolin 飾），在超市遇到單親媽媽愛黛兒（Adele Wheeler，Kate Winslet 飾）和她的兒子亨利，法蘭克挾持這對母子，威脅愛黛兒帶自己回家。勞動節週末長假發生的這一連串事件，改變了三人的命運和人生。

Frank: I'd take twenty more years just to have another three days with you.
我願意用二十年的自由，來換取多跟妳相處三天的時光。

Labor Day

《麥迪遜之橋》

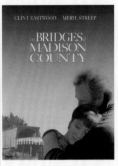

1965 年，在愛荷華州麥迪遜郡，寂寞的義大利裔家庭主婦法蘭西絲卡（Francesca，Meryl Streep 飾）在丈夫與孩子們外出時，遇到來當地拍攝廊橋的攝影師羅勃（Robert，Clint Eastwood 飾），兩人迅速墜入愛河。他們相處的四天，成為法蘭西絲卡生命中的祕密。

Robert: It seems right now that all I've ever done in my life is making my way here to you.
現在看來，我這輩子所做的一切，都只是為了與妳相遇。

Bridges of Madison County

《金色池塘》

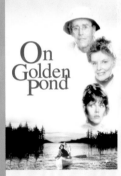

退休的老教授諾曼（Norman，Henry Fonda 飾）與妻子埃塞爾（Ethel，Katherine Hepburn 飾）回到金色池塘畔的故居度過晚年，面臨著年老的各種危機。諾曼有天從外面回來，告訴妻子自己竟然在再熟悉不過的家鄉差點迷了路，感嘆自己漸漸衰老，並陷入深深的恐懼與無助中，於是妻子安慰他並說了這段話：

Ethel: Listen to me, mister. You're my knight in shining armor. Don't forget it. You're going to get back on that horse, and I'm going to be right behind you, holding on tight, and away we're gonna go, go, go!
聽我說，先生，你永遠都是我的白馬王子，別忘了這點。有一天你還能再騎上馬，而我也會坐在你背後，緊抱著你，天涯海角，我們一起前進，前進，前進！

On Golden Pond

《大地英豪》

1757 年，英法兩國為了爭奪殖民地，在北美洲的哈德遜河一帶開戰，英國上校的兩個女兒科拉（Cora，Madeleine Stowe 飾）與愛麗絲前往戰地探望父親，途中被法軍的同盟休倫族印第安人綁架，英國軍方的偵查員與莫西幹族人去營救她們。這段臺詞，是男主角鷹眼（Hawkeye，Daniel Day-Lewis 飾）要女主角科拉向休倫族印第安人暫時投降以求保命時說的話：

Hawkeye: You stay alive, no matter what occurs! I will find you. No matter how long it takes, no matter how far, I will find you.
不論發生什麼事，妳要活著！我會找到妳的。不論要多久時間、多遠距離，我會找到妳。

The Last of the Mohicans

《魔戒首部曲：魔戒現身》

在古老的中土世界，哈比族人佛羅多巴金斯得到一個代表邪惡勢力的魔戒，邪惡的黑暗魔君索倫知道後，準備奪回魔戒。佛羅多在夥伴的陪伴下，踏上毀滅魔戒的征程。路上有遊俠亞拉岡、精靈公主亞玟等正義力量的保護和幫助。亞玟（Arwen，Liv Tyler 飾）與人皇亞拉岡（Aragorn，Viggo Mortensen 飾）相戀，決定放棄精靈長生不死的生命，對亞拉岡說了這段臺詞：

Arwen: I would rather share one lifetime with you than face all the ages of this world alone. I choose a mortal life.
我寧願和你共度短暫的一生，也不願孤獨地面對世間無盡的歲月。我選擇成為凡人。

The Lord of the Rings: Fellowship of the Ring

《手札情緣》

年邁的諾亞（Noah，Ryan Gosling 飾）日復一日來到療養院探望罹患阿茲海默症的艾麗（Allie，Rachel McAdams 飾），讀日記給她聽，娓娓道出往事，讓艾麗回想起他們兩人之間的愛情。這句臺詞是兩人年輕時來到海邊，艾麗在海中戲水時，告訴諾亞自己的前世可能是隻鳥，像海鷗一樣飛翔，諾亞回了她這句話：

Noah: If you're a bird, I'm a bird.
如果妳是隻鳥，那我也是隻鳥。

The Notebook

《北非諜影》

二次大戰期間，神秘的美國人李克（Rick，Humphrey Bogart 飾）在卡薩布蘭卡經營一家酒吧。一日，捷克的反納粹領袖維克和妻子伊爾莎（Ilsa，Ingrid Bergman 飾）來到酒吧，希望找到管道拿到通行證離開卡薩布蘭卡。李克見到伊爾莎時，發現是他日思夜念的昔日戀人。最後李克決定幫他們夫婦離開卡薩布蘭卡，在機場送他們離開時，李克對伊爾莎說了這句臺詞：

Rick: Here's looking at you, kid.
永誌不忘。

Casablanca

直視對方，讓女生害羞的英文說話術

Here's looking at you, kid! 這句電影《北非諜影》中的經典台詞，在電影中分別在巴黎相識、車站離別、酒吧重聚，還有機場告別時出現。這句臺詞最常見的中譯版是：「永誌不忘」。而字面的意思則是：「我正看著你，孩子」，也可以意譯為，「我的眼裡一直有你」、「你一直在我心裡」。

關於這句臺詞，還有段小插曲，劇本裡原本寫的是 Here's good luck to you. 鮑嘉把臺詞改了。傳聞當時在拍戲的空檔，鮑嘉在教英格麗玩撲克牌時，經常說 Here's looking at you. 這句話。而這句話應該跟撲克牌的術語有關，當你拿到國王、王后和騎士這三張「人面牌」（face card）時，已經是勝券在握，亮牌時就可以說：「他們（這幾張臉）都在看著你（Here's looking at you.）」。將這句話巧妙融合了敬酒詞 Here's to you. 成了劇中經典臺詞。鮑嘉對這句即興發揮的臺詞似乎情有獨鍾，因為在他另一部電影《午夜》Midnight 也出現過。

《命運規劃局》

美國紐約州聯邦眾議員大衛（David，Matt Damon 飾），邂逅芭蕾舞老師伊莉（Elise，Emily Blunt 飾），兩人墜入愛河，卻突然出現一群自稱「命運規劃局」的幹員，阻撓大衛與伊莉的姻緣。大衛不甘心任由命運被擺布，誓言要掌握自己的命運，在穿越一道神秘的任意門之前，詢問伊莉是否要跟他一起走。

David: OK, I can go through this door, alone. You'll never see me or the people chasing us again.

好吧，我可以自己穿越這道門，妳就再也見不到我，也不會再有人追我們。

Or you can come with me, and I don't know what's on the other side, but I'd know you'd be next to me.

或者，妳可以跟我走，我不知道過了這道門後會發生什麼事，但我知道妳會在我身邊。

And that's all I wanted since the minute I met you.

這是我從第一眼見到妳後，就一直想要的。

Elise: I'm coming with you.

我跟你走。

The Adjustment Bureau

《紅磨坊》

改編自歌舞劇的電影版，由伊旺麥奎格（Ewan McGregor）和妮可基嫚（Nicole Kidman）飾演男女主角克利斯汀（Christian）和莎婷（Satine）。十九世紀末，來自中產階級的年輕人克利斯汀，獨自來到巴黎闖天下，在蒙馬特區的紅磨坊與紅牌歌舞明星莎婷相識相戀，兩人的身分，加上貴族的介入，這場愛情故事注定以悲劇告終。這句臺詞是歌舞劇中最終曲《天荒地老》*Come What May* 其中一段歌詞。

Storm clouds may gather and stars may collide, but I love you, until the end of time.

風起雲湧，星辰隕滅，我依然愛你到天荒地老。

Moulin Rouge

《鐵達尼號》

1912 年，年輕美貌的貴族少女蘿絲（Rose，Kate Winslet 飾）隨著母親和未婚夫搭上豪華的鐵達尼號巨輪，邂逅了年輕畫家傑克（Jack，Leonardo DiCaprio 飾），兩人墜入愛河。這段對白是在鐵達尼號撞上冰山而沉船之時，傑克讓蘿絲爬上一塊浮板，自己則抓著浮板，泡在水裡，要蘿絲答應他活下去。

Jack: Winning that ticket, Rose, was the best thing that ever happened to me…it brought me to you. And I'm thankful for that, Rose. I'm thankful.

贏到那張船票，蘿絲，是我有生以來最棒的事，是它讓我遇見妳。我感激這件事，蘿絲，很感激。

You must do me this honor, Rose. Promise me you'll survive. That you won't give up, no matter what happens, no matter how hopeless. Promise me now, Rose, and never let go of that promise.

妳一定要答應我一件事，蘿絲，答應我妳會活下去，絕不放棄，不管發生什麼事，不管希望多渺茫。現在就答應我，蘿絲，千萬別忘記這個承諾。

Rose: I promise.

我答應你。

Jack: Never let go.

絕不放棄。

Rose: I'll never let go, Jack. I'll never let go.

我絕不放棄，傑克，絕不放棄。

Titanic

《暮光之城：無懼的愛》

《暮光之城》系列描述的是女高中生貝拉（Bella，Kristen Stewart 飾）與帥氣的吸血鬼愛德華（Edward，Robert Pattinson 飾）之間的浪漫愛情故事。因父母離異，貝拉隨父親來到小鎮生活。在新學校裡，貝拉發現庫倫家族的人舉止詭異，很是神秘。在實驗課上，她遇到庫倫家族中的愛德華，被他俊朗的外表和出眾的談吐吸引。此時，小鎮裡接連發生死亡事件。在一次意外中，愛德華救出貝拉時，貝拉發現他擁有異於常人的能力，開始懷疑他就是殺人兇手。愛德華向她坦白，自己是吸血鬼，而兇手另有其人。

Edward: I can't read your mind. You have to tell me what you're thinking.
我無法讀妳的心，告訴我妳在想什麼。

Bella: That I'm afraid.
我很害怕。

Edward: Good.
很好。

Bella: I'm not afraid of you. I'm only afraid of losing you, like you're going to disappear.
我不是怕你，我唯一害怕的是失去你，我感覺你就要消失了。

Edward: You don't know how long I've waited for you.
妳不知道我等了妳多久。

Bella: I'd rather die than to stay away from you.
寧可死別，絕不生離。

Edward: That's what you dream about? Being a monster?
這就是妳的夢想？當一個怪物？

Bella: I dream about being with you forever.
我的夢想是永遠跟你在一起。

Twilight

風靡一時的《暮光之城》

電影《暮光之城》系列改編自美國暢銷小說家史蒂芬妮梅爾（Stephenie Meyer）的同名作品，共有四集，分別是《暮光之城》Twilight、《暮光之城：新月》New Moon、《暮光之城：蝕》Eclipse、《暮光之城：破曉》Breaking Dawn。

梅爾的《暮光之城》系列其實是正反評價兩極的作品，不過，由於小說內容充滿許多少女情懷般的戀愛情節，帥氣的吸血鬼愛上平凡的女孩，俊男美女，加上浪漫愛情等元素，因此深受美國廣大青少女喜愛，成為死忠書迷。她的處女作《暮光之城》出版時，便被書店票選為 2005 年最佳新秀作家之一，更被媒體譽為「J.K. 羅琳第二」。

梅爾是虔誠的摩門教徒，畢業於美國猶他州的楊百翰大學，擁有英文學士學位，目前居住於亞歷桑那州。她曾坦言自己不吸菸、不喝酒，有別於與一般人對好萊塢文化的印象。她早年結婚生子後，放棄了當律師的夢想，留在家裡做全職媽媽，結果寫出《暮光之城》一系列暢銷小說，而且之前沒有寫作經驗。

據說梅爾寫出《暮光之城》的靈感，來自於她所做的一個夢。夢中她見到一對少男少女在一片草原上交談，少女相貌平凡，少年卻擁有驚人的美貌。梅爾直覺這名少年不是普通人，而是一名吸血鬼。有趣的是，身為虔誠的摩門教徒，她不允許自己看限制級的電影，就算是她最欣賞的演員詹姆斯麥艾維（James McAvoy）所主演的《刺客聯盟》也一樣不看。但她所寫的《暮光之城》，卻是描述邪惡、血腥的吸血鬼，與一名人類少女共譜一場禁忌之戀的故事。

《暮光之城 2：新月》

被比喻為「美版瓊瑤小說」、「美版花系列」的《暮光之城》系列，內容主要著墨於男女主角之間的情愛糾葛，電影中當然也少不了運用大量的浪漫對白，來刻畫出男女主角之間濃烈的情感。

Bella: I needed to make you see me once. You had to know that I was alive. You didn't have to feel guilty or anything. I can let you go now.

我必須再讓你見到我一次，讓你知道我還活著。你不必感到內疚什麼的。我現在就放你走。

Edward: You never had to let it go. I just couldn't live in a world where you don't exist.

妳不用放什麼走。我就是不能活在一個沒有妳的世界。

Bella: But you said....

但你說……。

Edward: I lied. I had to lie and you believe me so easily.

我騙妳的，我不得已撒謊，而且妳這麼輕易就相信我了。

Bella: Because it doesn't make sense for you to love me. I'm nothing...human.

因為你沒理由愛我。我什麼都不是，只是一個凡人。

Edward: Bella, you're everything to me. You're everything.

貝拉，妳是我的全部，我的全部。

Edward: Bella, the only reason why I left is because I thought I was protecting you. So that you could have a chance at a normal, happy life.

貝拉，我離開妳只有一個原因，我以為我這麼做，是在保護妳。讓妳有機會過上正常的幸福生活。

Bella: It was so easy for you to leave.

對你來說，離開是輕而易舉的事。

Edward: Leaving you was the hardest thing I've done in 100 years. I swear, I will never fail you again.

離開妳是我這一百年來所做過最困難的事。我發誓，我再也不會辜負妳了。

Edward: So how come Jacob Black gets to give you a gift, and I don't?

為什麼雅各可以送妳禮物，我就不能？

Bella: Because I have nothing to give back to you.

因為我沒什麼可以回贈你。

Edward: Bella, you give me everything just by breathing.

貝拉，妳只要活著就是讓我擁有一切。

The Twilight Saga: New Moon

《電子情書》

凱薩琳（Kathleen，Meg Ryan 飾）在紐約經營母親留下的小書店，書店已有四十年歷史。但附近新開張了一家大型的連鎖書店，危及到小店生意，大書店的老闆喬（Joe，Tom Hanks 飾）成為凱薩琳的眼中釘。兩人在現實中是互看不順眼的競爭對手，卻不知彼此是用電子郵件互訴心事的最佳筆友。最後他們終於相認時，凱薩琳對喬說了這句話。

Kathleen: I wanted it to be you, I wanted it to be you so badly.

我希望那是你，我多希望那是你。

You've Got Mail

電子情書

《電子情書》的片名其實是一個置入性行銷的手法，英文原名 *You've Got Mail*，是美國網路公司「美國線上」（AOL）的用戶在收到新郵件時，會聽到的招牌問候語。

除了 1998 年的《電子情書》，1990 年的《跳火山的人》*Joe Versus The Volcano*，以及 1993 年的《西雅圖夜未眠》*Sleepless in Seattle*，梅格萊恩都是和湯姆漢克搭檔演出，因此兩人被觀眾認為是最佳銀幕情侶。時隔十六年，這對黃金搭檔又再度合作，由梅格萊恩首次轉戰導演，執導電影《綺色佳》*Ithaca*，湯姆漢克則擔任製片，兩人也會在電影中飾演夫妻。影片背景設定在二戰時期的美國，描述一個男孩的青春成長故事，預計 2015 年底上映。

Meg Ryan 梅格萊恩

© s_bukley / Shutterstock.com

Showbiz Words

soap opera 肥皂劇

指長期播放，有著連貫劇情的電視戲劇節目，類似台灣的連續劇。被稱為「肥皂」劇是因為這類節目原本多由肥皂廠商贊助，並在節目間隔播放以家庭主婦為目標客群的洗滌產品廣告。由於許多人認為「肥皂劇」有貶低之意，因此又稱其為日間劇（daytime drama）。

America's Sweetheart 美國甜心

sweetheart 這個字可以表示「情人」，也常當作對家人或朋友的親暱稱呼。America's Sweetheart 是美國影劇媒體經常頒給當時最受歡迎女星的封號，尤其是常演浪漫喜劇的女星。最早被封為 America's Sweetheart 的女星，是二十世紀初活躍於美國影壇的加拿大女星瑪麗畢克馥（Mary Pickford）。近年繼梅格萊恩之後，常被媒體封為 America's Sweetheart 的女星，還有茉莉亞羅勃茲、珍妮佛安妮斯頓、珊卓布拉克等人。

- Could you pass me the salt, sweetheart?
  小甜心，可以把鹽遞給我嗎？

🎧 5

Meg Ryan was born on November 19, 1961 in Fairfield, Connecticut, the daughter of a math teacher and an English teacher. Her mother, who had once acted, [1]**fostered** her young daughter's interest in acting. Ryan acted in TV commercials to support herself while studying [2]**journalism** at New York University, and dropped out one semester short of graduating when her acting career began to [3]**take off**.

Ryan's first success was as Betsy Stewart in the soap opera *As the World Turns* (1982 to 1984). Next, after a small part in the [4]**megahit** *Top Gun* (1986), she starred opposite her future ex-husband Dennis Quaid in *Innerspace* (1987) and *D.O.A.* (1988). But it was 1989's *When Harry Met Sally…* that made Meg Ryan a [5]**household** name. The hit romantic comedy, famous for the scene where her character fakes an [6]**orgasm** in a crowded New York [7]**deli**, won her a Golden Globe [8]**nomination** and earned her the title of America's Sweetheart.

This success led to a string of successful rom-coms in the 1990s. Highlights include *Sleepless in Seattle* (1993) and *You've Got Mail* (1998), both of which paired her with Academy-Award winner Tom Hanks, won her two more Golden Globe nominations. Not wanting to be [9]**typecast**, Ryan has also [10]**delved into** other [11]**genres**, such as action thriller *Proof of Life* (2000) opposite *Gladiator* star Russell Crowe, [12]**erotic** thriller *In the Cut* (2003) and [13]**boxing** drama *Against the Ropes* (2004). Taking her career to the next level, Ryan will both direct and star in the 2015 drama *Ithaca*.

© Featureflash / Shutterstock.com

梅格萊恩於 1961 年十一月十九日出生在美國康乃狄克州的費爾菲德市，父母分別為數學及英文老師。她的母親曾演過戲，因此培養了年幼女兒對演戲的興趣。萊恩於紐約大學研讀新聞學時曾演出多部電視廣告以賺取開銷，不過在演藝事業起飛之際、於畢業前一學期自學校輟學。

萊恩於肥皂劇《隨著世界運轉》（1982-1984）中飾演貝西史都華一角而初嘗成功滋味。接下來，在超級鉅片《捍衛戰士》（1986）中跑龍套後，她先後於《驚異大奇航》（1987）和《死亡漩渦》（1988）裡與將來的前夫丹尼斯奎德大演對手戲。不過使梅格萊恩成為家喻戶曉巨星的，則是 1989 年的《當哈利碰上莎莉》。這部賣座浪漫喜劇的著名場景、就是其角色在一間擁擠的紐約餐館裡假扮性高潮，不但使她得到金球獎提名，更為她贏得美國甜心的封號。

該片的成功促成她於 1990 年代接演一連串賣座的浪漫喜劇電影。最著名的包括《西雅圖夜未眠》（1993）以及《電子情書》（1998），兩部電影皆和奧斯卡獎得主湯姆漢克搭檔演出，她也因此兩度獲得金球獎提名。不願被定型的萊恩也嘗試了其他電影類的演出，像是與《神鬼戰士》男星羅素克洛共演的動作驚悚片《千驚萬險》（2000）、情色驚悚電影《凶線靈異第六感》（2003）、以及拳擊劇情片《奮力一擊》（2004）。欲將電影事業帶往下一階段的萊恩，更將執導並主演 2015 年上映的劇情片《綺色佳（暫譯）》。

Tongue-tied No More

short (of sth.) 不足，達不到（某事）

short 當副詞有「短缺」的意思，而 short of sth. 則是指（某事）不足，或者沒有達到特定情況；另外也有「除了……之外」之意。

A: Could you lend me 20 dollars?
　你可以借我二十元嗎？

B: I would, but I'm short of cash.
　我願意借你，但我身上現金不夠。

A: Do you have enough to buy a ticket?
　你的錢夠買票嗎？

B: No. I'm three dollars short.
　不夠。我還差三元。

Vocabulary Bank

1) **foster** [ˋfɔstɚ] (v.) 培養，促進
The writing contest was started to foster young writers.
舉辦這個作文比賽是為了培養年輕作家。

2) **journalism** [ˋdʒɝnəl͵ɪzəm] (n.) 新聞學系，新聞業
After a long career in journalism, James will be retiring in August.
在長期從事新聞業之後，詹姆斯即將在八月退休。

3) **take off** [tek ɔf] (phr.) 起飛；蔚為風潮，大受歡迎
The star's career took off when she was nominated for an Oscar.
那位明星在獲奧斯卡提名後星路大開。

4) **megahit** [ˋmɛgə͵hɪt] (n.) 非常成功或受歡迎的作品（電影、小說、唱片等）
The singer performed all her megahits at the concert.
這位歌手在演唱會上演出所有她最大歡迎的歌曲。

5) **household** [ˋhaʊs͵hold] (a.) 家喻戶曉的
Google has become a household word.
谷歌已經成為家喻戶曉的名詞了。

6) **orgasm** [ˋɔr͵gæzəm] (n.) 性高潮，極度興奮
Many people are unable to achieve orgasm.
許多人無法達到性高潮。

7) **deli** [ˋdɛli] (n.) 熟食店，小吃店
That deli makes tasty sandwiches.
那家熟食店的三明治很好吃。

8) **nomination** [͵nɑməˋneʃən] (n.) 提名
The actress has received many Oscar nominations.
那位女演員多次得到奧斯卡提名。

9) **typecast** [ˋtaɪp͵kæst] (n.)（演員）定型，一再扮演同類型角色
The actor was tired of being typecast as a villian.
這位演員對於老是扮演反派角色感到厭倦。

10) **delve (into)** [dɛlv] (v.) 探索，探究
The documentary delves into the history of World War II.
這部紀錄片深入探討第二次世界大戰的歷史。

11) **genre** [ˋʒɑnrə] (n.)（藝文作品的）類型
What's your favorite genre of literature?
你最喜愛哪一類型的文學作品？

12) **erotic** [ɪˋrɑtɪc] 性愛的，色情的
The museum has an exhibition of erotic art.
這間博物館有個情色藝術的展覽。

13) **boxing** [ˋbɑksɪŋ] (n.) 拳擊運動
Boxing is a dangerous sport.
拳擊是一項危險的運動。

Nicholas Sparks

尼可拉斯史派克

© Featureflash / Shutterstock.com

Nicholas Sparks was born in Omaha, Nebraska on December 31, 1965. After moving from place to place while his father completed graduate school, the family finally settled in Sacramento, California, where Nicholas graduated from high school at the top of his class. Also a [1]**gifted** athlete, he was accepted to the University of Notre Dame on a [2]**track** scholarship. It was a track injury in his freshman year that got Nicholas started as a writer. While he was stuck at home [3]**recuperating** that summer, his mother suggested that he write a book. The result was *The Passing*, a horror novel that was never published.

In 1988, Nicholas met his future wife, Catherine, and graduated with [4]**honors**. The two married the following year, but [5]**tragedy** struck just six weeks later when his mother died in a horse-riding accident. When his next novel was also rejected by publishers, Nicholas held a string of jobs to make ends meet. After eventually becoming a salesman in North Carolina, he decided to make a last attempt at writing. It took him just six months to complete *The Notebook*, but it wasn't until two years later that a young [6]**literary** agent [7]**rescued** his [8]**manuscript** from the slush pile. Published in October 1996, this tragic romance novel, which was inspired by the 60-year marriage of his wife's grandparents, hit the **New York *Times* Best Seller list** within a week of its [9]**release**.

When this success was followed by another tragedy—his father's death in a car crash—he wrote another novel, this one inspired by his parents' relationship. A story about love after [10]**grief**, *Message in a Bottle* was not only a [11]**bestseller**,

Showbiz Words

New York Times Best Seller list
《紐約時報》暢銷書排行榜

《紐約時報》暢銷書排行榜出自於每週日出刊的《紐約時報書評》(The New York Times Book Review)，從一九四二年四月九日起刊登至今，是美國最具公信力的暢銷書排行榜之一。主要分類有印刷書與電子書類 (print & e-books)、精裝書類 (hardcover)、平裝書類 (paperback)、電子書類 (e-books)、建議與其他類 (advice & misc.)、童書類 (children's)、圖畫書類 (graphic books) 等。J.K. 羅琳的《哈利波特》系列與史帝芬妮梅爾的《暮光之城》系列都是榜上常客。

slush pile 成堆的稿件
這是出版界的專門用語，指作家沒有經過經紀人，自行投遞到出版社的稿件。通常這種會被成堆放在編輯桌上，幾乎沒有出版希望。

© Phil Stafford / Shutterstock.com

but also became a [12]**hit** movie starring Kevin Costner. Since then, Nicholas has written a new romance novel nearly every year, many of which have also been made into movies, including *A Night to Remember, Nights in Rodanthe, Dear John* and *The Lucky One*.

1965 年十二月三十一日，尼可拉斯史派克出生於美國內布拉斯加州的奧馬哈。他的父親在攻讀研究所之際，一家人也多處搬遷，最後全家在加州沙加緬度定居下來，而尼可拉斯也在此地以該屆最高分自高中畢業。由於本身也是出色的運動員，他因此獲得聖母大學提供徑賽獎學金而入學。而使尼可拉斯開始寫作的契機，卻也是他大一時在跑道上受傷之故。當年暑假他困在家裡養傷時，他母親建議他提筆寫書，其成果就是一本從未出版、名為 *The Passing* 的恐怖小說。

1988 年，尼可拉斯遇見了他未來的妻子凱瑟琳，同時也以優異成績畢業。兩人於隔年結婚，不過僅六週後家中就遭逢不幸，當時他母親意外墜馬身亡。他的第二本小說也被出版商打回票後，尼可拉斯嘗試了多種工作來維持家計。最後他在北卡羅來納州當起業務，此時他決定給予寫作最後一次機會。他只花了六個月的時間就完成了《手札情緣》，不過一直要到兩年後才由一位年輕的出版經紀人從成堆投稿中將他的稿子挖掘出來。這本靈感源自他太太祖父母六十年婚姻的愛情悲劇小說於 1996 年十月發行，推出後的一週內便登上《紐約時報》暢銷書排行榜。

當他的成功再次被另一件不幸打擊——他的父親於車禍中喪生，他又寫了另一本小說，這次是啟發自他父母的感情婚姻。描寫喪偶後的重拾愛情，《瓶中信》不只是一本暢銷書，還被搬上大銀幕，成為一部由凱文科斯納主演的賣座電影。自此之後，尼可拉斯幾乎每年都會推出一本新的愛情小說，當中有許多都被改拍電影，包括《留住一片情》、《羅丹薩的夜晚》、《最後一封情書》及《幸運符》。

Tongue-tied No More

make ends meet 維持生計

此片語照字面上解釋是「使兩端相接」，大家可以想成記帳時「收入」與「支出」兩欄的數字至少要「入能敷出」，才不會還沒到月底就月光光、心慌慌，所以 make ends meet 可解釋為「收支平衡、勉強餬口」等。

A: How's the pay at your company?
   你在這間公司的薪資待遇如何？
B: Pretty bad. I'm barely making enough to make ends meet.
   很差。我賺的錢少到幾乎無法維持生計。

Vocabulary Bank

1) **gifted** [ˋgɪftɪd] (a.) 有天賦的
   My brother is more musically gifted than I am.
   我哥比我有音樂天份。

2) **track** [træk] (n.) 徑賽運動，跑道
   Joseph was on the track team in high school.
   喬瑟夫高中時是田徑隊的。

3) **recuperate** [rɪˋkupəˌret] (v.) 休養，康復
   How long did it take you to recuperate after your accident?
   你發生意外後花了多久時間才康復？

4) **honors** [ˋɑnəz] (n.) 優異成績，graduate with honors 即「以優異成績畢業」
   Kevin was an honors student in high school.
   凱文在高中是模範生。

5) **tragedy** [ˋtrædʒədi] (n.) 悲劇，慘事，災難
   (a.) tragic 悲慘的
   It's a tragedy that so many people are out of work.
   這麼多人都沒工作，真是個悲劇。

6) **literary** [ˋlɪtəˌrɛri] (a.) 文學的，文藝的
   The novel has been praised by literary critics.
   這部小說深受文學評論家的讚賞。

7) **rescue** [ˋrɛskju] (v./n.) 營救，解圍
   The fireman rescued the girl from the burning building.
   消防員從起火的大樓中救出那個女孩。

8) **manuscript** [ˋmænjəˌskrɪpt] (n.) 手稿，原稿
   The author has almost completed the manuscript of his new novel.
   那位作者已經快完成他的新小說手稿了。

9) **release** [rɪˋlis] (n./v.) 發表，發行
   The band's new album is scheduled for release in July.
   那個樂團的新專輯預計會在七月發行。

10) **grief** [grif] (n.) 悲痛，悲傷
   The boy's death caused his parents great grief.
   那位男孩的死讓他的父母悲痛萬分。

11) **bestseller** [ˋbɛstˋsɛlə] (n.) 暢銷的商品
   This novel has been a bestseller for several years.
   這部小說熱賣好幾年了。

12) **hit** [hɪt] (a.) 流行的，熱門的
   Have you heard Jolin Tsai's latest hit single?
   你有聽過蔡依林的最新單曲嗎？

史派克看電影

不同於某些小說家，史派克對自己的小說改編電影總是保持開放、樂觀其成的態度。
他曾說，自己是透過寫小說來講故事，讀者讀了小說後，自然會對故事產生自己的想像，
而電影是另一種說故事的方式，改編電影中所呈現、
反應的也同樣是讀者對小說故事的某種想像罷了。

史派克的改編電影中有許多讓觀眾難忘的鏡頭，
譬如《手扎情緣》大雨中Ryan Gosling把Rachel McAdams高舉擁吻，令人刻骨銘心；
《最後一封情書》Channing Tatum與Amanda Seyfried一前一後坐在沙洲蘆葦草中，
依依不捨的擁抱……經典浪漫畫面不勝枚舉。
現在換個角度，讓熱衷觀賞自己小說改編電影的史派克，來告訴你他最喜歡的經典電影畫面。

Message in the Bottle《瓶中信》(1999)

It was far and away the most surreal experience I've ever had because it was first.
看這片時我覺得非常超現實，因為這是被拍的第一部電影。

這部片我最喜歡的一幕是男主角老爸 Paul Newman、女主角 Robin Wright、男主角 Kevin Costner，三人坐在房子前的長廊聊天，Paul Newman「虧」女主角說：
If I was 100 years younger, you'd be in big trouble.（要是我年輕個一百歲，妳就要當心了。）

A Walk to Remember《留住一片情》(2002)

The movie we watch most frequently in my house is A Walk To Remember…I think the message there is wonderful.
看這片時我覺得非常超現實，因為這是被拍的第一部電影。

這部片有很多幕都很棒，但我會選男主角 Shane West 在車上幫女主角在肩膀弄上刺青貼紙的那幕。我很喜歡他努力想幫女主角 Mandy Moore 在來時不多的日子裡完成一點夢想的舉動。

The Notebook 《手扎情緣》(2004)

We gotta go with the rain. Gotta go with kissing in the rain!
這幕非得下大雨。一定得是大雨中的吻戲！

即將結婚的女主角 Rachel McAdams 回到故鄉見年少時的情人 Ryan Gosling 了結舊情，卻意外與男主角重燃愛火。Ryan Gosling 激動的在大雨中對女主角說：It wasn't over for me! It still isn't over!（我們之間對我來說從沒結束過，現在這樣也不算結束！）拜託，觀眾都是為了這幕大雨中的吻戲來看電影的！

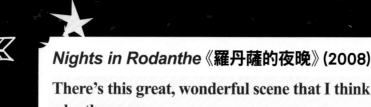

Nights in Rodanthe《羅丹薩的夜晚》(2008)

There's this great, wonderful scene that I think symbolizes who they are….

有一幕很棒、很美，我覺得這幕象徵了男女主角是怎樣的人

夜晚中，海邊獨棟民宿裡唯一的客人 Richard Gere 和獨居的女主人 Diane Lane 各自站在樓上和樓下的陽台上，看著屋子下方海水沖刷著沙灘。單一的畫面中，我卻同時看到了兩人的寂寞與孤獨。

Dear John《最後一封情書》(2010)

To me, that's a wonderful scene because the art of writing is going away. Everyone is emailing now.

對我來說這是很棒的一幕，因為親手寫信的文化已慢慢消失。現在大家都寄 email 了

人在軍中的 Channing Tatum 正在讀女友 Amanda Seyfried 從遠方寄來的信，畫面伴隨著 Amanda 口述信件的聲音」是我最喜歡的一幕。故事所設定的 911 事件前後時期，大概也是人沒們仍相當依賴美國郵政的最後一段時期了。現在大家都改用 skype 或 email 聯繫。

The Last Song《最後一曲》(2010)

…, and that's moment when she grows up

那幕中，她成熟長大了

父母分居的叛逆少女 Miley Cyrus 到爸爸的海邊小屋度暑假，卻得知爸爸將不久於人世，又氣又餒，她心中滿是對爸爸不敬的罪惡感，傷心的跟前來海邊小屋的媽媽說：I can't go. I have to stay.（我不能走，我必須留在這）。這是我最喜歡的一幕。

The Lucky One《幸運符》(2012)

…by the time the film reached that point, it was exactly what you were hoping for both characters.

電影演到此時，剛好也就是你希望看到兩人如此發展的時刻

美國軍人 Zac Efron，回到美國並找到了在伊拉克作戰時所拾獲照片中的女主角 Taylor Schilling，男主角細雨綿綿中跟她在屋後激烈擁吻，那幕非常非常令人血脈賁張。

The Best of Me《有你，生命最完整》(2014)

I think the forties are an incredibly interesting decade in life for most people.

四十幾歲是大多數人生命中最有趣的十年。

人從十幾、二十歲一直到四十歲以前，大多認為自己的夢想總有實現的一天，而年過半百之後則會了解想做的事不一定辦得到。卡在兩段時期中間的四十歲，便是人們開始理解人生窘境，卻還不想接受事實的一段有趣時期。這部片是我嘗試撰寫內戰時期的劇情小說 *Deliverance Creek* 後，重返拿手愛情題材的浪漫小說。

史派克式浪漫電影新作預告
The Longest Ride（2015）

知名導演 Clint Eastwood 兒子 Scott Eastwood 飾演一位職業牛仔，並在某次表演時結識大學女生 Britt Robertson。電影講述兩個完全不同世界的人，試圖在一段充滿矛盾、考驗的關係中得到圓滿愛情。本片將在 2015 年 4 月上映。

The Choice（2016）

改編自史派克 2007 年同名小說，敘述比鄰而居的兩人一見鍾情的浪漫故事。分別由 Benjamin Walker 與 Teresa Palmer 擔任男女主角，此片於 2014 年 10 月開拍，將於 2016 年上映。

愛到卡慘死

梁山伯與祝英台、羅密歐與茱麗葉、
小姐愛流氓、蘿絲愛傑克……
溫莎公爵為了美人捨棄江山、
貝拉愛上吸血鬼連命都得賠上！
原本不愛都沒事，愛上之後慘事接踵而至──
雖然你讓我很淒慘，但我就是愛你！

來看看電影史上「不是冤家不聚頭」的案例，
學學他們聽起來像在抱怨，卻能顯露愛意的
浪漫說話術。

《愛上波莉》

魯本菲佛（Reuben Feffer，Ben Stiller 飾）是保險公司的風險精算師，卻無法幫自己避開人生危機，先是新婚妻子在度蜜月時就紅杏出牆，離婚之後又愛上喜歡冒險、生活一團亂的女子波莉（Polly，Jennifer Aniston 飾）。為了波莉，原本飲食清淡的魯本硬跟著吃辣，搞得上吐下瀉。

Reuben Feffer: Since we have been together I have felt more uncomfortable, out of place, embarrassed, and just physically sick than I have in my entire life. But I could not have gone through that, I could not have thrown up 19 times in 48 days if I was not in love with you.
我們在一起之後，是我這輩子最尷尬、不自在、丟人現眼，身體不適的時候。這四十八天裡我吐了十九次，要不是因為我愛妳，我不可能熬得過來。

Along Came Polly

《四個畢業生》

懷抱電影夢的大學應屆畢業生里萊娜（Lelaina Pierce，Winona Ryder 飾）正在拍攝一部紀錄片，記錄同窗兼室友特洛伊戴爾（Troy Dyer，Ethan Hawke 飾）等三名年輕人的生活。里萊娜後來認識有線電視年輕主管麥可（Michael Grates，Ben Stiller 飾），兩人開始約會，麥可有意幫她安排紀錄片公開播放，但里萊娜卻發現自己無法忽略與特洛伊之間的感情……。

Lelaina: I was really going to be somebody by the time I was 23.
我原本想要在二十三歲時出人頭地。
Troy: Honey, all you have to be by the time you're 23 is yourself.
親愛的，妳到二十三歲時需要做的就是妳自己。
Lelaina: I don't know who that is anymore.
我已經不知道自己是誰了。
Troy: I do. And we all love her. I love her. She breaks my heart again and again, but I love her.
我知道。而且我們都愛她。我愛她。她一而再、再而三的讓我心碎，但我愛她。

Reality Bites

Ben Stiller
愛情片草食男

長相英俊的 Ben Stiller 是浪漫喜劇常客，他都演一些容易為愛受傷的平凡魯蛇，像是讓他一炮而紅的 *There's Something about Mary*《哈啦瑪麗中》，他是暗戀校花十多年的癡情男；在 *Along Came Polly*《愛上波莉》當中，他是一切靠數字做判斷的失婚精算師；*Meet the Parents*《門當父不對》系列裡，因為姓 Focker（與 fucker 諧音）及男性護士職業而備受嘲笑的他，必須想盡辦法證明自己。

大家對 Ben Stiller 的印象，就是那個一臉正經卻很好笑的喜劇演員。但在現實生活中，他是影視雙棲的得獎導演、製作人、編劇及演員，*Reality Bites*《四個畢業生》是 Ben Stiller 第一部執導的電影，受到相當高的評價。不過他在本片飾演一位青年才俊，並不搞笑。

Jennifer Aniston 浪漫愛情緋聞女王

身材玲瓏、笑容燦爛的珍妮佛安妮斯頓擔綱演出許多浪漫愛情片,但最讓人印象深刻的,還是電視影集 *Friends*《六人行》當中的傻大姐 Rachel Green,以及她的離婚緋聞。不幸的是,當初闖入的第三者安潔莉娜裘麗(Angelina Jolie)與前夫布萊德比特(Brad Pitt)人氣歷久不衰、話題不斷,每次他們成為鎂光燈焦點,八卦記者都不忘順便提一下珍妮佛的現況,還老愛拿她跟裘麗一較高下。

雖然跟高調放閃的布裘戀比起來,珍妮佛好像老是略遜一籌,但稍稍值得安慰的是,在她壯烈離婚之後,市面上出現了 Team Aniston(安妮斯頓支持者)及 Team Jolie(裘麗支持者)T 恤,買安妮斯頓的支持者是裘麗的四倍。

《同床異夢》

布魯克(Brooke,Jennifer Aniston 飾)和蓋瑞(Gary,Vince Vaughn 飾)這對怨偶決定分手,卻因不願意搬離共同購買的屋子,展開一場荒謬的趕人大戰。雙方搞到最後精疲力盡,終於能心平氣和討論彼此的關係,布魯克不懂為何自己為愛付出那麼多,卻沒有得到任何回報。

Brooke: I just don't know how we got here. Our entire relationship, I have gone above and beyond for you, for us.
我真不明白我們是怎麼走到這步田地。在這段婚姻當中,我為了你、為了彼此費盡心力。

I've cooked, I've picked your shit up off the floor, I've laid your clothes out for you like you're a four-year-old.
我煮飯燒菜、我跟在你後面收拾地上的髒亂、我把你當四歲小孩一樣,把衣服擺出來給你穿。

I support you, I supported your work. If we ever had dinner or anything I did the plans, I take care of everything.
我支持你,支持你的工作。如果我們要外出晚餐或做其他的事,是我在規劃,我包辦所有的事。

And I just don't feel like you appreciate any of it. I don't feel you appreciate me. All I want is to know, is for you to show me that you care.
而我不覺得你對哪個有感激之情。我不覺得你感激我。我只不過是想知道,想要你表現出你在意。

Gary: Why didn't you just say that to me?
妳為什麼不直接跟我說?

Brooke: I tried. I've tried.
我試過了。我已經試過了。

Gary: Never like that. You might have said some things that meant to imply that, but I'm not a mind reader.
沒有像剛剛那樣說過,妳或許說過什麼想要暗示,但我又不會讀心術。

The Break-Up

《愛情藥不藥》

傑米蘭道(Jamie Randall,Jake Gyllenhaal 飾)是一位把妹無往不利的藥廠業務,在拜訪醫生的時候遇到美麗的病人梅姬(Maggie,Anne Hathaway 飾),兩人陷入熱戀的同時,梅姬的帕金森氏症持續惡化⋯⋯。

Jamie: Let's just say in some alternate universe, there's a couple that's just like us, OK?
我們就假設有另一個宇宙吧,那裡有一對跟我們一模一樣的情侶,好嗎?

Only she's healthy and he's...he's perfect. And their world is about how much money they're gonna spend on vacation, or who's in a bad mood that day, or whether they feel guilty about having a cleaning lady.
只不過女的很健康,男的⋯⋯很完美。在他們的世界裡,要煩惱的是度假要花多少錢,或那天某人心情欠佳,或是請清潔婦來打掃不會感到愧疚。

I don't want to be those people. I want us. You. This.
我不想要成為他們。我要的是我們。是妳。是眼前這一切。

Love and Other Drugs

《如果能再愛一次》

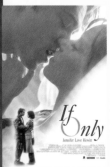

到英國學音樂的小提琴才女莎曼珊（Samantha，Jennifer Love Hewitt 飾）愛上英國年輕人伊恩（Ian，Paul Nicholls 飾），深愛莎曼珊的伊恩一心為事業打拚，不懂如何表達感情，讓莎曼珊決定忍痛分手回國。慘的是女主角衝出去搭上計程車，就出車禍死了！這讓男主角痛不欲生，他能得到再愛一次的機會嗎？

Ian: I guess what I'm trying to say is...I want to soldier on. I really do. OK?
我試著想說的是……我想要堅持下去。我真的想要。好嗎？

Samantha: No.
不好。

Ian: No what?
什麼不好？

Samantha: I don't...want to soldier on. Ian, if I were to stay in London now, it would be for you. For us. And I would do that in a heartbeat if I knew we were really special.
我……不想要堅持下去。伊恩，如果我繼續留在倫敦，會是為了你，為了我們。我會毫不猶豫，如果我知道我們的關係真的很特別。

Ian: We are.
我們是啊。

Samantha: Really? You never tell me how you feel or talk about yourself. You don't want to meet my family. You forgot my graduation. We run into my favorite student and you act as if he has something *contagious.
真的嗎？你從不跟我說你的感覺，或是談論你自己。你不想見我的家人。你忘記我的畢業典禮。當我們碰到我最鍾愛的學生，你卻對他避之唯恐不及。

Samantha: Ian, I know you have the best intentions, but I feel like I'm a really high second priority to you. That hurts. And the worst part is I'm starting to get used to it.
伊恩，我知道你沒有惡意，但我覺得自己只被你視為第二順位當中相當重要的項目。我很傷心。最糟的是我已經開始習慣了。

Ian: I don't understand.
我不懂。

Samantha: I know. That's what kills me. If there had just been one day, Ian, one day where nothing else matters but us.
我知道。那就是我最難過的事。真希望有那麼一天，伊恩，有那麼一天我們不被任何事情干擾，只有彼此。

Ian: I adore you.
我非常喜歡妳。

Samantha: I don't want to be adored, I want to be loved. I can't do this anymore.
我不想要被非常喜歡，我想要被愛。我不能再這樣下去了。

*contagious [kən`tedʒəs] (a.)（疾病等）傳染性的

If Only

羅曼死英文教室

If Only《如果能再愛一次》對白當中的 soldier on 表示「堅持下去」。soldier 這個字大家都知道是「阿兵哥」，一般都認為當兵辛苦，必須聽命行事，因此在這邊當動詞，就有即使遇到困難、覺得無聊，還是繼續做下去的意思。

A: I was sure that player was going to leave the field after he got injured.
我原本以為那名選手受傷後會離開球場。

B: Yeah, but he soldiered on and finished the game!
是啊，但他還是堅持完成比賽！

對白中的 have the best intentions，intentions 是指「（做一件事的）本意」也可以說 have good intentions 或 with the best (of) intentions，表示「一片好意」。

A: Jason always seems to mess things up when he tries to help.
傑森好像每次想幫忙都會搞砸。

B: I know, but at least he has good intentions.
對啊，但至少他是好意。

請各位翻到上一頁，看看 *The Break-Up*《同床異夢》對白當中的 above and beyond，這個片語也可以說 go above and beyond the call of duty，call 和 duty 都有「職責」的意思。above 是「在……之上」，beyond 是「在……之外」，高度跟廣度都超出職責所在的範圍，當然就是被一個人當兩個人用，所做的事超出應負的責任。也可以說 go above and beyond one's duty。

A: Why did Cindy get the Employee of the Month award?
辛蒂為什麼可以獲得本月最佳員工獎？

B: She deserved it. She always goes above and beyond the call of duty.
她應得的。她總是鞠躬盡瘁。

《絕配冤家》

安蒂（Andie，Kate Hudson 飾）是雜誌的兩性專欄作家，但她希望除了戀愛建議之外，能寫些言之有物的內容。安蒂的主管給她一個緊急任務，只要她能以自身經驗寫一篇利用女人約會常犯錯誤即可在十天內把男友嚇跑的報導，她以後寫稿就能擁有更多自主權。無奈的是，安蒂挑的實驗對象與她實力旗鼓相當：廣告公司主管班（Ben，Matthew McConaughey 飾）剛跟重要客戶打賭，要讓一個女人在十天內死心踏地愛上他。

Ben: Where's the sexy, cool, fun, smart, beautiful Andie that I knew? The one that wanted to be a serious journalist?
我之前認識的那個性感、有個性、風趣、聰明、美麗的安蒂跑哪去了？想成為嚴肅新聞工作者的那位？

You're up, you're down, you're here, you're there, you're like a fricking one woman circus.
妳這個人瞻之在前，忽焉在後，遠在天邊，近在眼前，根本是活生生的一人女子馬戲團。

本片另一段對白也被視為浪漫經典，不過屬於心碎類型，兩個明明愛得要死的人卻死鴨子嘴硬，不肯向對方低頭，反而繼續互相傷害：

Ben: That's what I was, huh? I was your guinea pig, somebody you can test your theories on.
那就是我，對吧？我是妳的白老鼠，供妳試驗妳的理論。

Andie: And I was just a girl somebody picked out in a bar.
而我不過是某人在酒吧泡上的女生。

Ben: Yeah, so what, big deal? Hell, now you can even use it as a little twist in your story.
是啦，那又怎樣，有什麼大不了？拜託，妳還可以把這個小插曲寫進妳的報導。

Andie: That's a good idea, maybe we should bet on it.
好主意，或許我們可以針對這點打個賭。

Ben: You know what, you did your job now Andie.
妳知道嗎，安蒂，妳完成任務了。

Andie: Yes I did
沒錯，我是完成了。

Ben: You wanted to lose a guy in 10 days. Congratulations, you did it. You just lost him.
妳想要在十天內失去一個男人，恭喜妳辦到了，妳剛剛失去他了。

Andie: No I didn't, Ben, 'cause you can't lose something you never had!
不，阿班，我沒有，因為一個人無法失去不曾擁有過的東西。

How to Lose a Guy in 10 Days

《27 件禮服的秘密》

珍（Jane，Katherine Heigl 飾）是個熱心助人的甜姐兒，已經當了二十七次伴娘卻一直輪不到她當新娘。這天她又要當伴娘，而且是連趕兩場，因此結識了痛恨婚禮卻以報導婚禮為生的記者凱文（Kevin，James Marsden 飾），他與熱衷婚禮的珍抬槓起來。這段對白中「愛到卡慘死」的是凱文眼中的新郎，不是本片男主角。

Jane: There's gotta be one thing about weddings that you like.
關於婚禮，一定有什麼是你喜歡的。

Kevin: Open bar.
免費喝酒。

Jane: No.
不會吧。

Kevin: [thinks for a moment] All right. So when the bride comes in and she makes her giant, grand entrance, I like to glance back at the poor bastard getting married. 'Cause even though I think he's an idiot for willingly entering into the last legal form of slavery...I don't know, he always looks really, really happy.
（想了一下）好吧。當新娘走進來，盛大進場的時候，我喜歡回頭瞄那個快要結婚的傢伙。因為儘管我覺得他願意走入僅存合法的奴役形式根本是白癡……不知道，新郎看起來總是非常、非常開心。

27 Dresses

《咆哮山莊》

英國文學家艾蜜莉勃朗特（Emily Brontë）這部黑暗的愛情小說被多次改編電影，這裡所選的是 1939 年拍攝的版本，由 Merle Oberon 飾演咆哮山莊主人的小女兒凱薩琳恩蕭（Catherine Earnshaw），與家中收容的流浪兒希斯克里夫（Heathcliff，Laurence Oliver 飾）相戀，最後卻選擇嫁給富家子弟，希斯克里夫對她由愛生恨持續終生，直至凱薩琳臨終仍不能原諒。

Heathcliff: Catherine Earnshaw, may you not rest so long as I live on! I killed you. Haunt me, then!
凱薩琳恩蕭，只要我活著，願妳都不得安息！我殺了妳。陰魂不散的糾纏我吧！

Haunt your murderer! I know that ghosts have wandered on the Earth. Be with me always. Take any form, drive me mad, only do not leave me in this dark alone where I cannot find you.
糾纏殺了妳的人！我知道鬼會在人世飄蕩。一直跟著我吧。以任何形式都行，把我逼瘋也好，就是不要把我一個人留黑暗之中找不到妳。

I cannot live without my life! I cannot die without my soul.
沒了妳我活不下去（妳是我的生命）！少了妳我無法死去（妳是我的靈魂）。

Wuthering Heights

《我心屬於你》

費絲（Faith，Marisa Tomei 飾）小時候玩占卜遊戲時，得知自己以後要嫁給 Damon Bradley，幾年後她去算命，算命仙又告訴她同一個名字。事隔多年，就在她已經淡忘此事，即將步入禮堂的前夕，得知未婚夫有一位名 Damon Bradley 的高中同學當天要前往義大利，費絲於是拋下一切追尋真命天子。她在那裡遇到一位自稱 Damon Bradley 的美國青年，兩人陷入熱戀，此時男方坦承他其實叫彼得（Peter，Robert Downey, Jr. 飾），費絲立刻翻臉，繼續上路尋找 Damon Bradley。深愛費絲的彼得一路相隨，最後真的找到一個叫 Damon Bradley 的人⋯⋯。

Peter: The only problem is me because I'm in love with her. I love her more than she'll ever know. But... you're a lucky, lucky man. You've got the right name! Goodbye, Faith. Hope you two work it out.
這裡唯一有問題的是我，因為我愛上她了。我比她所能想像的還要愛她。但⋯⋯你是個非常、非常幸運的人。你取對名字了！再見了費絲。希望你們倆能開花結果。

Only You

《愛在午夜希臘時》

席琳（Celine，Julie Delpy 飾）和傑斯（Jesse，Ethan Hawke 飾）這對夫妻接受朋友招待，在風景如畫的希臘海濱度假，讓他們有機會深談，卻將過去幾年來對彼此的不滿都翻了出來。

Jesse: Good luck finding somebody to put up with your shit for more than, like, six months. OK?
我祝妳好運，希望妳找到能夠忍受妳那些狗屁倒灶超過六個月的人。可以了吧？

But I accept the whole package, the crazy and the brilliant. All right?
但我全盤接受，不論是讓人抓狂的，還是美妙絕倫的。好嗎？

I know you're not gonna change and I don't want you to. It's called accepting you for being you.
我知道妳不會改，我也不想要妳改。這就叫做接受原本的妳。

Before Midnight

Ms. Dreamy 完美女朋友

貴族氣息可人兒
Lily Collins
莉莉柯林斯

Lily Collins, daughter of pop singer Phil Collins, was born in England and grew up in L.A. after her parents' divorce. Although she first acted in the BBC series *Growing Pains* when she was just two, Lily became interested in journalism as a teenager, writing articles for teen magazines and working as a TV correspondent and host. But with her stunning looks—people say she looks like a young Audrey Hepburn—it was only a matter of time before she got into modeling and acting. After a small part in 2009's *The Blindside*, Lily was cast as Snow White in 2012's *Mirror Mirror*, a role that brought her worldwide attention.

© Featureflash / Shuttershock.com

莉莉柯林斯出生英國，父親為流行歌手菲爾柯林斯，父母離異後於洛杉磯成長。雖然莉莉年僅兩歲時便在英國廣播公司的影集 *Growing Pains* 中演出，卻在青少年時期對新聞工作產生興趣，除了替青少年雜誌撰稿之外，更擔任電視特派記者及主持人。但外貌出眾的她（許多人說她長得像年輕的奧黛麗赫本），進入模特兒界及演藝圈也只是時間早晚的事。在 2009 年的電影《攻其不備》擔任小角後，莉莉於 2012 年的《魔鏡，魔鏡》獲選擔綱白雪公主，使她揚名國際。

影星小檔案

全　名：Lily Jane Collins
生　日：March 18, 1989
身　高：165 cm
出生地：英國薩里郡吉爾福德
　　　　（Guildford, Surrey）
成名作：《魔鏡，魔鏡》*Mirror, Mirror*

最受喜愛的搖滾第二代

莉莉柯林斯有名的老爸菲爾柯林斯，是全球發行團體及個人專輯銷售上億的三位暢銷音樂人之一（其他兩位分別是披頭四成員保羅麥卡尼，以及流行樂之王麥克傑克遜）。雖然沒有跟隨厲害的爸爸走上音樂之路，莉莉柯林斯光靠甜美的外貌與名門出身的好氣質，輕易成為近年鎂光燈焦點。穿著打扮得宜，能寫作也能演戲的南加大高材生也讓她成為難得觀眾緣與媒體緣都好的美少女星二代。

莉莉的男友名冊

讓人有童話故事中公主錯覺的小莉莉，身旁的緋聞男友也真都是白馬王子類型。肌肉猛男型 Taylor Lautner(《暮光之城》的狼人)、笑容迷人陽光男 Zac Efron 都在莉莉「前男友名單」上。不過美國大男孩似乎已經不對莉莉胃口，最近莉莉似乎迷上帶點優雅陰鬱氣息的男生，例如一起演出電影，戀情也最長久的頹廢感英國男模 Jamie Campbell Bower，以及澳洲新星 Thomas Cocquerel。

© Helga Esteb / Shuttershock.com

© Photo Works / Shuttershock.com

© Jaguar PS / Shuttershock.com

45

《BJ 單身日記》

三十拉警報的英國女子布莉姬（Bridget Jones，Renée Zellweger 飾）是個少根筋的出版社助理，她立志要找到如意郎君，卻情不自禁醉心於花心上司丹尼爾（Daniel Cleaver，Hugh Grant 飾）的曖昧，心碎之後受到事業有成但個性高傲的童年玩伴馬克達西（Mark Darcy，Colin Firth 飾）幫助，卻老是跟他不對盤，又常在他面前出糗……。

Mark: I don't think you're an idiot at all. I mean, there are elements of the ridiculous about you. Your mother's pretty interesting. And you really are an *appallingly bad public speaker. And, um...you tend to let whatever's in your head come out of your mouth without much consideration of the *consequences.

我完全不認為妳是個白癡。我是說，妳有些方面讓人啼笑皆非。令堂相當有趣。妳非常不擅長上臺講話。還有妳……經常不計後果想到什麼就講什麼……。

Mark: I realize when I met you at the turkey curry buffet, that I was unforgivably rude, and wearing a reindeer jumper that my mother had given me the day before. But the thing is, um...what I'm trying to say, very *inarticulately, is that, um...in fact, perhaps despite appearances, I like you, very much.

我發覺從一開始在火雞咖哩餐會上遇見妳時，那時候我非常無禮，還穿著我媽前一天送我的麋鹿毛衣。但重點是，呃……我是想要說，雖然口齒不清，但是，呃……事實上，或許儘管表面上看不出來，我喜歡妳，非常喜歡妳。

Bridget: Ah, apart from the smoking and the drinking and the vulgar mother...and the verbal *diarrhea.

啊，撇開我抽菸、喝酒，還有低俗的媽媽……以及說話一發不可收拾。

Mark: No, I like you very much. Just as you are.

不，我非常喜歡妳。就喜歡原原本本的妳。

*appallingly [əˋpɔlɪŋlɪ] (adv.) 駭人聽聞的
*consequence [ˋkɑnsə͵kwɛns] (n.) 後果
*inarticulately [͵ɪnɑrˋtɪkjəlɪtlɪ] (ad.) 口齒不清地
*diarrhea [͵daɪəˋriə] (n.) 拉肚子。
在此以 verbal diarrhea 形容口無遮攔

Bridget Jones's Diary

Colin Firth 影視史上最成功的「達西先生」

Jane Austen 的小說 *Pride and Prejudice*《傲慢與偏見》於 1813 年出版，兩百年來廣受歡迎，光是英國國家廣播公司（BBC）就拍過五次，其中 1995 年由柯林弗斯主演的版本，被公認為改編得最好且最受歡迎的一版，《BJ 單身日記》作者海倫費丁（Helen Fielding）更因受到這部電視劇啟發，以柯林弗斯的達西先生為本寫出暢銷小說，後來搬上大銀幕再度由他詮釋達西這個角色，柯林弗斯從此踏上國際巨星之路。

2013 年，BBC 出資的電視廣播網 UKTV 為了慶祝新頻道 Drama（戲劇）開播，暨《傲慢與偏見》出版兩百年，還在倫敦海德公園的九曲湖（Serpentine Lake）當中重現「英國電視戲劇史上最令人印象深刻的場景」——達西出水，這一幕就是出自柯林弗斯主演的 1995 年版《傲慢與偏見》。而九曲湖畔也正是 Jane Austen 經常流連散步的地方。

© taylorherringpr/www.flickr.com

Julia Stiles YA 片常客

認識 Julia Stiles 之前，先聊一下什麼是 YA 片。YA 是 young adult 的縮略，原本是文學的分類，一般指上高中到大學畢業之間，年齡約為十四到二十一歲上下，並沒有一定的標準，後來成為美國電影類型之一。

就內容來說，YA 片都是以美國年輕人的校園生活為題材，啦啦隊長（cheerleading captain）、啦啦隊員（cheerleader）、運動健將、遜咖（nerd）、宅男（geek）是這類電影常見的角色，情節大多圍繞在考試、愛情、升學、就業的煩惱，往往以校友返校（homecoming）、期末舞會（prom）為大結局場景。

《對面惡女看過來》改編自莎士比亞的

《馴悍記》，是 Julia Stiles 首挑大樑的作品，大獲好評之後，又參與另外兩齣莎翁劇改編電影 Hamlet《哈姆雷特》（2000 年版）及另一部《奧塞羅》改編的 YA 片 O《千方百計》，讓她被影評封為「新生代莎翁劇女王」。後來她又接演 Mona Lisa Smile《蒙娜麗莎的微笑》及 The Prince and Me《麻雀變王妃》，都在片中飾演傑出女大生。

哥倫比亞大學畢業，主修英國文學的 Julia Stiles 是演舞台劇起家，不但戲演得好，也善寫劇本。但可不要以為她只是文青一枚，她在叫好又叫座的青少年街舞電影 Save the Last Dance《留住最後一支舞》當中所有舞蹈都是親自上陣，沒有替身喔！

《對面惡女看過來》

本片是由莎士比亞 The Taming of the Shrew《馴悍記》改編的 YA 浪漫喜劇。高中校花碧安卡的爸爸明令，除非她那眼高於頂、超難相處的女性主義者怪咖姊姊凱特（Kat，Julia Stiles 飾）先交到男朋友，否則碧安卡不準約會。為此，愛上碧安卡的卡麥隆（Cameron，Joseph Gordon-Levitt 飾）開始想盡辦法幫凱特物色對象，終於讓一個校園大怪咖派崔克（Patrick，Heath Ledger 飾）去約凱特，一開始碰一鼻子灰的派崔克打動了凱特的心，讓她當眾唸出這段話，也就是英文片名 10 Things I Hate About You 的由來。

Kat Stratford: I hate the way you talk to me, and the way you cut your hair.
我痛恨你跟我講話那副德性，還有你可怕的髮型。

I hate the way you drive my car.
我痛恨你那樣開我的車。

I hate it when you stare.
我痛恨你瞪著我看。

I hate your big dumb combat boots, and the way you read my mind.
我痛恨你那雙粗重的戰鬥靴，還有你能看透我在想什麼。

I hate you so much it makes me sick; it even makes me rhyme.
我恨你恨到要生病，恨你恨到講話押韻。

I hate it, I hate the way you're always right.
我好恨，我痛恨你總是對的。

I hate it when you lie.
我痛恨你說謊。

I hate it when you make me laugh, even worse when you make me cry.
我痛恨你逗我笑，更痛恨你讓我哭。

I hate it when you're not around, and the fact that you didn't call.
我痛恨你不在我身邊，還有你不打電話給我。

But mostly I hate the way I don't hate you. Not even close, not even a little bit, not even at all.
但我最痛恨的，是我不恨你。根本不恨，一點也不恨，完完全全不恨。

10 Things I Hate About You

Brad Pitt

布萊德
彼特

© cinemafestival / Shutterstock.com

🎧 10

Born in Shawnee, Oklahoma in 1963, Brad Pitt was raised in Springfield, Missouri in a 1)**conservative** Baptist family. While attending Kickapoo High School, he was on the tennis, golf and swimming teams, and took part in school 2)**debates** and musicals. Although Pitt studied journalism at the University of Missouri, he decided that he didn't want a nine-to-five job, and 3)**dropped out** just two weeks before 4)**graduation** to move to L.A. and **try his luck** at acting.

But Pitt's luck wasn't good, and he worked all kinds of jobs to support himself, including driving 5)**strippers** to parties and dressing as a chicken for a fast food restaurant. He 6)**eventually** started getting small parts in soap operas and TV series, and made his film debut in the 1989 7)**slasher** *Cutting Class*. His big **break** came two years later in the hit road movie *Thelma & Louise*, where he plays a charming criminal, a role that made him a sex symbol. Pitt's 8)**acclaimed** performance in 1992's period drama *A River Runs Through It* proved that he was more than just a pretty face, but it was 1994's vampire romance *Interview with the Vampire* and period drama *Legends of the Fall* that 9)**established** him as a major star.

Pitt continued to 10)**broaden** his range, appearing in thriller *Seven*, 11)**fantasy** romance *Meet Joe Black* and romantic comedy *The Mexican*. He even established himself as an action star in the blockbuster *Troy*. But Pitt may be even more famous as a 12)**celebrity**. After he left his wife Jennifer Aniston when he fell in love with Angelina Jolie on the set of *Mr. & Mrs. Smith*, **Brangelina** became a worldwide 13)**phenomenon**. The couple finally got married in 2014, and still find time to make movies when they're not too busy looking after their six children.

Showbiz Words

Brangelina 布裘戀
媒體在報導超級名人情侶檔時，每次都要把兩個人的名字寫出來實在很麻煩，乾脆創一個字來當作代稱。Brangelina 就是將布萊德彼特 (Brad Pitt) 與安潔莉娜裘莉 (Angelina Jolie) 的姓名首字結合。以下是其他例子：

- **Tomkat 湯凱戀**
Tom Cruise + Katie Holmes，即阿湯哥及前阿湯嫂凱蒂
- **Billary 比拉戀**
Bill Clinton + Hillary Clinton，前美國總統柯林頓及夫人希拉蕊
- **Zanessa 柴妮莎戀**
Zac Efron + Vanessa Hudgens，柴克艾弗隆及前女友凡妮莎哈金絲
- **Bennifer 班妮佛戀**
Ben Affleck + Jennifer Garner / Jennifer Lopez，班艾佛烈克跟現任妻子珍妮佛加納，以及舊愛珍妮佛羅培茲。剛好前後兩任都叫 Jennifer，因此現在跟老婆珍妮佛加納這段便被稱 Bennifer 2

© Debby Wong / Shutterstock.com

布萊德彼特於 1963 年出生在美國奧克拉荷馬州肖尼市的保守浸信會家庭中，在密蘇里州的春田市長大。就讀於奇嘉布高中時，他不但身為網球、高爾夫及游泳隊的一員，還參與學校辯論會和音樂劇表演。雖然小布後來念密蘇里大學新聞系，不過他決定自己不想做一般朝九晚五的工作，因此在離畢業僅有兩週時退學、搬到洛杉磯試試星運。

不過小布並沒有那麼走運，而且還做過各種工作好養活自己，包括開車載脫衣舞孃參加派對，以及穿上公雞裝為速食餐廳宣傳。他最終開始有機會在肥皂劇及電視影集中出演小角，並以 1989 年的血腥恐怖片《翹課》初登大銀幕。兩年後的賣座公路電影《末路狂花》更令他星途大開，片中他所飾演的迷人罪犯一角使他一舉成為性感偶像。而在 1992 年的時代劇《大河戀》中，小布的精彩演出證明他不是空有漂亮臉蛋而已，不過一直要到 1994 年的吸血鬼愛情電影《夜訪吸血鬼》及時代劇《真愛一世情》這兩部作品，才真正確立他的巨星地位。

小布繼續開拓他的戲路，出演了驚悚電影《火線追緝令》、奇幻愛情片《第六感生死緣》、以及愛情喜劇《危險情人》。他甚至在賣座鉅片《特洛伊：木馬屠城》中奠定自己的動作巨星地位。不過小布或許更以其名人身分聞名於世。他因拍攝《史密斯任務》而與安潔莉娜裘莉墜入愛河，導致他和前妻珍妮佛安妮斯頓分手，爾後這段布裘戀遂成為全球話題。這對佳偶終於在 2014 年訂下終身，並且在照顧六位兒女的閒暇之餘還能找出時間繼續拍片。

Tongue-tied No More

try one's luck 碰碰運氣
這個片語用來表達做了某件事情，希望得到成功的結果。

A: I haven't met anybody on that dating site.
我在那個交友網站上沒遇到任何對象。
B: Maybe you should try your luck on another site.
也許你該到另一個網站碰碰運氣。

break 機會
俚語的 break 是特別指「大好的機會」、「幸運的轉折」。

A: Have you guys signed with a label yet?
你們和任何唱片公司簽約了嗎？
B: No, we're still waiting for our big break.
沒有，我們還在等待我們的大好機會。

 11

Vocabulary Bank

1) **conservative** [kən`sɜvətɪv] (a./n.) 保守的，傳統的；保守派人士
Saudi Arabia is a very conservative country.
沙烏地阿拉伯是一個非常保守的國家。

2) **debate** [dɪ`bet] (n./v.) 辯論，爭議
Which side are you on in the global warming debate?
你是全球暖化爭議的哪一方？

3) **drop out** [drɑp aʊt] (phr.) 輟學
My parents would kill me if I dropped out of school.
若是我輟學，爸媽肯定會殺了我。

4) **graduation** [ˌgrædʒu`eʃən] (n.) 畢業
Are your parents coming to the graduation ceremony?
你父母會來參加畢業典禮嗎？

5) **stripper** [`strɪpɚ] (n.) 脫衣舞孃
Tanya never told her husband that she used to work as a stripper.
譚雅從來沒有告訴她的丈夫，她以前曾當過脫衣舞孃。

6) **eventually** [ɪ`vɛntʃuəli] (adv.) 最後，終究
Allen and Grace plan to get married and have children eventually.
艾倫和葛麗絲打算最後還是要結婚生子。

7) **slasher** [`slæʃɚ] (n.) 砍殺電影（亦作 slasher movie），砍人的兇手
That slasher was too violent for my taste.
那部砍殺電影對我來說太暴力了。

8) **acclaimed** [ə`klemd] (adj.)（尤指對藝術成就的）受到讚揚的
The acclaimed orchestra is performing at the concert hall tonight.
大受讚揚的交響樂團今晚將在音樂廳裡表演。

9) **establish** [ɪ`stæblɪʃ] (v.) 創辦，建立
The university was established in 1926.
此大學建立於 1926 年。

10) **broaden** [`brɔdən] (v.) 使…變寬闊
Going to college will broaden your mind.
上大學將會寬闊你的視野。

11) **fantasy** [`fæntəsi] (a./n.) 奇幻（作品）
What's your favorite fantasy novel?
你最喜歡的奇幻小說是什麼？

12) **celebrity** [sə`lɛbrɪti] (n.) 名人，名流
Have you heard the latest gossip about that celebrity?
你有聽說那位名人最近的八卦嗎？

13) **phenomenon** [fə`nɑməˌnɑn] (n.) 意想不到、非凡的人事物，現象
Jeremy Lin became a basketball phenomenon almost overnight.
林書豪在籃球壇上幾乎是一夜成名。

最動人的告白

告白、互訴情衷，往往是愛情片中最重要的環節，所有的暗戀、曖昧和猜疑都在告白的那一刻得到釋放。毋需講得驚天地泣鬼神，只要憑著一顆真心，就能讓對方感受到自己的心意。

以下這些經典告白台詞，有的浪漫，有的笨拙，有的單刀直入，有的拐彎抹角，但都充滿著真摯的誠意和情感，讓觀影者也不禁沈浸在這些字句的浪漫氣氛中。

《吸血鬼：真愛不死》

公元 1462 年，德古拉伯爵（Count Dracula，Gary Oldman 飾）受命征討入侵君士坦丁堡的土耳其人，在他奮戰之時，卻傳出他早已戰死沙場的消息，他的妻子伊莉莎白誤信謠言，自殺身亡。當德古拉戰勝歸鄉，等著他的卻是妻子冰冷的屍首，他怪罪上帝，從此化身成為不死的吸血鬼，等待他的愛妻輪迴轉生，再與她重逢。

Dracula: I have crossed oceans of time to find you.
我跨越浩瀚的時間之海來尋找妳。

— Dracula

© cinemafestival / Shutterstock.com

Gary Oldman 老男人的魅力

蓋瑞歐德曼的姓氏是 Oldman，因此常被戲稱為「老男人」。這位英國實力派演員在台灣的知名度並不高，但其實很多電影裡都看得到他的蹤影。其中最廣為人知的就是《哈利波特》系列中的天狼星了。還有或許你沒認出來，他也是諾蘭 (Christopher Nolan) 執導蝙蝠俠系列中憨厚老實的高登局長。而他所飾演的德古拉公爵則被認為是影史上最迷人的吸血鬼。蓋瑞演技精湛，無論是任何扮相、任何性格的角色都能駕馭，演什麼像什麼，說是老戲精一點也不為過！

《金陵十三釵》

故事背景設定在 1937 年的南京大屠殺，當時南京遭日軍大舉入侵，全境滿目瘡痍，慘不忍睹，期間被凌辱的女孩不計其數。日軍後來還強徵女學生去日軍慶功會上表演，一群以玉墨為首的風塵女子們決定要代替女學生踏上這條不歸路。

Shujuan: Are you going to fall in love with me?
你要愛上我了嗎？

John: I already have.
我已經愛上妳了。

The Flowers of War

《有你，生命最完整》

道森（Dawson，James Marsden 飾）和亞曼達（Amanda，Michelle Monaghan 飾）高中時曾經相戀，卻因家世懸殊而分開。分手二十年後，兩人因參加共同好友塔克的喪禮而再次相遇，過去的甜蜜歷歷在目，道森對亞曼達還是一往情深，但亞曼達已經結婚，兩人的感情究竟還有沒有一絲絲可能？還是只能將這份愛默默藏在內心最深處？

Dawson: There was so much you wanted to do.
妳想做的事情真多。

Amanda: I wanted to do it with you! I blame you for thinking that you knew what was best for me when it was you that was best for me.
我想和你一起做！我討厭你明明最適合我，卻還要自以為知道誰最適合我。

The Best of Me

《騎士風雲錄》

十四世紀的英格蘭是個階級分明的封閉社會，出身卑下的威廉（William，Heath Ledger 飾）從小立志成為一名騎士，由於身分限制，對他來說是不可能達成的夢想，但威廉還是不放棄，勤練劍術。在一次機會下，威廉冒充貴族身分，參加各地的比武大賽，靠著精湛的劍術，不僅贏了騎士比武大賽，還贏得貴族女子喬絲琳（Jocelyn，Shannyn Sossamon 飾）的芳心。

William: May I ask your name, my lady? Or perhaps angels have no names, only beautiful faces.
小姐，可以請教妳的芳名嗎？還是天使沒有名字，只有美麗的臉龐。

A Knight's Tale

羅曼死英文教室

《壁花男孩》對白當中一句是：It's really sweet and everything, but you can't just sit there...。這裡要討論的，是 and everything 到底是什麼意思。

其實，這是口語中常見的用法，沒什麼意思，就類似中文「諸如此類」、「……是沒錯啦」，如果後面搭配 but，重點是後面接的句子，也就是 and everything 前面說什麼都無所謂，要緊的是 but 後面的意見。

A: How did your date with Jason go?
你和傑森的約會怎麼樣？

B: Well, he's nice and everything, but we didn't really hit it off.
這個嘛，他是不錯啦，但我們並不來電。

《壁花男孩》

害羞又內斂的查理（Charlie，Logan Lerman 飾）常被同學欺負，封閉的他總是在一旁默默觀察大家，不敢主動和人交朋友。直到認識了珊（Sam，Emma Watson 飾）和珊的哥哥派翠克（Patrick，Ezra Miller 飾）這兩個高年級學生，使查理的高中生活開始有了轉變。他們接納查理進入他們的圈子，讓他嚐到友誼與初戀的美好，然而就在珊和派翠克即將畢業邁入大學之際，查理心中的陰影又開始浮現……。

Charlie: We accept the love we think we deserve.
我們總是接受自認為配得起的愛。

Sam: Then, why didn't you ever ask me out?
那你怎麼都沒問我要不要和你約會？

Charlie: I, uh...I just didn't think that you wanted that.
我……呃……我只是沒想到妳會想這麼做。

Sam: Well, what did you want?
那你想幹嘛？

Charlie: I just want you to be happy.
我只是想要妳快樂。

Sam: Don't you get it, Charlie? I can't feel that.
你還不懂嗎，查理？我感覺不到你喜歡我。

It's really sweet and everything, but you can't just sit there and put everybody's lives ahead of yours and think that counts as love.
這樣很甜蜜，但你不能光是坐在那裡，把別人的人生看得比自己更重要，然後認為這算是愛。

I don't want to be somebody's *crush. I want people to like the real me.
我不想只是某人的暗戀對象。我要有人能喜歡真正的我。

Charlie: I know who you are, Sam. I know I'm quiet, and I know I should speak more, but if you knew the things that...that were in my head most of the time, you'd know what it really meant.
我認識真正的妳，珊。我知道我總是很沈默，也知道我應該多開口。但妳要是知道我的腦海中都是些什麼事，妳會知道這對我來說是什麼意思。

How much we're alike, and how we've been through the same things. And you're not small. You're beautiful.
我們兩個有多相似，我們都經歷過相同的事情。還有妳並不渺小，妳很美麗。

*crush [krʌʃ] (n.) 暗戀、迷戀（的對象）

The Perks of Being a Wallflower

《愛情避風港》

身世成謎的凱蒂（Katie，Julianne Hough 飾）來到一個陌生的港口，遇見了帶著兩個孩子的單親爸爸艾力克斯（Alex，Josh Duhamel 飾），朝夕相處的兩人逐漸產生情愫，艾力克斯的兩個孩子也開始接受凱蒂。只是沒想到凱蒂竟然是被警察追捕的通緝犯，艾力克斯能夠接納她並幫助她嗎？

Katie: He's gonna find me.
他會找到我。

Alex: If you're in some kind of trouble, we can fix it. I love you, and I can't let you go. There's no safer place for you than here with me.
如果妳遇上什麼麻煩，我們可以一起處理。我愛妳，不能讓妳走。沒有哪裡比跟我在一起還安全。

本片最神奇之處，在於有已故妻子幫忙告白的喬段：

Jo: To the woman my husband loves. If you're reading this, then it must be true, he loves you without a shadow of a doubt or else he wouldn't have given this to you. I can only hope that you feel the same way about him that he does about you.
給我丈夫深愛的女人。如果妳正在讀這封信，那麼他一定很愛你，沒有一絲猶疑，否則他也不會把這封信交給妳。我只期望妳也對他有一樣的感覺。

I wanted to write this letter because I wanted you to know one very important thing; I'm so glad he's found you. I only wish I could be there some how to met you, and maybe in some ways I am.
我寫這封信是因為我想告訴妳一件重要的事，我很開心他找到了妳。我唯一的希望就是我能夠親自見妳一面，搞不好，我已經借由某種方式見到妳了。

Safe Haven

《生命中的美好缺憾》

改編自同名小說，海瑟（Hazel，Shailene Woodley 飾）是名癌末的十六歲少女，在父母的強迫之下參加了病友分享會，認識了另一名開朗積極的癌症患者奧古斯都（Augustus，Ansel Elgort 飾），相知相惜的倆人墜入情網，他們之間的愛情也奇蹟般地療癒著彼此的心。

Gus: I am in love with you. And I know that love is just a shout into the *void, and that *oblivion is *inevitable, and that we're all doomed, and that one day all of our labors will be returned to dust. And I know that the sun will swallow the only Earth we will ever have. And I am in love with you.
我愛上妳了。我知道愛很虛幻，遺忘是必然的，我們都難逃命運的劫難，總有一天我們所有的努力都將化作虛無，我也知道太陽總有一天會吞噬掉我們唯一的地球。但我還是愛上妳了。

***void** [vɔɪd] (n.) 虛空，虛無
***oblivion** [ə`blɪvɪən] (n.) 遺忘，淹沒
***inevitable** [ɪn`ɛvətəbəl] (a.) 不可避免的

The Fault in Our Stars

be doomed 註定要失敗

形容詞 doomed 意為「命中註定，終會失敗、死亡、毀滅的」，be doomed 就是指「完蛋了」的意思，同樣意思的片語還有 ill-fated

A: *That new restaurant went out of business in just four months.*
那間新餐廳四個月前才歇業。

B: *With a location like that, it was doomed from the start.*
在那樣的地點開店，歇業的命運從一開始就註定了。

《好友萬萬睡》

不想要有穩定男女關係的潔咪（Jamie，Mila Kunis 飾）和她的客戶兼好友狄倫（Dylan，Justin Timberlake 飾）協議成為不帶複雜情感的枕邊伴侶，維持了一段有性無愛的朋友關係。只是在時間的催化下，狄倫發現自己似乎愛上了潔咪，這段關係該如何發展下去？狄倫可以不再只是潔咪的「好朋友」嗎？

Dylan: Look, I can live without ever having sex with you again.
我跟妳說，我可以再也不要跟妳上床。

[潔咪露出驚訝的神色]

Dylan: It'll be really hard.
這樣會很困難。

[潔咪熱淚盈眶地看著狄倫]

Dylan: Hey, I want my best friend back. Because I'm in love with her.
嘿，我想要我最好的朋友回來，因為我愛上她了。

— Friends with Benefits —

Justin Timberlake 賈斯汀提姆布萊克

生於 1981 年的賈斯汀是以迪士尼童星的身份出道，後來加入男孩團體「超級男孩」（'N Sync）並擔任主唱，在 2002 年單飛後推出多張個人專輯，成績斐然，成功從團體偶像晉升為巨星歌手，期間陸續接演多部電影，包括《社群網站》（The Social Network）、《好友萬萬睡》（Friends with Benefits）和《終點站》（In Time）等，表現亮眼。

《妳是我今生的新娘》

此部英式愛情喜劇描述男主角查爾斯（Charles，Hugh Grant 飾）因為對婚姻有恐懼，遲遲不敢踏入婚姻。在經歷過三場婚禮和一場葬禮後，查爾斯對婚姻有了不同的體悟，終於決定要在第四場婚禮中與他心中唯一的摯愛凱莉（Carrie，Andie MacDowell 飾）告白。但問題是，他以為凱莉已經嫁做人婦（但其實沒有），因此講得吞吞吐吐，不斷自問自打臉：

Charles: Ehm, look. Sorry. Well, this is a very stupid question, but I just wondered, by any chance, ehm, eh, I mean obviously not because I guess I've only slept with 9 people, but…I just wondered… I really feel, in short, to *recap it slightly in a clearer version, eh, I think I love you, and, I just wondered by any chance you wouldn't like to… No, no, no of course not. I'm an idiot, he's not… Excellent, excellent, fantastic, eh, I was gonna say lovely to see you, sorry to disturb… Better get on…
呃，聽著，不好意思，嗯，這是個笨問題，但我只是想知道，有沒有可能，嗯，我是說顯然不是因為我只睡過九個人，但……我只是想說……我真的覺得，總之，重點是…呃，我想我愛妳，然後，我只是想知道妳有沒有可能會想……不不不，當然不是的。我是白癡，但他不是……。好極了好極了，太好了，呃，我本來只是想說很高興看到妳，抱歉打擾……我最好走了……。

Carrie: That was very romantic.
剛才好浪漫喔。

* **recap** [ˈrikæp] (v.) 重新講重點

— Four Weddings and a Funeral —

《新娘百分百》

安娜（Anna，Julia Roberts 飾）是好萊塢當紅明星，某日走進威廉（William，Hugh Grant 飾）在倫敦的書店買書，不過這並不是他倆羅曼史的起點，浪漫故事是從威廉把柳橙汁打翻在安娜身上開始。意外擦出愛情火花的倆人，會因懸殊的身分地位而使這段感情無疾而終嗎？

William: I live in Notting Hill. You live in Beverly Hills. Everyone in the world knows who you are, my mother has trouble remembering my name.
我住諾丁山。妳住比佛利山莊。全世界的人都認識你，我連自己的媽媽都快記不得我叫什麼名字。

Anna: I'm also just a girl, standing in front of a boy, asking him to love her.
我只不過是一個女生，站在一個男生面前，請求那個男生愛她。

Notting Hill

© Kobby Dagan / Shutterstock.com

Drew Barrymore 和 Adam Sandler 這對銀幕情侶合作次數多到一個奇怪的程度，兩人分別在 1998 年《婚禮歌手》*The Wedding Singer*、2004 年《我的失憶女友》*50 First Dates*，及 2015 年《當我們混在一起》*Blended* 三部浪漫喜劇當中擔綱演出，儘管這三部片的影評都普普甚至欠佳，卻都開出破億美金的全球票房。

身為喜劇演員的 Adam Sandler 拍片時常即興演出，但氣質猶如鄰家女孩般的 Drew Barrymore 就是有辦法面不改色的繼續演下去，這點當年執導《婚禮歌手》的導演 Frank Coraci 印象深刻，這或許也就是大家一再看兩人合作的電影卻不會膩的原因吧！

羅曼死英文教室

《我的失憶女友》對白當中的 hold me back from... 這個說法可以學起來。

hold back 這個片語表示「阻止」、「控制局勢繼續發展」、「使無法達成」，當我們說 hold (sb./sth.) from...，就是「害（某人事物）無法……」的意思。

A: Why don't Jeff and Alison want to have kids?
為什麼傑夫和艾莉森不想要孩子？
B: They're afraid having kids would hold them back in their careers.
他們害怕生孩子會阻撓他們的事業。

《我的失憶女友》

亨利（Henry，Adam Sandler 飾）是個超級花花公子，直到他遇見了讓他一見傾心的露西（Lucy，Drew Barrymore 飾）後，他才決定收起玩心，只是沒想到隔天亨利再度碰見露西時，她卻完全不認得他。原來是一年前的一場車禍，造成露西短期記憶受損，使她的記憶永遠停留在發生車禍前，亨利每天都要設法讓露西重新愛上他一次……。

Henry: You erased me from your memories because you thought you were holding me back from having a full and happy life. But you made a mistake.
妳把我從你記憶中抹去，因為妳覺得我會因為你失去我原本快樂的生活，但是妳錯了。

Being with you is the only way I could have a full and happy life. You're the girl of my dreams…and apparently, I'm the man of yours.
我只有跟妳在一起才會快樂。妳是我的夢中情人……看樣子，我也是妳的夢中情人。

Lucy: Henry. It's nice to meet you.
亨利，很高興認識你。

Henry: Lucy. It's nice to meet you too.
露西，我也很開心認識妳。

50 First Dates

肌肉美男
Channing Tatum
查寧坦圖

Born in Alabama and raised in Mississippi, Channing Tatum was an athletic child, excelling at sports and martial arts. Tatum went to college on a football scholarship, but soon dropped out and worked odd jobs around Tampa, Florida, including a stint as a male stripper. He next moved to Miami, where an encounter with a talent scout led to modeling and commercial work. After dancing in a Ricky Martin video and playing small parts in movies, his dancing skills won him the lead in the 2006 romantic dance film *Step Up*. The hunky star has since appeared in hits like romantic drama *Dear John* and comedy *Magic Mike*, based on his own experiences as a stripper.

© Helga Esteb / Shuttershock.com

查寧坦圖生於美國阿拉巴馬州、並在密西西比州成長，自小便體格健壯的他擅長運動及武術。坦圖因獲得美式足球獎學金而進入大學就讀，但不久後便休學並在佛羅里達坦帕市到處打臨工賺錢，包括短暫當起脫衣舞男。他接著搬至邁阿密，在當地遇見某位星探而成為模特兒並參與電視廣告演出。在瑞奇馬丁的 MV 中擔任舞者以及接演幾個電影小角後，他的跳舞技巧使他在 2006 年的舞蹈愛情片《舞出真我》裡贏得擔綱主角的機會。這位高大健美的男星自此便出現在多部賣座電影裡，像是浪漫愛情片《最後一封情書》及喜劇電影《舞棍俱樂部》，後者正是根據他身為脫衣舞男時的經歷改編而成。

影星小檔案

全　　名：**Channing Matthew Tatum**
生　　日：**April 26, 1980**
身　　高：**185 cm**
出 生 地：美國阿拉巴馬州
感情狀態：已婚
成 名 作：《卡特教頭》*Coach Carter*

路過千萬不要錯過
Magic Mike 保證「顧眼睛」

© s_bukey / Shuttershock.com

© Featureflash / Shuttershock.com

這部由查寧圖坦、俊俏新星艾利克帕帝佛、魅力影帝馬修麥康納，三大好萊塢型男「肌」情演出的脫衣舞男片，不管男女都想要尖叫的猛男組合，光是預告片就讓人想對銀幕塞小費，影評也給予正面評價「熟悉的故事在此片變為獨樹一格的新電影，絕對不只那些 beefcake（猛男）好看而已！」《舞棍俱樂部》繼 2012 年開出好票房後，2015 將上演續集《舞棍俱樂部 XXL》，還沒看過第一集的趕快租來看！

The Sexiest Dad Alive 柔情壯漢

因戲《舞出真我》而與 Jenna Dewan 相戀結婚，婚後即使接連與大眼名模 Amanda Seyfried、古典美女 Winora Ryder 以及浪漫愛情女王 Rachel McAdams 拍攝愛情片，都守身如玉，完全沒緋聞傳出。

© Featureflash / Shuttershock.com

疼愛老婆出名的 Channing 最近跟 Jenna 生了個小女兒，Jenna 甚至多次公開表示老公除了一路給予絕對支持外，一有空在家，換尿布、餵奶等育兒瑣事通通包辦，就是為了讓太太好好休息。難怪美國時人雜誌封 Channing 為「世上最性感奶爸」了！

Shirley MacLaine
莎莉麥克蓮

莎莉麥克蓮身兼演員、歌手、舞者和作家。她於 1955 年首次演出希區考克電影《怪屍案》The Trouble with Harry 即獲得金球獎年度最佳新晉女演員獎，1960 年與傑克李蒙（Jack Lemmon）合演獲五項奧斯卡獎的《公寓春光》讓她聲名大噪，更因本片第二度獲奧斯卡最佳女主角提名，可惜最後輸給伊麗莎白泰勒（Elizabeth Taylor）。

莎莉麥克蓮影藝生涯中曾獲四度奧斯卡最佳女主角提名，於 1983 年以《親密關係》Terms of Endearment 奪下大獎，多才多藝的她並於 2000 年自導自演《神童布魯諾》Bruno，年過八十的她至今仍活躍於演藝圈，且時有新作推出。

《公寓春光》

巴德（Bud Baxter，Jack Lemmon 飾）為了鞏固自己的工作，將自己居住的公寓借給他的上司，讓他能和他的情婦法藍（Fran Kubelik，Shirley MacLaine 飾）約會，沒想到上司幽會的人是竟是自己暗戀的對象……。巴德的這段感情會有結果嗎？利用不光明手段來升遷，真的是巴德想要的嗎？

Bud:Miss Kubelik, one doesn't get to be a second *administrative assistant around here unless he's a pretty good judge of character, and as far as I'm concerned you're tops. I mean, decency-wise and otherwise-wise.
庫貝利克小姐，除非能精準判斷別人的品性，要在這裡當上副行政助理是不可能的。就我的觀點來看，妳實在太好了。我指的是端莊得體，其他方面也是。

* **administrative** [əd`mɪnɪˌstretɪv] (a.) 管理的，行政的

The Apartment

《西城故事》

湯尼（Tony，Richard Beymer 飾）和瑪莉亞（Maria，Natalie Wood 飾）彼此相愛，卻因身處不同幫派而被百般阻撓。故事設定在曼哈頓的西區，因為爭奪地盤，當地的噴射機幫和來自波多黎各的鯊魚幫勢不兩立。不被接受的愛戀引發兩幫派間更多的械鬥，湯尼和瑪莉亞於是決定要遠走高飛，他們會成功嗎？

Tony: You're not thinking I'm someone else?
妳不會覺得我是別人？
Maria: I know you are not.
我知道你不是。
Tony: Or that we've met before?
還是我們有遇過嗎？
Maria: I know we have not.
我確定沒有。
Tony: I felt, I knew something never before was going to happen, had to happen. But this is so much more.
我能感覺到，我知道有些從未發生過的東西即將發生。但現在遠遠超過我的想像。

West Side Story

《西城故事》最初是一齣百老匯音樂劇，直到 1961 年才被翻拍成電影，情節是《羅密歐與茱莉葉》的翻版，只不過加入更多美國現實社會中的元素，如暴力、少年犯罪以及種族歧視等，使得這部電影更為寫實，諷刺意味相當濃厚。

《窗外有藍天》

露西（Lucy，Helena Bonham Carter 飾）在表姐的陪同下到佛羅倫斯去旅行，因自己的房間看不見窗外的風景，而認識旅館的其他房客喬治（George，Julian Sands 飾）和他的父親，喬治父子很熱情地和露西交換房間，沒想到這一交換，居然牽起了露西和喬治兩人之間的紅線。只是兩人的身分地位懸殊，再加上露西已有未婚夫，他們的感情能修成正果嗎？

George: He's the sort who can't know anyone *intimately, least of all a woman. He doesn't know what a woman is.

他這種人無法跟任何人親近，尤其是女人。他不懂女人。

He wants you for a *possession, something to look at, like a painting or an ivory box. Something to own and to display. He doesn't want you to be real, and to think and to live. He doesn't love you.

他想擁有妳，只是想有個東西可欣賞，就像是一幅畫作或是個象牙盒。想擁有某個東西並展示。他根本不希望妳真的存在，不希望妳有自己的想法和生活。他根本不愛妳。

But I love you. I want you to have your own thoughts and ideas and feelings, even when I hold you in my arms. It's our last chance.

但是我愛妳，我希望妳擁有妳自己的想法和感覺，甚至是將妳擁在懷裡時也一樣。這是我們的最後機會。

*intimately [ˈɪntəmɪtli] (adv.) 親密地

*possession [pəˈzɛʃən] (n.) 財產，所有物

A Room with a View

《當哈利遇上莎莉》

哈利（Harry，Billy Crystal 飾）和莎莉（Sally，Meg Ryan 飾）兩人的愛情觀大不相同，哈利認為男人沒辦法和女人當普通朋友；而莎莉卻覺得男女之間可以有純友誼。這對原本互相看不順眼的男女分隔五年後再度相遇，對彼此的感覺似乎都有些不同了。到底男女之間有沒有純友誼？而哈利和莎莉之間又是不是純友誼呢？

Harry: I love that you get cold when it's 71 degrees out. I love that it takes you an hour and a half to order a sandwich. I love that you get a little *crinkle above your nose when you're looking at me like I'm nuts. I love that after I spend the day with you, I can still smell your perfume on my clothes. And I love that you are the last person I want to talk to before I go to sleep at night.

And it's not because I'm lonely, and it's not because it's New Year's Eve. I came here tonight because when you realize you want to spend the rest of your life with somebody, you want the rest of your life to start as soon as possible.

我喜歡妳會在外面只有（華氏）七十一度（攝氏二十二度）時發冷；我喜歡妳花一個半小時只為了點一份三明治；我喜歡妳皺著鼻子看著我，彷彿我是個瘋子；我喜歡跟妳相處一整天後，還能在我的衣服上聞到妳留下的香水味；我喜歡晚上睡前妳是我最想講話的對象。

這絕不是因為我很孤單，也絕不是因為今天是跨年夜。今晚我出現在這裡，是因為當一個人了解到自己找到了想共度餘生的人，就會儘可能地想快點跟她開始。

Sally: You see? That is just like you, Harry. You say things like that, and you make it impossible for me to hate you.

看吧？哈利，這就是你，你會講這樣的話，讓我沒辦法討厭你。

*crinkle [ˈkrɪŋkəl] (v.) 縮，皺

When Harry Met Sally

《愛在心裡口難開》

患有強迫症的作家梅爾文（Melvin，Jack Nicholson 飾）是個孤僻的人，對於自己看不順眼的人事總會加以刁難。他討厭隔壁鄰居賽門；到餐廳只有服務生卡蘿（Carol，Helen Hunt 飾）能為他點菜。沒想到這兩個人卻意外地打破梅爾文的心防，讓他逐漸打開他封閉的內心……。

Melvin: I might be the only one who appreciates how amazing you are in every single thing that you do, and…I watch them, wondering how they can watch you bring their food, and clear their tables and never get that they just met the greatest woman alive. And the fact that I get it makes me feel good, about me.

我應該會是那個唯一能體會到妳所做的每一件事情有多棒的人，我看著他們，想著他們為什麼可以看著妳送餐、收拾餐桌，卻不知道剛才遇到這世上最好的女人。我能夠了解這件事，這讓我覺得自己很棒。

As Good As It Gets

《第六感生死緣》

死神的化身為喬布萊克（Joe Black，Brad Pitt 飾）出現在影視大亨威廉（William，Anthony Hopkins 飾）的眼前。見到死神的威廉知道自己壽命將至，卻沒想到喬居然愛上自己的小女兒蘇珊（Susan，Claire Forlani 飾），人神殊途，喬應該帶走他深愛的女子，還是應該將她繼續留在人間？

Susan: Tell me you love me now.
告訴我你現在愛我。

Joe: I love you now. I love you always.
我現在愛妳。我永遠都會愛妳。

Meet Joe Black

百鍊鋼化作繞指柔

《愛在心裡口難開》這部電影更所為人知的經典台詞無非就是梅爾文告訴卡蘿：「為了妳，我想成為更好的人」(You make me want to be a better man.)。原本是個患有強迫症的機車男，卻在遇見卡蘿之後，願意為了她成為一個很棒的人，這就是愛情給人的正面能量，難怪此部電影堪稱浪漫愛情經典中的經典了。

《今天暫時停止》

氣象播報員菲爾（Phil，Bill Murray 飾）奉命到一座小鎮報導一年一度的二月二日土撥鼠日，採訪過程中，所有人都領教到他的壞脾氣，搞得大家雞飛狗跳。當夜，採訪團隊因為大風雪而被迫在當地停留一日，不料隔天起床，菲爾竟發現自己被困在二月二日這一天，他該如何擺脫這詭異的情境？

Phil: You like boats, but not the ocean. You go to a lake in the summer with your family up in the mountains. There's a long wooden dock and a boathouse with boards missing from the roof, and a place you used to crawl underneath to be alone. You're a sucker for French poetry and rhinestones. You're very generous. You're kind to strangers and children, and when you stand in the snow you look like an angel.

妳喜歡船但不喜歡海。在夏天妳會和妳的家人到山裡的湖邊，那裡有個很長的木製碼頭，還有屋頂少一塊木板的船庫，妳都會爬到底下自己待著。妳對於法國詩詞和水鑽非常著迷。妳很慷慨，妳對陌生人和小孩子總是很友善。當妳站在雪裡，看起來像天使一樣。

Rita: How are you doing this?
你怎麼會知道這些？

Phil: I told you. I wake up every day, right here, right in Punxsutawney, and it's always February 2nd, and there's nothing I can do about it.

我告訴過妳啦。我每天醒來都在這裡，都在旁蘇托尼，而且時間都是二月二日，我也沒辦法逃脫。

Groundhog Day

《雲端情人》

在人際溝通完全仰賴電子的未來社會，心思細膩的西奧多（Theodore，Joaquin Phoenix 飾）在偶然的機會下認識了完全「人」性化、且會不斷進步的人工智慧系統──莎曼珊（Samantha，Scarlett Johansson 飾）。莎曼珊天天陪伴著西奧多，使西奧多不知不覺陷入情網，居然愛上這個軟體中的「她」，這段人與科技發展出的不尋常愛情，結果會是如何？

Theodore: I've never loved anyone the way I love you.

我從來沒有像愛妳這樣愛過一個人。

Samantha: Me too. Now we know how.

我也是。現在我們知道要如何去愛了。

Theodore: Even if you come home late and I'm already asleep, just whisper in my ear one little thought you had today. Because I love the way you look at the world. And I'm so happy I get to be next to you and look at the world through your eyes.

就算妳晚歸時，我已經睡著了，還是輕聲在我耳邊說一件妳今天發生的事吧。因為我愛妳看世界的方式。而且我很開心能夠有妳在我身旁，用妳的眼睛帶我看這個世界。

Her

史嘉蕾
獻「聲」談愛

在《雲端情人》中，史嘉蕾喬韓森雖沒現身，但卻成功地用充滿磁性的獨特嗓音完美詮釋人工智慧系統──莎曼珊這個角色，令大家驚艷。雖然金球獎認為聲音演出無法角逐獎項，但導演史派克瓊斯（Spike Jones）依然十分讚許史嘉蕾的表現，他表示，厲害的演員就算只憑聲音，也能演出各種情緒，傳達情感，使觀眾真正感受到他們角色之間產生的互動連結和愛意。

《愛是您，愛是我》

距離 2003 年的耶誕節只剩五個星期，發生在倫敦的八個故事，交織出精彩的浪漫喜劇。故事以這八個看似獨立卻又有些微妙關聯的愛情故事穿插而成。由休葛蘭、連恩尼遜、綺拉奈特莉、柯林佛斯……等多名英國明星領銜主演。

以下是本片令人最印象深刻的兩個場景。第一個是暗戀朋友新婚妻子的馬克（Mark，Andrew Lincoln 飾）決定把想說的話寫在紙板上，在耶誕夜跑去告白：

Mark: But for now, let me say—without hope or agenda, just because it's Christmas and at Christmas you tell the truth—to me, you are perfect. And my *wasted heart will love you. Until you look like this. Merry Christmas.

現在請讓我說，我不抱任何希望或企圖，只因今天是聖誕節，而聖誕節是個說實話的節日，對我來說，妳很完美，而我如癡如醉的心將會一直愛妳，直到妳變成這樣（紙板上是木乃伊的照片）。耶誕快樂。

*wasted [ˋwestɪd] (a.)（因病或放蕩而）枯槁的

第二個浪漫告白場景，是赴法國鄉間寫作的英國作家傑米（Jamie，Colin Firth 飾）開車送幫他打理生活，只會講葡萄牙語的清潔婦奧瑞莉亞（Aurélia，Lúcia Moniz）回家路上的這段：

Jamie: It's my favorite time of day, driving you.

（英文）我一天中最愛的時刻就是送妳回家。

Aurélia: It's the saddest part of my day, leaving you.

（西班牙文）而離開你卻是我一天中最傷心的事。

Love Actually

Drew 茱兒芭莉摩
Barrymore

© DFree / Shutterstock.com

Showbiz Words

blockbuster 賣座電影、暢銷書

blockbuster 這個字源自二次世界大戰，指的是一種威力強大、能將敵方陣營摧毀的巨型炸彈，後來引申表示廣受歡迎、風靡一時、叫好又叫座的電影、戲劇、唱片、書……等。相反的，若是某個戲劇或是電影失敗到一踢糊塗則會用 bomb 這個字，bomb 是「炸彈」的意思，因此用被炸彈炸過後出現一片死寂的殘破模樣來形容票房成果。其他「熱賣大作」的表達還有：

- megahit 賣座電影、唱片
- smash hit 廣受歡迎的電視劇、產品
- bestseller 暢銷書、產品
- chartbuster 熱門唱片、歌曲

lead 主角

lead 當動詞時表「引導、帶領」，在電影用語中就是指「主角、主要的演員」。

相關字彙還有

- leading actor / man, male lead 男主角
- leading actress / lady, female lead 女主角
- leading role 男 / 女主角
- star 男 / 女主角

〔13〕

Born in L.A. to John Drew Barrymore of the famous Barrymore acting family and Jaid, an [1]**aspiring** actress, Drew Barrymore got her first role—in a dog food commercial—when she was just 11 months old. After making her big screen [2]**debut** at five with a small part in the 1980 sci-fi [3]**flick** *Altered States*, she was cast as Gertie in the blockbuster *E.T.*, a role that instantly made her one of Hollywood's top child stars. In 1984, Barrymore won a Golden Globe [4]**nomination** for *Irreconcilable Differences*, in which she plays a young girl who [5]**divorces** her parents.

But [6]**despite** her fame, Barrymore's childhood was less than ideal. Her mom kicked her dad out before she was born, and her first memory of him is being thrown across the room by him when she was three. Her mom started taking her to wild parties before she was ten, and by the age of 14 Barrymore was in [7]**rehab** for drugs and [8]**alcohol**. But this experience actually helped her career. She wrote the [9]**autobiography** *Little Girl Lost* the next year, and began playing bad girl roles in movies like *Poison Ivy* and *Guncrazy*, which won her another Golden Globe nomination.

By the age of 20, Barrymore was all grown up. She started a production company, Flower Films, and began producing many of the films she starred in, including hits like *Charlie's Angels* and *Donnie Darko*. She also [10]**transformed** from bad girl to romantic lead, starring in successful rom-coms like *The Wedding Singer, 50 First Dates* and *He's Just Not That Into You*. Although she's stated that she's [11]**bisexual**, Barrymore has been married three times, first to bar owner Jeremy Thomas for two months, next to comedian Tom Green for five months, and finally to art [12]**consultant** Will Kopelman since 2012.

© Featureflash / Shutterstock.com

茱兒芭莉摩出生於洛杉磯，父親為著名演藝世家芭莉摩家族中的約翰德魯芭莉摩，母親潔德則是一位想成名的女演員。她在十一個月大時就得到生平第一個角色，出演一部狗食廣告。1980 年五歲時於科幻片《變形博士》初登大銀幕之後，她便獲選演出強檔鉅片《E.T. 外星人》中的歌蒂一角，令她瞬間成為好萊塢的頂尖童星。1984 年，芭莉摩以《舞台》一片獲得金球獎提名，當中她飾演一位欲斷絕親子關係的年輕女孩。

雖然成名甚早，不過芭莉摩的童年生活並不理想。她的母親在她出生之前就將她爸爸趕出門，而她對父親最早的記憶竟是自己三歲時被他扔到房間另一端。十歲之前芭莉摩就開始被媽媽帶去參加各種狂歡派對，到了十四歲時自己也因毒品及酗酒問題而遭到勒戒。不過這段經歷卻有助於她的演藝生涯。她於隔年出版了自傳《迷失的小女孩》，並開始在《慾海潮》和《賭命狂花》等電影中演出壞女孩的角色，後者也為她再次贏得金球獎提名。

到了二十歲的時候，芭莉摩已經相當成熟。她成立了花卉電影這間製片公司，開始製作許多她親自主演的電影，包括《霹靂嬌娃》及《怵目驚魂 28 天》等暢銷影片。她也從壞女孩的角色成功轉型為浪漫電影的主角，主演了《婚禮歌手》、《我的失憶女友》、《他其實沒那麼喜歡妳》等賣座愛情喜劇。雖然她表示自己為雙性戀，不過芭莉摩也曾三度結婚，第一段與酒吧老闆傑瑞米湯瑪斯的婚姻僅維持兩個月，接著跟諧星湯姆格林則撐了五個月，最後於 2012 年下嫁藝術顧問威爾科波曼直至現在。

 14

Vocabulary Bank

1) **aspiring** [əˋpaɪrɪŋ] (a.) 有意成為…的，有抱負的
Many aspiring actors work as waiters.
許多有意成為演員的人都在做服務生。

2) **debut** [deˋbju] (n./v.) 首度演出，處女秀
The singer's debut television performance was a huge success.
此歌手在電視節目上的首次登台相當成功。

3) **flick** [flɪk] (n.) （口）電影
My girlfriend dragged me to see another chick flick last night.
我女友昨晚又拖我去看浪漫溫馨片。

4) **nomination** [ˌnɑməˋneʃən] (n.) 提名
The actor has received many Oscar nominations.
那位演員多次得到奧斯卡提名。

5) **divorce** [dɪˋvors] (v./n.) 離婚
Mark's wife refuses to divorce him.
馬克的太太拒絕跟他離婚。

6) **despite** [dɪˋspaɪt] (prep.) 雖然，儘管
The concert was held despite the bad weather.
雖然天候不佳，演唱會仍照常舉辦。

7) **rehab** [ˋrihæb] (n.) （菸酒、毒品等）勒戒，治療
The star spent two months in rehab last year.
那位明星去年花了兩個月勒戒。

8) **alcohol** [ˋælkəˌhɔl] (n.) 酒，酒精
The restaurant applied for a license to serve alcohol.
這間餐廳申請了提供酒精飲料的許可證。

9) **autobiography** [ˌɔtəbaɪˋɑgrəfi] (n.) 自傳
Have you read Benjamin Franklin's autobiography?
你讀過富蘭克林的自傳嗎？

10) **transform** [trænsˋfɔrm] (v.) 改變，改觀
Technology has transformed the way we live and work.
科技改變了我們的生活與工作方式。

11) **bisexual** [baɪˋsɛkʃuəl] (a./n.) 雙性戀（的）
Many famous actors and singers are bisexual.
許多著名演員和歌手都是雙性戀。

12) **consultant** [kənˋsʌltənt] (n.) 顧問
Our company is considering hiring a management consultant.
我們公司正考慮聘用一位管理顧問。

搭訕經典

莫等待，莫依賴，白雪公主不會從天上掉下來！
看到中意的對象，
與其等待天雷勾動地火的瞬間，
不如主動創造彼此認識的機會。

以下「搭訕破冰句」都出自電影對白，
原本不一定用於搭訕，但只要學起來巧加運用，
一定能讓你的愛情運勢大開！

Want to know how I got these scars?
想知道我這些疤是怎麼來的嗎？
── *The Dark Knight*《黑暗騎士》

你以為我是醫美專家？還是皮膚科醫師？

I've never wanted a human's blood so much before.
我從沒像現在這麼渴望一個人的血。
── *Twilight*《暮光之城》

你以為只要學羅伯派汀森（Robert Pattinson，飾演帥哥吸血鬼愛德華）講話，女生就會買單嗎？

Wanna play a game? You can be Little Red Riding Hood and I'll be the Big Bad Wolf.
想不想玩個遊戲？妳可以當小紅帽，我來當大野狼。
── *Twilight*《暮光之城》

不如你來當大野狼，我來當大獵槍吧。真是夠了！

Are you tired? You have been flying through my mind nonstop!
妳累不累？妳一直在我的腦海中飛個不停！
── *Planes*《飛機總動員》

基本上，所有冷笑話都不適合用來搭訕。

絕對 NG 搭訕

Just relax and let your mind go blank. That shouldn't be too hard for you.
儘管放輕鬆讓腦中一片空白。那對妳來說一定不會太難。
── *Avatar*《阿凡達》

在酒吧中勸人頭腦放空、心情放輕鬆，嗯，蠻貼心的，但千萬不要嘴賤加上後面這句啊！

I could find the whole meaning of life in those sad eyes.
在那雙哀傷的眼睛裡，我能找到人生全部的意義。
── *Waitress*《情迷窩心批》

或許有人覺得這句又憂鬱又浪漫，但正常女生碰到不認識的人跟她說這種話，只會覺得他是肖ㄟ吧？

I don't know how to put this, but I'm kind of a big deal.
我不知道該怎麼說，但是我算是個大人物。
── *Anchorman*《銀幕大角頭》

put 在這裡當「說」的意思。如果不知道該怎麼說，就不要說囉，大人物先生。

You're not too smart, are you? I like that in a man.
你不是很聰明，對吧？我喜歡有這種特質的男人。
── *Body Heat*《體熱》

如果覺得對方看起來還不錯，只是搭訕的方法很破，可以這樣回答。

Your hat has sequins.
妳的帽子上有小亮片。
── *The 40-Year-Old Virgin*《40 處男》

sequin ['sikwɪn] 原本是一種古代的金幣，現在指衣服上裝飾的小亮片。這句根本是沒話找話講，只會讓人覺得你這個人很無聊。也難怪本片說這句話的男主角是「40（歲）處男」了！

Hello, gorgeous.
哈囉，美女。
—— *Funny Girl*《妙女郎》

應該沒人會討厭被叫美女吧。

You are everything I never knew I always wanted.
我都不知道我一直想要的就是妳。
—— *Fools Rush In*《傻愛成真》

這……真是嘴巴太甜了吧！？

Now what's a nice girl like you doing in a place like this?
像妳這樣的好女孩在這種地方做什麼？
—— *You Only Live Twice*《雷霆谷》

你以為誇人家 nice girl 有種欣賞內在美的 fu，不會給人色鬼的噁心感覺嗎？其實這句英文很俗氣，要用開玩笑的語氣講，如果正經八百說這句話，會讓人啼笑皆非。

Today, I consider myself the luckiest man on the face of the earth.
今天，我覺得自己是地球表面最幸運的男人。
—— *The Pride Of The Yankee*《洋基之光》

為什麼呢？當然是因為遇見眼前的真命天女囉！

I know what I want, because I have it in my hands right now. You.
我知道我要的是什麼，因為現在就在我的手中：妳。
—— *P.S. I Love You*《P.S. 我愛妳》

這句最適合用在跳舞的場合。跳舞牽手只是社交禮儀，但說出這句話，你跟她就是友達以上，戀人未滿囉！

Your eyes are amazing, do you know that? You should never shut them, not even at night.
妳的眼睛美得驚人，妳知道嗎？妳應該永遠不要閉眼睛，即使是在夜晚。
—— *Unfaithful*《出軌》

具體說出美的地方，尤其是靈魂之窗——眼睛，感覺多麼脫俗高雅。

I've always depended on the kindness of strangers.
一直以來都只有陌生人會對我好。
—— *A Streetcar Named Desire*《慾望街車》

如果你今天在夜店裡百發不中，眼看就要槓龜，就裝可憐試試看這句吧！

Mrs. Robinson, you're trying to seduce me. Aren't you?
羅賓森太太，妳想要引誘我。沒錯吧？
—— *The Graduate*《畢業生》

使用這句的前提，一是那女生明顯大你很多歲，二是你真的喜歡大姊姊類型的冶豔女生，否則小心惹禍上身啊。再來就是要視情況把 Mrs. Robinson 改為 Ms. Lee、Ms. Chen 等等。

I would give anything if you were two people, so I could call up the one who is my friend and tell her about the one I like so much.
但願妳能變成兩個人就好了，這樣我就可以打電話給當我朋友的妳，跟妳說我有多喜歡另一個妳。
—— *Broadcast News*《收播新聞》

這裡的角色扮演，是請對方一人分飾兩角。

I used to live like Robinson Crusoe, shipwrecked among eight million people. But one day I saw a footprint in the sand and there you were.
我一直過得像魯濱遜克魯索，在八百萬茫茫人海中沈船。但有一天，我在沙灘上看到一個腳印，妳就站在那裡。
—— *The Apartment*《公寓春光》

Robinson Crusoe 是小說《魯濱遜漂流記》的主角，敘述因船難漂流荒島二十八年的故事。

You know what I heard when I first met you? Beeeeoooo! Beeeeooooo! Beeeeooooo! Beeeeooooo! That's an ambulance, come to take me away, 'cause the sight of you stopped my heart. Beeeeeoooooooooooooo.
妳知道我第一次看到妳時，聽到什麼聲音嗎？嗶嗚！嗶嗚！嗶嗚！嗶嗚！那是救護車的聲音，來載我的，因為妳的身影讓我心跳停止。嗶嗚！
—— *A Night at the Roxbury*《舞翻天》

擅長模仿各種汽機車聲、蟲鳴鳥叫的人，儘管把參加選秀會的本領拿出來，說不定能虜獲芳心喔。

Swoon—I'll catch you.
暈過去吧——我會接住妳。
—— *The English Patient*《英倫情人》

這次你扮演的角色是大情聖，而對方就快要拜倒在你的西裝褲底下了。

Can you keep a secret? I'm trying to organize a prison break. I'm looking for, like, an accomplice. We'd have to first get out of this bar, then the hotel, then the city, and then the country. Are you in or are you out?
妳能保密嗎？我正在計劃逃獄。我在找，呃，一個共犯。我們第一步得先離開這間酒吧，然後走出這個飯店，接著是這座城市，最後是這個國家。妳要不要加入？
—— *Lost in Translation*《愛情不用翻譯》

罪犯類型對一些女生代表致命的吸引力，不過相信你這樣講不會有人真以為你是罪犯，而是會覺得你這個人挺有趣的吧。

Was that cannon fire, or is it my heart pounding?
剛剛那是大砲發射的聲音嗎？還是我的心跳聲？
—— *Casablanca*《北非諜影》

除了假裝聽到救護車的聲音，還可以假裝聽到大砲聲呢！

You know, it's dangerous for you to be here in the frozen foods section—because you could melt all this stuff.
妳知道嗎，妳待在冷凍食品區太危險了——因為妳會讓這裡的東西都融化。
—— *My Blue Heaven*《貴客光臨》

看到穿著火辣的性感女孩在超市或便利超商出沒，這句話就可以上場了。

When I think of why I make pictures, the reason that I can come up with just seems that I've been making my way here. It seems right now that all I've ever done in my life is making my way here to you.
當我思索自己為何攝影，所能想到的理由似乎就是讓我找到這裡。現在看來，我這輩子做的每一件事，就是讓我來這裡找到妳。
—— *The Bridges of Madison County*《麥迪遜之橋》

如果你是玩單眼相機的文青，剛好可以藉口幫對方照相，想辦法找機會說出這段話。

Fasten your seatbelts. It's going to be a bumpy night.
安全帶繫好了。今天晚上可刺激了。
—— *All About Eve*《彗星美人》

搭夜班巴士返鄉過年嗎？若是剛好有可愛女生坐你旁邊，不妨試試這句話。

Drop that zero and get with the hero.
別管那隻狗熊，到英雄這邊來吧。
—— *Cool as Ice*《他酷得像冰》

zero（無足輕重的小角色）跟 hero 只有一個字母之差，意思卻是天差地別。發現想要搭訕的對象，最煞風景的莫過於旁邊有護花使者了。這句話不只能讓你化阻力為助力，還能展現非凡的自信。

What you're about to see is totally classified....
妳即將看到的是絕對機密……。
—— *Transformers*《變形金剛》

獻寶之前用這句增加神秘感，會讓人覺得你這個人很有趣喔！

Wanna see my spaceship?
你想看我的太空船嗎？
—— *The Hitchhiker's Guide to the Galaxy*《星際大奇航》

萬一你沒有太空船，可以把 spaceship 換成 Mercedes（賓士車）、Harley Davidson（哈雷機車）、CD collection……等任何想要獻寶的東西。

讓知識為你加分

You give me premature ventricular contractions. You make my heart skip a beat.
你害我心律不整。你讓我的心漏跳了一拍。
—— *No Strings Attached*《飯飯之交》

這句話與知識有關的部分，在於用了比較難的英文字：
premature [͵primə`tjʊr] (a.) 倉促的，過早的
ventricular [vɛn`trɪkjələ] (a.) 心室的
contraction [kən`trækʃən] (n.) 收縮
三個字加起來是「心律不整」的意思。

You know how they say we only use ten percent of our brains? I think we only use ten percent of our hearts.
妳知道據說我們只用了一成的智力嗎？我覺得我們只用了一成的心。
—— *Wedding Crashers*《婚禮終結者》

講話帶統計數字，聽起來比較聰明。

You know what you are? You're God's answer to Job, y'know? You would have ended all argument between them. I mean, he would have pointed to you and said, "Y'know, I do a lot of terrible things, but I can still make one of these."
妳知道妳是什麼嗎？妳是上帝給約伯的答案，懂嗎？妳可以終結他們之間的爭執。我的意思是，上帝可以指著妳說，「你知道嗎，我是做了很多很可怕的事，但我還是有造出這樣的東西。」
—— *Manhattan*《曼哈頓》

〈約伯記〉在聖經中占了四十二章，純就故事內容來看，上帝對約伯反反覆覆做了許多無理的事，讓人覺得這個上帝太可怕了。這句電影對白就是利用這個典故來凸顯眼前女子的美好——不論這個世界再怎麼糟，上帝造了妳，就是給我最大的恩典。

I couldn't help but notice that you look a lot like my next girlfriend.
我沒辦法不注意到，妳長得有夠像我下一任女友。
—— *Hitch*《全民情聖》

能講這種話的人臉皮實在很厚，但聽起來挺有趣的。

I want to buy you food, I want to buy you corn dogs, I want to buy you anything.
我想要買東西給妳吃，我想要買炸熱狗給妳，要我買什麼給妳都好。
—— *Kids*《衝擊年代》

死皮賴臉硬是要為小姐服務，最後應該都會得逞吧。

Are you stalking me? Because that would be super.
妳是在跟蹤我嗎？要是真的可就太棒了。
—— *National Lampoon's Van Wilder*《留級之王》

明明是自己故意製造巧遇，卻賴對方在跟蹤你。

Dave: Do you have a cell phone I could use?
妳有手機可以借我嗎？
Ronnie: Why?
幹嘛？
Dave: Someone's got to call God and let him know one of his angels is missing.
得有人打電話給上帝，跟祂說祂有一個天使掉在這裡。
—— *Couples Retreat*《伴侶度假村》

雖然片中女主角 Ronnie 接下來說 Wow, that is the worst line I've ever heard.（這是我聽過最爛的搭訕。）但其實網上很多人都在求這句台詞，應該是因為爛歸爛，但讓人印象深刻吧。

If I win, I get to take you home. If you win, you can come home with me.
如果我贏，我可以帶妳回家。如果妳贏，妳可以跟我回家。
—— *Trees Lounge*《傷心樹屋》

這不是油嘴滑舌，什麼才是油嘴滑舌？

Mr. Dreamy 夢幻情人

性感熟男
George Clooney
喬治克隆尼 🎧 15

George Clooney was born in Lexington, Kentucky to a TV talk show host and a beauty queen. Although Clooney acted in sketches on his dad's show as a kid, he became more interested in baseball in high school. But after failing to go pro and dropping out of college, he decided to give acting another try. After a decade of small TV parts, he finally got his break on the hit medical drama *ER*. This led to film roles, and his appearance opposite Jennifer Lopez in the 1998 crime comedy *Out of Sight* marked the beginning of a long collaboration with director Steven Soderberg, which has included hits like *Ocean's Eleven*. After years of dating actresses and models, Clooney married human rights lawyer Amal Alamuddin in 2014.

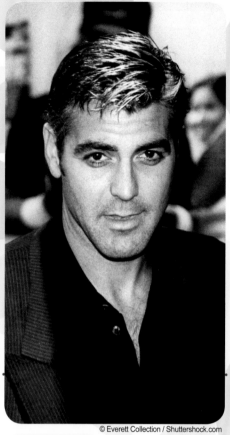

© Everett Collection / Shuttershock.com

喬治克隆尼出生於美國肯塔基州萊辛頓市，父親是電視脫口秀的主持人，母親則為選美皇后。雖然克隆尼小時候會在父親節目的短劇中演出，高中時期的他卻對打棒球較感興趣。不過在無法成為職業球員、而且大學又輟學之後，他決定再次試著走演員這條路。在電視圈跑了十年的龍套後，他終於在熱門的醫院影集《急診室的春天》中一嘗走紅滋味。克隆尼因此獲邀飾演電影角色，而他與珍妮佛羅培茲於 1998 年的犯罪喜劇《戰略高手》裡的搭檔演出，也開啟了他和導演史蒂芬索德柏的長期合作，當中包括《瞞天過海》等賣座強片。多年來換過無數女星及模特兒女友後，克隆尼終於在 2014 年情定人權律師艾默阿拉穆丁。

影星小檔案

全　　名：**George Timothy Clooney**
生　　日：**May 6, 1961**
出 生 地：美國肯塔基州
感情狀態：已婚

同場加映
啊～讓人好有安全感的大叔們小檔案

有些人喜歡細皮嫩肉、白白淨淨的文青，有些人則喜歡肌肉發達的猛男，還有些人是大叔控，特別欣賞有成熟韻味的中年男子。到底這些熟男有什麼魅力，居然能擁有這麼廣大的粉絲市場？快一同來瞧瞧吧！

Liam Neeson 連恩尼遜

有看過《即刻救援》的人都知道，連恩在這部電影裡真是太威了，被封為「地表最強老爸」的他，為了從綁匪手中營救心愛的女兒，不惜上山下海，隻身直搗虎穴，最終憑著機智和俐落的身手成功救出女兒，整部戲緊湊刺激，讓觀眾大呼過癮之餘，心裡也不禁 OS：這麼 man 這麼有安全感的男人上哪兒找啊！

© vipflash / Shuttershock.com

Pierce Brosnan 皮爾斯布洛斯南

這位前 007 演員向來是少女心中的偶像，不單單只因為他俊俏的外表，還有他不願被偶像包袱束縛，在《媽媽咪亞》中搞笑加唱歌的新鮮嘗試，更難能可貴的是，他是演藝圈中難得潔身自愛，沒什麼花邊新聞的愛妻好男人，日前狗仔還拍到他與身材發福的妻子在路邊甜蜜擁吻，兩人結髮多年，感情仍舊如膠似漆，真是羨煞旁人啊！

© Featureflash / Shuttershock.com

I wanna shake you naked and eat you alive.
我想把妳搖晃到衣服都掉光了，再生吞活剝把妳吃了。
—— *Zandalee*《禁情遊戲》

有誰看過這部電影嗎？竟然只列輔導級耶。

Skylar: You were hoping to get a goodnight kiss?
你是在期待我跟你親親說晚安嗎？
Will: I was hoping to get goodnight laid.
我是在期待上床道晚安。
—— *Good Will Hunting*《心靈捕手》

約會之後送女生回到家門口，或許可以碰碰運氣，學麥特戴蒙在片中的角色說這句話。

Take me to bed or lose me forever.
帶我上床，否則我就永遠離開你。
—— *Top Gun*《捍衛戰士》

大家不要懷疑，這句話可是美國甜心梅格萊恩在片中的台詞喔！

I don't exactly know what I am required to say in order for you to have intercourse with me. But could we assume that I said all that. I mean essentially we are talking about fluid exchange right? So could we just go straight to the sex?
我不知道我應該說什麼適當的話，讓妳跟我性交。但我們可不可以假裝我該說的都說了。我是說，實際上我們在討論的就是交換體液，不是嗎？所以我們可不可以直接上床？
—— *A Beautiful Mind*《美麗境界》

羅素克洛在片中飾演精神分裂的數學家，也只有瘋到一定程度的天才，才有辦法說這種話又不被呼巴掌吧。

I really wish that you'd come home with me. You're so cute and I'm really good in bed, believe me. You smell good, too.
我真希望妳能跟我回家。妳好可愛，而我床上功夫了得，不騙妳。妳聞起來也好香。
—— *Leaving Las Vegas*《遠離賭城》

尼可拉斯凱吉在片中飾演醉鬼，難怪能說得這麼直接啊！

How would you like to have a sexual experience so intense it could change your political views?
妳想不想要體驗一次火辣辣的性愛，激烈到可以改變妳的政治立場？
—— *The Sure Thing*《校門外》

與其終日政黨惡鬥，不如大家就來愛與和平吧！

You're good looking, you got a beautiful body, beautiful legs, beautiful face, all these guys in love with you. Only you've got a look in your eye like you haven't been fucked in a year.
妳很美，身材漂亮，一雙美腿，臉蛋標緻，每個男人都愛妳。只不過妳的眼神透露已經一年沒人跟妳上床了。
—— *Scarface*《疤面煞星》

艾爾帕西諾在片中飾演凶狠的毒販，這句話一聽就是大哥才有的「愧靠（口氣）」！

出奇制勝

I may be the outlaw, but you're the one stealing my heart.
我或許作奸犯科，但妳偷走了我的心。
—— *Thelma and Louise*《末路狂花》

outlaw 是「亡命之徒，罪犯」的意思。在片中，年輕俊美的布萊德彼特飾演利用青春肉體洗劫師奶的小混混，他給熟女下蠱的工具就是這句話。

I don't bite, you know...unless it's called for.
我不會咬人，你知道嗎……除非有那個必要。
—— *Charade*《謎中謎》

奧黛麗赫本在片中想引誘卡萊葛倫跟她一起回家時，說了這句話。儘管已經是 1963 年的電影，這句對白仍深受現在的英美女性觀眾喜愛，被評選為影史最性感對白。

I hate to see you go, but I love to watch you leave.
我很不想看妳走，但我喜歡望著妳的背影。
—— *Face/Off*《變臉》

如果你擔心女孩一去不回，說這句話保證能讓她回頭看你一眼。

That's a nice dress—where's the rest of it?
那件洋裝很漂亮，但其他的布跑到哪裡去了？
—— *Internal Affairs*《流氓警察》

如果看到穿著暴露的開朗女生，可以試試這一句。

We gotta get you out of those wet clothes and into a dry martini.
我們得先幫妳脫掉那一身濕衣服，再來一杯乾馬丁尼。
—— *Beerfest*《酒國英雄榜》

這裡是在玩 wet 和 dry 的文字遊戲。martini 這款雞尾酒是由琴酒（gin）及苦艾酒（vermouth）調成，不過各種廠牌的苦艾酒甜度不一，用不甜的苦艾酒（dry vermouth）調成的馬丁尼，就是 dry martini。

Reggie: You're blocking my view.
你擋住我了。
Peter: Oh. which view would you prefer?
喔，妳想看哪一邊？
Reggie: The one you're blocking.
你擋住的那一邊。
—— *Charade*《謎中謎》

故意找人抬槓，也算是一種引起對方注意的招數。順道一提，這裡的 Roggie 可是奧黛麗赫本演的唷！

I see you're drinking 1%. Is that 'cause you think you're fat? 'Cause you're not. You could be drinking whole if you wanted to.
我看到妳在喝低脂牛奶。是因為妳覺得自己太胖嗎？妳不胖。妳可以喝全脂牛奶都沒問題。
—— *Napoleon Dynamite*《拿破崙炸藥》

不管你打算說什麼，跟女生講話出現「胖」這個字是很危險的。但也正因為如此，她一定會注意到你。

Ma'am, in the leopard print dress, you have an amazing rack.
小姐，穿豹紋洋裝那位，妳的胸部真棒。
—— *The Hangover*《最後大丈夫》

敢穿豹紋又有好身材的美女可遇不可求，怎能不把握機會？

Your husband told me you were the most beautiful woman he'd ever seen, but he didn't say anything about the most beautiful woman I'd ever seen.
妳丈夫有說妳是他見過最美的女人，但他沒說妳是我見過最美的女人。
—— *Intolerable Cruelty*《真情假愛》

喬治克隆尼在片中飾演顛倒黑白的離婚律師，反被委託人的下堂妻色誘的故事。如果你看上的對象是人妻，可以參考這句。願老天保佑你。

Richard Gere 李察基爾

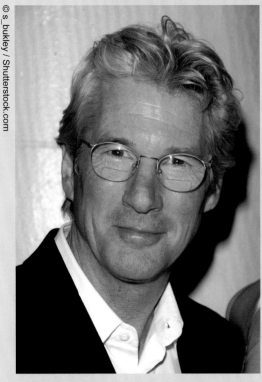

Richard Gere was born in Philadelphia on August 31, 1949 to Homer, an ¹⁾**insurance** ²⁾**salesman** and Doris, a ³⁾**housewife**. As a boy, he played the trumpet and competed in ⁴⁾**gymnastics**, the latter earning him a scholarship to UMass Amherst. Gere majored in ⁵⁾**philosophy** and drama, but as his interest in acting grew, he decided to drop out and become a professional actor. In 1973, he won the lead role in a London production of *Grease*. Gere's screen ⁶⁾**breakthrough** came in 1977 when he played a young street ⁷⁾**hustler** in the erotic drama *Looking for Mr. Goodbar*.

With starring roles in films like *American Gigolo* (1980) and *An Officer and a Gentleman* (1982), Gere established himself as a Hollywood leading man and sex symbol in the 1980s. But with little interest in the Hollywood lifestyle, he began ⁸⁾**turning down** blockbuster roles and devoting his time to ⁹⁾**humanitarian** ¹⁰⁾**causes**. The actor spent time working with ¹¹⁾**refugees** in Central America, and began supporting human rights in Tibet after meeting the Dalai Lama. Gere established the Tibet House in 1987 to help ¹²⁾**preserve** Tibetan culture, and was later ¹³⁾**banned** from presenting at the Academy Awards after expressing his support for Tibetan ¹⁴⁾**independence** onstage.

But Gere couldn't stay away from Hollywood forever. In 1990, two hit movies—crime thriller *Internal Affairs* and romantic comedy *Pretty Woman*—put him right back on top of the A-list. The latter, with Gere starring as a successful businessman opposite Julia Roberts as a prostitute, was so successful that it led to leading roles in a string of romantic films, including *Runaway Bride* (1999), *Autumn in New York* (2000) and *Nights in Rodanthe* (2008). Now in his 60s, the actor is still as sexy as ever and has no plans to retire.

Showbiz Words

sex symbol 性感偶像

sex symbol 這個字眼最早出現在一九五〇年代中期，代表對大眾具有性吸引力的名人，經常以票選排名的形式出現在時尚、八卦雜誌當中。一開始都是電影明星，但隨著時代演進，現在包括樂團歌手、模特兒、運動員，甚至政治人物都可能入列。不過 sex symbol 最著名的例子是瑪麗蓮夢露 (Marilyn Monroe)，她甚至被 BBC（英國國家廣播公司）評為永不隕落的好萊塢性感偶像。

李察基爾於 1949 年八月三十一日出生在美國費城，父親荷馬是一位保險業務員，母親桃樂絲則為家庭主婦。青少年時期的他愛演奏喇叭並參加體操比賽，後者更令他獲得獎學金進入麻省大學安默斯特分校就讀。基爾的主修為哲學和戲劇，不過隨著他對演戲的興趣日益濃厚，他決定休學以成為專業演員。 1973 年，他於倫敦的《火爆浪子》音樂劇演出中獲得擔綱主角的機會。不過基爾到了 1977 年才闖入大銀幕，在情色劇情片《尋找顧巴先生》中飾演一個年輕的街頭騙徒。

於 1980 年《美國舞男》及 1982 年《軍官與紳士》等電影中飾演主角後，基爾確立了自己身為 1980 年代好萊塢領銜男星及性感偶像的地位。不過由於對好萊塢的紙醉金迷不感興趣，他開始婉拒鉅片邀約、轉而將時間奉獻給人道服務。這位男星到中美洲協助難民，並且在與達賴喇嘛會晤後開始支持西藏的人權運動。基爾於 1987 年設立了西藏之家這個組織來維護西藏文化，之後也因於台上聲援西藏獨立而被禁止主持奧斯卡頒獎典禮。

不過基爾無法永遠置身於好萊塢之外。1990 年的兩部賣座電影——犯罪驚悚片《流氓警察》及愛情喜劇《麻雀變鳳凰》——再次將他推向一線男星之列。基爾於後者飾演一位成功的商業人士，與詮釋妓女的茱莉亞羅勃茲大演對手戲。該片的成功也使他領銜主演一連串的愛情電影，包括 1999 年的《落跑新娘》、2000 年的《紐約的秋天》、以及 2008 年《羅丹薩的夜晚》。雖然這位男星已年屆六十，不過他仍性感依舊、絲毫沒有任何退休的打算。

Tongue-tied No More

drop out 退學，退出

drop out 除了字面上的意思「掉出來」，也表示「停止參與，退出」，運用在學業上就是「向學校申請退學」。

A: So how was the marathon?
　馬拉松比賽跑得怎麼樣？

B: Not so great—I dropped out halfway through.
　不太好，我跑到一半就退出了。

如果只是因故暫時「休學」，則是 (take a) leave of absence。

A: I want to travel around the world, but I don't want to wait till I graduate.
　我想要環遊世界，但是不想等到畢業才去。

B: In that case, you should take a leave of absence.
　既然這樣的話，你應該休學。

 17

Vocabulary Bank

1) **insurance** [ɪnˋʃʊrəns] (n.) 保險
Do you have fire insurance on your home?
你的房子有保火災險嗎？

2) **salesman** [ˋselzmən] (n.)（男）推銷員，業務員
You should never trust a used car salesman.
絕對不能相信二手車推銷員。

3) **housewife** [ˋhaʊsˌwaɪf] (n.) 家庭主婦，複數為 housewives
Lisa doesn't want to be a housewife like her mother.
麗莎不想像她的媽媽一樣當家庭主婦。

4) **gymnastics** [dʒɪmˋnæstɪks] (n.) 體操（運動）
Gymnastics requires great balance and agility.
體操運動需要絕佳的平衡感和靈活度。

5) **philosophy** [fɪˋlɑsəfɪ] (n.) 哲學
There aren't many career options for philosophy majors.
哲學系學生的就業選項不多。

6) **breakthrough** [ˋbrekˌθru] (n.) 突破，重大進展
Police are still waiting for a breakthrough in the investigation.
警方還在等待調查的突破性進展。

7) **hustler** [ˋhʌslɚ] (n.) 騙子，妓女（男）
The poor neighborhood was filled with hustlers and drug dealers.
這個貧窮的社區充滿了騙徒和販毒者。

8) **turn down** [tɝn daʊn] (phr.) 拒絕，否決
I asked Kelly out, but she turned me down.
我約凱莉出去，但是她拒絕了。

9) **humanitarian** [hjuˌmænəˋtɛrɪən] (a./n.)
人道主義的；人道主義者，慈善家
Many countries provide humanitarian aid to Africa.
許多國家對非洲提供人道救助。

10) **cause** [kɔz] (n.)（人努力支持的）理想，目標，事業等
I'm willing to donate money if it's for a good cause.
如果立意良善，我願意捐錢。

11) **refugee** [ˋrɛfjʊˌdʒi] (n.) 難民
Thousands of refugees fled across the border.
成千上萬的難民從邊界逃離。

12) **preserve** [prɪˋzɝv] (v.) 保存，保藏
The government has been criticized for not doing enough to preserve historical sites.
政府因對古蹟維護做得不足而被批評。

13) **ban** [bæn] (v./n.) 禁止，取締
The city is considering banning smoking in restaurants.
這個城市考慮禁止人們在餐廳抽菸。

14) **independence** [ˌɪndɪˋpɛndəns] (n.) 獨立，自主
American independence is celebrated on the 4th of July.
七月四號是慶祝美國獨立的日子。

伍迪艾倫
Woody Allen

Showbiz Words

Emmy Awards 艾美獎

艾美獎為美國電視圈的年度重要盛事,其中艾美獎又可細分為黃金時段艾美獎 (Primetime Emmy Award)、日間時段艾美獎 (Daytime Emmy Award) 及運動艾美獎 (Sports Emmy Award)……等不同類別,而這些獎項皆由分屬於不同機構的會員投票選出。

Emmy 一名源自早期電視攝影機中常見的 image orthicon tube(圖像正析映像管),簡稱為 immy,因其與電視圈息息相關,於是便將獎項命名為與 immy 諧音的 Emmy,且沿用至今。

standup 單口相聲

又稱 stand-up comedy,是一種在台上連續說許多短笑話來娛樂眾人的表演,內容大多是預先設定好的,不像 talk show(脫口秀)多為即興創作。

- The comedian is developing a new standup routine.
  那位諧星正在發想一套新的單口相聲表演。

star 主演

文中出現的另一個字 costar,是由表「共同,一起」的字首 co- 加上 star,即是「共同主演 (v.)」、「共同主演的演員 (n.)」。star 當一般名詞可以指「明星」,當動詞時,star (in) 則代表「由……主演」。

- Johnny Depp has starred in many hit movies.
  強尼戴普已經主演過很多賣座的電影。

🎧 18

Allen Stewart Konigsberg was born on December 1, 1935 to Martin and Nettie, both children of Jewish [1]**immigrants**. The young Allen became [2]**fascinated** with movies after his mother took him to see *Snow White and the Seven [3]Dwarves*. But Allen soon discovered that his true talent was [4]**comedy**, and his parents' frequent arguments in their small Brooklyn apartment **provided him with** [5]**material** for the jokes he loved to tell. By the time he was in high school, he was making [6]**pocket money** selling his jokes to local newspapers. After graduating, Allen [7]**enrolled** at New York University to study film, but dropped out in his first year.

It didn't matter, though—by the age of 19, Allen, now going by the name Woody, was making more money than both his parents combined writing comedy [8]**scripts** for popular TV shows like *Caesar's Hour* and *The Ed Sullivan Show*. While his five years writing for TV brought him success and even an **Emmy** nomination, he eventually got tired of writing for other people and decided to **try his hand at standup** comedy. Developing for himself the role of a nervous [9]**intellectual**—which would often be mistaken for his real personality—Allen was soon performing in Manhattan nightclubs and on television. He became a [10]**playwright** as well, writing *Don't Drink the Water* and *Play It Again, Sam*, which he **starred** in. Allen also had a brief romance with his costar, Diane Keaton, who would later become his [11]**muse**.

艾倫史都華康尼斯堡出生於 1935 年十二月一日,父母馬丁和內蒂同為猶太移民的子女。小時艾倫被母親帶去看《白雪公主》之後,便深深為電影所著迷。不過艾倫很快就發現自己的真正天賦在喜劇,於是父母經常在布魯克林狹小公寓裡爭吵的內容就成為他愛說的笑話題材。等到艾倫上高中時,他已經在向當地報社兜售笑話來掙零用錢。高中畢業後,艾倫進入紐約大學研習電影,但讀沒一年就休學了。

© catwalker / Shutterstock.com

Vocabulary Bank

1) **immigrant** [ˈɪmɪɡrənt] (n./a.) 移民（的）
Carlos is the son of Mexican immigrants.
卡洛斯是墨西哥移民之子。

2) **fascinate** [ˈfæsə.net] (v.) 著迷，使神魂顛倒
Roberta has always been fascinated by Asian culture.
蘿貝塔總是被亞洲文化所吸引。

3) **dwarf** [dwɔrf] (n.) 侏儒，矮子
Is that character played by a child or a dwarf?
那個角色是由小孩還是侏儒扮演？

4) **comedy** [ˈkɑmədi] (n.) 喜劇
Kelly likes to watch Jim Carrey comedies.
凱莉喜歡看金凱瑞的喜劇。

5) **material** [məˈtɪrɪəl] (n.) 素材，資料，工具
All students have access to university library materials.
所有學生都能使用大學圖書館的資料。

6) **pocket money** [ˈpɑkɪt ˈmʌni] (n.) 零用錢
Kevin got a part-time job after school to earn pocket money.
凱文放學後去打工，賺取零用錢。

7) **enroll** [ɪnˈrol] (v.)（註冊）入學；入伍
How many students are enrolled at the college?
那所大學有多少學生註冊入學？

8) **script** [skrɪpt] (n.)（戲劇、電影等）劇本
The director rejects most of the scripts he is offered.
那名導演把人家提供的大部分劇本都推掉了。

9) **intellectual** [.ɪntəˈlɛktʃuəl] (n.) 知識分子；知識（分子）的，（需）智力的
The café is a gathering place for artists and intellectuals.
這間咖啡館是藝術家和知識份子聚集的地方。

10) **playwright** [ˈple.raɪt] (n.) 劇作家
Shakespeare is England's most famous playwright.
莎士比亞是英國最有名的劇作家。

11) **muse** [mjuz] (n.) 繆思，（帶來靈感的）女神、人
The artist's lover was his muse for many years.
這位藝術家的愛人是多年來帶給他靈感的繆思女神。

不過這其實也不太要緊，如今改用「伍迪」這個名字的艾倫到了十九歲時，已經在幫《西澤時間》及《艾德蘇利文秀》等熱門電視節目撰寫笑哏，收入甚至超過了他父母的薪水總和。雖然為電視撰稿的五年間令他名利雙收，甚至還得到艾美獎提名，不過他最終還是厭倦了替別人寫稿，決定自行嘗試表演單口相聲。艾倫將自己的角色設計成一個神經兮兮的知識份子（這常被人誤會是他的真實性格），並很快在各大曼哈頓夜總會和電視節目登台演出。他同時還當起了劇作家，寫下了《別喝生水》和自己主演的《獸頭鵝》。艾倫還與共同領銜主演的黛安基頓傳出一段短暫戀情，日後她也成為艾倫創作靈感來源的繆思女神。

Tongue-tied No More

provide sb. with sth. 提供某人某物
provide 是「提供」，如果要表達「提供某人某物」的話，後面的介系詞必須接 with，也就是「provide sb. with sth.」。但如果要把句子反過來說成「提供某物給某人」，則是「provide sth. to sb.」，也可用 for 替換 to。

- The hotel provides its guests with clean towels every day.
飯店每天提供客人們乾淨的毛巾。
- The soup kitchen provides hot meals for the homeless.
熱食站會提供熱食給遊民。

try one's hand at...（某人）試試身手
表「初次嘗試某事物」。

A: What do you plan on doing after you retire?
你退休後打算幹嘛？

B: I may try my hand at writing a novel.
我可能會試試看寫小說。

When Allen was asked to write the script for *What's New, Pussycat?*, he **jumped at the chance** to work in film. But he was so disappointed with the comedy when it came out in 1965 that he swore he'd only write another script if he could direct it himself. The movie was a **box-office** success, so he soon had his chance. Allen's debut as director was 1966's *What's Up, Tiger Lily?*, which was actually an existing Japanese spy movie that he provided with new English dialogue, turning it into a comedy about a search for the world's best egg salad recipe. This led to Allen directing and starring in a [1)]**string** of comedies in the early '70s, including *Bananas*, a film version of *Play It Again, Sam, Sleeper* and *Love and Death*, many [2)]**costarring** Diane Keaton, even though they were no longer a couple.

While most of Allen's previous films had been successes, it was 1977's *Annie Hall* that would [3)]**define** his career. With himself as a [4)]**comedian opposite** Keaton in a role written just for her, he created a story about a [5)]**quirky** couple that set the standard for modern romantic comedies. After another successful film with Keaton, 1979's *Manhattan*, Allen found a new muse—and life partner—in Mia Farrow. The two would make 13 movies together, including well-received romances like *The Purple Rose of Cairo* (1985), *Hannah and Her Sisters* (1986) and *Husbands and Wives* (1992). Although Allen and Farrow's [6)]**partnership** ended when the actress discovered he was having an affair with her [7)]**adopted** daughter, the director has since found new muses like Scarlett Johansson, Penelope Cruz and Cate Blanchett. Now almost 80, Allen continues to make a new film nearly every year. But in his own words, "I don't want to achieve [8)]**immortality** through my work, I want to achieve it by not dying."

Showbiz Words

box-office 賣座的，票房的
名詞 box office 是指電影院或劇院的售票處，而 box-office 則為形容詞「賣座的」或「票房的」。

- All the director's movies have been box-office hits.
  這個導演拍的電影全部都很賣座。

opposite 演對手戲
opposite 最常作形容詞，表「相反的，對立的」，在跟影視有關的文章中，也常作介系詞，表「與……演對手戲」。

- Tom Cruise starred opposite his wife in *Far and Away*.
  湯姆克魯斯在《遠離家園》中和他老婆演對手戲。

當艾倫獲邀編寫《風流紳士》的劇本時，他緊緊把握住這個參與電影製作的機會。不過當這部喜劇於 1965 年上映時，他卻對片子大失所望，甚至發誓只有自己能執筒導演時才會再次編劇。結果該片票房成績相當亮眼，因此他的機會迅速降臨。艾倫執導的首部作品是 1966 年的《野貓嬉春》，這其實是一部已經發行的日本間諜電影，被艾倫配上全新的英文對白後變成了喜劇片，內容是尋找全世界最棒的雞蛋沙拉食譜。他也因此而在 70 年代初執導並主演一連串喜劇片，包括《傻瓜大鬧香蕉城》、《獸頭鵝》的電影版本、《傻瓜大鬧科學城》以及《愛與死》，黛安基頓也在當中多部片子共同主演，即便當時兩人不再成雙成對。

雖然艾倫先前的多數片子都相當成功，不過要到 1977 年的《安妮霍爾》才奠定了他的電影人生。在片中，艾倫飾演一位喜劇演員，而女主角則是專為黛安基頓量身打造，他筆下這對古怪情侶的故事，為現代浪漫喜劇電影樹立了基準。1979 年再與基頓共同合作另一部佳片《曼哈頓》之後，艾倫找到

了一位新的繆思女神及人生伴侶──米亞法羅。兩人共同合作了十三部電影，包括 1985 年的《開羅紫玫瑰》、1986 年的《漢娜姊妹》以及 1992 年的《賢伉儷》等廣受好評的愛情片。雖然法羅發現艾倫和她的養女有染而導致兩人的合作關係結束，但這位導演此後仍持續找到新女神，像是史嘉蕾喬韓森、潘妮洛普克魯茲以及凱特布蘭琪等人。現年將近八十的艾倫依然幾乎每年都會拍新片，但如同他自己所說：「我不願透過我的作品而永垂不朽，我只想靠著不死來做到這點。」

Language Guide

Woody Allen 的繆思女神

Diane Keaton 戴安基頓
少數以西裝褲裝闖蕩好萊塢的知性女星，與 Woody Allen 合作的《安妮霍爾》Annie Hall，讓兩人同時獲得奧斯卡獎肯定。

Mia Farrow 米亞法羅
與 Woody Allen 合作關係最長的女星，可惜並未如其他眾多女星一樣得到奧斯卡獎。

Penélope Cruz 潘妮洛普克魯茲
這位西班牙美女靠著與 Woody Allen 合作的《情遇巴賽隆納》Vicky Cristina Barcelona 得到奧斯卡最佳女配角獎，後來又在《愛上羅馬》To Rome with Love 當中合作。

Rachel McAdams 瑞秋麥亞當斯
曾參與 Woody Allen 執導超大卡司（除了奧斯卡影帝 Adrien Brody、影后 Marion Cotillard、連法國第一夫人 Carla Bruni 都赫然在列！）電影《午夜・巴黎》Midnight in Paris。

Scarlett Johansson 史卡蕾喬韓森
與 Woody Allen 在《愛情決勝點》Match Point、《遇上塔羅牌情人》Scoop 兩片當中合作，兩人非常投契，成為忘年的莫逆之交。

Cate Blanchett 凱特布蘭琪
與 Woody Allen 合作《藍色茉莉》Blue Jasmine 讓她一舉奪下奧斯凱最佳女主角。

Emma Stone 艾瑪史東
Woody Allen 最新合作的女星，除了與奧斯卡影帝 Colin Firth 合作的《魔幻月光》Magic in the Moonlight，還有另一部與 Joaquin Phoenix（瓦昆菲尼克斯）合作的電影《非理性的人》Irrational Man 即將發行上映。

 21

Vocabulary Bank

1) **string** [strɪŋ] (n.) 一串，一系列
The band had a string of hits in the 1990s.
該樂團在 1990 年代有一系列暢銷作品。

2) **costar** [ˋkoˌstɑr] (v./n.) 合演（的演員）
The two actors have costarred in several films.
這兩位演員共同主演好幾部片。

3) **define** [dɪˋfaɪn] (v.) 界定，使明確
You shouldn't let your job define you as a person.
你不該讓你的工作來界定你是什麼人。

4) **comedian** [kəˋmidɪən] (n.) 諧星，喜劇演員
Jim Carrey is my favorite comedian.
金凱瑞是我最喜歡的喜劇演員。

5) **quirky** [ˋkwɜki] (a.) 古怪的，奇特的
Robert has a quirky sense of humor.
羅伯有很古怪的幽默感。

6) **partnership** [ˋpɑrtnɚˌʃɪp] (n.) 合作關係，合夥關係
The two companies formed a partnership to develop the product.
這兩間公司為了生產產品而建立了合作關係。

7) **adopt** [əˋdɑpt] (v.) 收養，接納
The couple can't have kids, so they've decided to adopt.
那對夫妻無法生育，所以他們決定領養小孩。

8) **immortality** [ˌɪmɔrˋtælɪti] (n.) 永生，不朽
Man has long dreamed of immortality.
人們亙古以來都夢想能夠長生不老。

Tongue-tied No More

jump at the chance 立刻把握機會
也可以說 jump at the opportunity，都很傳神的形容遇到機會不但趕緊把握，還跳上去緊緊抱著不放的樣子。

A: Will you go to that school if you can get in?
如果你進得去的話，你會去讀那間學校嗎？
B: Yeah. I'd jump at the chance!
會啊。我會立刻把握機會！

1977

Annie Hall《安妮霍爾》

說到 Woody Allen，就不得不提這部獲得最佳影片、導演、原創劇本、女主角等四大獎的奧斯卡經典之作。該片劇情簡單，描述神經質又愛碎碎念的艾維（Alvy，Woody Allen 飾）和與他個性大相逕庭的安妮（Annie Hall，Diane Keaton 飾），兩人從相知相戀到分手，這段情感由濃轉淡的戀愛過程。當中不斷採用倒敘和插敘的手法，加上細碎的呢喃，並藉由兩個角色的個性差異（艾維尖酸機車，安妮爛漫活潑）來創造戲劇張力，對白和敘事方式都頗具實驗性，隱含了許多發人深省的議題，但又不像其他藝術片艱澀難懂，值得觀影者細細品味。

由以下這段對白可充分看出艾維喜好諷刺挖苦的個性：
Annie Hall　: **It's so clean out here.** 這外面好乾淨喔。
Alvy Singer : **That's because they don't throw their garbage away, they turn it into television shows.** 那是因為他們不把垃圾丟掉，他們把垃圾做成電視節目。

1978

Interiors《我心深處》

伍迪艾倫向大師柏格曼（Ingmar Bergman）致敬的作品。描述紐約一對夫婦和三個女兒的家庭故事。黛安基頓飾演的雷納塔（Renata）是一位在文壇嶄露頭角的詩人，丈夫是位不得志的作家，在這個角色中，她不但要安撫丈夫，還得應付原生家庭父母的感情問題，以及和兩個姊妹共同承受母親偏執個性所帶來的壓力。雖然艾倫在該片中改變了以往諷刺幽默的敘事風格，轉而採向嚴肅深沉的表現方式，然而當中隱含的悲觀主義和現實主義，卻是一脈相承的。

永遠的安妮——黛安基頓

黛安基頓生於 1946 年，年輕時度過一段放縱的日子，後來因主演舞台劇被伍迪艾倫發掘，兩人惺惺相惜，在合作初期曾短暫交往。之後雖然分手，依然是伍迪艾倫電影中的常客。1977 年的《安妮霍爾》讓黛安拿下人生第一座奧斯卡影后，也讓伍迪艾倫拿下最佳導演。兩人友好的情誼至今不變，甚至在伍迪艾倫獲得 2014 年金球獎的終身貢獻獎時，也是由黛安娜基頓代他出席領獎。

© Rena Schild / Shutteersttock.com

素人影評怎麼看《我心深處》

Probably the best of Allen's Bergman tributes.
可能是艾倫向柏格曼最棒的致敬之作。

An Allen film that is seldom mentioned. It pales in comparison to Annie Hall but it is a very strong film thanks to the ladies involved.
這部艾倫的片很少被拿來討論。拿它來和《安妮霍爾》比的確是稍嫌黯淡，不過好在有片中這些女演員，讓它成為一部後勁很強的電影

(資料取自 http://www.rottentomatoes.com)

鬼才導演 Allen

近年作品

1979

Manhattan《曼哈頓》

繼《安妮霍爾》後另一浪漫經典之作。故事內容在描述四十二歲的知名電視台編劇艾薩克（Isaac，Woody Allen 飾），因為前妻發現自己是同性戀而與他離婚，隨後他便與十七歲的嫩妹崔西交往，然後又與好友的情婦勾搭上，全片就以紐約曼哈頓為背景，圍繞在他與三個女子周旋的故事中，藉由這些混亂和困擾，試圖揭開當中所隱含的愛情真相。

1986

Hannah and Her Sisters《漢娜姐妹》

描述大姊漢娜（Hannah，Mia Farrow 飾）二姊荷莉（Holly，Dianne Wiest 飾）和小妹李（Lee，Barbara Hershey 飾），這三名個性截然不同的姊妹，與他們身邊男性所發展出的複雜感情關係。伍迪艾倫自己在片中軋上一腳，飾演漢娜神經兮兮的電視製作人前夫。全片藉由漢娜姊妹的故事，以輕鬆幽默的方式來探討婚姻與家庭的課題。

繼黛安基頓後，米亞法洛與伍迪艾倫的愛恨情仇顯然糾葛許多，除了爆出伍迪艾倫與養女順宜有染，更誇張的是他與米亞的女兒也跳出來指證伍迪在小時候曾經性侵她，針對這起醜聞，他看似豁達的表示：To have been the lead character in a juicy scandal—a really juicy scandal l—that will always be a part of what people think of when they think of me. It doesnt't bother me. It doesn't please me. It's a non-factor. But it's a true factor.

（在這麼有料的醜聞中擔綱主角——以後當人們想到我時，永遠都會想到這個部分——真的是很有梗的醜聞。這並不會對我造成困擾。也不會讓我開心。這不是什麼重要的事，但卻會造成實質上的影響。）

2005

Match Point《愛情決勝點》

克里斯（Chris，Jonathan Rhys Meyers 飾）是一名網球教練，因緣際會下認識了富家子湯姆（Tom，Matthew Goode 飾），並與他的妹妹克洛伊（Chloe，Emily Mortimer 飾）結婚，然而克里斯卻深深被湯姆的女友諾拉（Nora，Scarlett Johansson 飾）吸引，還讓她意外懷孕。諾拉不斷要求克里斯離婚，然而克里斯這時才發現，原來他並沒有那麼愛諾拉，他還寧可為了自己的前途，待在克洛伊身邊，於是他決定痛下殺手，解決諾拉，以鞏固他安穩的生活。

2006

Scoop《遇上塔羅牌情人》

一名美國新聞系學生桑卓拉（Sandra，Scarlett Johansson 飾）到英國遊玩，在欣賞魔術表演的過程中，看到已故記者喬伊的鬼魂，鬼魂告訴她有關塔羅牌連續殺人魔的內幕，希望她能繼續循線追查下去。而根據種種跡象顯示，貴族彼得萊曼（Peter Lyman，Hugh Jackman 飾）的嫌疑最大，於是桑卓拉決定色誘他來查明真相，不料兩人一方面諜對諜，處心積慮算計彼此，卻又難抵愛情魔力，雙雙墜入情網。

影響 Woody Allen 的三位電影人

英格瑪柏格曼
Ingmar Bergman

瑞典名導，擅長處理宗教、孤獨、人性等深沉抑鬱的問題，取景也幾乎都在他的家鄉瑞典，因此瑞典冬日永夜的黑暗封閉，以及荒涼蕭瑟的景致，都在其作品中留下鮮明的印記。伍迪艾倫曾讚他「可能是自電影藝術發明以來最偉大的電影藝術家」。其代表作有《第七封印》、《野草莓》等。

費德里柯費里尼
Federico Fellini

義大利藝術電影導演，亦身兼演員及作家。他早期是畫家，後來才投身電影，因此其電影作品的藝術成分很高，多充滿夢境、魔幻、潛意識等元素，屬超現實主義風格。其電影作品不但一直被視為經典，也啟迪了許多同期和後期的電影人，除了伍迪艾倫外，還有馬丁史柯西斯、大衛林區等都深受其影響。代表作有《大路》、《卡比莉亞之夜》等。

查理卓別林
Charlie Chaplin

英國著名的喜劇演員及反戰人士，後期亦投身擔任導演，是現代喜劇電影的先驅，不少藝人的表演都深受他的啟發。他的招牌造型就是戴著高帽，身穿一件窄小的禮服，再配上特大號的鞋子和褲子，手拄拐杖，留著一撇小鬍子。只要講到早期的默片，大多數人都會聯想到這號人物。

2011

Midnight in Paris 《午夜巴黎》

由爵士樂、巴黎雨景和夜景所交織成的迷人奇幻故事。男主角吉兒（Gil，Owen Wilson 飾）原本在加州擔任好萊塢編劇，不過內心一直想嘗試寫純文學，並且深深為巴黎著迷，他與未婚妻伊妮絲（Inez，Rachel McAdams 飾）婚前來巴黎旅遊，不料意外穿越時空，遇見過去許多有名的文人作家，讓他的內心有了微妙的變化，而他與未婚妻的分歧也逐漸顯現……。

2013

Blue Jasmine 《藍色茉莉》

婚姻觸礁後，原本因嫁入豪門而養尊處優的貴婦茉莉（Jasmine，Cate Blanchett 飾），也開始為自己的經濟狀況發愁。她決定從紐約搬到舊金山的妹妹家中展開新生活，在這裡，她偏偏又愛上了一個正處於經濟低潮的男人，沒有辦法從欠債中脫身。在決定是不是要愛這個男人之前，茉莉必須在心理上接受舊金山這個城市，並且好好檢視自己的人生，重新認識自己。

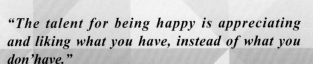

"The talent for being happy is appreciating and liking what you have, instead of what you don'have."

快樂的訣竅在於欣賞並喜歡你所擁有的，而非你所沒有的。

"If you want to make God laugh, tell him about your plans."

如果你想讓上帝發笑，那就告訴祂你的計劃。

"If you're not failing every now and again, it's a sign you're not doing anything very innovative."

如果你沒有偶爾失敗的話，那麼這意味著你沒有在做什麼創新的事。

Woody Allen 伍式風格

伍迪艾倫的電影都充滿他的個人風格，例如他習慣在片頭使用一種老式英文字體——windsor，以及大多數的電影都充滿絮絮叨叨的碎念，並且習慣用尖酸幽默的方式去傳達深沉的議題……等。名詞加上 -esque 結尾，可轉化成「某種風格」的意思，例如 DaVinci-esque　就是「有達文西風格的」，而 Woody Allenesque 就是專屬於伍迪的「伍式風格」了。

Directed by
Woody Allen

Quotes Woody Allen

伍迪艾倫特別喜歡在電影中探討的三大主題：
愛、性與死亡，也在他的單人脫口秀、著作、受訪當中，
留下許多關於生命與宗教的名言。

About Love

Even as a kid I always went for the wrong women. When my mother took me to see *Snow White*, everyone fell in love with Snow White. I immediately fell for the wicked queen.
我從小就老是愛錯女人，我媽帶我去看《白雪公主》時，大家都愛上白雪公主，我卻對巫婆皇后一見鍾情。

I'm such a good lover because I practice a lot on my own.
我是個很優質的情人，因為我常常自己練習。

Bisexuality doubles your chances of a date on a Saturday night.
雙性戀讓你在週六夜晚有約會的機會增加了一倍。

About Sex

The difference between sex and death is, with death you can do it alone and nobody's going to make fun of you.
性跟死亡的差別在於死亡可獨力完成，而沒有人會取笑你。

Sex without love is an empty experience. But as empty experiences go, it's one of the best.
沒有愛的性只是空虛的體驗。但是對空虛的體驗來說，它是數一數二的。

Sex between a man and a woman can be wonderful, provided you can get between the right man and the right woman.
男女之間的性愛可以很美妙，前提是要找對讓你被夾在中間的男女。

About Life

In my next incarnation I want to live my life backwards. You start out dead and get that out of the way. Then you wake up in an old people's home feeling better every day. You get kicked out for being too healthy, go collect your pension, and then when you start work, you get a gold watch and a party on your first day. You work for 40 years until you're young enough to enjoy your retirement. You party, drink alcohol, and are generally promiscuous, then you are ready for high school. You then go to primary school, you become a kid, you play. You have no responsibilities, you become a baby until you are born. And then you spend your last nine months floating in luxurious spa-like conditions with central heating and room service on tap, larger quarters every day and then Voila! You finish off as an orgasm!

下輩子，我要倒著活一遍。從死而復生，在一個療養院裡醒來，感覺身體一天比一天好。後來因為太健壯被趕出去領養老金，並開始工作，在工作第一天，你收到一只金錶，還有一場為你辦的派對（編註：金錶為美國職場常見的退休禮物，還會有歡送派對）。工作四十年，等到你夠年輕時，就去享受退休生活。你終日飲酒作樂，結交很多性伴侶（編註：影射美國大學生活），接著準備上中學、上小學，變成一個小孩，只知道玩。你不必負責任，你變成小嬰兒，直到你出生。接下來九個月，你住在跟水療館一樣有中央空調、全天候客房服務的奢華環境中，房間一天比一天寬敞。終於！你的生命在一次高潮之中結束！

About Death

It's not that I'm afraid to die, I just don't want to be there when it happens.
我並不是怕死，我只是希望死亡發生時，我不在場。

On the plus side, death is one of the few things that can be done just as easily lying down.
講到優點，死亡是躺下來一樣容易做的少數事情之一。

There are worse things in life than death. Have you ever spent an evening with an insurance salesman?
生命中還有比死亡更糟的事。你曾經一整個晚上都跟保險業務員在一起嗎？

Life is full of misery, loneliness and suffering—and it's all over much too soon.
生命充滿了不幸、孤單和痛苦——而且結束得太快。

You can live to be a hundred if you give up all the things that make you want to live to be a hundred.
如果你放棄所有讓你想要活到一百歲的那些東西，你就可以活到一百歲。

About Religion

Standing in a garage no more makes you a car than standing in a church makes you a Christian.
站在車庫裡，你不會變成一輛車，就像站在教堂裡，你不會變成基督徒。

God is silent. Now if only man would shut up.
上帝靜默不語。要是人也閉嘴就好了。（編註：《聖經》多處出現上帝訓示當祂靜默不語時，並不代表祂不存在的章節。）

Some guy hit my fender the other day, and I said unto him, "Be fruitful, and multiply." But not in those words.
前幾天開車有人從後面撞我，我對他說「要生養眾多、遍滿地面」。不過是用其他的說法。（編註：原典出自《聖經》〈創世紀〉。伍迪艾倫的意思是他用 fuck 罵人。）

從此過著幸福快樂的日子

經典愛情片常常以告白或求婚的場景收尾，男女主角深情相擁，眾人簇擁叫好，全片在浪漫的背景音樂下告終……。Well……雖然大家心知肚明，現實生活中不可能有這麼好康的事，但就是因為跟現實差距很大，這些浪漫電影的情節才會讓人心嚮往之啊！所以有人說電影是 **great escape**，能讓人忘卻煩惱，沉浸在情節當中，忘乎所以。

《麻雀變鳳凰》

愛德華（Edward Lewis，Richard Gere 飾）是個商業大亨，僱用名叫薇薇安（Vivian Ward，Julia Roberts 飾）的應召女郎當他的女伴一週，陪他出席各大商宴場合。不料兩人竟假戲真做。

Vivian: I'm gonna treat you so good, you're never gonna let me go.
我要好好寵你，寵到你再也不讓我走。

Pretty Woman

《阿甘正傳》

在成長過程中飽受冷眼與霸凌的低智者阿甘，與自幼結識的摯友珍妮（Jenny Curran，Robin Wright 飾）重逢，這段青梅竹馬的友誼是否能克服智商差異與世俗眼光，順利昇華為愛情，開花結果？珍妮對此猶豫了……。

Forrest Gump: Why don't you love me, Jenny?
珍妮，妳為什麼不愛我？
[珍妮沈默不語]
Forrest Gump: I'm not a smart man…but I know what love is.
我不是個聰明的人……但我知道什麼是愛。

Forrest Gump

《絕配冤家》

安蒂（Andie，Kate Hudson 飾）是雜誌的兩性專欄作家，但她希望除了戀愛建議之外，能寫些言之有物的內容。安迪的主管給她一個緊急任務，只要她能以自身經驗寫一篇利用女人約會常犯錯誤即可在十天內把男友嚇跑的報導，她以後寫稿就能擁有更多自主權。只可惜安蒂挑的實驗對象與她實力旗鼓相當：廣告公司主管班（Ben，Matthew McConaughey 飾）剛跟重要客戶打賭，要讓一個女人在十天內死心踏地地愛上他。

Ben: Where you going?
妳要去哪兒？

Andie: Ben, it's the only place l can go and write what l want to write.
班，只有去那裡我才能寫我想寫的東西。

Ben: No, I'm not buying that. You can write anywhere. l think you're running away.
才怪，我不相信。妳在哪裡都能寫。我覺得妳是想逃跑。

Andie: Why don't you save your mind games for your next bet, ok? l am not running away.
何不把你的心理分析遊戲留到下次打賭呢？我才沒有逃跑。

Ben: Bullshit.
亂講。

Andie: Excuse me?
你說什麼？

Ben: You heard me. Bullshit.
妳聽到我說的了。我說亂講。

Andie: You callin' my bluff?
你是說我在虛張聲勢嗎？

Ben: You bet l am.
沒錯，我肯定是。

How to Lose A Guy in 10 Days

《時空旅人之妻》

亨利（Henry DeTamble，Eric Bana 飾）有著能穿梭時空的特殊體質，是一名時空旅人，克萊兒（Clare Abshire，Rachel McAdams 飾）從小就認識他了，兩人相知相戀，然而亨利無法控制自己何時會突然穿越到別的時空，克萊兒常要面對他無預警的消失、在重要時刻缺席，但兩人卻堅信彼此的愛能克服一切，決定結為連理……。

Henry: I never wanted to have anything in my life that I couldn't stand losing. But it's too late for that. It's not because you're beautiful and smart. I don't feel alone anymore. Will you marry me?
我這輩子從來不想擁有捨不得失去的東西。但現在已經回不去了。不是因為妳這麼美又這麼聰明。而是我再也不覺得孤單。妳願意嫁給我嗎？

Clare: No.
不要。

[亨利驚訝地看著她]

Clare: I didn't mean that. I just wanted to try it, to say it, to *assert my own sense of free will, but my free will wants you.
我沒那個意思。我只是想試著說那句話看看，要宣示我的自由意志，但我的自由意志想要你。

Henry: So it's a yes?
所以妳答應了？

Clare: Yes, of course.
是啊，當然。

*assert [ə`sɝt] (v.) 確立，主張擁有

The Time Traveller's Wife

《愛‧重來》

里歐（Leo，Channing Tatum 飾）和佩姬（Paige, Rachel McAdams 飾）這對新婚夫妻遇上了嚴重的車禍，使得佩姬失去近期一年的記憶，里歐為了幫助心愛的妻子恢復記憶，努力找尋兩人相愛的「證據」給佩姬看，而其中一項就是結婚當天兩人說這段誓詞的錄影畫面：

Paige: I vow to help you love life, to always hold you with tenderness and to have the patience that love *demands, to speak when words are needed and to share the silence when they are not and to live within the warmth of your heart and always call it home.
我發誓要幫你熱愛生命，永遠溫柔地抱著你，用愛人所需的耐心來對待你，需要用言語表達時就開口，不需要時就靜靜待在一旁，你溫暖的心間會是我永遠的家。

Leo: I vow to *fiercely love you in all your forms, now and forever. I promise to never forget that this is a *once in a lifetime love. I vow to love you, and no matter what challenges might carry us apart, we will always find a way back to each other.
我發誓要瘋狂愛妳，無論妳變成什麼樣，直到永遠。我答應妳永不忘記這段千載難逢的愛。我發誓要愛妳，無論任何挑戰將我們拆散，我們總會找到彼此。

*demand [dɪ`mænd] (v. / n.) 要求，需求
* fiercely [`fɪrslɪ] (adv.) 極度地，強烈地
*once in a lifetime 此生僅有，千載難逢

The Vow

《親親小媽》

育有一子一女的路克（Luke Harrison，Ed Harris 飾）與賈姬（Jackie Harrison，Susan Sarandon 飾）離婚後，伊莎貝（Isabel Kelly，Julia Roberts 飾）成為路克的現任妻子，孩子們為了坦護自己的生母，處處與伊莎貝作對，然而就在伊莎貝得知賈姬罹患癌症之後，兩人關係開始有了轉變，為了心愛的家人，努力找尋相處的平衡點。

Luke: Even when things are hard and you feel like giving up, you have to hang on to that decision, that choice to love each other. Even if it's only by a thread. I let that thread break once. This time, it won't. Will you marry me?
即使有時候情路坎坷，你會很想放棄，但還是要堅持自己所做的決定，也就是相愛的決定。即便一不小心就會錯過。我曾經錯過一次。這次我不會再放手了。妳願意嫁給我嗎？

Stepmom

《傲慢與偏見》

背景設於 18 世紀的英國，班奈特一家五位千金從小就被教育要釣個金龜婿，在帥氣多金的賓利先生（Mr. Bingley，Simon Woods 飾）與友人達西先生（Mr. Darcy，Matthew Macfadyen 飾）搬到附近後，這家人的生活有了翻天覆地的變化，而其中一位千金伊麗莎白（Elizabeth Bennet，Keira Knightley 飾）和達西先生之間因身份背景所產生錯綜複雜的情愛糾葛，則是本故事的主軸。

Pride & Prejudice

Darcy: If, however, your feelings have changed, I will have to tell you: you have *bewitched me, body and soul, and I love…I love…I love you. I never wish to be parted from you from this day on.

如果……如果有可能，妳感覺變了，我必須告訴妳：妳讓我整個人，我的身體、我的靈魂都神魂顛倒，我愛……我愛……我愛妳。從今以後再也不想和妳分開。

*bewitch [bɪˈwɪtʃ] (V.) 使陶醉，使銷魂

同場加映
第一次求婚失敗慘劇重播

Darcy: Miss Elizabeth, I have struggled in vain and can bear it no longer. These past months have been a *torment. I came to Rosings only to see you. I have fought against judgment, my family's expectation, the *inferiority of your birth, my rank. I will put them aside and ask you to end my *agony.

伊麗莎白小姐，我痛苦掙扎了好久，再也無法忍受了。這幾個月來一直備受煎熬。我來羅辛斯莊園只為了見妳一面。我挺身對抗他人的批判、我家人的期望、妳低下的出生和我的地位，這些我都會置之不理，只求妳能了結我的痛苦。

Elizabeth: I don't understand.
我不懂你的意思。

Darcy: I love you, most *ardently. Please do me the honor of accepting my hand.
我愛妳，熱情滿溢地愛妳。請讓我有幸能執妳之手。

Elizabeth: Sir, I appreciate the struggle you have been through, and I am very sorry to have caused you pain. It was unconsciously done.
先生，我可以體會您的為難，造成您的痛苦，我感到非常抱歉。我是無意的。

Darcy: Is this your reply?
這就是妳的回答？

Elizabeth: Yes, sir.
是的，先生。

Darcy: Are you laughing at me?
妳在嘲笑我嗎？

Elizabeth: No.
我沒有。

Darcy: Are you rejecting me?
妳是在拒絕我？

Elizabeth: I'm sure the feelings which hindered your regard will help you overcome it.
我肯定那些讓你打退堂鼓的顧慮會幫你克服這種感覺。

*torment [ˈtɔrmɛnt] (n.) 痛苦，苦惱
*inferiority [ɪnˌfɪrɪˈɑrətɪ] (n.) 劣等，低下
*agony [ˈæɡənɪ] (n.) 極度痛苦，（情感的）爆發
*ardently [ˈɑrdəntlɪ] (adv.) 熱烈的，燃燒般的

《理性與感性》

隨著一家之主去世，達斯伍一家被迫搬離諾倫莊園，到鄉下過著清苦的生活。個性內斂堅毅的大女兒艾莉娜（Elinor，Emma Thompson 飾）歷盡千辛萬苦，終於與心上人愛德華（Edward，Hugh Grant 飾）結為連理。

Edward: My heart is, and always will be, yours.
我的心，從現在直到永遠，都屬於妳。

Sense and Sensibility

《新娘不是我》

茉莉安（Julianne，Julia Roberts 飾）與麥克（Michael，Dermot Mulroney 飾）是多年好友，曾開玩笑說若兩人二十八歲前還沒找到另一半，就要結婚。不料就在期限快到之時，麥克告訴茉莉安他要結婚了，還邀請茉莉安當伴娘，茉莉安頓時驚覺自己其實早就愛上了麥克，於是決定要從中作梗，搶回新郎。

Julianne: Michael...I've loved you for nine years, I've just been too arrogant and scared to realize it, and...well, now I'm just scared. So, I realize this comes at a very *inopportune time, but I really have this *gigantic favor to ask of you. Choose me. Marry me. Let me make you happy. Oh, that sounds like three favors, doesn't it?

麥克……我已經愛了你九年了，我只是太高傲又太怕意識到這件事，還有，嗯……我現在只有害怕。所以即便我知道時機非常不恰當，但我有個天大的忙要請你幫幫我。選擇我吧。娶我吧。讓我給你幸福。噢，聽起來像是三個忙，對不對？

***inopportune** [ˌɪnˌɑpəˈtjun] (a.) 不適當的，時機不對的
***gigantic** [dʒaɪˈgæntɪk] (a.) 巨大的，龐大的

My Best Friend's Wedding

《史密斯任務》

約翰史密斯（John Smith，Brad Pitt 飾）和珍史密斯（Jane Smith，Angelina Jolie）這對互相隱瞞身份的間諜夫妻，最新任務居然是要幹掉自己的枕邊人？接下任務後，不只是自己的殺手生涯，這對伴侶的感情也受到考驗……。

Counselor: On a scale of one to ten, how would you rate the happiness of your marriage?
評分為一到十，你覺得你們婚姻的幸福指數是多少？

Jane: Eight.
八吧。

John: Wait. Could you clarify? Is ten the highest? Ten being perfectly happy and one being totally miserable, or...?
等等。你能說清楚一點嗎？十分最高是吧？十分代表非常美滿、一分是糟到極點，還是……。

Counselor: Just respond instinctively.
憑直覺回答就好。

John: OK, ready?
好吧，準備好囉？

Jane, John: Eight.
八分。

Mr. & Mrs. Smith

回不去了，還是祝你幸福……

雖然安潔麗娜和小布因為《史密斯任務》搭上線，讓安潔麗娜被冠上狐狸精的罵名，但也許是兩人外型真的是太相配了，感情也算穩定，觀眾的輿論似乎也從謾罵、唱衰轉為祝福。

不過小布的原配珍妮佛（Jennifer Aniston）可沒有因此自暴自棄變成怨婦，走出前夫出軌陰霾的她日前也大方放閃，與現任小他兩歲的男友賈斯汀瑟魯（Justin Theroux）聯袂出席頒獎典禮，也傳兩人好事將近，看來這段婚外情的各當事人都 move on 了，也祝福他們都幸福美滿囉。

《婚禮歌手》

羅比（Robbie Hart，Adam Sandler 飾）是一位婚禮歌手，被青梅竹馬的未婚妻拋棄後，認識了已訂婚的喜宴服務生茱莉亞（Julia Sullivan，Drew Barrymore 飾），

兩人朝夕相處後戀情萌芽，為了阻止茱莉亞嫁給他人，羅比千里迢迢追到拉斯維加斯，企圖以他自創的情歌打動佳人芳心……。

Robbie:

I wanna make you smile whenever you're sad
Carry you around when your arthritis is bad
All I wanna do is grow old with you.
每當妳難過失意，我會讓妳破涕為笑，
當妳關節炎發作，我會揹著妳上山下海，
我最想做的事就是和妳白頭偕老。

I'll get your medicine when your tummy aches
build you a fire if the furnace breaks
Oh it could be so nice, growing old with you.
當妳肚子痛，我幫妳拿藥，
暖爐壞掉，我幫妳升火，
喔！和妳白頭偕老會是多美好的事。

I'll miss you, kiss you, give you my coat when you are cold.
Need you, feed you, I'll even let you hold the remote control...
Oh I could be the man to grow old with you.
I wanna grow old with you.
我會想念妳、親吻你、當妳冷時為妳披上我的大衣
需要妳，餵妳，甚至讓妳佔走電視遙控器
喔！我可以成為那個與妳白頭偕老的人
我想要和妳白頭偕老

The Wedding Singer

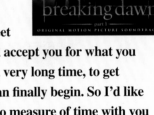

Adam Sandler
呆呆情聖

亞當山德勒出生於美國猶太家庭，小時候立志要當消防員，後來在紐約大學取得藝術學位。進入演藝圈後，早期大多扮演瘋癲、搞笑的角色，例如《阿呆闖學府》*Billy Madison*、《呆呆向前衝》*The Waterboy* 等，雖然成了票房巨星，但也拿了不少「金酸莓獎」，直到後來才慢慢碰觸一些稍為內斂、嚴肅的議題，例如《真情快譯通》*Spanglish* 和《命運好好玩》*Click* 等，雖然不是走浪漫帥哥路線，但是對感情的那股執著傻勁兒仍舊虜獲觀影者的心。

《暮光之城：破曉 1》

歷經千辛萬苦的貝拉（Bella Swan，Kristen Stewart 飾）和愛德華（Edward Cullen，Robert Pattinson 飾）終於要結婚了，婚禮賓客都期待見證這幸福的一刻，愛德華在眾人面前說出這段令人感動的宣言：

Edward: It's an *extraordinary thing to meet someone who you can bare your soul to and accept you for what you are. I've been waiting, for what seems like a very long time, to get beyond what I am. With Bella I feel like I can finally begin. So I'd like to *propose a toast to my beautiful bride. No measure of time with you will be long enough. But let's start with forever.

遇見一個能讓你赤裸裸地展現自己靈魂、並且全盤接受你的人，是件不凡的事。我一直在等待，等了好久，為了超越自己。和貝拉在一起後，我覺得我終於可以開始了。所以我要向我美麗的新娘敬酒。和妳在一起多久都不夠。我們就從永恆開始吧。

* **extraordinary** [ɪk`strɔrdə͵nɛri] (a.) 特別的
* **propose a toast** (phr.)（提出）敬酒

The Twilight Saga:
Breaking Dawn
Part 1

怪怪甜心美少女
Emma Stone
艾瑪史東

© s_bukley / Shuttershock.com

Born in 1988, Emma Stone was raised Catholic on her parent's golf resort in Arizona. After getting into drama in middle school, she moved to L.A. with her mom at the age of 15 to pursue acting. A few small TV parts led to a lead role in the Fox drama *Drive*. Stone made her film debut as Jonah Hill's love interest in 2007's Superbad, followed by roles in other comedies like *The House Bunny*. Her breakthrough came when she co-starred with Matthew McConaughey in the romantic comedy *Ghosts of Girlfriends Past*, and has since starred in hits like *Crazy, Stupid, Love* and *The Amazing Spider-Man*, whose co-star, Andrew Garfield, she's now dating.

艾瑪史東出生於 1988 年，自小在亞歷桑納州爸媽經營的高爾夫度假中心以天主教的方式培養長大。初中接觸戲劇表演之後，她便和母親搬至洛杉磯以追求演藝生涯。她在接演幾個電視劇小角色後，進而在福斯電視台的《不法駕駛》擔綱主角。2007 年，史東於《男孩我最壞》中在大銀幕上初試啼聲，飾演喬納希爾的心儀對象，接著還參與了《女郎我最兔》等其他喜劇片的演出。在與馬修麥康納共演的浪漫喜劇電影《舊愛找麻煩》中，史東有了突破性表演，此後更出演《熟男型不型》及《蜘蛛人：驚奇再起》等賣座影片，而後者的同戲男星安德魯加菲爾德則是她目前的交往對象。

影星小檔案

全　名：**Emily Jean Stone**
生　日：**November 6, 1988**
身　高：**168 cm**
出生地：美國亞利桑納州
成名作：《舊愛找麻煩》
Ghosts of Girlfriends Past

© Glynnis Jones / Shuttershock.com

《破處女王》，羞得自己都不敢看

艾瑪史東首挑大樑演出的《破處女王》不但票房成績亮眼，她也因此片獲得金球獎最佳女主角提名。雖然這是一部不折不扣的青春校園片，但電影中談論青少年性與愛迷思與價值觀，對天主教家庭的長大的艾瑪來說還是太辛辣，更何況自己在電影中飾演一位跟很多男生上床的「萬萬睡女王」！艾瑪自己都承認：「《破處女王》首映日我買了晚餐回家吃。」

「網」上情人也為之傾心

新版蜘蛛人，英國籍新星安德魯加菲爾德曾如此形容艾瑪史東：「她是我認識最充滿活力的人，在她身邊總是歡笑不斷。除此之外，她的美麗和才華更是一般人所夢寐以求的。」親密愛人都這麼說了，還能不封艾瑪史東為「完美女朋友」代表人物嗎？

© s_bukley / Shuttershock.com

《愛情限時簽》

瑪格麗特（Margaret Tate，Sandra Bullock 飾）是個惡名昭彰，沒人惹得起的惡魔女主管，身為加拿大人的她，因為美國工作簽證已經過期，必須趕快獲得美國公民身份才能保住飯碗，因此強迫平常被她當奴隸的助理萊恩（Andrew Paxton，Ryan Reynolds 飾）與她假結婚，萊恩當然不會放過整瑪格麗特的大好機會，於是要求她當街下跪求婚。

Andrew: Now, ask me nicely.
現在，好好地求我。

Margaret: "Ask you nicely" what?
「好好地求你」什麼？

Andrew: Ask me nicely to marry you, Margaret.
好好地求我娶妳，瑪格麗特。

Margaret: What does that mean?
什麼意思？

Andrew: You heard me. On your knee.
妳聽到我說的了。跪下吧。

Margaret: Fine. Does this work for you?
好啦。[跪下] 這樣可以了嗎？

Andrew: Oh, I like this. Yeah.
噢，我喜歡。太好了。

Margaret: Will you marry me?
你願意娶我嗎？

Andrew: No. Say it like you mean it.
不行。要心甘情願地說。

Margaret: Andrew?
安德魯？

Andrew: Yes, Margaret?
什麼事，瑪格麗特？

Margaret: Sweet Andrew?
安德魯小親親？

The Proposal

Andrew: I'm listening.
我在聽。

Margaret: Would you please, *with cherries on top, marry me?
拜託拜託，求求你，跟我結婚好嗎？

Andrew: OK. I don't appreciate the sarcasm, but I'll do it. See you at the airport tomorrow.
好吧。雖然我不太喜歡妳語帶反諷，但我會娶妳的。明天跟妳在機場見了。

> ***with cherries on top**　拜託求求你
> 這句話常用在拜託別人幫忙，或是請求別人原諒的情境下，主要是為了加強語氣，通常是小孩子比較常這樣說。

同場加映

本片其實有兩場求婚戲，以下這段是男主角在兩人墜入愛河後的正式求婚：

Andrew: Three days ago, I loathed you. I used to dream about you getting hit by a cab.
三天前，我恨妳入骨。我曾經幻想妳被計程車撞。

Then we had our little adventure up in Alaska and things started to change. Things changed when we kissed, and when you told me about your tattoo, even when you checked me out when we were naked.
然後我們在阿拉斯加來了場小冒險，事情有了轉變。就在我們接吻後，還有妳跟我說妳刺青的故事，甚至在兩人沒穿衣服妳打量我時，一切都變了。

But I didn't realize any of this, until I was standing alone...in a barn...wifeless. Now, you could imagine my disappointment when it suddenly dawned on me that the woman I love is about to be kicked out of the country. So Margaret, marry me, because I'd like to date you.
但我都沒有意識到這些，直到我隻身一人……站在穀倉裡，沒了老婆。現在妳能夠想像當我突然發現我深愛的女人要被踢出國，我有多失落了吧。所以，瑪格麗特，嫁給我吧，因為我想和妳約會。

《留住一片情》

蘭登（Landon Carter，Shane West 飾）是個桀驁不遜的少年，喜歡惹事生非，某次意外讓一名同學癱瘓，被判服社區勞役，除了要教附近的孩子讀書，還要參與學校的話劇演出，在話劇排練的過程中，愛上了牧師的女兒潔咪（Jamie Sullivan，Mandy Moore 飾），潔咪單純溫柔的個性漸漸改變了蘭登，兩人譜出一段觸動人心的愛情故事。

Landon: Do you love me?
妳愛我嗎？
[潔咪點頭]
Landon: Will you do something for me, then?
那妳可以幫我個忙嗎？
Jamie: Anything.
任何事都可以。
Landon: Will you marry me?
請妳嫁給我好嗎？
[潔咪露出微笑，親吻蘭登]

A Walk to Remember

《美麗蹺家人》

梅蘭妮（Melanie Smooter，Reese Witherspoon 飾）是從阿拉巴馬到紐約發展的新興服裝設計師，男友是紐約市長的公子安德魯（Andrew Hennings，Patrick Dempsey 飾），某天男友在蒂芬妮珠寶店向她求婚，她情不自禁地答應了，但其實她早先在家鄉已有一段婚姻，為了嫁給紐約市長之子，她必須重返家鄉辦離婚手續，卻發現自己無法忘懷過去的種種……。

Andrew: Melanie Carmichael...will you marry me?
梅蘭妮卡蜜科……妳願意嫁給我嗎？
Melanie: Are you sure? I mean, a-a-are you really sure? Because if you're not sure, we could just go back to the car.
你確定嗎？我是說……你……你肯定？因為要是你不確定的話，我們可以先回車上。
Andrew: You know I never do anything rash. And I usually never ask a question I don't already know the answer to. So, at the risk of being rejected twice, I'm gonna ask you again. Will you marry me?
妳也知道我從不匆促下決定。我通常也不會問我其實不知道答案的問題。所以，冒著被二次打槍的風險，我要再問妳一次。妳願意嫁給我嗎？
Melanie: Yes!
我願意！

同場加映
梅蘭妮與傑克兒時的嬉笑誓詞
Melanie: Why would you want to marry me for, anyhow?
你到底為什麼想娶我？
Jake: So I can kiss you anytime I want.
因為那樣我就能隨時親妳。

梅蘭妮悔婚經典台詞
Melanie: The truth is I gave my heart away a long time ago, my whole heart, and I never really got it back.
事實是我很久以前就把我的整顆心給了出去，而且一直都沒收回來。

Sweet Home Alabama

《阿凡達》

「阿凡達計劃」是要將人類戰士的 DNA 與潘朵拉星球的納美人融合，創造出阿凡達戰士潛入潘朵拉星球，幫助人類掠奪資源。自願參與計劃的癱瘓退役軍人傑克（Jake Sully，Sam Worthington 飾）在潘朵拉星球重獲新生，也愛上了納美人女子妮蒂芮（Neytiri，Zoe Saldana 飾）。

Neytiri: And you may choose a woman. We have many fine women. Ninat is the best singer.
你可以選一個女人。我們有的是優質女人。妮娜唱歌唱得最好。

Jake: Well, I don't want Ninat.
但我不想要妮娜。

Neytiri: Beyral is a good hunter.
貝洛是優秀的獵人。

Jake: Yeah, she is a good hunter.
是啊，她是很棒的獵人。

[妮蒂芮開始擔心地轉頭看他]

Jake: I've already chosen. But this woman must also choose me.
我已經選好了。但必須要這個女人也選擇我。

[妮蒂芮笑了]

Neytiri: She already has. I am with you now, Jake. We are mated for life.
她早就選了。我與你相屬了，傑克。我們是天生一對。

Avatar

《愛是您，愛是我》

這部經典聖誕愛情片的導演理查克特斯（Richard Curtis）是 *Notting Hill*《新娘百分百》、*Bridget Jones's Diary*《BJ 單身日記》、*Four Weddings and a Funeral*《你是我今生的新娘》等經典愛情片的編劇，因此不但眾星雲集，多線主角的故事各自發展又彼此交匯，更製造了許多浪漫經典場景及對白。片中為情所困的小男孩山姆（Sam，Thomas Sangster 飾）在看完一部愛情電影之後，做了這句總結。

Sam: But you know, the thing about romance is...people only get together right at the very end.
你也知道，浪漫片就是這樣……大家都要到最後才能在一起。

Love Actually

《他其實沒那麼喜歡你》

劇情圍繞在幾位年輕女性的愛情故事上，當中不斷探討女人在感情上常有的迷思：到底男人怎樣才是真的喜歡妳？常說甜言蜜語？常和你約會、煲電話粥？每次見面都滾床單？該片由 Jennifer Aniston、Drew Barrymore、Ben Affleck、Scarlett Johansson 等好萊塢巨星聯合主演，藉由一段段互相交織的關係和遭遇來呈現愛情的消長和轉變，也引領觀眾思索愛的本質。

Neil: I love you so much, so much. I want to make you happy. I need to make you happy for me to even have a shot at being happy too.
我好愛妳，如此愛妳。我想令妳幸福。我得令妳快樂，才能獲得擁有幸福的機會。

[尼爾拿出戒指]

Neil: Will you marry me?
妳願意嫁給我嗎？

Beth: Yes. Of course, yes.
我願意。當然願意。

He's Just Not That Into You

《征服偶像》

羅莎琳（Rosalee，Kate Bosworth 飾）和好友彼德（Pete，Topher Grace 飾）一起在鎮上的超市工作，羅莎琳向來很仰慕好萊塢明星泰德漢姆頓（Tad Hamilton，Josh Duhamel 飾），某次她幸運地獲得與泰德漢姆頓約會的機會，兩人陷入熱戀，泰德漢姆頓甚至願意為她放下明星光環，追隨她到小鎮生活，這樣的發展讓暗戀她的彼德焦急萬分……。

Pete: You have six smiles. Did you know that? One when something really makes you laugh. And one when you're just laughing out of politeness. One when you're making plans and one when you're making fun of yourself. One when you're uncomfortable and one when you're talking about your friends.

妳有六種微笑。妳知道嗎？一種是真心覺得好笑的笑容。一種是出於禮貌的笑容。計劃事情的笑、自嘲的笑。還有當妳感到不自在時也會有一種笑容，談到朋友時又是另一種笑容。

Win a Date with Tad Hamilton!

同場加映

情敵相見不眼紅，大器讓愛

彼德去找泰德漢姆頓，準備成全他們

Pete: I'm telling you, she is more of a treasure than you could possibly know. She is not just some wholesome, small town girl, some like, good for you breath of fresh air. Tad, she is a wonderful person with a huge heart. And the kind of beauty that a guy only sees once, you know? So, Tad, if there is even a chance that you could break her heart, please, just for her sake, walk away, man.

我告訴你，她比你所知道的任何一樣珍寶都還珍貴。她可不是什麼隨便的鄉下女孩，不是讓你喘口氣的新鮮空氣。泰德，她是個好心腸的人。她的純真是百年難得一見的，你知道嗎？所以，泰德，如果你有朝一日可能會傷她的心，拜託，行行好，離開她吧。

Tad: I could never break Rosalee's heart, ok?

我永遠也不會傷羅莎琳的心，好嗎？

Pete: Good. Because if you do I swear to God I will tear you to pieces with my bare hands.

很好。因為如果你真的這樣做的話，我對天發誓會徒手把你碎屍萬段。

Tad: You're a good guy, Pete.

你真是個好人，彼德。

Pete: Well, yes. Apparently not good enough.

呃，是啊。但顯然還不夠好。

《亂世佳人》

本片描述美國南北戰爭期間，塔拉莊園莊主么女郝思嘉（Scarlett O'Hara，Vivian Leigh 飾）與玩世不恭的白瑞德（Rhett Butler，Clark Gable 飾）之間的情愛糾葛。幾經戰亂，白瑞德與一直愛慕的郝思嘉再度相遇，而她已經二度守寡。

Rhett: I can't go all my life waiting to catch you between husbands.

我不能一輩子都不斷錯過單身的妳。

Gone with the Wind

《落跑新娘》

艾克（Ike，Richard Gere 飾）是《紐約時報》的專欄作家，在經歷過不愉快的婚姻後，喜歡對女人冷嘲熱諷，一天聽聞有個叫瑪姬（Maggie，Julia Roberts 飾）的女子有結婚恐懼症，總在步入紅毯的那一刻突然落跑，艾克決定親自拜訪瑪姬所在的小鎮，針對這號人物做個專題報導，結果卻愛上故事的主人……。

Ike: Look, I guarantee there'll be tough times. I guarantee that at some point, one or both of us is gonna want to get out of this thing. But I also guarantee that if I don't ask you to be mine, I'll regret it for the rest of my life, because I know, in my heart, you're the only one for me.

聽著，我肯定會有一些艱難的時刻。我肯定在某些時候，我們其中一人會打算離開對方。但我也可以肯定，要是我不把妳訂下來，我餘生都會在後悔中度過，因為我知道，在我心深處，只有妳是唯一。

Runaway Bride

瑞秋麥亞當斯
Rachel McAdams

© Everett Collection / Shutterstock.com

Any current list of Hollywood **"it" girls** is sure to include Rachel McAdams. This beautiful [1)]**blonde** not only has the looks audiences like, but also the acting [2)]**chops** directors [3)]**crave**. Born in Ontario, Canada in 1978, McAdams' first love was figure skating. As a teenager, however, she gave up the ice for the stage. McAdams appeared in several Shakespeare productions before attending York University, where she earned a degree in theater. After graduation, she began working in Canadian TV, and before long had set her sights on Hollywood.

McAdams' first U.S. role was in the 2002 body [4)]**swap** comedy *The Hot Chick*, starring Rob Schneider. But movie audiences really started to take notice of the [5)]**up-and-coming** young actress when she played Regina George in the 2004 Lindsay Lohan [6)]**vehicle** *Mean Girls*. This [7)]**breakout** performance was followed later that year by a leading role in *The Notebook*, a romantic drama about [8)]**forbidden** love. McAdams and co-star Ryan Gosling showed a real [9)]**chemistry** on-screen, which famously translated into a romantic relationship off-screen.

Away from the [10)]**set**, environmental issues are a passion for McAdams. The actress doesn't even own a car, choosing to bike or take public transportation instead. Her movie career has [11)]**motored** ahead though, thanks to strong performances in the Sherlock Holmes [12)]**franchise** and the 2013 romantic comedy-drama *About Time*, among others. Up next, fans will get to see McAdams star in the much-anticipated second **season** of HBO's acclaimed drama, *True Detective*, set to [13)]**air** in summer 2015.

Showbiz Words

"It" girl
如果你關注時尚消息，一定常常在時尚或穿搭雜誌上看見 "It" girl 這個字。It girl 指的是走在時尚尖端、甚至引領流行趨勢的女孩；她們不一定是演員，也可能是名媛、模特兒、或是因穿搭別具風格而知名的部落客或素人。而時尚趨勢變換迅速，每隔幾年、甚至幾個月就會出現另外一個成為鎂光燈寵兒的新 It girl。近幾年的英國名模 Agyness Deyn 和 Cara Delevingne、演員 Emma Watson 和 Lily Collins 都是女孩們最想成為的 It girls！

season 季
歐美的影集會分「季」，每一季的集數約為 10 到 25 集（episode）不等，通常從九、十月播映到隔年三或四月。分季的原因和收視率有關，若收視率、廣告等反應不佳，則會在下一季做劇情調整或考慮是否開拍。

要說到目前當紅的好萊塢女星，瑞秋麥亞當斯絕對榜上有名。這位金髮美女的外貌不但極富觀眾緣，演技更是眾家導演所讚賞。麥亞當斯於 1978 年出生加拿大安大略省，一開始所鍾情的嗜好為花式溜冰。不過到了青少年時期，她卻為了舞台表演而高掛冰鞋。在進入約克大學攻讀戲劇之前，麥亞當斯已出演了幾部莎翁劇碼，畢業後也順利打入加拿大電視圈，不久後更將目標放眼於好萊塢。

麥亞當斯的首部美國電影為 2002 年由勞勃許奈德主演的身體互換喜劇《小姐好辣》。不過一直要到 2004 年主打琳賽蘿涵的《辣妹過招》中，觀眾才透過蕾吉娜喬治一角而真正開始注意到這位嶄露頭角的年輕演員。在這項突破性演出的同年稍晚，她又主演了一部描寫禁忌之愛的愛情電影《手札情緣》。麥亞當斯與共同主演的雷恩葛斯林在銀幕上顯得非常來電，而銀幕下兩人的假戲真做也轟動一時。

大銀幕之外，麥亞當斯熱衷於環保議題。這位女星甚至沒有自己的私家車，而是選擇騎乘自行車或搭乘大眾交通工具。不過她的演員生涯依舊快速推進，這點要歸功她於《福爾摩斯》系列及 2013 年愛情喜劇《真愛每一天》等片中的出色表演。麥亞當斯接著將主演預定於 2015 年暑期播映的《無間警探》第二季，屆時粉絲們又可以在這部廣受期待的 HBO 精彩影集裡看見她的芳蹤。

Tongue-tied No More

before long 不久之後
這個慣用語的意思等同於 soon，但是通常只放在句子的開頭或結尾，這點與 soon 的用法不太相同。例：

She got used to her new life in New York before long.
= Before long, she got used to her new life in New York.
= She soon got used to her new life in New York.
　她不久之後就習慣了紐約的新生活。

set one's sights on sth. 目標放在…、志在…、
set 是「放置、設定」，sight 則是「視野，眼界」；因此 set one's sights on sth. 直譯是將目光放在某處，引伸為「以某事為目標」。

A: What are you planning to do after you graduate?
　你畢業後打算做什麼？
B: I've set my sights on law school.
　我的目標是進入法律學院就讀。

Vocabulary Bank

1) **blonde** [blɑnd] (n.) 金髮女人
Do you know if Debbie is a natural blonde?
你知道黛比到底是不是天生金髮嗎？

2) **chops** [tʃɑps] (n.) 在特定領域的卓越技巧或傑出表現（尤指音樂、戲劇等）
I wanted to be in a band, but I didn't have the chops.
我想要加入樂團，但是我沒什麼演奏技巧。

3) **crave** [krev] (v.) 渴望
Pregnant women often crave pickles.
孕婦常會想吃酸黃瓜。

4) **swap** [swɑp] (n./v.) 交換，調換
Can I swap seats with you?
我可以和你換位子嗎？

5) **up-and-coming** [ˋʌpændˏkʌmɪŋ] (n.) 嶄露頭角的，很有前途的
The record company signs a lot of up-and-coming artists.
這間唱片公司簽下了許多潛力新星。

6) **vehicle** [ˋviɪkəl] (n.)（特別適合某表演者的、為特定演員製作的）電影，戲劇
The movie is just another Tom Cruise vehicle.
這不過是又一部為湯姆克魯斯量身打造的電影。

7) **breakout** [ˋbrekˏaʊt] (a.) 突破性的
The actor became a big star after this breakout role.
這名演員在出演這個突破性角色後成為巨星。

8) **forbidden** [fəˋbɪdən] (a.) 禁止的，禁忌的
Smoking is forbidden in all areas of the building.
整棟建築物都禁止吸菸。

9) **chemistry** [ˋkɛmɪstrɪ] (n.)（人與人之間的）來電，冒出火花
The lack of chemistry between the two stars ruined the movie.
這兩位演員之間缺乏火花，毀了這部電影。

10) **set** [sɛt] (n.) 攝影棚，拍攝現場
The director called for silence on the set.
導演要片場安靜下來。

11) **motor (ahead)** [ˋmotə] (v.)（口）快速前進、增長
The stock market motored ahead in January.
股票市場在一月快速成長。

12) **franchise** [ˋfræntʃaɪz] (n.) 系列作品，授權商品
What's your favorite movie in the Star Wars franchise?
你最喜歡《星際大戰》系列的哪一部？

13) **air** [ɛr] (v.) 播送，播放
The classical music show airs every evening at 8 p.m.
古典樂節目每天晚上八點播放。

不在乎天長地久，只在乎曾經擁有。欲語相思何處寄？

人性起伏、情愛糾葛、世事無常，真愛難了。老天爺往往讓真愛一瞬間在戀人眼神交會中發生，卻要戀人們用盡半生的輾轉去成全真愛的樣貌。或許真愛中的戀人們，流光輕拋，轉身無悔，只是徒留了半生的遺憾，與一生的懸念。

愛與不愛之間，讓人不知所措，也讓人彷徨無依，直到那一天的來臨，戀人們才在恍惚間，看見了真愛的身影。

《生命中的美好缺憾》

圍繞著年輕癌症患者的愛情與親情，並以恰如其分的歡笑及淚水交織出 16 歲癌症末期病人海瑟（Hazel，Shailene Woodley 飾）與因癌症而只剩半條腿的奧古斯都（Augustus，暱稱 Gus，Ansel Elgort 飾）一段短暫卻閃亮的愛情故事。海瑟與奧古斯都共通的溝通暗號是問對方「OK？」，因為對他們來說，一般人認為最普通的 OK 已是再好也不過的狀態了。他們的家人與朋友也同時跟著兩人一起探索與體悟，即使愛的意義如此虛無，卻真實深刻的影響人的每一分一秒；「珍惜現在」就是實踐愛的最佳方法。

海瑟坐在車上，讀著她最喜愛並曾親自登門拜訪過的作家 Van Houten 交給自己的的信紙：一封奧古斯都寫給海瑟的信，充滿對海瑟的真情告白，並希望能說服 Van Houten 幫忙修改這封信。海瑟就這麼躺在後院草地上，仰望星空，讀著奧古斯都的信。

Gus: You don't get to choose if you get hurt in this world but you do have a say in who hurts you. And I like my choices. I hope she likes hers. Okay, Hazel Grace?

人生中無法避免被傷害，但你可以選擇由誰來傷害你，而我很喜歡我的選擇。我希望海瑟也喜歡她的選擇。OK 嗎，海瑟？

[海瑟把信拿近自己，抬頭對著星空回答]

Hazel: OK.

OK。

[海瑟微笑地閉上眼]

奧古斯都的好朋友 Isaac 因為癌症必須切除眼球，然而 Isaac 女友卻因此提出分手，既生氣又失望透頂的他找奧古斯都與海瑟抱怨，說當初山盟海誓都是虛假，海瑟卻說出一番人們對誓言的誤解。

Hazel: Sometimes people don't understand the promises that they're making when they make them.

人們往往不了解自己所許的承諾意義何在。

Isaac: I know, but, I just feel like such a loser. I still have her necklace on.

我明白，但我就是覺得很孬。我到現在還戴著她給的項鍊。

Hazel: Take it off. 拿下來啊。

Isaac: Dude, take that off! 兄弟，把項鍊拿掉！

[Issac 從脖子上扯斷項鍊]

Hazel: Yeah!

耶！

The Fault in Our Stars

Hazel: I fell in love with him the way you fall asleep: slowly, and then all at once.
我跟他墜入情網的方式跟睡著的過程很像，一開始很緩慢，然後剎那間沉沉入睡。

Hazel: Like all real love stories ours will die with us, as it should. You know, I'd kind of hoped that he'd be the one eulogizing me. Because there's really no one else...
但就像所有的愛情故事般，我們的故事將隨著我們死亡而逝去。我反而希望是他來悼念我，因為我也沒有別人了。

[海瑟輕柔嘲笑自己]

Hazel: Yeah, no. Um...I'm not gonna talk about our love story, because I can't. So, instead, I'm gonna talk about math. I am not a mathematician, but I do know this. There are infinite numbers between zero and one. There's point-one, point-one-two, and point-one-one-two, and...and an infinite collection of others. Of course, there is a bigger infinite set of numbers between zero and two, or between zero and a million. Some infinities are simply bigger than other infinities. A writer that we used to like taught us that.

對了，不，我沒有要講我們的愛情故事，因為我辦不到，所以我要改談數學。我並非數學家，但我知道 0 到 1 之間存有無限多個數字，從 0.1、0.12、0.112……一直到無限多。0 到 2 之間，甚至是 0 到百萬之間，又有更大的無限多。某些無限多一定會遠大於其他的無限多，一位我們曾喜歡的作家這麼告訴我們。

You know, I want more numbers than I'm likely to get. And, God, do I want more days for Augustus Waters than what he got.
我希望自己生命的天數可以再多一點，天啊，我也多希望奧古斯都能有更多時日。

[海瑟看著奧古斯都，淚水從臉上滑落]

But, Gus, my love, I cannot tell you how thankful I am, for our little infinity.
不過，奧古斯都，我的摯愛，我非常非常感激能擁有我們之間這些小小的「無限」。

[海瑟試著繼續講完悼詞]

You gave me a forever, within the numbered days. And for that, I am...I am eternally grateful. I love you so much.
我會永遠感謝著你，在我有限的日子裡，你給了我永恆。我好愛好愛你。

Gus: I love you, too. 我也愛妳。

雪琳伍德莉 & 安賽爾埃爾葛特

出生加州的大女孩雪琳，年紀輕輕便展現過人演技，加上俏麗外形與性格大方，讓很多人認為她與珍妮佛羅倫斯的特質相像。雪琳的電影生涯才剛開始，但 2014 年演出的兩部熱門小說改編電影《分歧者》與《生命中的美好缺憾》，早已奠定她「能文能武」演技派新星地位。

同樣在這兩部 2014 重要電影中演出的安賽爾埃爾葛特有著傻傻的笑容、開朗的個性，渾身散發鄰家大男孩氣息，無疑是新一代「暖男」代表。《生命中的美好缺憾》裡奧古斯都一角，更讓他瞬間打敗羅伯派丁森，成為青少年最喜愛的偶像。

這兩位《分歧者》兄妹與《生命中的美好缺憾》最佳銀幕情侶私底下互動如何？安賽爾透露，其實他超怕惹雪琳生氣的！這個大男生真的很可愛！

《真愛挑日子》

從相識開始所展開近 20 年「友達以上，戀人未滿」友誼的艾瑪（Emma，Anne Hathaway 飾）和達斯（Dexter，Jim Sturgess 飾）陪伴彼此走過懵懂的歲月，到最後確定彼此就是自己生命中無可取代的另一半。艾瑪是平凡的女孩，達斯則是高富帥類型的風雲人物，大學四年中彼此互不相識，卻在畢業舞會當晚產生火花，因此這兩人約定好每年 7 月 15 日這天一定得排除萬難見面……。

這是電影中，最經典感人的時光回顧。入學就暗戀達斯的艾瑪，畢業派對酒後兩人沒機會達陣，只是相擁入眠到天亮，醒來隔天便到附近小山丘上散步。還是隻小鴨女的艾瑪，對於有機會與達斯相識並共度一晚感到幸運與感動，想要把握當下的感動：

1988 年 7 月 15 日，艾瑪和達斯共眠醒來後的那個早上

Emma: I don't want you thinking I'm bothered or anything about last night. I don't want your phone number, or letters or postcards. I don't want to get married to you. Definitely don't want to have your babies. Whatever happens tomorrow, we've had today. And if we should bump into each other sometime in the future, well that's fine too. We'll be friends.
我不想要你覺得我會在意昨晚發生的事。我不要你給我電話號碼、或寫信和明信片給我。我沒要嫁給你，更沒想要跟你生孩子。無論明天發生什麼事，我們擁有今天。如果以後，某一天我們無意中相遇，那也很好，我們就會當朋友。

Dexter: Yeah. right.
噢，這樣啊。

[達斯把手搭在艾瑪肩上]

Dexter: Or on the other hand.
又或者是……。

Emma: Go on. 你說。

Dexter: Well, my parents don't arrive until later.
呃，我爸媽晚點才會到家。

Emma: So? 所以？

Dexter: So, my flat's empty. If you want to...finish what we started.
所以我家沒人在。如果妳還想把我們還沒做完的事做完……。

Emma: What, sober?
什麼？沒喝醉做嗎？

Dexter: And in daylight.
而且是在光天化日之下。

[艾瑪微笑]

Emma: Race you!
看誰先到！

[他們嬉笑著跑下山。]

羅曼死英文教室

艾瑪說的「不論明天怎樣」，就跟這課的主題「不在乎天長地久」想表達的意思一樣，而這意思在英文裡就用這個句型：whatever, S + V…

· whatever 當副詞連接詞用時等於 no matter what「不論什麼事 / 物」，使用時要與主要子句間以逗點相隔。
Whatever happens, you know you can count on me.
= No matter what happens, you know you can count on me.
不管發生什麼事，你知道有我讓你依靠。

· whatever 也可當複合關係代名詞使用，義同 anything (that)「所有……的東西」，與主要子句間就不需要逗點。類似用法還有 whichever（不論哪種）、whoever（不論是誰）whenever（不論何時）wherever（不論何處）。
Whatever it takes to win her heart, I'm willing to do.
= Anything (that) it takes to win her heart, I'm willing to do.
為了得到她的芳心，什麼我願意做。

One Day

達斯正在咖啡廳工作時聽到有人進門，是艾瑪之前有緣無份的男友伊恩，那天碰巧是 2009 年 7 月 15 日。伊恩想告訴達斯，艾瑪跟自己在一起的時候，他早知道達斯一直都是艾瑪心裏最重要的人。

Ian: I hate today. Fifteenth of July.
我真討厭今天，7 月 15 日。

Dexter: St. Swithin's day. It's uh...it's a tough one.
聖斯威辛日，的確是個難度過的節日。

Ian: I never noticed it before, but it was always there. Just waiting, lurking. I used to hate you too. Quite violently actually, Dexter. No! I'm sorry, but only...because she lit up with you, just in a way that she never did with me and it used to make me so angry because I...I didn't think that you deserved her. Can I say this?
以前從沒注意到這天，不過它一直存在、悄悄等著到來。我以前很恨你，滿激烈的恨意，達斯。啊，抱歉抱歉，只不過……她總是因為你容光煥發，她跟我在一起時從沒那樣過，讓我好生氣，因為我……我覺得你根本配不上她。我可以繼續說嗎？

Dexter: Yeah, go on.
請繼續。

Ian: She made you decent, and in return, you made her so happy, so happy. And I will always be grateful to you for that. And on that bombshell...
她讓你人變好，而你讓她很快樂，非常快樂。我會一直為此對你心存感激，雖然我講了這麼多莫名其妙的話……。

[達斯笑了]

Ian: Back to the sticks! There's my lot out there.
回頭講講我平凡無奇的生活吧！我的妻兒在那邊。

[伊恩指向坐在咖啡廳外面的太太和兩個小孩]

Dexter: Oh!
哇！

Ian: Yeah, I know!
對，我知道！

Dexter: So, listen. You know, we'll...we'll stay in touch. I'll give you a call.
嗯，我們……我們應該保持聯絡。我會再打電話給你。

Ian: No, I don't think that's necessary. I think we're done here. Come here!
不用啦，沒那個必要了。我們之間就此結束吧。過來一下！

[伊恩抱了抱達斯]

Ian: Good luck, mate. Alright?
朋友，祝你好運，好嗎？

Dexter: You too. Thank you.
你也是。謝謝。

羅曼死英文教室

St. Swithin's Day 聖斯威辛日

你知道嗎？聖斯威辛日是一個與天氣有關的古老英國民間節日，訂立在每年 7 月 15 日這天，預告著英國雨季即將到來，請大家注意出門要帶傘。

聖斯威辛原是英國溫徹斯特郡的主教，跟一般基督教聖徒一樣，被記載為樂善好施之人，其他也沒什麼特別之處。據傳說，聖斯威辛死後依照他的遺願，被埋葬在教堂外面。不料 100 年後有位主教想把它的屍骨移至教堂內，以示紀念，並指定 7 月 15 日這天遷移墳墓。沒想到遷移當天開始下起大雨，而且一下就是 40 天，民間就流傳著「聖斯威辛顯靈阻擾遷移」的說法，這個計劃就此告吹。這節日和聖斯威辛的名字在一千多年後還被大家記得，主要是因為這首民謠：

St. Swithin's Day if thou dost rain 聖斯威辛日若降雨
For forty days it will remain 之後的四十天都會一直下雨
St. Swithin's Day if thou be fair 聖斯威辛日若天晴
For forty days 'twill rain no more 之後的四十天都不會有雨

Anne Hathaway
安海瑟薇

飾演女主角安娜的安海瑟薇（Anne Hathaway），生於美國紐約，2013 年以《悲慘世界》*Les Misérables* 獲得奧斯卡最佳女配角獎，被譽為「茱莉亞羅勃茲和奧黛莉赫本的綜合體」。她曾因篤信天主教而想成為修女，後來因哥哥是同性戀而放棄了這個夢想，並脫離天主教。她說：「如果有宗教不支持我哥哥對愛的選擇，我也不支持那個宗教。」她在李安執導的《斷背山》*Brokeback Mountain* 中飾演男同性戀者的妻子露琳 Lureen 一角，演技獲得肯定，也因為對同性戀者和同性婚姻公開表示支持，成為男同性戀者心目中偶像的少數女演員之一。

《派特的幸福劇本》

患有躁鬱症的派特（Pat，Bradley Cooper 飾）在精神病院治療 8 個月出院後一心想與前妻重修舊好，決心改頭換面成為前妻心中的好老公，卻意外認識嗑藥過度的蒂芬妮（Tiffany，Jennifer Lawrence 飾）。儘管派特擺明自己有老婆，蒂芬妮仍頻頻出現，幾近死纏爛打的想要跟派特在一起。從沒想過可以幸福的兩人，最後卻意外得到幸福的降臨。

Pat: **The only way you can meet my crazy… was by doing something crazy yourself. Thank you. I love you. I knew it the minute I met you. I'm sorry it took so long for me to catch up. I just got stuck.**

唯一能和我的瘋狂相抗衡的，是妳自己做瘋狂的事。謝謝妳。我愛妳。從遇見妳的那一刻我就知道了。對不起我花了這麼久時間才搞懂，我之前腦袋卡住了。

The Silver Linings Playbook

《跳躍時空的情書》

原本住在湖邊小屋裡，即將離去到大醫院工作的凱特（Kate，Sandra Bullock 飾）留了一封信給下一任屋主，而收到信的卻是年輕不得志，住在湖邊小屋中的亞歷（Alex，Keanu Reeves 飾）。時空相隔 2 年的兩人因通信而發展出戀情，並刻意安排一場未來的會面，但凱特卻沒有等到亞歷出現。心碎的凱特認為情已逝，寫了一封信給亞歷。

Kate: **…, I drove myself to the lake house looking for any kind of answer and I found you and I let myself get lost, lost in this beautiful fantasy where time stood still. But it's not real, Alex.**

我把車開到湖邊小屋尋找答案，我卻發現了你，而且迷失了自己，迷失在這段時光依舊的美麗幻夢之中。但這卻不真實，亞歷。

Kate: **I have to learn to live the life that I have got. Please don't write anymore. Don't try to find me. Let me let you go.**

我必須學著去過我現在的生活。請不要再寫信給我，別來找我。讓我忘記你。

The Lake House

《為愛朗讀》

二次大戰時，一位 15 歲男孩麥可（Michael，德籍演員 David Kross 飾）愛上了一位 36 歲的美麗少婦漢娜（Hannah，Kate Winslet 飾）。漢娜雖也對麥可心動，但礙於保守時代的眼光，常常故意拒麥可於門外。上學無法跟漢娜見面的麥可，一放假就狂奔去找思念已久的漢娜，然而在電車上漢娜刻意無視他，使他大發脾氣，而後又覺得自己不該對漢娜如此失禮。

Michael: **I didn't mean to upset you.** 我不是故意惹你生氣的。

Hanna: **You don't have the power to upset me. You don't matter enough to upset me.** 你沒有惹我生氣的能耐。你沒重要到會讓我生氣。

Michael: **I don't know what to say. I've never been with a woman before. We've been together four weeks, and I can't live without you. I can't. Even the thought of it kills me.** 我不懂該怎麼表達。我從沒跟女人在一起過。我們在一起過了四週，現在我無法沒有妳，真的無法。就連想到會沒有妳都讓我快死掉。

Michael: **Is it true what you said? That I don't matter to you?** 你說的是認真的嗎？我對妳來說並不重要？

[漢娜坐在浴盆裡，搖了搖頭]

Michael: **Do you forgive me?** 妳能原諒我嗎？

[漢娜看著他，然後點點頭]

Michael: **Do you love me?** 那妳愛我嗎？

The Reader

Mr. Dreamy 夢幻情人

海灘男孩兄弟檔
Chris & Hemsworth
克里斯、連恩漢斯沃

🎧 25

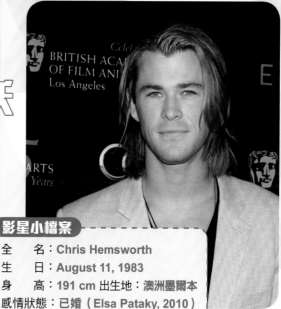

Growing up in Melbourne, Australia, Chris Hemsworth spent his free time surfing with his older brother Luke and younger brother Liam. In his late teens, Chris followed Liam into television, getting his start on the hit Australian soap opera *Home and Away*. After a small role in 2009's *Star Trek*, Chris moved to L.A. to try his luck in Hollywood, taking Liam with him. They both tried out for the lead in *Thor*, but Chris got the part, making him an instant star. But don't feel bad for Liam—he landed the role of Miley Cyrus' love interest in the romantic drama *The Last Song*, and is now famous for playing Gale Hawthorne in the *Hunger Games* series.

影星小檔案

全　　名：**Chris Hemsworth**
生　　日：**August 11, 1983**
身　　高：**191 cm** 出生地：**澳洲墨爾本**
感情狀態：**已婚（Elsa Pataky, 2010）**
成 名 作：**《雷神索爾》*Thor***

© Helga Esteb /
Shuttershock.com

成長於澳洲墨爾本的克里斯漢斯沃，每當閒暇之餘就會跟哥哥路克和弟弟連恩一起到海邊衝浪。克里斯於青少年晚期跟隨連恩的腳步進入電視圈，在澳洲熱門的肥皂劇《聚散離合》中開啟了演員生涯。克里斯於 2009 年的《星際爭霸戰》出演小角後，便帶著連恩一同搬至洛杉磯、到好萊塢闖蕩星途。兩人雙雙試鏡角逐《雷神索爾》的男主角，克里斯最後雀屏中選，令他瞬間成為知名巨星。不過千萬不要替連恩感到惋惜，他後來於愛情電影《最後一首歌》中得到演出機會、飾演（＋迪士尼小天后）麥莉希拉的戀人，目前則因詮釋《飢餓遊戲》系列中的蓋爾霍桑而走紅影壇。

影星小檔案

全　　名：**Liam Hemsworth**
生　　日：**January 13, 1990**
身　　高：**191 cm**　出生地：**澳洲墨爾本**
成名作：**《最後一曲》*The Last Song***

© Joe Seer /
Shuttershock.com

© Helga Esteb / Shuttershock.com

打造索爾般體魄

為了演出高壯魁武的索爾，克里斯被要求增重將近 10 公斤。要練出大塊又漂亮的肌肉，他說「多吃、多休息、多運動」三者缺一不可。除了攝取高蛋白，還要吃大量高纖蔬菜水果；不停變化健身重量、組數、次數，讓肌肉無法適應訓練強度，最後還要搭配充足休息。

演索爾前從沒上過健身房的克里斯說：如果你有規律健身，就已經比我剛開始時還厲害了！

《雲端情人》

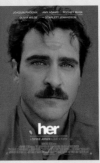

設定特殊的科幻愛情片，講述近未來世界中，專門幫忙撰寫 email、電子卡片的西奧多（Theodore，Joaquin Phoenix 飾），雖然能替客戶寫出最感人肺腑的信件，但自己的婚姻卻無法維持。心碎的他決定暫把語音作業系統莎曼莎（Samantha，Scarlett Johansson 配音）當作排解寂寞、療癒情傷的對象。莎曼莎熱情又風趣，無形卻溫柔地陪伴著西奧多，兩人墜入情網，轉變為一段美麗、哀傷的浪漫愛情故事。

凱薩琳（Catherine，Rooney Mara 飾演）是西奧多從小相伴到結婚，確以離婚收尾的前妻。在經歷與莎曼莎超越形體的情感之後，西奧多終於提筆為自己寫一封給前妻的信。

隨著「人工智慧」莎曼莎不斷進化，西奧多身為有形體人類的短缺漸漸浮現，他的溝通與思考層級跟不上莎曼莎，身體只能一次出現在一個地方，更無法「永生」跟莎曼莎在一起。面對無法彼此共築未來，莎曼莎心痛地決定離開。

Theodore: Where are you going?
妳要到哪去？
Samantha: It's hard to explain, but if you get there, come find me. Nothing will be able to tear us apart then.

我要去的地方很難解釋清楚，但若你找到了那裡，要來找我。到那時候，再也沒有任何事情能拆散我們。

Theodore: Dear Catherine, I've been sitting here thinking about all the things I wanted to apologize to you for. All the pain we caused each other. Everything I put on you. Everything I needed you to be or needed you to say. I'm sorry for that. I'll always love you 'cause we grew up together and you helped make me who I am. I just wanted you to know there will be a piece of you in me always, and I'm grateful for that. Whatever someone you become, and wherever you are in the world, I'm sending you love. You're my friend to the end. Love, Theodore.

親愛的凱薩琳：我一直坐在這裡，想著所有我想跟妳道歉的事。所有我們給對方造成的傷害，那些我加諸於妳的指責、一切我以前想要妳做到及說的話，我好抱歉。我會永遠愛著妳，因為我們曾一起成長，因為妳讓我成為今天的我。我只想讓妳知道，妳將永遠是我的一部份，對此我心存感激。不論妳日後成為怎樣的人，或身在世界的任何角落，我都會將我的愛傳送給妳。妳是我一輩子的朋友。愛妳的西奧多。

Her

導演 Spike Jonze 把大明星改頭換面變成「小清新」

《雲端情人》題材前衛，講述科技發達的近未來，人心的空虛與寂寞，從海報設計到電影名稱，都讓人覺得這是部小成本的獨立電影，但其實本片演員各個大有來頭。你肯定知道貫穿本片的性感「女聲」是赫赫有名的史嘉蕾喬韓森（Scarlett Johansson），其他還有哪些扮相模素，讓人驚呼「差太多了吧！」的大明星呢？

神鬼戰士暴君＝深情大叔西奧多：
記得神鬼戰士裡處心積慮要滿門抄斬羅素克洛一家的羅馬暴君嗎？來自波多黎各的喬昆菲尼克斯（Joaquin Phoenix）除了會演戲以外，也是個音樂人。

龍紋身的女孩＝高知識份子前妻
全身穿洞又刺青的反社會份子，變身成家庭教育拘謹的高知識份子，真不知道這部片的選角人員是怎麼選的！更令人無法想像的是擁有義大利、愛爾蘭血統的魯妮瑪拉（Rooney Mara）居然是個富家千金！不得不敬佩她為演戲而犧牲的決心！

性感女騙子＝清秀紅粉知己
《瞞天大佈局》中美豔勾魂的艾美亞當斯（Amy Adams）在本片也是素到不行，飾演西奧多的談心好友。艾美另一個為人所知的角色是《曼哈頓奇緣》裡從童話王國中落入現實世界的公主。

實習女醫師＝熱情風騷的相親對象
因演出影集《怪醫豪斯》而名聲大噪的奧利維亞魏爾德（Olivia Wilde），是美國演員兼模特兒，其他知名電影作品還有《創：光速戰記》以及《星際飆客》。

已習慣莎曼莎隨時陪伴的西奧多，有天突然呼叫不到莎曼莎，通訊工具上甚至顯示「找不到作業系統」，讓西奧多心急如焚。再次與莎曼莎搭上線後，西奧多從她的話語中發現自己可能已不是「作業系統」莎曼莎唯一的「使用者」了。

Theodore: Do you talk to someone else while we're talking?
我們在說話的時候，妳也在跟其他人說話嗎？
Samantha: Yes. 是的。
Theodore: Are you talking with someone else right now? People, OS, whatever….
妳現在有沒有同時跟其他人、作業系統之類的在講話？

Samantha: Yeah. 有的。
Theodore: How many others? 多少人？
Samantha: 8,316. 八千三百一十六人。
Theodore: Are you in love with anybody else?
妳有愛上其他人嗎？
Samantha: Why do you ask that? 為何這麼問？
Theodore: I don't know. Are you? 我不知道。有嗎？
Samantha: I've been thinking about how to talk to you about this.
我一直在思考怎麼跟你解釋。
Theodore: How many others? 多少人？
Samantha: 641. 六百四十一人。

《斷背山》

在農場畜牧的艾尼斯（Ennis，Heath Ledger 飾）結識了相貌俊美、活潑愛笑的傑克（Jack，Jake Gyllenhaal 飾）。在完全無法接受同性愛情的 60 年代，兩人雖相愛，但隨後便各自結婚生子，並相約每年見面一起釣魚。然而傑克想與艾尼斯共築未來的渴望越發強烈，提出同居，卻遭無法放下世俗觀感的艾尼斯無情拒絕，兩人因此大爆口角。

Jack Twist: Tell you what, we could've had a good life together, fucking' real good life! Had us a place of our own. But you didn't want it, Ennis! …You count the damn few times we have been together in nearly twenty years and you measure the short fucking leash you keep me on, and then you ask me about Mexico and tell me you'll kill me for needing something I don't hardly never get. You have no idea how bad it gets! I'm not you… I can't make it on a couple of high-altitude fucks once or twice a year! You are too much for me Ennis, you son of a whoreson bitch… I wish I knew how to quit you.
告訴你好了，我們大可好好一起共度未來，過著他媽的好生活，擁有自己的農場，但你卻全都不要，艾尼斯！數數看這 20 年來我們才見面幾次，你又不想給我自由，問我去墨西哥幹嘛，還要為了我很少得到的親密關係（傑克到墨西哥召妓）說要把我幹掉。你不懂我會有多難耐！我不是你，我無法靠每年一兩次深山的幽會撐下去！你真是夠了，艾尼斯，你這王八蛋……我真希望我知道如何把你戒掉。

Ennis Del Mar: Well why don't you? Why don't you just let me be, huh? Because of you, Jack, that I'm like this. I'm nothing… and nowhere.
那你為何不這麼做？你為何不放過我？是你讓我變成這樣的。什麼也不是，哪裡也容不下。

Brokeback Mountain

《班傑明的奇幻旅程》

班傑明（Benjamin，Brad Pitt 飾）出生外貌是 80 歲的老人，卻逆時光成長為茁壯的青年，與美麗的芭蕾舞伶黛西（Daisy，Cate Blanchett 飾）經歷始終有緣無份的相遇與離別，但卻相互在心裡留下越來越深的情愫。輾轉 20 幾年後，兩人終於在彼此生命中對的時刻再度重逢。

Daisy: We're meeting in the middle….
我們終究在生命的中間遇見彼此
Benjamin: We finally caught up with each other…
我們終於趕上彼此了……。
Benjamin: I want remember us just as we are now.
我想好好記住我們現在的樣子。

The Curious Case of Benjamin Button

Reese Witherspoon 瑞絲薇斯朋

© Everett Collection / Shutterstock.com

🎧 26

Born on March 22, 1976 in New Orleans, Reese Witherspoon was raised in Nashville after four years in Germany, where her father worked for the U.S. military. She began modeling at seven and was soon appearing in local TV [1]**commercials**. Witherspoon's parents nicknamed her "Little [2]**Type A**" for her [3]**drive** to achieve, a quality that would help her get into Stanford, where she studied English literature. But the [4]**lure** of Hollywood proved stronger, and she quit her studies after one year to become an actress.

After [5]**auditioning** for a small part in the 1990 drama *The Man in the Moon*, she was instead offered a leading role, and her performance was well received by [6]**critics**. Following more [7]**solid** performances in *Fear* (1996) and *Cruel Intentions* (1999), Witherspoon won the role that would make her a big star: Elle Woods in the hit 2001 comedy *Legally Blonde*. Her winning [8]**streak** continued with the 2002 rom-com *Sweet Home Alabama* and 2005 Johnny Cash bio-pic *Walk The Line*. Witherspoon's acclaimed portrayal of June Carter Cash opposite Joaquin Phoenix earned her a number of major awards, including a Best Actress Oscar. Recent films like 2007 political [9]**thriller** *Rendition* and 2014 [10]**biographical** drama *Wild*, which won her another Oscar nomination, continue to show her range as an actress.

When Witherspoon isn't [11]**delighting** audiences on the silver screen, she's kept busy by her three children and growing career as head of her own production company. In addition to *Wild*, she also produced the hit 2014 thriller *Gone Girl*. This talented filmmaker will no doubt continue to **make her mark on** Hollywood for years to come.

Showbiz Words

bio-pic 傳記電影

為 biographical picture 的簡稱，這裡的 picture 指的是「電影」，等同於 film，也可稱 biographical film，即電影情節在講述某位名人的一生，但是由演員來飾演該位名人，劇情也會稍經改寫，與本人親自現身的紀錄片不一樣。

A: What's the name of that bio-pic about Mark Zuckerberg?
那部馬克佐伯格的傳記電影叫什麼？

B: I think it's called *The Social Network*.
好像叫《社群網站》吧。

© Joe Seer / Shutterstock.com

瑞絲薇斯朋與她的子女 Ava 與 Deacon 在星光大道合影留念。

瑞絲薇斯朋於 1976 年三月二十二日出生在美國紐奧良市，年幼時因父親為駐德國的美軍服務而在當地住了四年，後來再回到美國納許維爾市繼續成長。她年僅七歲時便開始擔任模特兒，隨後不久開始在地方性的電視廣告亮相。由於薇斯朋渾身充滿使命必達的幹勁，因此她父母暱稱她為「A 型小公主」，而這樣的特質也幫助她進入史丹佛大學就讀英語文學。不過好萊塢的誘惑顯然更為強烈，她僅僅一年後就放棄學業，立志成為一名演員。

薇斯朋參加 1990 年劇情片《月中人》中一個小角色的試鏡，不過卻獲邀擔綱主角，而她的表現也頗受影評讚賞。在 1996 年《致命的危機》及 1999 年《危險性遊戲》展現更多精湛的演技之後，薇斯朋獲得了日後令她成為巨星的角色——2001 年賣座喜劇《金法尤物》中的艾兒伍茲。而她也靠著 2002 年愛情喜劇《美麗蹺家人》及 2005 年描寫強尼凱許的傳記片《為你鍾情》，將她的成功表現延續下去。薇斯朋與瓦昆菲尼克斯同台飆戲、精采詮釋瓊恩卡特凱許的演技也為她奪得多項大獎，其中包括一座奧斯卡最佳女主角獎。較為近期的電影，像是 2007 年政治驚悚片《關鍵危機》和令她再次獲得奧斯卡提名的 2014 年傳記劇情片《那時候，我只剩下勇敢》，都繼續展現她身為演員的寬廣戲路。

沒有在大銀幕上娛樂觀眾之餘，薇斯朋仍是片刻不得閒，因為她不但是三個小孩的母親，同時還經營一間日益成長的製片公司。除了《那時候，我只剩下勇敢》一片，她也製作了 2014 年的強檔驚悚電影《控制》。這位才華洋溢的電影人在未來的日子裡，肯定還會在好萊塢中持續留下她的印記。

Tongue-tied No More

make one's mark on... （某人）對……留下影響

make / leave remark on... 表「在某方面造成影響」，也可說 make / leave its mark on... 或 make / leave a mark on...。

A: The new sales manager is really making a mark on the department.
新來的業務經理對部門影響滿多的。
B: Yeah. Sales have really improved in the last few months.
對啊。這幾個月的業績成長好多。

Vocabulary Bank

1) **commercial** [kə`məʃəl] (n.) 電視廣告
This channel has too many commercials.
這頻道廣告太多了。

2) **Type A** (phr.) 〔心〕A 型性格（指積極進取、好強、要求完美的人）
Leaders often have Type A personalities.
領導者通常都是 A 型性格。

3) **drive** [draɪv] (n.) 幹勁，決心
You don't have the drive it takes to succeed in business.
你沒有事業成功所需具備的衝勁。

4) **lure** [lur] (n.) 誘惑力，吸引力
The lure of easy money led the man to a life of crime.
不勞而獲的誘惑迫使那名男子走向犯罪的一生。

5) **audition** [ɔ`dɪʃən] (n.) 試鏡，試演，試唱
Did you pass your audition for the play?
你有通過那齣戲的試鏡嗎？

6) **critic** [`krɪtɪk] (n.) 評論家，批評家
Thomas is a restaurant critic for a local paper.
湯瑪仕替當地的報紙撰寫食評。

7) **solid** [`sɑlɪd] (a.)（口）（指）不錯的，水準之上的
Our football team has a solid defense.
我們足球隊的防守很強。

8) **streak** [strik] (n.) 連續的狀態
I've been having a streak of bad luck lately.
我最近一直很衰。

9) **thriller** [`θrɪlə] (n.) 驚悚片，驚悚小說
Jenny likes to read thrillers and mystery novels.
珍妮喜歡讀驚悚小說和奇幻小說。

10) **biographical** [ˌbaɪə`græfɪkəl] (a.) 傳記的，傳記體的
The writer mostly writes biographical novels.
這位作者大多寫傳記體小說。

11) **delight** [dɪ`laɪt] (v.) 使高興，取悅
The magician delighted the kids with his tricks.
魔術師的戲法把孩子們都逗樂了。

愛在曖昧不明時

想愛而不敢愛、或不能愛，於是造就出一段段欲說還休、躊躇隱忍的愛情故事，這也是以下四部電影的共同點。遲遲不踏出那一步的愛情，是害怕而逃避？還是為了不違背道義？不論如何，故事中的主人翁，最終都是帶著悔意，思念著過往而度過餘生。

《花樣年華》

1962 年的香港，報館編輯周慕雲與妻子搬進一棟多數是上海人居住的公寓，與在日商公司上班的陳先生和他太太蘇麗珍成為鄰居。後來周慕雲和蘇麗珍兩人發現自己的配偶與對方的配偶有婚外情，兩人之間也產生了微妙的感情。

《花樣年華》的中文片名源自於 1946 年電影《長相思》中的主題曲，由周璇所唱。而英文片名 In the Mood for Love 則源自於 1935 年的知名爵士樂，I'm in the Mood for Love 這首英文歌的中文版也被譯為《花樣年華》，由美國知名作曲家吉米麥克修（Jimmy McHugh）作曲，百老匯知名編劇作家朵洛西菲爾茲（Dorothy Fields）作詞。據說導演王家衛原本要為電影的英文片名取為「Secrets」（秘密），但坎城影展方面說，已有多部電影名稱帶有「secret」的字眼，而王家衛當時正好聽到 I'm in the Mood for Love 這首英文歌，於是決定借用中文歌名《花樣年華》為片名。

Chow Mo-wan: **It's me. If there's an extra ticket...would you go with me?**
是我。如果多一張船票，妳願不願意跟我一起走？
Su Li-zhen: **It's me. If there's an extra ticket...would you go with me?**
是我。如果有多一張船票，你會不會帶我一起走？

It is a restless moment. She has kept her head lowered...to give him a chance to come closer. But he could not, for lack of courage. She turns and walks away.
（旁白）那是一種難堪的相對，她一直羞低著頭，給他一個接近的機會。他沒有勇氣接近，她轉身，走了。

He remembers those vanished years. As though looking through a dusty window pane, the past is something he could see, but not touch.
那些消逝了的歲月，彷彿隔著一塊積著灰塵的玻璃，看得到，抓不著。他一直在懷念著過去的一切。
Su Li-zhen: **Why did you call me at the office today?**
今天為什麼打電話到我公司？
Chow Mo-wan: **I just wanted to hear your voice.**
我只想聽聽妳的聲音。

Chow Mo-wan: **In the old days, if someone had a secret they didn't want to share...you know what they did?**
我問你，從前有些人，心裡有了秘密，而且不想被人知道，知道他們會怎麼做？
Ah Ping: **I have no idea.**
我怎麼知道。
Chow Mo-wan: **They went up a mountain, found a tree, carved a hole in it, and whispered the secret into the hole. Then they covered it with mud, and left the secret there forever.**
他們會跑到山上找一棵樹，在樹上挖一個洞，然後把秘密全說進去，再用泥把洞封上。那秘密會留在樹裡，沒有人知道。

Chow Mo-wan: That handbag I saw you with yesterday...where did you buy it?
昨天妳拿的皮包，不知道在哪裡能買到？

Su Li-zhen: Why do you ask?
你為什麼這麼問？

Chow Mo-wan: It looked so elegant. I want to get one for my wife.
沒有，我只是看著款式很別緻，想買一個送給太太。

Su Li-zhen: Mr. Chow, you're so good to your wife!
周先生，你對太太可真細心。

Chow Mo-wan: Not really! My wife is so fussy. Her birthday is some days away. I don't know what to get her. Could you buy one for me to give her?
哪裡，她這個人很挑剔。過兩天是她生日，不知道買些什麼送給她。妳能幫我買一個嗎？

Su Li-zhen: Maybe she wouldn't want one just exactly the same.
如果是一模一樣的，她可能會不喜歡的。

Chow Mo-wan: You're right, I didn't think of that. A woman would mind?
對了，我倒是沒想到。女人會介意嗎？

Su Li-zhen: Yes, especially since we're neighbors.
會的，特別是隔壁鄰居。

Chow Mo-wan: Do they come in other colors?
不知道有沒有別的顏色？

Su Li-zhen: I'd have to ask my husband.
那得要問我先生才知道。

Chow Mo-wan: Why?
為什麼？

Su Li-zhen: He bought it for me on a business trip abroad. They aren't on sale here.
那個皮包是我先生在外地工作時買給我的。他說香港買不到。

Chow Mo-wan: Then never mind.
啊，那就算了吧。

In the Mood for Love

從題材、人物名稱和感情主線來看，《2046》與《花樣年華》是前後相承的。有段述說「將心中秘密埋封在樹洞裡」的臺詞，就同時出現在《花樣年華》與《2046》中。片名「2046」是劇中主角入住的旅館房間號碼，但對香港來說還有另一層意義。電影拍攝當時是香港回歸中國的 1997 年，中共承諾香港 50 年不變，而 50 年過後就是 2046 年。《2046》的片名也很有可能參考了 1959 年美國的一部電視影集《陰陽魔界》The Twilight Zone，劇中描述一名男子自 2046 年起，被獨自流放到一個遙遠的小行星，並和一個被送來陪伴他的機器人談戀愛，劇情架構和《2046》有些類似。

《2046》

1966 年，周慕雲回到香港，搬進一間旅館的 2047 號房間，遇到了住在 2046 號房間的幾個女人。為了告別過去，他開始寫一部名為《2046》的小說。小說中的人只要搭上了前往 2046 的列車，就可以找回失去的記憶。但到了西元 2046 年，那班神秘列車依舊定期開往 2046。

Chow Mo-wan: Love is all a matter of timing. It's no good meeting the right person too soon or too late. If I'd lived in another time or place, my story might have had a very different ending.
其實愛情是有時間性的，認識得太早或太晚都是不行的，如果我在另一個時間或空間認識她，這個結局也許會不一樣。

Chow Mo-wan: Everyone who goes to 2046 has the same intention—they want to recapture lost memories. Because in 2046 nothing ever changes. But nobody knows if that is true or not, because no one has ever come back.
去 2046 的乘客都只有一個目地，就是找回失去的記憶。因為在 2046，一切事物永不改變。沒有人知道這是不是真的，因為從來沒有人回來過。

Chow Mo-wan: When the peony blooms, she stands tall. Does she mean "no" or "yes"?

一若牡丹盛開，她站起身來，走了，留下既非「是」又非「否」的答案。

Chow Mo-wan: I once fell in love with someone. I couldn't stop wondering if she loved me back. I found an android that looked just like her. I hoped she would give me the answer.

我曾經愛上一個人，我想知道她到底喜不喜歡我。我發現這個機器人很像她，我開始嘗試在她身上尋找答案。

Chow Mo-wan: Maybe one day you'll escape your past. If you do, look for me.

如果有一天妳可以忘掉過去，記得來找我。

Chow Mo-wan: As I recall, that's the very last time we saw each other.

在我的記憶裡，那個晚上是我們最後一次見面。

Chow Mo-wan: In love you can't bring on a substitute.

愛情是沒有替代品的。

Chow Mo-wan: Do you remember you asked me if there was anything I wouldn't lend? I've given it a lot of thought and now I know there is one thing I'll never lend to anyone.

妳還記得嗎？妳以前問過我，有什麼東西我不借。我也想了很久，現在我才知道，原來有些東西，我永遠也不會借給別人。

Bai Ling: I don't get it. Where does all that fun get you? If you find the right person, why waste time on the others?

我就不明白，你們怎麼那麼喜歡逢場作戲？有個好的足夠了，何必擔誤時間呢？

Chow Mo-wan: If I find the right person? A man like me has nothing much except free time. That's why I need company.

那還得找到才行，我這個人什麼都沒有，有的就是時間，我總得找點什麼事來打發時間吧。

Bai Ling: So people are just time fillers to you?

拿人家填空檔啊？

Chow Mo-wan: I wouldn't say that. Other people can borrow my time to.

也不能這麼說，要說我把自己借給別人。

Bai Ling: And tonight? Are you borrowing me, or am I borrowing you?

那今天晚上，算你借給我還是我借給你啊？

Chow Mo-wan: No difference. Maybe I borrowed you earlier, now you're borrowing me.

隨便啦，上半夜當妳借給我，下半夜當我回借給妳好了

Bai Ling: Ridiculous.

少來這一套。

《臥虎藏龍》

劍客李慕白攜青冥寶劍拜訪女鏢頭俞秀蓮，托她將寶劍送往京城，交給鐵貝勒。寶劍被盜，俞秀蓮追查之下，發現與邊關要將之女玉嬌龍有關。而玉嬌龍幾年前隨父親往邊關赴任途中，車隊遇上山賊首羅小虎搶去她的梳子，玉嬌龍不惜一切追蹤羅小虎，反被羅小虎劫往山寨，兩人私訂終身。玉嬌龍隨父回京後，被許配給富貴人家，但在大婚當天離家出走。李慕白來到京城，與俞秀蓮聯手，要將寶劍追回。

《臥虎藏龍》
續集開拍

改編自武俠小說系列「鐵鶴五部」的《臥虎藏龍》，是由中港台美合拍的華語武俠電影，由李安執導，更代表台灣奪得第 73 屆奧斯卡最佳外語片獎。拍攝預算為 1700 萬美元的《臥虎藏龍》，在全世界的票房共累計 2 億 1350 萬美元，在美國的票房也有 1 億 2800 萬美元，成為美國史上最賣座的外語電影，對不愛看外國字幕的美國人來說是一項創舉，導演李安也因此成了全世界的焦點。

電影版權所屬的好萊塢公司已在坎城影展上宣布開拍續集《臥虎藏龍 2 青冥寶劍》，導演則換成袁和平，並預計於今年 8 月上映。

Yu Xiu-lian: Mu-bai, hold on. Give me some hope.

慕白，守住氣，給我一點希望。

Li Mu-bai: Xiu-lian....

秀蓮……。

Yu Xiu-lian: Save your strength.

別動氣。

Li Mu-bai: My life is departing. I've only one breath left.

生命已經到了盡頭，我只有一息尚存。

Yu Xiu-lian: Use it to meditate. Free yourself from this world as you have been taught. Let your soul rise to eternity with your last breath. Do not waste it...for me.

用這口氣練神還虛吧。解脫得道，元寂永恆，一直是武當修道的願望。提升這一口氣，達到你這一生追求的境地。別放下、浪費到我身上。

Li Mu-bai: I've already wasted my whole life. I want to tell you with my last breath that I've always loved you. I'd rather be a ghost drifting by your side as a condemned soul than enter heaven without you...because of your love, I will never be a lonely spirit.

我已經浪費了這一生，我要用這口氣對妳說，我一直深愛著妳。我寧願遊蕩在你身邊，做七天的野鬼，跟隨你，就算落進最黑暗的地方。我的愛，也不會讓我成為永遠的孤魂。

Li Mu-bai: Xiu-lian, the things we touch have no permanence. My master would say: there is nothing we can hold onto in this world. Only by letting go can we truly possess what is real.

秀蓮，我們能觸摸的東西沒有永遠。師父一再地說：把手握緊，裡面什麼也沒有；把手鬆開，你擁有的是一切。

Yu Xiu-lian: Mu-bai, not everything is an illusion. My hand...wasn't that real?

慕白，這世間不是每一件事都是虛幻的，剛才你握著我的手，你能感覺到它的真實嗎？

Li Mu-bai: Your hand, rough and callused from machete practice. All this time, I've never had the courage to touch it. The martial arts world is a world of tigers and dragons, full of corruption.

I tried sincerely to give it up but I've brought us only trouble.

你的手冰涼涼的，那些練刀練出來的硬繭，每一次我看見，都不敢觸摸。秀蓮，江湖裡臥虎藏龍，人心裡何嘗不是？刀劍裡藏凶，人情裡何嘗不是？我誠心誠意地把青冥劍交出來，卻帶給我們更多的麻煩。

Yu Xiu-lian: To repress one's feelings only makes them stronger.

壓抑只會讓感情更強烈。

Li Mu-bai: I can't hold back my feelings either. I want to be with you...just like this. It gives me a sense of peace.

我也阻止不了我的慾望，我想跟妳在一起。就像這樣坐著，我反而能感到一種平靜。

Luo Xiao-hu: When I was a boy, one night I saw thousand shooting stars. I thought, where did they all go? I'm an orphan. I used to look for stars alone. I thought if I rode to the other end of the desert, I'd find them. I've been riding in the desert ever since.

小的時候，有一天夜裡，我看見天上落下千萬顆星星。我想，它們都落到哪裡去了呢？我是個孤兒，我就一個人去找星。我想，如果我騎馬到了沙漠的另一頭，我就可以找到它們。從那以後我就一直在大漠中奔馳。

Yu Jiao-long: And so, the little boy grew up. He couldn't find the stars, so he stole my comb.

後來那個小男孩長大了，星星找不到，就來搶我的梳子。

Luo Xiao-hu: Out here, you always fight for survival. You have to be part of a gang to stand a chance. Slowly, your gang becomes your family. All that Dark Cloud stuff is just to make my life easier.

在大漠中，要活著就要不停地拚殺，大家要聯合起來才有機會活下去，你的同夥就成了自己的家。那個「半天雲」的名字，只是一個讓人更容易活下去的迷。

Yu Jiao-long: So you're still that little boy looking for shooting stars.

所以你在心裡頭還是個小男孩兒，在尋找那些流星？

Luo Xiao-hu: I'm a man. And now I've found the brightest star of all.

我是一個男人了，而且，我已經找到了最亮的一顆星了。

Crouching Tiger, Hidden Dragon

紅磨坊

故事背景發生在十九世紀末的巴黎蒙馬特區，富豪在當地的紅磨坊一擲千金、藝術家來此尋求靈感、貧民在此找尋翻身的機會。鋼琴詩人克利斯汀（Christian，Ewan McGregor 飾）來紅磨坊實現創作夢，浪漫的他愛上出身寒微的歌舞紅星莎婷（Satine，Nicole Kidman 飾），試著讓莎婷了解什麼是自由、什麼是美、什麼是愛。

Satine: Besides, I can't fall in love with anyone.
更何況，我不能跟任何人墜入情網。

Christian: Can't fall in love? But, a life without love, that's...terrible!
不能墜入情網？但是，少了愛的生命，簡直……太可怕了！

Satine: No, being on the street, that's terrible.
不，露宿街頭才叫可怕。

Christian: No! Love is like oxygen!
不對！愛就像氧氣！

Satine: What?
什麼？

Christian: Love is a many splendored thing. Love lifts us up where we belong. All you need is love!
愛是更超凡入聖的東西。愛將我們提升到應有的層次。妳我所需要的，就是愛！

Moulin Rouge!

羅曼死英文教室

《紅磨坊》當中有許多向音樂界致敬的橋段，光是此處節錄的這小小一段就出現許多名曲：

• *Love Is Like Oxygen* 是 1978 年英國樂團 Sweet 的同名歌曲。

• *Love Is A Many Splendored Thing* 是 1955 年同名電影《生死戀》的主題曲，曾獲奧斯卡最佳原創歌曲。

• *Love Lifts Us Up Where We Belong* 出自 1982 年電影《軍官與紳士》主題曲，曾獲奧斯卡最佳原創歌曲，原本只是電影配樂，改編後由 Joe Cocker 及 Jennifer Warnes 主唱的歌曲成為暢銷經典名曲。

• *All You Need Is Love* 是披頭四（the Beatles）的名曲，由 John Lennon 與 Paul McCartney 共同創作。

《我的藍莓夜》

紐約某夜裡，到咖啡廳找男友的伊莉莎白（Elizabeth，Norah Jones 飾）發現男友劈腿，憤而將男友鑰匙留給老闆傑洛米（Jeremy，Jude Law 飾）。事實上，傑洛米收藏了一整罐分手男女的鑰匙，包括他自己的。伊莉莎白開始習慣每夜到咖啡店點一塊沒人點的藍莓派，跟老闆聊天。

Elizabeth: So what's wrong with the blueberry pie?
藍莓派不好吃嗎？

Jeremy: There's nothing wrong with the blueberry pie. Just… people make other choices. You can't blame the blueberry pie, just…no one wants it.
藍莓派並不是不好吃，只是大家選了其他的口味。不能說藍莓派不好，只是沒人點來吃。

Elizabeth: Are they still left untouched at the end of the night?
晚上打烊時一樣還是剩下很多藍莓派嗎？

Jeremy: Yep, more or less.
對阿，差不多都是那樣。

Elizabeth: Then why do you keep making them?
那你為什麼還繼續做藍莓派？

Jeremy: Well, I always like having one around, just in case you pop in and fancy a slice.
我總喜歡留著一份藍莓派，以防你哪天會想來吃一塊。

My Blueberry Nights

骨感美女
Keira Knightley
綺拉奈特莉 🎧28

Born in London to an actor and a playwright, Keira Knightley asked for her own agent at the tender age of three. Her parents agreed when she was six, and she began acting on TV a year later. Knightley won her first Hollywood role as Padmé Amidala's double in *The Phantom Menace* because of her strong resemblance to Natalie Portman. After starring in the blockbuster Pirates of the Caribbean movies alongside Johnny Depp, she became the top choice for period dramas, appearing in acclaimed films like *Pride & Prejudice*, *Atonement* and *The Imitation Game*. Knightley married James Righton, vocalist of the indie rock band Klaxons in 2013, and is now pregnant with her their child.

出生於倫敦、父母分別為演員及劇作家的綺拉奈特莉，年僅三歲就開口希望自己能有專屬經紀人。她的爸媽於她六歲時答應，隔年她便開始在電視上演出。奈特莉的第一個好萊塢角色是《星際大戰首部曲：威脅潛伏》中佩咪艾米達拉的替身，原因是她與娜塔莉波曼的長相極為相似。在與強尼戴普共同主演《神鬼奇航》賣座系列之後，她成為時代劇的首選女星，演出了《傲慢與偏見》、《贖罪》及《模仿遊戲》等備受好評的電影。奈特莉於 2013 年嫁給了獨立搖滾團體「悲鳴樂團」的主唱詹姆斯萊頓，目前正懷有她的第一個寶寶。

© Joe Seer / Shuttershock.com

影星小檔案

全　　名：**Keira Christina Knightley**
生　　日：**March 26, 1985**
出 生 地：英格蘭特丁頓
感情狀態：已婚
成 名 作：《神鬼奇航》*Pirates of the Caribbean*

© Everett Collection / Shuttershock.com

平胸又怎樣？休想替我「加工」！

身材骨感的綺拉奈特莉並沒有傲人的上圍，不過她不但不在意，反倒堅持攝影時要如實呈現她身材的自然曲線，千萬不能用修圖軟體「加工」，對於自己之前在電影《神鬼奇航》*Pirates of the Caribbean* 的宣傳海報上被過分修圖，她感到十分不快，感嘆地說：「這些經過大量修飾的失真照片正是物化女性的元凶！在這樣的風氣下，我們如何能欣賞到不同體態的美？」這位小妮子不但有著美麗精緻的臉龐，以及許多好萊塢女星所沒有的古典氣質，更重要的是她還是位身體力行的女權主義者，善用她的知名度來導正偏頗的社會風氣。

綺拉奈特莉竟是「格雷」前女友

© cinemafestival / Shuttershock.com

很重視私人空間的綺拉奈特莉，對感情生活十分低調，但其實她在 2003 到 2005 年間曾與《格雷的五十道陰影》中的格雷——傑米道南（Jamie Dornan）交往。現在綺拉都已經嫁作人婦了，這段昔日戀情才浮出檯面，可見她有多會藏！

Colin Firth

柯林佛斯

Showbiz Words

wardrobe department
（劇團或電影公司）服裝部

電影或戲劇的製作，除了鎂光燈下的導演及演員外，工作人員更是功不可沒的幕後英雄。一般電影劇組（film crew）都會有燈光（lighting）、美術（art）、服裝（wardrobe）等不同的部門。wardrobe department又可稱為 costume department，負責設計及製作劇中角色的服裝，而他們對角色必須有深入的了解，才能夠設計出適合角色個性及年代的衣著。

 29

Colin Firth was born on September 10, 1960 in the village of Grayshott in the South of England. Firth's parents were both university teachers, and the family moved [1]**frequently** for work, living in Nigeria, the U.S. and different parts of the U.K. before finally [2]**settling** in the city of Winchester. Although he began acting in school plays at the age of five, he didn't develop a real interest until he **had a crush on** his drama teacher when he was 14. This interest became so strong that Firth dropped out of college at 18 and moved to London to [3]**pursue** an acting career.

After working in the **wardrobe department** at the National Theatre, Firth enrolled at Drama Centre London, where he studied for three years. While playing Hamlet at the Drama Centre, he was [4]**spotted** by playwright Julian Mitchell, who gave him a starring role in the 1983 West End [5]**production** of *Another Country*. Firth was also chosen to star in the screen [6]**adaptation** of *Another Country* the following year, marking his film debut. While this was followed by a number of film and TV roles, it wasn't until he played the [7]**haughty** Mr. Darcy in the 1995 BBC adaptation of *Pride and Prejudice* that he became a household name.

Firth's [8]**interpretation** of Mr. Darcy proved so popular that the character was brought back as Mark Darcy in the 2001 hit romantic comedy *Bridget Jones's Diary*, a modern [9]**version** of *Pride and Prejudice*. Although this led to further romantic roles in movies like the *Bridget Jones* [10]**sequel** and *Love Actually*, the actor has found his greatest success in serious dramas. Firth received his first Academy Award nomination as a [11]**gay** British [12]**professor** in 2009's *A Single Man*, and won a Best Actor Oscar playing George VI in *The King's Speech* two years later.

© Helga Esteb / Shutterstock.com

Vocabulary Bank

1) **frequently** [ˈfrikwəntli] (adv.) 經常地，時常
Gary frequently disagrees with his parents.
蓋瑞和父母經常意見不合。

2) **settle** [ˈsɛtəl] (v.)（使）定居，（使）安頓下來
Many Italian immigrants settled in New York.
許多義大利移民都在紐約定居。

3) **pursue** [pəˈsu] (v.) 從事，追求
Allen wants to pursue a career in real estate.
艾倫想要從事房地產事業。

4) **spot** [spɑt] (v.) 看見，發現，注意到
The police spotted the suspect driving a stolen car.
警察發現駕駛贓車的嫌疑犯。

5) **production** [prəˈdʌkʃən] (n.) 戲劇演出
The Drama Department is putting on a production of *Hamlet* this fall.
戲劇學院將在這個秋天演出《哈姆雷特》。

6) **adaptation** [ˌædæpˈteʃən] (n.) 改編，改寫
The director is working on an adaptation of *Macbeth*.
那位導演正致力於《馬克白》的改編。

7) **haughty** [ˈhɔti] (a.) 高傲的，自大的
I could tell by his haughty expression that he didn't like me.
從他那自大的表情看得出來，他並不喜歡我。

8) **interpretation** [ɪn.tɜprəˈteʃən] (n.) 詮釋，解釋
The actor's interpretation of Hamlet won him several awards.
那位演員所詮釋的哈姆雷特為他贏得一些獎項。

9) **version** [ˈvɝʒən] (n.) 版本
Which version of Windows do you have on your computer?
你的電腦是安裝哪一版本的 Windows 軟體？

10) **sequel** [ˈsikwəl] (n.) 續集
I think the sequel's even better than the original.
我覺得續集還比第一集更好。

11) **gay** [ge] (a./n.) 同性戀的；同性戀
Do you have any gay friends?
你有任何同性戀朋友嗎？

12) **professor** [prəˈfɛsɚ] (n.) 教授
The professor gave a lecture on Russian history.
這位教授發表俄國歷史的演講。

柯林佛斯於 1960 年九月十日出生在英國南部的格雷夏村。佛斯的雙親皆為大學老師，因此全家人常因工作之故四處搬遷，曾待過奈及利亞、美國和英國各地，最後才在溫徹斯特市安住下來。雖然他年僅五歲就開始在學校話劇中演出，不過卻沒有對演戲培養多大興趣，直到他在十四歲時暗戀上戲劇老師。佛斯對演戲的愛好變得十分強烈，他甚至在十八歲那一年自大學輟學，好搬到倫敦追求演藝生涯。

佛斯先是到皇家國立劇場的戲服部門工作一陣子，然後進入倫敦戲劇中心就讀三年。他在戲劇中心飾演哈姆雷特時被劇作家朱利安米謝爾發掘，並給予機會在 1983 年倫敦西區上演的《同窗之愛》擔任主角。隔年佛斯又雀屏中選、擔綱演出電影版的《同窗之愛》而初登大銀幕。雖然他此後接演了不少電影和電視角色，不過要等到他在 1995 年英國廣播公司製作的《傲慢與偏見》影集中扮演高傲的達西先生，這才成為家喻戶曉的明星。

佛斯所詮釋的達西先生相當受歡迎，以至於這個角色在現代版的《傲慢與偏見》、也就是 2001 年的賣座浪漫喜劇《BJ 單身日記》中，以馬克達西的身分被搬上大銀幕。雖然佛斯因此在《BJ 單身日記》續集和《愛是您・愛是我》等電影中接演更多浪漫角色，不過這位演員最為成功的表演還是在嚴肅的劇情片裡。佛斯於 2009 年的《摯愛無盡》裡飾演一位同性戀英國教授而首度獲得奧斯卡提名，兩年後再以《王者之聲：宣戰時刻》中詮釋英王喬治六世的精采表現而獲得奧斯卡最佳男主角獎。

Tongue-tied No More

have a crush on sb. 暗戀某人，對某人動情
crush 在口語中有「暗戀」的意思，當我們說 have a crush on sb. 或 get a crush on sb. 就表示對某人產生心動、迷戀的感覺。

A: I hear Cindy has a crush on our history teacher.
我聽說辛蒂很暗戀我們的歷史老師。

B: Eww, gross!
唷，好噁喔！

111

Jane 珍奧斯汀
Austen

位於英國漢普郡的珍奧斯汀博物館 (Jane Austen's House Museum)

© Featureflash / Shutterstock.com

Language Guide

Hampshire 珍奧斯汀的故鄉

漢普郡位於英國東南方，是英國 48 個名譽郡（ceremonial county）之一，郡治為溫徹斯特（Winchester），並有南安普頓（Southampton）和普次茅斯（Portsmouth）兩大沿海城市。除了珍奧斯汀之外，漢普郡也是著名作家狄更斯（Charles Dickens）的出生地。

而喬頓（Chawton）這個小村落位於東漢普郡，珍奧斯汀在這裡度過生命中的最後八年。當時她和母親、姊姊住在被稱為 Chawton Cottage 的小屋中，在此修改《理性與感性》、《傲慢與偏見》、《曼斯菲爾德莊園》的手稿，並完成接下來的三部著作。如今這棟小屋已成為博物館 Jane Austen's House Museum，收藏珍奧斯汀的手稿和遺物，供珍迷們緬懷這位偉大的作家。

🎧 31

Jane Austen was born on September 16, 1775 in Steventon, a small village in the county of Hampshire in southern England. The seventh of eight children, Jane grew up in a large, happy family. Although her Oxford-educated father and [1]**aristocratic** mother both came from [2]**landed gentry**, the family was **by no means** wealthy. Unusual for their time, Jane's parents believed that all their children—including their two daughters—should receive a formal education. Unfortunately, her father's [3]**modest** salary as [4]**minister** of the local church was only enough to provide Jane and her older sister Cassandra with two years of study at a [5]**boarding school** in Reading. But the education she received after returning home would prove even more valuable.

Given full [6]**access** to her father's [7]**extensive** library, and with her father and older brothers as guides, Jane began reading all the important novels, poetry and histories of the day. [8]**Inspired** by authors like Samuel Johnson and Henry Fielding, at the age of 12 she began writing stories, poems and plays for her family's [9]**amusement**. Works that survive from that time include *Love and Friendship*, a [10]**parody** of romantic novels of her day, which she found too [11]**sentimental**. By her late teens, Jane had decided that she wanted to become a professional writer, possibly inspired by her experiences attending balls and other social events at great houses around the Hampshire countryside. It was at such an event that she met Tom Lefroy, a young Irish law graduate, at the age of 20. The two soon fell in love, but neither had the wealth required for marriage, so Lefroy's parents made sure that they never saw each other again.

珍奧斯汀於 1775 年九月十六日出生在英國南部漢普郡的小村落史蒂文頓。八個小孩中排行老七的她，自小在一個和樂融融的大家庭中成長。珍的雙親皆來自坐擁土地的仕紳家族，父親畢業自牛津大學、母親則屬貴族世家，但他們一家人卻一點也不富有。不同於當時一般想法，珍的父母認為他們的所有孩子──包括兩個女兒──都應接受正式教育。不幸的是，他父親身為當地教堂牧師的微薄薪水，僅能供珍和姐姐卡珊卓拉在雷丁鎮的寄宿學校就讀兩年而已。不過事後證明，她返家後在家中受到的教育更加重要。

珍獲准取閱她父親豐富的藏書，再加上她父親和兄長們的從旁引導，她開始閱讀起當時所有重要的小說、詩詞和史書。深受塞繆爾詹森與亨利菲爾丁等作家的啟發，年僅十二歲的她開始寫起故事、詩作和劇本以娛樂家人。這個階段仍流傳至今的的創作包括《愛與友誼》，這是一本反諷作品，嘲弄她認為過於多愁善感的當代愛情小說。到了青少年時代後期，珍決定成為一位全職作家，這或許是因為她在漢普郡鄉間的莊園參加各種舞會等社交場合的經驗而起。她正是在這類的場合中，於二十歲那一年邂逅了湯姆勒弗伊，一位年輕的愛爾蘭法律畢業生。兩人迅速墜入愛河，但雙方都沒有足夠的錢成親，於是勒弗伊的父母出手干預，確保他們從此不會再度碰面。

© tristan tan / Shutterstock.com
© irisphoto1 / Shutterstock.com
© irisphoto1 / Shutterstock.com

英國於 1975 年發行珍奧斯汀紀念郵票，票面上的人物為《諾桑覺寺》凱瑟琳莫蘭

《傲慢與偏見》達西先生

《艾瑪》艾瑪及她的父親伍德豪斯先生

Tongue-tied No More

by no means 絕不、一點也不

means 當名詞用是指「手段、方法」，by no means 代表「絕不，一點也不」的意思；另外常見 means 的用法還有 by all means（用盡各種方法）

A: Was your trip to Europe expensive?
你的歐洲行花了很多錢嗎？
B: It was by no means cheap, but it was worth it.
真的一點都不便宜，但是很值得。

Vocabulary Bank

1) **aristocratic** [ə,rɪstə`krætɪk] (a.) 貴族的，儀態高貴的
The actress comes from an aristocratic family.
那位女演員出身貴族家庭。

2) **landed gentry** (n.) 鄉紳
England's landed gentry began to decline in the 20th century.
英國的鄉紳階級自二十世紀開始沒落。

3) **modest** [`mɑdɪst] (a.) 不太多的，適度的
It's hard to support a family on such a modest salary.
這樣微薄的薪水很難養活一家人。

4) **minister** [`mɪnɪstə] (n.) 牧師，神職人員
The minister at our church is retiring next year.
我們教堂的牧師明年就要退休了。

5) **boarding school** (n.) 寄宿學校
Kevin's parents sent him to a Catholic boarding school.
凱文的爸媽送他到天主教寄宿學校讀書。

6) **access** [`æksɛs] (n.)（可以）使用，（可以）取得
Few students in Africa have access to computers.
在非洲只有少數學生有電腦可用。

7) **extensive** [ɪk`stɛnsɪv] (a.) 廣泛的，廣大的
Out professor has extensive knowledge of Greek history.
我們的教授對希臘歷史有相當廣泛的了解。

8) **inspire** [ɪn`spaɪr] (v.) 激勵，賦予…靈感
inspiration [,ɪnspə`reʃən] (n.) 靈感
Our trip to France inspired us to take French lessons.
法國之旅激勵我們報名法文課程。

9) **amusement** [ə`mjuzmənt] (n.) 娛樂，娛樂活動，趣味
Steve plays the guitar just for his own amusement.
史提夫玩吉他只是為了自娛。

10) **parody** [`pærədi] (n./v.) 諧仿，嘲仿
The movie is a parody of popular scary movies.
這部電影是對熱門恐怖電影的諧仿。

11) **sentimental** [,sɛntə`mɛntəl] (a.) 多愁善感的，傷感的
The singer recorded an album of sentimental love songs.
這位歌手錄了張感傷情歌專輯。

Language Guide

珍奧斯汀的愛情名言

當我們討論愛情，我們討論的是……？沒有人知道愛情究竟是什麼，但你也許可以從文學作品中找到一些解答。珍奧斯汀的六部小說，無一不是以婚姻和愛情為主題，而其中不乏詼諧、幽默或嘲諷的語句，即使到了二十一世紀的今天，仍然值得渴望愛情的善男信女們參考。

Sense and Sensibility

- If I could but know his heart, everything would become easy.

  如果我能看穿他的心，一切就會簡單得多。

Pride and Prejudice

- It is a truth universally acknowledged, that a single man in possession of a good fortune, must be in want of a wife.

  這是一個舉世公認的事實：每個黃金單身漢，都缺個老婆。

Mansfield Park

- Good-humored, unaffected girls will not do for a man who has been used to sensible women. They are two distinct orders of being.

  對於一個和聰慧的女性交往慣了的男人來說，溫和、單純的女孩是不夠的。她們屬於不同的等級。

Emma

- I lay it down as a general rule, Harriet, that if a woman doubts as to whether she should accept a man or not, she certainly ought to refuse him.

  哈麗葉，我有一條原則：如果一個女人無法決定是否要接受一個男人，那麼她就該拒絕他。

Northanger Abbey

- Friendship is certainly the finest balm for the pangs of disappointed love.

  友情無疑是情傷最好的撫慰。

Persuasion

- I hate to hear you talk about all women as if they were fine ladies instead of rational creatures. None of us want to be in calm waters all our lives.

  我厭惡聽到你這樣談論女人，彷彿她們都只能是養尊處優的淑女，而不是理性的生物。我們沒有人想要平淡的度過一生。

After this experience, Jane **threw herself into** her writing, completing the rough [1]**drafts** for what would eventually become her first two novels—*Sense and Sensibility* and *Pride and Prejudice*—in her early 20s. It was likely no [2]**coincidence** that these novels [3]**explored** the themes of love, marriage and class in an unsentimental manner. In 1800, when Jane was 25, her father retired and moved to the [4]**resort** town of Bath with his wife and daughters. But Jane disliked town life, and without inspiration her writing nearly came to a stop. When her father died, the family lived with a series of relatives until her brother Edward, who had married into a wealthy family, provided them with a small house on his Hampshire [5]**estate** in 1809.

Back in the countryside she loved, Jane began writing again, completing final drafts of *Sense and Sensibility* and *Pride and Prejudice*. With help from her brother Henry, a London banker, she had the two novels published to modest success. But because Jane published her works [6]**anonymously**, they didn't bring her any fame. Over the next few years, she [7]**put out** *Mansfield Park* and *Emma*, both of which were well received. But just as Jane was completing her next novel and starting another, she suddenly fell ill and died soon after in 1817, at the age of 41. On her [8]**tombstone** at Winchester [9]**Cathedral**, there was no mention of her [10]**profession**. Henry arranged to have Jane's last two novels, *Northanger Abbey* and *Persuasion*, published as a set later that year, finally revealing her true identity in a biographical note. But Jane was largely forgotten until her nephew James published *A Memoir of Jane Austen* in 1896. Critics have since recognized her literary [11]**genius**, and she is now considered one of the greatest English novelists of all time.

在如此傷心的經歷後，珍全心投入寫作之中，並在二十出頭完成了兩本著作的草稿，也就是後來成為她頭兩本小說的《理性與感性》及《傲慢與偏見》。而這兩本小說以毫不感情用事的方式探索愛情、婚姻和階級等主題，似乎一點也不顯得意外。1800 年，當珍芳齡二十五之時，她父親因退休而攜妻帶女搬遷至巴斯這座度假小鎮。但珍厭惡城鎮生活，而缺乏靈感的結果也導致她幾乎停筆寫作。珍的父親過世後，他們一家人接連投奔多位親戚，直到她與有錢人家結親的哥哥愛德華於 1809 年在他的莊園裡找了間小房子供他們居住。

回到自己所鐘愛的鄉間生活，珍再度開始提筆創作，完成了《理性與感性》及《傲慢與偏見》的定稿。在身為倫敦銀行家的哥哥亨利協助下，她找人發行了這兩本小說，市場上也小有佳績。但由於珍是以匿名方式出版她的創作，因此並未替她帶來任何名聲。在接下來的數年間，她先後出版了頗受好評的《曼斯菲爾德莊園》和《艾瑪》。不過正當珍即將完成下一本小說並開

始另一本之際，她卻突然染病，不久之後便於 1817 年辭世，享年四十一歲。她位於溫徹斯特大教堂的墓碑上並未提及她的職業。亨利於當年稍後安排以成套方式出版珍的最後兩本小說——《諾桑覺寺》與《勸導》，且終於在作者生平簡介裡透露了她的真實身分。不過在珍的外甥於 1896 年出版《珍奧斯汀回憶錄》之前，她幾乎為世人所遺忘。後來文評家不但認同了她的文采，她如今也被公認是有史以來最偉大的英國小說家之一。

Tongue-tied No More

throw oneself into... 全心投入某事

動詞 throw 是「投擲、拋」的意思，而 throw oneself into sth. 就表示某人把自己投入某事，全心專注於這件事上。

A: What did Frank do after his divorce?
　　法蘭克離婚後都在做什麼？
B: He threw himself into his work.
　　他全心投入他的工作。

珍奧斯汀葬於溫徹斯特大教堂

 34

Vocabulary Bank

1) **draft** [dræft] (n./v.) 草稿；草擬
Have you finished the final draft of your paper?
你完成論文的最終稿了嗎？

2) **coincidence** [koˋɪnsɪdəns] (n.) 巧合
What a coincidence that we both wore the same shirt today!
真巧，我們今天穿同樣的衣服！

3) **explore** [ɪkˋsplor] (v.) 瞭解，探究，探索
You should explore your options before you choose a major.
在選擇主修科系之前，你應該先探索所有可選擇的科目。

4) **resort** [rɪˋzɔrt] (n.) 度假村，度假勝地
We spent our vacation at a beach resort in Hawaii.
我們在夏威夷的海灘度假村度假。

5) **estate** [ɪˋstet] (n.) 地產，莊園
The estate includes a big house, a tennis court and swimming pool.
這個莊園包含了一間大房子、網球場和游泳池。

6) **anonymously** [əˋnɑnɪməsli] (adv.) 不具名地，匿名地
anonymous [əˋnɑnɪməs] (a.) 不具名地，匿名地
The hotline allows people to report crimes anonymously.
這支熱線提供大眾匿名通報犯罪事件。

7) **put out** [put aut] (phr.) 出版，發行
I hear Mariah Carey is putting out a new album.
我聽說瑪麗亞凱莉要發行新專輯了。

8) **tombstone** [ˋtum.ston] (n.) 墓碑，墓石
Can you read what's written on this tombstone?
你讀得懂這座墓碑上寫了什麼嗎？

9) **cathedral** [kəˋθidrəl] (n.) 大教堂
Notre Dame is France's tallest cathedral.
聖母院是法國最高的大教堂。

10) **profession** [prəˋfɛʃən] (n.)（受過專門訓練的）職業
I'm considering a career in the legal profession.
我在考慮以法律專業為職業。

11) **genius** [ˋdʒinjəs] (n.) 天賦，天才
The artist's genius was only recognized after his death.
這位藝術家的天才直到死後才被人認可。

最浪漫文學家——珍奧斯汀

改編影視作品

Sense and Sensibility《理性與感性》

《理性與感性》是珍奧斯汀於 1811 年發表的首部作品。書中主角為達斯伍姐妹，長姐艾蓮娜（Elinor Dashwood）代表「理性」，個性穩重、內斂，即使因愛情傷透了心，仍為了他人著想而壓抑自身情感；妹妹瑪麗安（Marianne Dashwwod）則代表「感性」，個性熱情、衝動，毫不掩飾自己的感情，更不顧一切愛上迷人但花心的男孩。珍奧斯汀透過對人性細微的觀察，描寫出個性截然不同的姐妹面對愛情時的態度。

《理性與感性》電影（1995）

1995 年的《理性與感性》是李安首部執導的英語片，分別由艾瑪湯普森（Emma Thompson）及凱特溫斯蕾（Kate Winslet）飾演姊姊艾蓮娜、妹妹瑪麗安；而兩姐妹的追求者愛德華（Edward）及布蘭登上校（Colonel Brandon）則由休葛蘭（Hugh Grant）和艾倫瑞克曼（Alan Rickman）擔綱。這部《理性與感性》被譽為最成功的珍奧斯汀作品改編電影，入圍了七項奧斯卡提名，最後由女主角兼任編劇的艾瑪湯普森得到最佳改編劇本的獎項。

《理性與感性》影集（2008）

由 BBC 拍攝的《理性與感性》迷你影集（miniseries）共有三個版本，分別拍攝於 1971、1981 及 2008 年，總長皆約三小時。2008 年版本的編劇 Andrew Davis 是著名的英國劇作家，他擅長文學作品改編，除了《理性與感性》外，也曾在 1995 年改編《傲慢與偏見》影集；而他也是「現代版《傲慢與偏見》」《BJ 單身日記》的編劇之一。

Pride and Prejudice《傲慢與偏見》

《傲慢與偏見》於 1813 年發表，是珍奧斯汀最廣為人知的作品。故事背景在十九世紀初的英國，當時多數女性無法受教育，自然也沒有工作能力，因此保障自己和家人生活的唯一方式就是找個好歸宿嫁了。也因此，家中有五個女兒的班奈特太太（Mrs. Bennet）最大的願望就是將女兒們嫁給有錢的紳士。這時富有的賓利先生（Charles Bingley）搬進附近的莊園，他和朋友達西先生（Fitzwilliam Darcy）引起班奈特一家的注意，之後也各自和大姐珍（Jane）、二姐伊麗莎白（Elizabeth）產生若有似無的情愫……。

《傲慢與偏見》電影（2005）

2005 年的《傲慢與偏見》由喬萊特（Joe Wright）執導，綺拉奈特莉（Keira Knightley）及馬修麥費狄恩（Matthew Macfadyen）分別飾演伊莉莎白、達西先生。由於 BBC 在 1995 年所拍攝的《傲慢與偏見》影集實在太過經典，電影版勢必做些更動才能和影集有所區隔；也因此編劇將時代背景由十九世紀初提前到十八世紀末，並強調班奈特一家的經濟處境，以和富裕的賓利及達西先生形成對比。

《傲慢與偏見》影集（1995）

BBC 在 1938 年播出首部《傲慢與偏見》改編影集，之後分別在 1938、1952、1958、1967、1980 和 1995 重新拍攝，因此《傲慢與偏見》可說是珍奧斯汀小說中最常被搬上螢幕的作品。而 1995 年播出的《傲慢與偏見》至今仍被視為影視史上的經典，柯林佛斯（Colin Firth）將達西先生詮釋得惟妙惟肖，已成為當代少女心目中傲嬌好男人的最佳代表，據說《BJ 單身日記》中的馬克達西（Mark Darcy）就是為他量身打造的角色呢。

愛情永遠是文學作品最常探討的主題，而珍奧斯汀筆下所刻劃的愛情，除了呈現男女間微妙的情感，也反映十八世紀末、十九世紀初的社會氛圍。雖然她只留下六部長篇小說，但其改編、翻拍的電影和戲劇不計其數，可見她的作品對現代的婚姻及愛情觀仍有不可抹滅的影響。

Mansfield Park《曼斯菲爾德莊園》

《曼斯菲爾德莊園》出版於 1814 年，是珍奧斯汀的第三部作品。主角芬妮（Fanny Price）家境貧困，從小就被送到曼斯菲爾德莊園和富有的貝特倫一家——姨丈托馬斯（Sir Thomas Bertram）、阿姨（Lady Bertram）以及他們的四名子女同住。長期寄人籬下的生活使芬妮的個性性格內向、自卑，在嬌寵而個性放蕩的表兄妹中，善良的表哥愛德蒙（Edmund Bertram）是芬妮唯一較親近的同伴，而芬妮對他的感激也隨著年紀增長轉為愛慕之情。某一天，多金又迷人的亨利（Henry Crawford）和瑪麗（Mary Crawford）兄妹來此作客，平靜的曼斯菲爾德莊園也因他們而掀起一陣波瀾。

· ·

《窈窕野淑女》（1999）

1999 年改編自《曼斯菲爾德莊園》的《窈窕野淑女》，看片名就知道和原著差異甚大，畢竟珍奧斯汀所設定的芬妮個性可是一點都不「野」。此片由加拿大前衛導演派翠西雅羅賽瑪（Patricia Rozema）執導，她大幅更動原著設定，在電影中強化了芬妮的個性，並將作者珍

奧斯汀的影子投射其中，使芬妮變得更獨立自主、有原則。除此之外，羅賽瑪也將原著中較隱晦的感情與金錢糾葛、甚至敏感的黑奴議題以較清楚的方式呈現於電影中，雖然不怎麼「忠於原著」，但也不失為一部大破大立的作品。

Becoming Jane《珍愛來臨》

（1999）

《珍愛來臨》並非由珍奧斯汀小說改編，而是根據珍奧斯汀研究者 Jon Hunter Spence 所著之 Becoming Jane Austen 所拍攝的傳記式電影。電影描述年輕的珍奧斯汀（Anne Hathaway 飾）遇見愛爾蘭法律學生勒弗伊先生（Tom Lefroy, James McAvoy 飾），起先兩人互看不順

眼，卻隨著相處時間增加、對文學藝術的討論，漸漸對對方產生好感。然而，奧斯汀的母親希望她嫁給有錢的衛斯理先生，而勒弗伊家境貧困，若要結婚也需經過身為經濟來源的舅舅同意……。《珍愛來臨》藉著參考珍奧斯汀的書信、作品詮釋她的情史，讓喜愛珍奧斯汀的讀者一窺這位經典作家的感情生活。

Emma《艾瑪》

《艾瑪》出版於 1815 年，是珍奧斯汀生前發表的最後一部作品。有別於《理性與感性》中的達斯伍姐妹、《傲慢與偏見》中的班奈特姐妹、以及《曼斯菲爾德莊園》中家境貧困的芬妮，艾瑪可說是珍奧斯汀筆下主角中，唯一不需為麵包煩惱或得依附婚姻而急著嫁掉的少女。富有而漂亮的艾瑪過著無憂無慮的生活，平時最大的樂趣便是為她的閨蜜們物色好男人。在成功嫁掉她的家庭老師後，艾瑪又開始為朋友哈麗葉（Harriet Smith）做媒，不料卻一次次失算，直到哈麗葉坦誠仰慕艾瑪的朋友奈特利（George Knightley）先生，艾瑪才發現自己對奈特利先生的情感……。

· ·

《獨領風騷》（1995）

珍奧斯汀在寫作 Emma 時，大概萬萬想不到這部作品會在日後被改編成高中校園喜劇《獨領風騷》（Clueless），成為 YA 片經典之一。這部改編自《艾瑪》的電影將故事背景搬到美國比佛利山莊的高中，而原著中女主角艾瑪則成了校園風雲人物雪兒（Cher，Alicia Silverstone 飾）。雪

兒是個富有但膚淺的高中女孩，對她來說，每天去學校的穿著打扮遠比數學考幾分重要。然而她也心地善良，除了極力促成兩位老師的緣份之外，也想幫助新同學泰（Tai，Brittany Murphy 飾）改頭換面，成為校園裡的明星人物。雪兒的繼兄喬許（Josh，Paul Rudd 飾）看不慣雪兒的無腦作風，老是和她鬥嘴，而他正是衍生自原著中奈特利先生的角色。

《艾瑪姑娘要出嫁》（1996）

1996 年的《艾瑪姑娘要出嫁》正是改編自珍奧斯汀第四本著作《艾瑪》。通常珍奧斯汀改編電影都由英國演員擔綱主角，《艾瑪姑娘要出嫁》卻由美國演員葛妮絲派特洛（Gwyneth Paltrow）出演；她特有的古典美氣質、以及模仿得無懈可擊的英國腔頗受好評，甚至有影迷以為她是英國

人呢！她也因此得到其他英國角色的演出機會，並在兩年後以《莎翁情史》（Shakespeare in Love）拿下奧斯卡最佳女主角獎項。

愛的控制慾

企圖改變對方，要對方的言行思想照著自己的期望走，那是真愛？還是其實愛上的只是幻想中的那個人？控制和佔有，最初或許是為了維繫兩人的感情，只是走到最後，這種方式往往演變成一道讓雙方陷入痛苦深淵的枷鎖。

驚悚愛情片
大導演
Adrian Lyne

《愛你九週半》和《致命吸引力》這兩部電影的導演艾德萊恩（Adrian Lyne），出生於英國，深受法國新浪潮電影的影響，擅長運用禁忌的男女關係題材，藉由電影給觀眾一個震撼的道德教育。除了《愛你九週半》和《致命吸引力》，他執導的知名作品還有《桃色交易》、《時空攔截》等。

充滿爭議性的《愛你九週半》，改編自半自傳式的同名小說。《致命吸引力》是艾德萊恩的第四部電影，這部電影在全球票房已累積達六億美元，被《時代雜誌》標榜為「反映近十年來時代精神的成功之作」（the zeitgeist hit of the decade），更獲得奧斯卡六項提名，包括最佳女主角、最佳女配角、最佳剪輯、最佳影片、最佳導演、最佳編劇。

《愛你九週半》

畫廊助理伊麗莎白（Elizabeth，Kim Basinger 飾）剛和丈夫離婚，偶然認識了華爾街經理人約翰（John，Mickey Rourke 飾），自信、主動的約翰讓伊麗莎白完全無法抵抗他的誘惑，和他玩起熱烈的性愛遊戲，兩人的關係也因此越來越複雜。

John: I don't want to meet anybody. I really don't want to meet anybody. I just want to be with you.
我不想再認識任何人，我真的不想認識任何人。我只想跟妳在一起。

I'll start the dishes. Let me tell you something. You don't do dishes. You don't ever have to do dishes. I'll do the dishes. And I'll buy the groceries. And I'll cook the food. And I'll feed you. And I'll dress you in the morning. And I'll undress you at night. And I'll bathe you. And I'll take care of you.
我來洗碗。我跟妳講，妳不用洗碗，永遠都不用。我來洗碗，我來買菜，我來煮飯。我餵妳吃飯。早上幫妳穿衣服，晚上幫妳脫衣服。我幫妳洗澡，我會照顧妳。

And you can see your friends in the daytime. I just want the nighttime, from now on, to be ours.
白天妳可以見朋友，我只要晚上⋯⋯從現在起⋯⋯晚上只屬於我們兩人。

John: Elizabeth, Elizabeth, I love you. Would you please come back, by the time I count to fifty? One….
伊麗莎白，伊麗莎白，我愛妳，在我數到五十之前，請妳回來好嗎？一⋯⋯。

John: Every time I see you, you're buying a chicken.
每次看見妳，妳都是在買雞。

Elizabeth: Every time I see you, you're smiling at me.
每次看見你，你都在對我微笑。

Elizabeth: How did you know? How did you know I'd respond to you the way I have?
你怎麼知道？你怎麼知道我會對你有如此的回應？

John: I saw myself in you.
因為我在妳身上看到自己。

9½ Weeks

《致命吸引力》

家庭幸福的已婚男子丹（Dan，Michael Douglas 飾），偶然跟女編輯亞莉絲（Alex，Glenn Close 飾）發生一夜情。丹想回歸正常的家庭生活，但表面成熟知性的亞莉絲，其實內心占有慾極為強烈，不願放手，並開始跟蹤他們一家，做出許多可怕行為。

Dan: Why are you trying to hurt me?
妳為什麼要傷害我？

Alex: I'm not trying to hurt you Dan, I love you!
我沒有要傷害你，丹，我愛你！

Dan: You what?
什麼？

Alex: I love you!
我愛你！

Dan: You don't even know me.
妳根本不認識我。

Alex: How can you say that?
你怎麼能這麼說？

Alex: I just wanna be a part of your life.
我只是想融入你的生活。

Dan: This is the way you do it, huh? Showing up at my apartment?
妳用這種方式？出現在我家？

Alex: Well, what am I supposed to do? You won't answer my calls, you change your number. I mean, I'm not gonna be ignored, Dan!
那我該怎麼做？你不接我的電話，又換了號碼。我是說，丹，你不能不理我。

Alex: Hello, Dan. Are you surprised? This is what you've reduced me to. I guess you thought you'd get away with it. Well, you can't. Because part of you is growing inside of me...and that's a fact, Dan, and you'd better start learning how to deal with it.
哈囉，丹。你驚訝嗎？是你害我變成這樣的。我猜你一定以為可以逃開，但是你沒辦法。因為我肚子裡已經有你的骨肉了……這是真的，丹，你最好要開始學著接受。

Alex: 'Cause, you know, I feel you. I taste you. I think you. I touch you. Can you understand? Can you? I'm just asking you to acknowledge your responsibilities. Is that so bad? I don't think so. I don't think it's unreasonable.
因為，你知道的，我感覺得到你，我感受得到你的氣息，我知道你的心思，我摸得到你。你懂嗎？懂嗎？我只是想要你負起你的責任。不好嗎？我不覺得。我不覺得這有什麼不合理。

Alex: And, you know, another thing is that...you thought you could just walk into my life and turn it upside down, without a thought for anyone but yourself.
而且，還有一件事……你以為你可以就這麼走進我的生活，把我的人生攪得亂七八糟，而不替人家著想，只考慮你自己。

Fatal Attraction

Glenn Close 銀幕壞女人

《致命吸引力》*Fatal Attraction* 中，最令人印象深刻、把當時整個中壯年世代男人嚇破膽的橋段，就是葛倫克蘿斯（Glenn Close）主演，由愛生恨的女主角亞莉絲（Alex）潛入男主角家中，把他女兒飼養的兔子給煮了！讓 bunny boiler（煮兔子的人）在英國成為通用俚語，表示「情緒不穩定、復仇心重、嫉妒心強、有控制欲的女人」。

葛倫克蘿斯一共三次被提名奧斯卡最佳女主角，其中兩片《危險關係》、《致命吸引力》當中，她都扮演令人毛骨悚然的壞女人，另外她最為大眾熟悉的角色——迪士尼真人版《一〇一忠狗》*101 Dalmatians* 當中想抓小狗來剝皮做大衣的庫伊拉（Cruella de Vil），更是壞到連狗都發抖。當今好萊塢最壞女人，葛倫克蘿斯應該是當之無愧了。

《危險關係》

葛倫克蘿斯（Glenn Close）飾演守寡的法國貴婦梅黛侯爵夫人（Marquise de Merteuil），因丈夫一生花心而存心報復，刻意在上流社會圈中挑撥感情、勾引人夫、破壞婚姻，作為對愛情的嘲諷。以下這段話，說明了她對愛情幻滅、只要能自保就不怕遊戲人間的「理論」：

Merteuil: When I came out into society I was 15. I already knew that the role I was condemned to, namely to keep quiet and do what I was told, gave me the perfect opportunity to listen and observe.
當我十五歲甫入社交圈，就已經知道我被賦予的角色，被要求必須貞靜、服從，這讓我有好好傾聽學習的機會。

Not to what people told me, which naturally was of no interest, but to whatever it was they were trying to hide. I practiced *detachment. I learned how to look cheerful while under the table I stuck a fork into the back of my hand. I became a *virtuoso of *deceit.
我學的不是人家告訴我的，那些全都無聊得要命，而是他們試圖遮掩的。我練習把自己抽離。我學會強顏歡笑，儘管在桌面下我恨得拿叉子戳手背。我成為騙人高手。

It wasn't pleasure I was after, it was knowledge. I consulted the strictest moralists to learn how to appear, philosophers to find out what to think, and novelists to see what I could get away with, and in the end, I *distilled everything to one wonderfully simple principle: win or die.
我追求的不是愉悅，而是知識。我向最嚴格的道德家請益應對進退之道，向哲學家學習思考，與小說家共商脫罪的手段，到了最後，我精煉出一條簡單而完美的原則：不是贏，就是死。

*detachment [dɪˋtætʃmənt] (n.) 超脫，客觀無私
*virtuoso [ˌvɝtʃuˋoso] (n.)（藝術、古董）行家，收藏家
*deceit [dɪˋsit] (n.) 欺詐
*distill [dɪsˋtɪl] (v.) 精煉，蒸餾

Dangerous Liaisons

《瘋流美之活人生切》

內向、自卑又有弱視的美（May，Angela Bettis 飾），從小就是沒有朋友的怪咖，孤僻成性的她長大後在獸醫院擔任外科助理，由於舉止怪異，都沒人敢接近她。後來認識了初戀對象亞當（Adam，Jeremy Sisto 飾），不料美對亞當的愛戀越來越深，行徑也越來越誇張，嚇跑了亞當，失戀的她萬念俱灰，倍感孤獨，甚至突發奇想來自己「訂做」一個好朋友……。

May: You don't think I'm weird?
你不覺得我很怪嗎？

Adam: I do think you're weird.
我是覺得妳很怪。

May: I knew that.
我知道。

Adam: I like weird. I like weird a lot.
我喜歡怪啊。我超喜歡怪的。

May: I'll bet you're wondering what I'm making! Okay, I'll tell you. I saw someone today. A boy.

[對著洋娃娃說] 我猜你在好奇我在做什麼對吧！好，我告訴你吧。我今天看到一個人。一個男生。

You know how when you meet someone... and you think you like them? And then, the more you talk to them, you see parts that you don't like. Like that guy on the bench. And sometimes, you end up not liking any parts at all.
你知道和某人相遇是怎麼回事嗎？你覺得你喜歡他，接著你越跟他們說話，就會發現你不喜歡他們的地方。就像是坐在長椅上的那個人一樣。有時候，到最後你會一點也不喜歡他們。

But this boy is different. I like every part of him. Especially his hands, they're beautiful.
但這男孩不一樣。他每個部分我都喜歡。尤其是他的雙手，好美喔。

[pause] Don't be mad, you've been my friend my whole life. And you see me, you always have, but... I need a real friend. Someone I can hold.
[停頓一下]
別生氣，你這輩子都是我的朋友。而且你總是這麼了解我，但是……我需要一個真的朋友。一個我能擁抱的人。

May

Sebastian: You amaze me.
妳令我大開眼界。

Kathryn: Eat me, Sebastian! It's okay for guys like you and Court to fuck everyone. But when I do it, I get dumped for innocent little *twits like Cecile. God forbid, I *exude confidence and enjoy sex.
去死吧，薩巴斯丁！你和寇特這種男生就可以到處睡。我這麼做，卻因為出現了個「純真無邪」的小白癡瑟茜害我被甩。天理何在，我只是散發自信而且喜歡性愛而已。

Do you think I relish the fact that I have to act like *Mary Sunshine 24/7 so I can be considered a lady? I'm the *Marcia Brady of the Upper East Side, and sometimes I want to kill myself. So there's your psychoanalysis, Dr. Freud. Now tell me, are you in... or are you out?
妳以為我甘心表現得像「全天候陽光美少女」那樣才能被當作淑女嗎？我是紐約的瑪西雅布萊蒂，有時候我想自殺。這就是你要的心理分析，佛洛伊德博士。現在告訴我，你到底要不要玩這遊戲？

Kathryn: You were very much in love with her. And you're still in love with her. But it amused me to make you ashamed of it. You gave up on the first person you ever loved because I threatened your reputation.
你深深地愛上了她。而且你現在還是很愛她。看你如此窘迫真是讓我開懷啊。你放棄了你第一次真正愛上的人，只因為我威脅會毀了你的名聲。

Don't you get it? You're just a toy, Sebastian. A little toy I like to play with. And now you've completely blown it with her. I think it's the saddest thing I've ever heard.
你還不懂嗎？你只是個玩具，薩巴斯丁。給我樂子的小玩具。現在你跟她玩完了。我覺得這真是我聽過最可悲的事了。

Sebastian: You spend all your time preaching about waiting for love. Well here it is. Right in front of you, and you're going to turn your back on it. So I guess we're just fucked. I'll move on. But you are going to have to live the rest of your life knowing that you've turned your back on love. And that makes you a hypocrite. Have a nice life.
妳花了老半天向我說教，說什麼要等待真愛。現在就是了啊。真愛就站在你面前，然後妳卻不理不睬。所以我想我們是玩完了吧。我會放下的。但妳會用盡整個餘生意識到妳將真愛拒之門外，把自己變成個虛偽的人。祝妳有個美好人生。

*twit [twɪt] (n.)（口）白癡，笨蛋
*exude [ɪɡˈzjud] (v.) 滲出，散發
*24/7 讀作 twenty-four seven，指「一周七天，一天二十四小時」，用來形容「隨時，一直」
*Marcia Brady 是七〇年代極受歡迎影集《脫線家族》（The Brady Bunch）當中的長女，是個美麗、成熟、好人緣的女孩，

Cruel Intentions

《危險性遊戲》

凱薩琳（Kathryn Merteuil，Sarah Michelle Gellar 飾）和薩巴斯丁（Sebastian Valmont，Ryan Phillippe 飾）是有錢人家的異姓姊弟，由於凱薩琳的男友看上了純真的瑟茜（Cecile Caldwell，Selma Blair 飾）而把她甩了，因此凱薩琳懷恨在心，慫恿薩巴斯丁把瑟茜教育成蕩婦，不過薩巴斯丁卻看上了新校長的女兒安妮（Annette Hargrove，Reese Witherspoon 飾），於是凱薩琳便跟薩巴斯丁打賭，若他能在開學前引誘安妮上床，凱薩琳便為薩巴斯丁提供一夜的性服務，於是一場危險性遊戲就此展開……。

有史以來最偉大的小說之一《危險關係》

《危險性遊戲》與《危險關係》都改編自十八世紀法國作家拉克洛（Pierre Choderlos de Laclos）的原著小說 Les Liaisons Dangereuses（即《危險關係》英文片名 Dangerous Liaisons）。《危險性遊戲》凱薩琳的角色原型即為《危險關係》的梅黛侯爵夫人。

這部以一百七十五封書信構成的小說，敘述梅黛侯爵夫人聽說曾經背棄她的情人即將娶她的親戚西賽兒（Cecile Volanges）為妻，咽不下這口氣的梅黛侯爵夫人找來之前的情人凡爾蒙子爵（Vicomte de Valmont），想讓他奪取西賽兒的貞操，以報當初被拋棄之仇。沒想到凡爾蒙子爵嫌任務太過簡單，而且他已經找上新的獵物——貞潔的杜薇法官夫人（Présidente de Tourvel），兩人於是打賭，只要子爵能夠白紙黑字拿到法官夫人愛上他的證據，梅黛夫人就再讓他成為入幕之賓。沒想到子爵真的愛上法官夫人，令梅黛夫人大為嫉妒，於是展開精心設計的毀滅行動……。

這部暢銷小說在十九世紀兩次被禁，卻一直深受喜愛、廣為流傳，不但受到瑪麗皇后珍藏、被米蘭昆德拉譽為有史以來最偉大的小說之一，直到近代還一直被改編成電影。除了上述兩部歐美電影，還包括韓國片《醜聞》（裴勇俊飾演凡爾蒙子爵）及華語片《危險關係》（張柏芝飾演梅黛夫人，章子怡飾演杜薇法官夫人）。

《第六感追緝令》

員警尼克（Nick，Michael Douglas 飾）負責一件搖滾舞星的兇殺案，在調查和審訊死者的女友凱薩琳（Catherine，Sharon Stone 飾）時，情不自禁迷上她，兩人玩起危險又刺激的遊戲。尼克發現她寫的一本小說中，殺人場景與兇殺案完全相同，直覺告訴他，凱薩琳就是兇手。

Nick: What's your new book about?
妳在寫什麼書？

Catherine: A detective. He falls for the wrong woman.
關於一個警探，他愛上不該愛的女人。

Nick: What happens to him?
他後來怎麼了？

Catherine: She kills him.
她殺了他。

Nick: Beating that machine can't be easy.
要通過測謊機並不容易。

Catherine: If I was guilty and I wanted to beat that machine, it wouldn't be hard. It wouldn't be hard at all. You took a lie detector test after you shot those two people, didn't you?
假如我有罪，想通過測謊機的話，那並不難，一點都不難。你槍殺那兩個人後，也測過測謊機了，不是嗎？

Nick: I passed.
我通過了。

Catherine: You see, we're both innocent, Nick.
看吧，尼克，我們都沒有罪。

Nick: You seem to know an awful lot about me.
看來妳知道我不少事。

Catherine: You know an awful lot about me.
是你知道我不少事。

Catherine: You shouldn't play this game.
你不該加入這場遊戲。

Nick: Why not? I like it.
何不呢？我喜歡這遊戲。

Catherine: You're in over your head.
但你力不從心。

Nick: Maybe, but this is how I'll catch my killer.
也許吧，但這是為了抓到兇手。

Catherine: I'm not going to confess all my secrets just because I have an orgasm. You won't learn anything I don't want you to know.
我不會因為性高潮就將我所有秘密和盤托出。我不想讓你知道的事，你就不會知道。

Nick: Yes, I will. Then I'll nail you.
我會知道的，到時我會揭穿妳。

Catherine: Nah. You'll just fall in love with me.
才不，你只會愛上我。

Nick: I'm in love with you already. But I'll nail you anyway. You can put that in your book.
我已經愛上妳了。但我還是會揭穿妳。妳可以將這個寫進妳的書。

Catherine: I finished my book.
我的書寫完了。

Nick: So how does it end?
那結局如何？

Catherine: I told you. She kills him. Goodbye, Nick.
我說過了，她殺了他。永別了，尼克。

Nick: Goodbye?
永別？

Catherine: Yeah. I finished my book. Didn't you hear me? Your character's dead. Goodbye. What do you want? Flowers? I'll send you an autographed copy.
是的。我的書寫完了，你沒聽清楚嗎？你的角色死了。永別了。你想要什麼？一束花嗎？我會寄一本我親筆簽名的書給你。

Basic Instinct

Sharon Stone 莎朗史東

莎朗史東（Sharon Stone）1992 年以電影《第六感追緝令》開始揚名國際，成為好萊塢首席性感女神，也憑此片獲得金球獎最佳戲劇類電影女主角。她在 1995 年又以《賭國風雲》*Casino* 獲得金球獎最佳戲劇類電影女主角。莎朗史東曾說自己是西藏流亡精神領袖達賴喇嘛的好朋友，不過，達賴喇嘛表示自己與莎朗史東僅是「點頭之交」。

《第六感追緝令》在舊金山拍攝期間，引來當地同性戀團體的示威抗議，因為片中女主角是雙性戀，不但被塑造成是凶殘的殺人兇手，還患有自戀傾向的精神疾病。為防止暴動發生，舊金山警局天天派出鎮暴警察到每一個拍攝現場巡邏。

哈佛知性女神
Natalie Portman
娜塔莉波曼 35

Born in Jerusalem to an Israeli father and American mother, Natalie Portman moved to the U.S. when she was three. Portman started taking dancing lessons the following year, and learned how to act at theater camp during summer vacations. After turning down an offer to model for Revlon, she made her film debut in Luc Besson's *The Professional* at the age of 12. Her striking performance as a hitman's assistant won her more roles, but it was her portrayal of Padmé Amidala in the new *Star Wars* trilogy that made her famous. And between takes, Portman even found time to complete a psychology degree at Harvard! More recently, she not only took home an Oscar for *Black Swan*, but also a husband, marrying her choreographer.

© Everett Collection / Shuttershock.com

娜塔莉波曼出生於耶路撒冷，父親是以色列人，母親是美國人，三歲時便搬到美國居住。隔年波曼開始學舞，暑假期間則於戲劇營學習表演。在婉拒來自露華濃彩妝公司的模特兒邀約後，她以十二歲之齡在盧貝松的《終極追殺令》中初登大銀幕。她在片中擔綱殺手助理的精采表現為她帶來更多演出機會，不過真正令她聲名大噪則是在新的《星際大戰》三部曲中飾演佩咪艾米達拉一角。在拍戲空檔之餘，波曼甚至還能找出時間完成哈佛大學的心理學課程並取得學位！波曼在前一陣子不僅以《黑天鵝》的演出抱回一座小金人，而且還抱得情郎歸，嫁給了她的編舞老師。

影星小檔案

全　　名：**Natalie Portman**
生　　日：**June 9, 1981**
出 生 地：以色列耶路撒冷
感情狀態：已婚
成 名 作：《星際大戰》Star Wars

© Mira John / Shuttershock.com

跟女神學「黑天鵝」瘦身法

本來就很苗條的娜塔莉，為了演出《黑天鵝》中清瘦的白天鵝，敬業的她藉由飲食和運動又瘦下九公斤，快來看看她是怎麼辦到的。
● 嚴格執行的素食菜單：蔬菜湯＋豆腐
● 持之以恆的運動：每週運動四次以上，每次一個半小時，運動項目包括皮拉提斯、飛輪有氧、游泳及瑜伽。
● 吃大量新鮮的蔬果和全麥食品，儘量避開精制澱粉，以蕎麥花蜜（buckwheat honey）替代糖類，並且吃黑巧克力來解饞。

© Featureflash / Shuttershock.com

性感黑天鵝──蜜拉庫妮絲

猶太裔的蜜拉庫妮絲 (Mila Kunis)，五官有著濃濃的異國風情，深棕色的頭髮與一雙電眼，不知迷倒多少男性觀眾，也讓女影迷們爭相學化她的招牌煙燻妝。她在《黑天鵝》中與納塔莉波曼大演對手戲，精湛的演出令她奪得威尼斯國際影展「最佳年輕女演員」的獎項，其後又出演賣座電影《奧茲大帝》(Oz the Great and Powerful，演藝之路扶搖直上，被譽為演藝圈中少數能與納塔利波曼匹敵的女演員。

《控制》

和妻子愛咪（Amy，Rosamund Pike 飾）結婚五週年紀念日當天，尼克（Nick，Ben Affleck 飾）發現妻子失蹤。尼克召開記者會並發出協尋公告，警方也在廚房中驗出愛咪的血跡。媒體後來控出尼克不但有婚外情，欠一大筆債，還有提高保單理賠金，種種跡象顯示兇手就是尼克。但兇手和屍體遲遲未尋獲，愛咪也一直下落不明。

電影《控制》改編自同名小說，原書名 Gone Girl（失蹤的女孩），除了點出故事內容的失蹤案主題，gone 這個字也有「無望」、「無可挽救」、「逝去」等意思，更能感受到作者為這部作品取名的深意。而中文片名《控制》，則呈現出女主角愛咪善於控制人心的性格，也點出電影的另一個主題：婚姻是控制人生的一道枷鎖。

原著作者吉莉安弗琳（Gillian Flynn）原本是《娛樂周刊》Entertainment Weekly 的記者，因經濟不景氣失業而開始在家寫小說，從 2006 年起出版了三本懸疑小說，除了《控制》，還包括《利器》Sharp Objects 和《暗處》Dark Places。美國女演員瑞絲薇斯朋讀過《控制》的原著小說後，對小說中探討經濟問題影響婚姻、家庭等社會議題的內容很感興趣，於是買下電影改編權，也想親自主演，只是導演最後屬意羅莎蒙派克擔任女主角。

電影開場獨白：

Nick: When I think of my wife, I always think of the back of her head. I picture cracking her lovely skull, unspooling her brain, trying to get answers.

當我想起我的妻子，我總會想起她的後腦勺，我想像著把她的頭顱給剖開，解開她的大腦，好讓我找到答案。

The primal questions of a marriage: What are you thinking? How are you feeling? What have we done to each other? What will we do?

婚姻的根本問題是：妳在想什麼？妳覺得如何？我們對彼此做了什麼？我們接下來會怎麼做？

Amy: Everyone told us and told us and told us—marriage is hard work. And compromise and more work. "Abandon all hope, ye who enter."

大家都一而再，再而三地告訴我們，婚姻需要靠努力維持，需要妥協，除了努力還是努力。『凡入此門者，當捨棄一切希望』（語出但丁《神曲》的「地獄篇」）。

Nick: You fucking cunt!

你這個臭婊子！

Amy: I'm the cunt you married. The only time you liked yourself was when you were trying to be someone this cunt might like. I'm not a quitter, I'm that cunt. I killed for you; who else can say that? You think you'd be happy with a nice Midwestern girl? No way, baby! I'm it.

那我也是你娶回家的婊子。你唯一喜歡你自己的時候，就是努力討我這個婊子喜歡的時候。我不是個半途而廢的人，我就是你口中的婊子。我為你殺人，還有誰可以這麼說？你跟一個中西部乖女孩在一起會快樂嗎？不可能啊，寶貝！你要的就是我。

Nick: Yes, I loved you and then all we did was resent each other, try to control each other. We caused each other pain.

是的，我愛過妳，但我們後來只會彼此怨恨，試著控制對方，給彼此帶來痛苦。

Amy: That's marriage.

這就是婚姻。

Amy: Nick, I don't get it. I don't get why you're daring me to be someone I don't wanna be. The nagging shrew, the controlling bitch. I'm not that person. I'm your wife.

尼克，我不懂，我不懂你為什麼要把我逼成一個嘮叨的潑婦、霸道的婊子，我不想變成那種人，我更不是那種人。我是你的老婆。

Gone Girl

Christian: What about you? I'd like to know more about you.
那妳呢？我想更瞭解你。

Anastasia: There's really not much to know about me. Look at me.
我沒什麼好瞭解的，看我這樣子。

Christian: I am.
我是在看妳。

Christian: Where have you been?
妳在哪裡？

Anastasia: Waiting.
等你。

Christian: It's about gaining your trust and your respect, so you'll let me exert my will over you. I will gain a great deal of pleasure, joy, even in your submission. The more you submit, the greater my joy—it's a very simple equation."
我要先贏得妳的信任和尊敬，這樣妳才會讓我為所欲為。當妳臣服於我，我會得到極大的快感和歡愉。妳越是順從，我就越是歡愉——這是非常簡單的對等關係。

Anastasia: And what would I get out of this?
那我會從中得到什麼？

Christian: Me.
我。

Anastasia: Why are you trying to change me?
你為什麼想改變我？

Christian: I'm not. It's you that's changing me.
我沒有，是妳在改變我。

Christian: Anastasia, I'm not a hearts and flowers kind of man, I don't do romance. My tastes are very singular. You should steer clear from me.
安娜塔希婭，我不是那種會付出真心和送花的男人，我不搞浪漫。我的口味比較特別。妳該和我保持距離。

There's something about you, though, and I'm finding it impossible to stay away. But I think you've figured that out already.
不過，妳身上有某種特質，我發現自己已經離不開妳了。但我想妳已經看出來了。

Anastasia: Then don't.
那就別離開。

Fifty Shades of Grey

作者 EL 詹姆絲（E. L. James），本名埃里卡倫納德（Erika Leonard）。2011 年出版處女作《格雷的五十道陰影》便一鳴驚人，在 11 周內突破一百萬冊，打破了美國作家丹布朗《達文西密碼》36 周的紀錄，還被《時代雜誌》選為 2012 年的百大風雲人物。

《格雷的五十道陰影：調教》、《格雷的五十道陰影 2：束縛》*Fifty Shades Darker*、《格雷的五十道陰影 2：自由》*Fifty Shades Freed* 三部曲在全世界銷售逾七千萬冊，其中 3500 萬冊在美國售出，在英國打破銷售最快的紀錄，也是首本突破百萬大關的 Kindle 電子書。

《格雷的五十道陰影》小說原本是詹姆絲從 2009 年開始，在《暮光之城》的粉絲同人創作網站（Fan Fiction）上，以筆名「Snowqueen's Icedragon」（雪女王的冰龍）發表的作品，所以也被稱為「暮光之城成人版」。因為是粉絲同人創作，所以最初沿用了暮光之城男女主角愛德華庫倫（Edward Cullen）和貝拉史旺（Bella Swan）等其他角色的名字，小說原名是「*Master of the Universe*」（宇宙的主宰），連載期間就已在網路上廣為流傳，後來更改角色名字和小說名稱，並大幅刪改內容後出版成書。對於這部小說造成的旋風，作者表示自己也感到很驚訝。作者形容這部小說三部曲是「我的中年危機，顯而易見。我所有幻想都在裡面了，就這樣。」

《格雷的五十道陰影》

主修文學的女大學生安娜塔希婭（Anastasia，Dakota Johnson 飾）為了完成校刊報導，前去採訪年輕企業鉅子克里斯欽格雷（Christian Grey，Jamie Dornan 飾）。安娜被年輕、俊帥、多金的格雷吸引，兩人迅速墜入情網。安娜塔希婭漸漸發現格雷不為人知的陰暗面，令她陷入高壓、控制，令人窒息卻又無法抗拒的愛情中。

Keanu Reeves 基努李維

© s_bukley / Shutterstock.com

🎧 36

Keanu Reeves was born on September 2, 1964 in Lebanon to an English mother and American father of Hawaiian, Chinese and Portuguese [1)]**ancestry**. When his parents divorced two years later, mother and son moved to Australia and then New York. His mother next married director Paul Aaron, and the family moved to Toronto, becoming Canadian citizens. But this second marriage only lasted a year, and his mother's third and fourth marriages would also end in divorce. The young Keanu didn't find [2)]**stability** at school either, attending four high schools in five years and dropping out at 17.

Keanu had enjoyed [3)]**hockey** and drama in school, but an injury ended his dream of a sports career. So he combined his two interests by playing a [4)]**goalie** in the 1986 drama *Youngblood*, which was filmed in Toronto. He next moved to L.A., where his stepfather Paul Aaron helped him **break into** Hollywood. After starring in the 1986 drama *River's Edge*, Keanu landed his breakout role—[5)]**clueless** teen Ted Logan in the comedy *Bill and Ted's Excellent Adventure*. But when he found himself being [6)]**cast** in a number of similar roles, he made an effort to expand his range, playing an FBI [7)]**agent** in *Point Break* and a male prostitute in *My Own Private Idaho*.

Although the 1994 action blockbuster *Speed* made Keanu an **A-list** star, he turned down the sequel—despite being offered $11 million—to play Hamlet in a small [8)]**theatrical** production. The actor showed the same lack of interest in money when he starred in the hugely successful *Matrix* [9)]**trilogy** several years later, giving two-thirds of his $150 million paycheck to the costume and special effects teams, who he considered the true stars. Since then, he's continued

Showbiz Words

A-list 一線（明星），A 咖

A-list 指的是「一線（明星）」，用來表示好萊塢目前當紅的或是票房保證的明星，這是好萊塢一位資深影劇記者詹姆斯烏爾姆（James Ulmer）以各項評比數據來衡量明星所做的排行，這個評比標準稱為烏爾姆量尺（Ulmer Scale）。當然，有一線就會有「二線」（B-list），甚至有「三線」（C-list），現今報章雜誌常說的「B 咖」概念便是由此而來的。最初烏爾姆量尺只有三個等級，但演藝圈其實還有許多比 C 咖行情更低的無名小卒，於是有人便創造出 D-list 來指那些名不經傳的超小牌演員。

to [10]**take on** new challenges, appearing in the romantic drama *The Lake House*, producing the documentary *Side by Side*, and directing the [11]**martial arts** film *Man of Tai Chi*.

基努李維於 1964 年九月二日出生於黎巴嫩，母親為英國人，父親則是擁有夏威夷、中國及葡萄牙血統的美籍人士。兩年後他的雙親離異，母子先是搬到澳洲居住，後來再到紐約。他的母親接著改嫁導演保羅艾倫，然後一家人遷往多倫多，並入籍加拿大。不過這次再婚僅維持一年而已，接下來的第三、四段婚姻同樣也以離婚收場。年輕的基努在學校的生活也不甚穩定，五年之間就換了四所高中，最後於十七歲時輟學。

學生時期的基努喜歡打曲棍球及演戲，不過某次受傷使他放棄追求運動生涯的夢想。因此他結合了這兩項嗜好，在 1986 年於多倫多拍攝的劇情片《血性小子》裡，飾演一位冰球守門員。接著他搬去洛杉磯，由他的繼父保羅艾倫協助帶他闖入好萊塢。於 1986 年主演劇情片《大河邊緣》後，基努在喜劇片《阿比阿弟闖天關》裡獲得令他爆紅的角色，飾演泰德羅根這個無厘頭的青少年。不過太多同類角色的邀約使他努力嘗試拓展戲路，於是他在《驚爆點》中飾演美國聯邦調查局探員，並在《男人的一半還是男人》裡詮釋一名男妓。

雖然 1994 年的動作鉅片《捍衛戰警》使基努成為一線紅星，他卻婉拒片酬高達一千一百萬美金的續集邀約，轉而到小型的劇場演出裡飾演哈姆雷特。數年後當他主演極為賣座的《駭客任務》三部曲時，這位男星又再次展現他淡泊的金錢觀，將一億五千萬美元片酬的三分之二贈送給服裝造型及特效小組，因為他認為這些人才是真正的幕後英雄。自此之後，他仍繼續接下各種新挑戰，主演浪漫愛情電影《跳越時空的情書》、製作紀錄片《基努李維之數位任務》、並且執導武打片《太極俠》。

© Jaguar PS / Shutterstock.com

Tongue-tied No More

break into sth. 順利進入（某行業或領域）
break 這個動詞是「打破」的意思，如果你 break into sth.，表示你突破重圍，順利進入某領域。

A: Why are you majoring in communication?
　為什麼你要主修傳播？
B: I want to break into broadcasting after I graduate.
　我畢業後想進入傳播業。

Vocabulary Bank

1) **ancestry** [ˈænsɛstrɪ] (n.) 祖先（統稱），血統
Humans and apes have a common ancestry.
人類和猿猴有相同的祖先。

2) **stability** [stəˈbɪlətɪ] (n.) 穩定（性），安定
The government is struggling to maintain economic stability.
政府正努力維持經濟安定。

3) **hockey** [ˈhɑkɪ] (n.) 曲棍球
The hockey player retired after he broke his jaw.
那位曲棍球選手摔斷下巴後就退休了。

4) **goalie** [ˈgolɪ] (n.) 守門員
The goalie is one of the most important players on the team.
那位守門員是球隊裡最重要的球員之一。

5) **clueless** [ˈkluləs] (a.) 一無所知的，愚蠢的
Most people are clueless about economics.
多數人對於經濟學一無所知。

6) **cast** [kæst] (v./n.) 選派⋯為角色；卡司，演員陣容
The actor was tired of being cast as a villain.
那位演員對於老是被選派為惡棍角色感到厭倦。

7) **agent** [ˈedʒənt] (n.) 幹員，探員，特務
The terror suspect was questioned by intelligence agents.
這名恐怖份子嫌犯被情報員審問。

8) **theatrical** [θɪˈætrɪkəl] (a.) 戲劇的
The Hollywood star started out as a theatrical actor.
那位好萊塢明星以劇場演員起家。

9) **trilogy** [ˈtrɪlədʒɪ] (n.) 三部曲
What's your favorite movie in the *Twilight* trilogy?
《暮光之城》三部曲中你最喜歡哪一集？

10) **take on** [tek ɑn] (phr.) 接受、承擔（挑戰、責任、任務等）
We're looking for employees who are willing to take on new challenges.
我們在尋找願意接受新挑戰的員工。

11) **martial art** [ˈmɑrʃəl ɑrt] (n.) 武術
Tae kwon do is the most popular martial art in the world.
跆拳道是世界上最熱門的武術。

英國大文豪
莎士比亞愛的語錄

莎士比亞是英國文學史上最傑出的戲劇家，也是西方文藝史上最傑出的作家和文學家之一。他流傳下來的作品有三十八部戲劇、一百五十五首十四行詩、兩首長敘事詩等其他詩歌，但關於他私人生活的記錄很少。有人懷疑「莎士比亞」可能是一個由多人集體創作而使用的筆名，還有人認為他的真實身份是貴族，甚至是英國女王伊莉莎白一世，因為莎士比亞的作品中有許多是描述宮廷貴族之事，辭藻運用典雅，不像是經常出入市井場所之人所寫得出來的。

《莎翁情史》

1593 年，失去寫作靈感的莎士比亞（Shakespeare，Joseph Fiennes 飾）遇到女扮男裝前來應徵演員的貴族女孩薇奧拉（Viola，Gwyneth Paltrow 飾），兩人相戀讓莎士比亞再度有了靈感，寫出《羅密歐與茱麗葉》的劇本。

《莎翁情史》這部電影雖然是在敘述莎士比亞的愛情故事，但實際上是虛構的故事。電影中大量融入莎士比亞的作品，包含角色、情節和對白的設計，都參考了莎士比亞的戲劇，尤其是《羅密歐與茱麗葉》。這部電影還榮獲1998 年度第 71 屆奧斯卡金像獎七項獎項，包括最佳影片、最佳女主角、最佳女配角、最佳原創劇本、最佳藝術指導、最佳服裝設計，和最佳配樂。而其中飾演伊莉莎白一世的茱蒂丹契（Judi Dench），在電影中雖然只有八分鐘左右的戲份，就讓她奪得了那一屆的最佳女配角獎。

Viola: [as Thomas Kent] Tell me how you love her, Will.
[女扮男裝成湯瑪士肯特] 威爾（莎士比亞的暱稱），告訴我，你有多愛她。

Shakespeare: Like a sickness and its cure together.
就像是犯病了，又像是吃了藥痊癒了。

Viola: I think the lady is wise to keep your love at a distance.
我想，小姐要和你的愛保持距離是明智之舉。

For what lady could live up to it close to, when her eyes and lips and voice may be no more beautiful than mine?
哪有小姐能不負你的期待，靠近細看，她的眼睛、嘴唇和聲音可能還不比我漂亮。

Besides, can a lady born to wealth and noble marriage love happily with a Bankside poet and player?
再說，一個注定要與貴族聯姻的千金小姐，怎麼能跟一個出生岸邊區的詩人和演員幸福相愛呢？

Shakespeare: Yes, by God! Love knows nothing of rank or riverbank!
可以，天地為證！愛是不分階級和門第的！

It will spark between a queen and the poor vagabond who plays the king and their love should be minded by each, for love denied blights the soul we owe to God! So, tell my lady, William Shakespeare waits for her in the garden!
女王和扮成國王的窮小子也能擦出愛情的火花，兩方也不容忽視，因為否定這樣的愛情，就是愧對上帝賜與我們的靈魂！好了，告訴你家小姐，威廉莎士比亞在花園裡等她！

Viola: But, what of Lord Wessex?
那魏瑟爵士（Viola 的婚約對象）怎麼辦？

Shakespeare: For one kiss, I would defy a thousand Wessexes!
為了一個吻，我可以對抗一千個魏瑟。

Shakespeare: You will never age for me, nor fade, nor die.
妳在我的心裡永遠不老、不凋零、不滅。

Shakespeare: Can you love a fool?
你會愛一個笨蛋嗎？
Viola: Can you love a player?
那你會愛一個演員嗎？

Viola: I loved a writer and gave up the prize for a sonnet.
我愛上一個作家，為了一首詩而放棄了大獎。
Shakespeare: I was the more deceived.
我才被騙得更深。
Viola: Yes, you were deceived, for I did not know how much I loved you.
是的，你被騙了，因為我不知道我是如此深愛著你。

Shakespeare: My story starts at sea, a *perilous voyage to an unknown land.
故事是從一片汪洋開始，那是一段冒險的旅程，朝著未知的陸地前進。

A shipwreck. The wild waters roar and heave. The brave vessel is *dashed all to pieces. And all the helpless souls within her drowned. All save one.
有一艘遇難的沉船，在波濤洶湧中載浮載沉。這艘英勇的船被撞成碎片，船裡所有無助的靈魂全數沉沒，只有一個獲救。

A lady. Whose soul is greater than the ocean, and her spirit stronger than the sea's embrace. Not for her a watery end, but a new life beginning on a stranger shore.
那是一位女子，她的靈魂比海洋廣闊，她的心靈比大海的懷抱更堅強。她的結局不會是沉入海底，而是在陌生的彼岸展開新生活。

It will be a love story. For she will be my heroine for all time. And her name will be Viola.
這會是一個愛情故事。而她，會是我一生中永遠的女主角。她的名字是薇奧拉。

***perilous** [ˋpɛrələs] (a.) 危險的，險惡的
***dash** [dæʃ] (v.) 擊碎，使（希望等）破滅

Shakespeare in Love

莎士比亞的秘密

莎士比亞除了劇本不斷被改編成電影，也有杜撰他生平故事的電影如《莎翁情史》，及另一部較晚近的作品《莎士比亞的秘密》Anonymous。

《莎士比亞的秘密》改編自美國作家卡雷爾（Jennifer Lee Carrell）的小說 The Shakespeare Secret（又名 Interred with Their Bones），於 2007 年出版，並於 2011 年由《明天過後》The Day After Tomorrow、《2012》災難片導演艾默里奇（Roland Emmerich）改編為電影。由於小說中結合真實歷史背景及虛擬情節的敘事技巧，時常被拿來和另一本暢銷小說《達文西密碼》The Da Vinci Code 比較，而卡雷爾也有「女版丹布朗」之稱。

在《莎翁情史》當中，Joseph Fiennes 飾演的莎士比亞是一位劇作家，所有劇本都是他搖筆桿寫出來的；但《莎士比亞的秘密》卻透過英國宮廷的驚悚鬥爭，對「莎士比亞是否真有其人」提出質疑。片中假設莎翁劇真正的創作者，其實是當時的牛津公爵愛德華（Edward de Vere，Rhys Ifans 飾），由於其貴族身份不允許他沉浸戲劇，愛德華只好暗地創作，便將作品交由他人發表。這部電影藉懸疑、禁忌之愛、宮廷鬥爭等元素，滿足世人對莎士比亞的臆測和想像。

語言學家將英文在歷史上的演變大致劃分為四個階段：
5 世紀到 11 世紀中期使用的是古英文（Old English）
11 世紀中期到 15 世紀是中古英文（Middle English）
16 世紀末和 17 世紀為早期現代英文（Early Modern English）
19 世紀開始使用至今的是現代英文（Modern English）

1590 年到 1613 年是莎士比亞創作的黃金時代，屬於早期現代英文，不論是單詞或文法都與現在我們所看到的英文有些不同。因此對現代人來說，閱讀莎士比亞的作品會比較吃力，外國人在學校裡學習或閱讀莎士比亞作品時，有時也會借助現代英文譯本。

以下三部電影對白，我會為大家找出莎士比亞原著的片段，供各位與現代英文做比較。

《羅密歐與茱麗葉》

《羅密歐與茱麗葉》是莎士比亞寫作生涯早期的愛情悲劇作品，常被誤認是四大悲劇，但其實莎士比亞的四大悲劇分別是《馬克白》Macbeth、《奧賽羅》Othello、《李爾王》King Lear 和《哈姆雷特》Hamlet。《羅密歐與茱麗葉》描述北義大利維洛那城（Verona）的兩大家族，蒙特鳩（Montague）和卡帕萊特（Capulet）是世仇，兩家的青年兒女相戀，但受到雙方家長阻撓，這對戀人最後以殉情告終。

Romeo: Did my heart love till now? Forswear it, sight! For I ne'er saw true beauty till this night.
❍現代英文
Did my heart ever love anyone before this moment? My eyes were liars, then! Because I never saw true beauty before tonight.
我的心在此刻之前有愛過人嗎？我的眼睛曾騙了我，我今晚才見識到什麼是真正的絕世佳人。

Juliet: O Romeo, Romeo, wherefore art thou Romeo? Deny thy father and refuse thy name, or if thou wilt not, be but sworn my love, and I'll no longer be a Capulet.
❍現代英文
Oh, Romeo, Romeo, why do you have to be Romeo? Forget about your father and change your name. Or else, if you won't change your name, just swear you love me and I'll stop being a Capulet.
哦，羅密歐、羅密歐，為什麼偏偏要叫羅密歐？否定你的父親，拋棄你的名字吧，若是你不情願，只要發誓做我的愛人，我就不再姓卡帕萊特。

Romeo: Shall I hear more, or shall I speak at this?
我該繼續聽下去，還是該回答她？

Juliet: 'Tis but thy name that is my enemy, thou art thyself though not a Montague. What is Montague? It is nor hand, nor foot, nor arm, nor face, nor any other part belonging to a man. Oh, what's in a name? That which we call a rose by any other word would smell as sweet; so Romeo would, were he not Romeo called, retain that dear perfection to which he owes without that title. Romeo, doff thy name! And for thy name, which is no part of thee, take all myself.
❍現代英文
It's only your name that's my enemy. You'd still be yourself even if you stopped being a Montague. What's a Montague anyway? It isn't a hand, a foot, an arm, a face, or any other part of a man. What does a name mean? The thing we call a rose would smell just as sweet if we called it by any other name.
只有那姓氏是我的仇敵，就算不姓蒙特鳩，你依然是你。蒙特鳩到底是什麼？不是手、不是腳、不是胳膊，也不是臉，不屬於人的任何部位。啊，名字有什麼關係呢？玫瑰不管叫什麼名字，氣味都一樣芳香。

Romeo would be just as perfect even if he wasn't called Romeo. Romeo, lose your name. Trade in your name—which really has nothing to do with you—and take all of me in exchange.
所以，羅密歐就算不叫羅密歐，就算改變稱謂，還是一樣珍貴完美。羅密歐，拋棄你的名字吧！用那不屬於你任何部位的名字，換取全部的我。

Romeo: Lady, by yonder blessed moon I swear. That tips with silver all these fruit-tree tops.。

🔊現代英文

Lady, I swear by the sacred moon above, the moon that paints the tops of fruit trees with silver.

小姐，我對著那將樹梢染成銀色的聖潔月亮發誓。

Juliet: O, swear not by the moon, the inconstant moon, who monthly changes in her circled orb, lest that thy love prove likewise variable.

🔊現代英文

Don't swear by the moon. The moon is always changing. Every month its position in the sky shifts. I don't want you to turn out to be that inconsistent too.

啊！不要拿月亮發誓，月亮變化無常，月月陰晴圓缺，你的愛恐怕也會生變。

Romeo: What shall I swear by?

那我拿什麼發誓？

Juliet: Do not swear at all. Or, if thou wilt, swear by thy gracious self, which is the god of my idolatry, and I'll believe thee.

🔊現代英文

Don't swear at all. But if you have to swear, swear by your wonderful self, which is the god I worship like an idol, and then I'll believe you.

不要發誓。假如你一定要發誓，拿你高尚的自己起誓就好，你是我心儀的偶像，這樣我就相信你。

Juliet: How camest thou hither, tell me, and wherefore? The orchard walls are high and hard to climb. And the place death, considering who thou art. If any of my kinsmen find thee here.

🔊現代英文

Tell me, how did you get in here? And why did you come? The orchard walls are high, and it's hard to climb over them. If any of my relatives find you here they'll kill you because of who you are.

告訴我，你怎麼會到這裡來，什麼到這裡來？花園的圍牆這麼高，是不容易爬上來的。要是我家人看到你，他們一定不讓你活命。

Romeo: With love's light wings did I o'erperch these walls. For stony limits cannot hold love out. And what love can do, that dares love attempt. Therefore thy kinsmen are no stop to me.

🔊現代英文

I flew over these walls with the light wings of love. Stone walls can't keep love out. Whatever a man in love can possibly do, his love will make him try to do it. Therefore your relatives are no obstacle.

我戴著愛的輕翼飛過圍牆，石牆是阻擋不了愛情的。為了愛我什麼都能做，愛能讓人鼓起勇氣，所以妳的家人也阻擋不了我。

Juliet: If they do see thee they will murder thee.

🔊現代英文

If they see you, they'll murder you.

要是他們看到你，一定會殺害你。

Romeo: Alack, there lies more peril in thine eye than twenty of their swords. Look thou but sweet and I am proof against their enmity.

🔊現代英文

Alas, one angry look from you would be worse than twenty of your relatives with swords. Just look at me kindly, and I'm invincible against their hatred.

唉！妳憤怒的眼神比他們二十把刀劍還厲害。用妳溫柔的眼神看著我，我就能戰勝他們。

Romeo and Juliet

《羅密歐與茱麗葉》是最常被翻拍和演出的莎士比亞戲劇之一，其中 1996 年的電影版 *Romeo + Juliet*，男女主角分別由李奧納多狄卡皮歐和克萊兒丹妮絲飾演。對白雖沒改多少，但導演將故事背景改到現代，地點改成「維羅納灘」（Verona Beach），是個虛構城市。兩個世仇家族的決鬥武器從刀劍變成槍械，有些角色的名字也做了改變。而蒙特鳩與卡帕萊特兩個貴族世家也改成類似義大利黑手黨，兩個幫派火拚不只是為了世仇，更是為了企業之爭。但蒙特鳩和卡帕萊特家族的獨子羅密歐（Leonardo DiCaprio 飾）與愛女茱麗葉（Claire Danes 飾），在一場舞會中一見鍾情並私定終身，這對戀人最後用殉情來換取兩家人的和解。

《仲夏夜之夢》

莎士比亞的知名喜劇《仲夏夜之夢》，敘述赫米亞（Hermia）不願順從父親的安排嫁給狄米奇（Demetrius），與另一名男孩拉山德（Lysander）私奔。赫米亞的好友海倫娜（Helena）將私奔之事告訴狄米奇，兩人先後追入森林裡。在夜晚的森林中，精靈仙王奧布朗（Oberon）與仙后提泰妮（Titania）吵架，於是命精靈帕克（Puck）將愛情花的汁液滴在仙后的眼皮上，讓她愛上一個變成驢子的村民波頓 (Bottom)。頑皮的精靈帕克又將愛情花的汁液滴在拉山德和狄米奇的眼上，讓兩人都愛上海倫娜，崩潰的赫米亞跑來找海倫娜算帳，三對情侶在森林裡上演了一場荒唐的愛情鬧劇。

Lysander:

Why should you think that I should woo in scorn?
Scorn and derision never come in tears:
Look, when I vow, I weep; and vows so born,
In their nativity all truth appears.
How can these things in me seem scorn to you,
Bearing the badge of faith, to prove them true?

❍ 現代英文

Why do you think I'm making fun of you when I tell you I love you?
為什麼妳會認為，我告訴你我愛妳，是在開妳玩笑呢？

People don't cry when they're mocking someone.
開玩笑是不會流著淚的。

Look, when I swear that I love you, I cry, and when someone cries while he's making a promise, he's usually telling the truth.
瞧！我發著誓說我愛妳時，是流著淚的！當人發誓時流著淚，都是在說實話。

How can it seem like I'm making fun of you, when my tears prove that I'm sincere?
明明淚水可以證明我的誠意，為什麼妳會覺得我在開妳玩笑？

Helena:

You do advance your cunning more and more.
When truth kills truth, O devilish-holy fray!
These vows are Hermia's: will you give her o'er?
Weigh oath with oath, and you will nothing weigh:
Your vows to her and me, put in two scales,
Will even weigh, and both as light as tales.

❍ 現代英文

You get trickier and trickier.
你越來越狡猾了。

You've made the same promises to me and to Hermia—they can't both be true! They must both be false.
當兩邊真話是互相矛盾的，那麼兩邊一定都是謊言。

The promises you're making to me belong to Hermia. Will you abandon her?
你對我說的誓言，都應該對赫米亞說，難道你將她拋棄了嗎？

If you weighed the promises you made to me against the promises you made to her, they'd come out the same—they both weigh nothing. They're lies.
把你對她和對我說的誓言，放在兩個天秤上，一定秤不出輕重來，因為兩邊都如空話一般輕浮。

A Midsummer Night's Dream

《仲夏夜之夢》是一部富有想像力的喜劇，精靈、森林、夢境與現實之間的元素，搭配怪誕的劇情和綺麗的幻境，被亂點鴛鴦的四位男女，譜出一段段陰錯陽差的愛恨糾葛，是莎士比亞的喜劇當中最複雜的一部，因此也少有人挑戰翻拍。

1999 年版的電影版由凱文克萊（Kevin Kline）飾演變成驢子的波頓，以及 1992 年在《蝙蝠俠大顯神威》*Batman Returns* 裡飾演貓女的蜜雪兒菲佛（Michelle Pfeiffer）飾演仙后提泰妮。導演為了拉近電影與觀眾的距離，將故事的時空背景拉到十九世紀末，讓海倫娜和拉山德騎著腳踏車私奔。除此之外，劇情方面幾乎是百分之百忠於莎士比亞的原著，對白也幾乎一字不差。

精靈系美男子
Orlando Bloom
奧蘭多布魯 38

© Featureflash / Shuttershock.com

Orlando Bloom was raised in Canterbury, England, where his parents ran a language school. Dyslexic as a child, he did poorly in school. But he excelled at drama, and decided he wanted to be an actor after watching a Paul Newman movie. Bloom moved to London at 16 to join the National Youth Theatre, and after receiving small TV and film parts, went on to study at the Guildhall School of Music and Drama. Days before graduating, he was cast as Legolas in the Lord of the Rings trilogy, a role that brought him worldwide fame. He next conquered Hollywood in the Pirates of the Caribbean series, becoming a teen heartthrob in the process. Offscreen, Bloom is a practicing Buddhist who enjoys extreme sports.

奧蘭多布魯成長於英格蘭的坎特伯雷鎮，父母於當地經營一所語言學校。幼時患有閱讀障礙症的他在學校裡表現不佳。不過他於戲劇方面的表現優異，並在觀賞保羅紐曼的電影後立志成為演員。布魯十六歲時為了加入英國青年劇團而搬至倫敦，在接演了幾個電視和電影小角色之後，繼續到市政廳音樂及戲劇學院深造。就在畢業前幾天，他獲選成為《魔戒》三部曲中的勒苟拉斯一角，使他走紅全球。接著他又以《神鬼奇航》系列的演出征服好萊塢，成為青少女的偶像。大銀幕之外的布魯是一位喜好極限運動的虔誠佛教徒。

影星小檔案

全　名：Orlando Jonathan Blanchard Bloom
生　日：January 13, 1977
身　高：180 cm
出生地：英國坎特伯利郡
成名作：《魔戒三部曲》
The Lord of the Rings Trilogy

《哈比人》美男大集合

奧蘭多布魯在《魔戒》中以帥氣脫俗的精靈弓箭手扮相射穿影迷的心之後，劇組在《哈比人》三部曲中，不但讓勒苟拉斯重返大銀幕，更加入另一強大「天菜」，勒苟拉斯的老爸，精靈王瑟蘭督伊（Lee Pace 飾演），再度迷惑影迷的眼睛。此外，矮人這邊也不是省油的燈，飾演索林的 Richard Armitage、奇力 Aidan Turner 都是戲外比戲裡更有魅力的大帥哥，連噴火龍的配音男優都找來紅透半邊天的 Benedict Cumberbatch 飾演。只能說《哈比人》的卡司誠意十足！（編劇就⋯⋯）

© Jaguar PS / Shuttershock.com

© Joe Seer / Shuttershock.com

© Jaguar PS / Shuttershock.com

《第十二夜》

莎士比亞最後一部浪漫喜劇《第十二夜》敘述薇奧拉（Viola）和西巴斯辛（Sebastian）是對雙胞兄妹，在一次船難中失散。為了尋找哥哥，薇奧拉女扮男裝成西薩里奧（Cesario），成為奧西諾公爵（Duke Orsino）的侍從。奧西諾公爵愛上奧麗維婭伯爵小姐（Olivia），派薇奧拉傳口信，奧麗維婭拒絕了奧西諾的情意，卻愛上了薇奧拉，薇奧拉愛的則是奧西諾。隨後西巴斯辛出現，巧遇奧麗維婭，她以為西巴斯辛是薇奧拉，展開了一段複雜的四角關係。

Orsino:
If music be the food of love, play on.
Give me excess of it that, surfeiting,
The appetite may sicken, and so die.
That strain again, it had a dying fall.
Oh, it came o'er my ear like the sweet sound,
That breathes upon a bank of violets,
Stealing and giving odor. Enough, no more.
'Tis not so sweet now as it was before.
O spirit of love, how quick and fresh art thou,
That, notwithstanding thy capacity
Receiveth as the sea, nought enters there,
Of what validity and pitch soe'er,
But falls into abatement and low price
Even in a minute. So full of shapes is fancy
That it alone is high fantastical.

➲現代英文

If it's true that music makes people more in love, keep playing. Give me too much of it, so I'll get sick of it and stop loving.

假如音樂是愛情的糧食，那就奏下去吧；儘量地奏下去，好讓愛情因過飽而噎死。

Play that part again! It sounded sad. Oh, it sounded like a sweet breeze blowing gently over a bank of violets, taking their scent with it.

又奏起這個調子來了！聽來讓人消沉。啊！耳畔的調子聽來多麼甜美，就像微風吹拂一叢紫羅蘭，把花香偷走，又把花香四處吹散。

That's enough. Stop. It doesn't sound as sweet as it did before. Oh, love is so restless! It makes you want everything, but it makes you sick of things a minute later, no matter how good they are. Love is so vivid and fantastical that nothing compares to it.

夠了！別再奏下去了！這調子現在聽來已經不像原來那樣甜美了。愛情的精靈呀！它是多麼輕盈而活潑；如大海般讓你包容一切，頃刻間卻又讓你厭倦一切，不論是多麼高貴的事物，也變得毫無價值。愛情就是這樣讓人猜不透，如夢如幻。

羅曼死英文教室

「第十二夜」一詞源自於基督教聖誕假期中的最後一夜，從聖誕節過後開始算起的第十二天是主顯節（Epiphany），而前一夜就是第十二夜。不過，《第十二夜》的劇情跟節日或聖誕節並沒有關連。在伊莉莎白時期的英國，主顯節已演變成狂歡作樂的日子，所以《第十二夜》是為了慶祝主顯節前夕而寫的劇本，劇情也設計得較歡樂、逗趣。

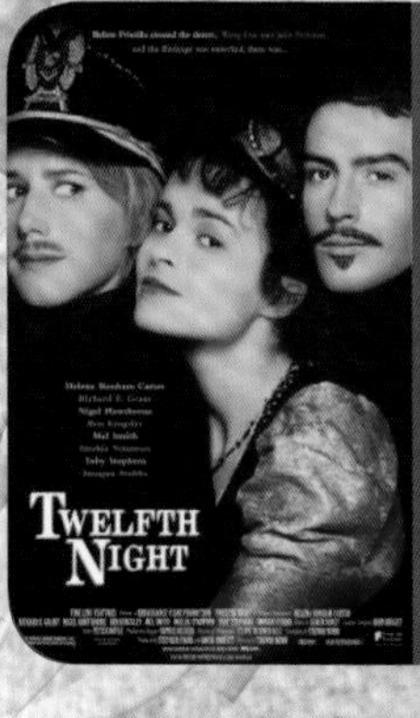

1996 年版的電影《第十二夜》由托比史蒂芬斯（Toby Stephens）、海倫娜寶漢卡特（Helena Bonham Carter）等人主演，除了將背景改到 19 世紀外，劇情、對白幾乎忠於原著。

2006 年的電影《足球尤物》*She's the Man* 也是以《第十二夜》為依據而改編，由亞曼達拜恩斯 (Amanda Bynes)、查寧塔圖 (Channing Tatum)、蘿拉琳賽 (Laura Ramsey) 和凡尼瓊斯 (Vinnie Jones) 主演，背景不但設在現代，場景也改成足球校隊，敘述高中女足校隊隊長薇奧拉在足球隊解散後，女扮男裝，代替雙胞胎哥哥西巴斯辛參加哥哥學校的足球隊，因而發生一連串趣事。雖然時空背景不一樣，但劇情中的四角戀愛關係，和原著《第十二夜》相同。

Olivia:

Thy tongue, thy face, thy limbs, actions, and spirit,

Do give thee fivefold blazon. Not too fast! Soft, soft!

Unless the master were the man. How now?

Even so quickly may one catch the plague?

Methinks I feel this youth's perfections

With an invisible and subtle stealth

To creep in at mine eyes. Well, let it be.

◉現代英文

Your way of talking, your face, your body, your behavior, and your sensitive soul all prove you're a gentleman.

你的語氣，你的臉，你的肢體、動作、精神，都可以證明你的高貴。

Ah, no. Calm down, calm down. If only his lord were more like him.

別這麼性急。慢慢來！慢慢來！除非主僕名分調換。

How strange I'm feeling! Can someone fall in love this quickly? I can feel this young man's perfection creeping in through my eyes like some kind of disease, slowly and invisibly. Oh, well.

真奇怪！這麼快就陷入了？我覺得這位少年的美妙之處，似乎正無聲無息地潛入我的眼中。好吧，就隨它去吧。

Viola:

A blank, my lord. She never told her love,

But let concealment, like a worm i' the bud,

Feed on her damask cheek. She pined in thought,

And with a green and yellow melancholy

She sat like patience on a monument,

Smiling at grief. Was not this love indeed?

We men may say more, swear more, but indeed

Our shows are more than will, for still we prove

Much in our vows, but little in our love.

◉現代英文

There was no story, my lord. She never told him she loved him. She kept her love bottled up inside her until it destroyed her, ruining her beauty.

一片空白而已，殿下。她從來沒說出她的愛，而是隱藏在心中，像蓓蕾中的蟲，侵蝕著她緋紅的臉頰。

She pined away. She just sat waiting patiently, sadly, smiling despite her sadness. Her complexion turned greenish from depression. Doesn't that sound like true love?

她因相思而憔悴，臉色發青泛黃，帶著憂鬱，像不朽的石碑一樣有耐性地等待著，悲傷地微笑著。這難道不是真的愛情嗎？

We men might talk more and promise more, but in fact we talk more than we really feel. We might be great at making vows, but our love isn't sincere.

我們男人也許更會表達、更會發誓，可是，我們表達的多，以行動證明真心實意的少；或許我們擅長山盟海誓，但我們的愛並不夠真誠。

Twelfth Night

羅曼死英文教室

看到這裡，你一定發現莎士比亞所用的英文和現代英文十分不同，難免造成閱讀上的困難；尤其時常出現的 thou, thee, thy, thine，到底代表什麼意思？其實它們正是現代英文中 "you" 和 "your" 的早期現代英文用法，只是不同「格」。看看以下的整理和例句，你會發現其實並不難！

主格 thou (you)

"Thou art more lovely and more temperate."
妳更加可愛，更加婉約。

受格 thee (you)

"Shall I compare thee to a summer's day?"
我應該把妳比作夏日嗎？

所有格 thy (your，後接子音開頭單字)

"Thy husband is thy lord, thy life, thy keeper."
妳的丈夫就是妳的神，妳的生命，妳的守護者。

所有格 thine (your，後接母音)

"To thine own self be true."
對你自己誠實。

Tom 湯姆漢克 Hanks

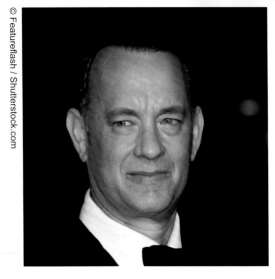

© Featureflash / Shutterstock.com

🎧 39

Born in Concord, California in 1956 to a [1]**chef** and a hospital worker, Tom Hanks had an [2]**unstable** childhood after his parents divorced when he was five. Finding direction in acting while in high school, he studied theater at Cal State, but dropped out to become an [3]**intern** at the Great Lakes Theater Festival in Cleveland. During his three years there, he learned about all [4]**aspects** of theater production, and won acclaim for his performances in Shakespeare plays. Hanks moved to New York in 1979 to audition on **Broadway**, but ended up playing a [5]**transvestite** on the TV **sitcom** *Bosom Buddies*. This led to a role as a man who falls in love with a [6]**mermaid** in the 1984 romantic comedy *Splash*, which [7]**launched** his Hollywood career.

After a string of [8]**flops** in the mid-'80s, Hanks had another hit with *Big* in 1988, playing a little boy who finds himself in a grown man's body. But the actor would find his greatest success as a leading man in the 1990s, starting with two blockbusters in 1993—romantic comedy *Sleepless in Seattle* and [9]**AIDS** drama *Philadelphia*, which won Hanks his first Oscar. And next year's *Forrest Gump* was an even bigger hit, winning six Oscars, including a second for Tom. Now one of Hollywood's top names, Hanks had his choice of projects. And he's chosen well, starring in megahits like war drama *Saving Private Ryan*, romantic comedy *You've Got Mail* and mystery thriller *The Da Vinci Code*. Not only is Tom Hanks the [10]**all-time** box office king, but he's also become a successful director and producer, and has even had an [11]**asteroid** named after him.

Showbiz Words

Broadway 百老匯

百老匯泛指聚集在紐約曼哈頓中城的劇院區 (Theater District) 與林肯中心 (Lincoln Center) 的劇院，是紐約的著名觀光景點，同與倫敦西區 (West End) 被譽為英語國家中最高等級的劇院區，尤以音樂劇演出而聞名，而歌劇魅影 (The Phantom of the Opera) 是在百老匯上演最多次的音樂劇。百老匯劇院均有超過五百個以上的座位，另外還有分為規模較小，比較具有實驗性質的外百老匯 (Off-Broadway) 與外外百老匯 (Off-Off-Broadway)。

sitcom 情境喜劇

sitcom 是 situation comedy 的縮寫，為喜劇的一種分類，通常有固定角色及辦公室、家庭等特定場景，並以幽默的對話貫穿全集。部分情境喜劇會有現場觀眾參與笑聲錄製，但也有許多是以預錄的罐頭笑聲取代。《六人行》(*Friends*)、《老爸老媽的浪漫史》(*How I Met Your Mother*) 都是非常受歡迎的情境喜劇。

© s_bukley / Shutterstock.com

湯姆漢克於 1956 年出生在美國加州的康科德市，父母分別為廚師與醫院員工，但兩人在他五歲時離異，導致他童年生活的不穩定。高中時期奠定志向為演戲的他，大學時於加州州立大學就讀戲劇系，不過後來卻輟學到克里夫蘭的五大湖戲劇節劇團當起實習生。在這裡工作的三年期間，他學到劇場製作的各種層面，並因莎翁劇碼的演出贏得不少讚譽。1979 年，漢克為了百老匯的試鏡而搬至紐約，不過最後卻在電視情境喜劇《親密夥伴》中飾演變裝者。他也因此得到機會，於 1984 年的愛情喜劇《美人魚》中飾演一位愛上美人魚的男子，就此展開他的好萊塢星途。

80 年代中期接演了一連串爛片後，漢克終於靠著 1988 年的《飛進未來》再度翻身走紅，片中的他飾演一名一夜長大的小男孩。不過 1993 年的兩部強檔巨片——愛情喜劇《西雅圖夜未眠》以及描述愛滋病患的劇情片《費城》——更令這位影星達到生涯顛峰、成為 90 年代首屈一指的男主角，後者還替他奪得首座奧斯卡獎。隔年的《阿甘正傳》更加熱門賣座，全片共拿下六座小金人，當中包括湯姆的第二座。成為好萊塢重量級人物的漢克，此時已能自己選角，而他都精心挑選，主演了戰爭電影《搶救雷恩大兵》、愛情喜劇《電子情書》、以及驚悚懸疑的《達文西密碼》等超級強片。湯姆漢克不僅是影史上的票房之王，也是相當成功的導演及製片，甚至還有一顆小行星是以他命名的呢。

© s_bukley / Shutterstock.com

Vocabulary Bank

1) chef [ʃɛf] (n.) 主廚
The chef at this restaurant is known for his desserts.
這間餐廳主廚的拿手招牌是甜點。

2) unstable [ʌnˋstebəl] (a.) 不穩的
The weather has been unstable lately.
最近的天氣有點不穩定。

3) intern [ˋɪn.tɜn] (n.) 實習生，實習醫生
Richard worked as a law office intern while going to law school.
理查在法學院就讀時，曾在法律事務所當實習生。

4) aspect [ˋæspɛkt] (n.) 方面，層面
Which aspects of your job are most challenging?
你的工作在哪一方面最具挑戰性？

5) transvestite [trænzˋvɛstaɪt] (n.) 人妖，變裝者
Did you see a transvestite show when you went to Thailand?
你去泰國的時候有沒有看人妖秀？

6) mermaid [ˋmɜ.med] (n.) 美人魚
The Little Mermaid is about a mermaid who falls in love with a human prince.
《小美人魚》是美人魚愛上人類王子的故事。

7) launch [lɔntʃ] (v.) 展開，發起
The police have launched an investigation into the murder.
警察已經對這起兇殺案展開調查。

8) flop [flɑp] (n.)（尤指電影，書等）失敗，慘敗
The director's last movie was a box-office flop.
那位導演最近的一部電影票房慘敗。

9) AIDS [edz] (n.) 愛滋病
Scientists are still working on a cure for AIDS.
科學家仍在致力尋找愛滋病的解藥。

10) all-time [ˋɔl.taɪm] (a.) 空前的，破紀錄的
Gas prices are at an all-time high.
油價來到了歷史新高。

11) asteroid [ˋæstə.rɔɪd] (n.) 小行星
Most asteroids are found between Mars and Jupiter.
大部分小行星都是在火星和木星之間發現的。

中國文化大學推廣教育部

國際語文中心九大語系　幫您累積財富和價值

英　日　韓　西　法　德　義　越　葡

基礎發音、會話綜合、商務專修、檢定證照、師資培訓、口譯筆譯

加薪升遷 企業外派 無往不利

成人外語第一品牌：文化推廣部ILI國際語文中心
http://my.sce.pccu.edu.tw/MS/Home.aspx
地址：台北市忠孝東路一段41號（捷運善導寺6號出口）
電話：(02)2700-5858 或 (02)2356-7356#9

不是藝術家，
也可以翻轉玩藝術！

0~ 80 歲都該認識的 37 幅藝術大師名畫

欣賞臨摹、塗塗畫畫

剪它貼它、改造惡搞

經典名畫✕個人 style

誰說你沒有藝術細胞？畫上去就好！

／藝術涵養、創意體驗、靈感刺激、培養想像力

／不只是著色！三十七幅經典畫作的名畫小檔案，鑑賞、創作一次滿足

／特別邀請創意人及讀者示範畫作，讓你發現「原來名畫還可以這樣玩？！」

／內頁採用適於上色的厚磅道林紙；畫完了，就是屬於你自己的名畫冊！

「好想畫畫喔！可是我是手殘的美術白痴⋯。」

「覺得好煩喔！想要找件能讓頭腦放空的事來做。」

不管是「星光燦爛的星夜」、「橋上吶喊著的扭曲人形」，或是「戴著珍珠耳環回眸的少女」⋯選一張喜歡的名畫，跟著原畫上色。拿起身邊任何可以用來創作的物品發揮創意。完成屬於自己獨一無二的作品。

◯ Yes24 網路書店藝術類熱銷超過二十週

◯ SBS 節目特別介紹創意書籍

書名｜**動手玩名畫：**
　　　跟著梵谷和他的朋友們，徹底解放你的創意！

定價｜**$320**

各界名人推薦

專文推薦	創意畫作示範
邱建一	**王建民** - 藝術家　／ **徐德寰** - 拾參樂團主唱小寶
藝術史學者 / 台北市立大學視覺藝術系助理教授	**Belle 莊蕙如** - 旅行繪畫家　（依姓氏筆畫排列）

復仇之路 回歸到起點

玩命關頭7

4月1日 隆重鉅獻

國賓給您最極致享受的飆速體驗

4/1(三)起全台國賓限量推出
玩命關頭七經典造型杯

VENGEANCE HITS HOME
FURIOUS7
ONLY IN CINEMAS

產品細節及售價請洽各影城

國賓會員獨享
紅利升等VIP影廳

指定影城:
林口/台南/義大

兌換細節請洽指定影城

國家圖書館出版品預行編目 (CIP) 資料

好萊塢 A 咖教你說愛電影英文：EZ TALK 總編嚴選特刊 /EZ 叢書館編輯部作 -- 初版 . --
臺北市：日月文化 , 2015.04
144 面 ; 21X28 公分
ISBN 978-986-248-459-3（平裝附光碟片）
1. 英語 2. 讀本

805.18　　　　　　　　　　104002419

EZ 叢書館

好萊塢A咖教你說愛電影英文：
EZ TALK總編嚴選特刊

作　　　者：EZ TALK 編輯部
總 編 審：Judd Piggott
筆　　　者：Judd Piggott、Jacob Roth
責 任 編 輯：陳思容、蔡佳勳
文 字 編 輯：葉瑋玲、韋孟岑、黃鈺琦、黃書英、曾婷瑄
美 術 設 計：管仕豪
內 頁 排 版：健呈電腦排版股份有限公司
錄 音 後 製：純粹錄音後製有限公司
錄 音 員：Michael Tennant、Meilee Saccenti

發 行 人：洪祺祥
第二編輯部
總編輯顧問：陳思容
第二編輯部
副總編輯：顏秀竹、葉瑋玲
法 律 顧 問：建大法律事務所
財 務 顧 問：高威會計師事務所

出　　　版：日月文化出版股份有限公司
製　　　作：EZ 叢書館
地　　　址：台北市大安區信義路三段151號8樓
電　　　話：(02) 2708-5509
傳　　　真：(02)2708-6157
網　　　址：www.ezbooks.com.tw
客 服 信 箱：service@heliopolis.com.tw

總 經 銷：聯合發行股份有限公司
電　　　話：(02)2917-8022
傳　　　真：(02)2915-7212
印　　　刷：科樂印刷事業股份有限公司
初　　　版：2015 年 4 月
定　　　價：350 元
I S B N：978-986-248-459-3

封面圖權（依名字開頭字母順序）：

Benedict Cumberbatch：Jaguar PS / Shutterstock.com
Chris Hemsworth：s_bukley / Shutterstock.com
Keira Knightley：Joe Seer / Shutterstock.com
Lily Collins：Featureflash / Shutterstock.com
Natalie Portman：Featureflash / Shutterstock.com
Woody Allen：Armando Brecciaroli / flickr.com

讀者基本資料

■姓名 ＿＿＿＿＿＿＿＿＿＿＿＿＿＿＿＿＿ 性別 □男 □女

■生日 民國 ＿＿＿＿＿年 ＿＿＿＿＿月 ＿＿＿＿＿日

■地址 □□□-□□（請務必填寫郵遞區號）

＿＿＿＿＿＿＿＿＿＿＿＿＿＿＿＿＿＿＿＿＿＿＿＿＿＿

■聯絡電話（日）＿＿＿＿＿＿＿＿＿＿＿＿＿＿＿＿＿

　　　　（夜）＿＿＿＿＿＿＿＿＿＿＿＿＿＿＿＿＿

　　　　（手機）＿＿＿＿＿＿＿＿＿＿＿＿＿＿＿＿

■E-mail ＿＿＿＿＿＿＿＿＿＿＿＿＿＿＿＿＿＿＿
（請務必填寫E-mail，讓我們為您提供VIP服務）

■職業
　□學生　□服務業　□傳媒業　□資訊業　□自由業　□軍公教　□出版業
　□商業　□補教業　□其他

■教育程度
　□國中及以下　□高中　□高職　□專科　□大學　□研究所以上

■您從何種通路購得本書？
　□一般書店　□量販店　□網路書店　□書展　□郵局劃撥

您對本書的建議⋯⋯

請傳真至 *02-2708-6157* 或投郵筒寄回，感謝你的配合！

日月文化出版股份有限公司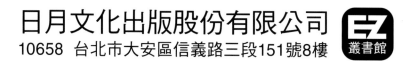
10658 台北市大安區信義路三段151號8樓